MW01488456

Unhappy Hunting Ground

Welcome to
Bartlesville
& WMO.

Jackie S.
Featherston
Moss

Unhappy Hunting Ground

A Historical Novel of Murder and Intrigue

Jamie S. Eccleston

Writer's Showcase
San Jose New York Lincoln Shanghai

Unhappy Hunting Ground
A Historical Novel of Murder and Intrigue

All Rights Reserved © 2000 by Jamie S. Eccleston

No part of this book may be reproduced or transmitted in any form or by any means, graphic, electronic, or mechanical, including photocopying, recording, taping, or by any information storage retrieval system, without the permission in writing from the publisher.

Writer's Showcase
an imprint of iUniverse.com, Inc.

For information address:
iUniverse.com, Inc.
5220 S 16th, Ste. 200
Lincoln, NE 68512
www.iuniverse.com

ISBN: 0-595-15665-7

Printed in the United States of America

DEDICATION

For my father, **J. F. Quinlan**, Oil Field Historian,

For my husband, **Ovia Wood**, who sustained my every effort.
For my children, **John and Beckie, Scott and Kelli, Julie and Eric**, and **Susie**.
For my grandchildren, **Quinton, Rylie, Evan, McKenzie**, and **John Ryan**.

For **Mary Hudson**, my sister and co-founder of Mary Martha Outreach

And for my special friends and consultants:

J. H. Hatfield, Author of *FORTUNATE SON, G. W. Bush and The Making of an American President;*
Pat and Gay Scudder, Oil Field and Indian Historians;
The late Edward Red Eagle, Assistant Chief of the Osages,
And the late Matthew Kane, Attorney and Osage County Historian

FOREWORD

By J.H. Hatfield

Picture in your mind a cross between the strong-willed 19th-century ranch matriarch Victoria Barkley on the sixties television western *Big Valley* and the equally tough but caring *Dr. Quinn Medicine Woman* as portrayed in the nineties by Jane Seymour. Now you have a fairly decent mental visualization of this book's author, Jamie S. Eccleston, whose own life reads like a novel.

The offspring of four generations of Irish Catholic oil men, this self-described "oil field brat" was born in Tulsa, Oklahoma in 1945, during the last year of World War II. A few months later her family moved to Osage County (better known as the Osage Indian Reservation), so when Jamie writes in this book about Irish oil barons as wild and bold as the seething Oklahoma land that spawned them, black gold gushing from the earth, Osage Indians becoming wealthy almost overnight, con men practicing their felonious craft, and the Roman Catholic Church's influence—the author *truly* knows firsthand about the land and the people she writes about in *Unhappy Hunting Ground*.

After graduating from the University of Wyoming with a degree in theatre, speech and English in the mid-sixties, Jamie married and subsequently gave birth to two boys and two girls in the short span of five years. And guess where she raised her family? Yes, back on the Osage Indian Reservation, where she weathered devastating prairie fires and (accompanied by the sheriff's deputy) chased down thieves and militant Indians who planned to torch her house after robbing her of everything she owned.

After eighteen years of marriage, Jamie and her husband divorced. Somehow this human hybrid of Victoria Barkley and Dr. Quinn, struggled to raise four children—by herself. During these years, oil promoters drilled on her Osage County land and when she foiled their swindling schemes, they attempted to have her murdered. She survived and was awarded record-setting damages because of a deal she cut with Denver-based oilmen, who had "pockets full of money and no brains."

In the late eighties, Jamie operated a gun shop in Osage County and became well-known throughout the state as the only blond gun runner in Oklahoma; she was raped and left for dead along the road; and kept her house from burning to the ground by pouring buckets of water down the stove pipe hole on an icy roof for eleven *long* minutes until the fire trucks finally arrived at her rural residence.

She also established her own charitable foundation to build an Indian Arts in Action center in Osage Hills State Park, which was funded by country-and-western concerts and rodeos and brought in millions of dollars to the struggling economies of several Oklahoma towns.

In the early nineties, Jamie sold her gun shop and moved to the foothills of the Ozarks in Eureka Springs, Arkansas, to be close to her only sister, Mary. They purchased the Sunnyside Bed and Breakfast, a 115-year-old Victorian house frequented by governor and soon-to-be president, Bill Clinton, and his wife and daughter. The Quinlan sisters ran the picturesque inn all by themselves, with Jamie doing the cooking and Mary cleaning a house that typically housed fourteen overnight guests. Scattered throughout the interior of the Sunnyside Bed and Breakfast were family heirlooms and "treasures" from four generations of Oklahoma oil men, such as a stuffed coyote in the howling position and a table that once belonged to the owner of Skelly Oil Company.

After selling the inn, Jamie was informed she had a tumor that was "probably cancerous" and was told to get her personal "affairs in order." Nine days later, surgeons operated and discovered it was benign.

It was during this time of personal introspection that she decided to begin writing the book that you now hold in your hands. Returning to her roots, Jamie moved back to her house in Osage County; married Ovia Wood, a former military officer and mayor of a neighboring Oklahoma town; and was given the Indian name "Me La Doea" (a moniker given to the oldest daughter in a family) when she was adopted into the Osage tribe by Assistant Chief and lifelong friend, Edward Red Eagle.

In 1998, Jamie and others founded a charitable foundation called "Mary Martha Outreach, Inc.," so-named for two of Christianity's most famous women. In the first two years of operation, the mission's 25,000 square foot building housed and provided 250,000 garments, 168 tons of food, 1,500 pieces of furniture and 10,000 meals to the poor and downtrodden in the community.

During the summer of wildfires in 2000, Jamie once again faced an all-consuming inferno of treetop jumping flames fanned by thirty-five-mile-per-hour winds. Although three nearby houses were destroyed and almost all of her acreage was turned to charcoal embers, her home for so many years in Osage County miraculously survived. And so did Jamie Eccleston.

Almost a year before, she had rescued my family and that was when I developed a close bond of friendship with this frontier woman. In the wake of the publication of the George W. Bush biography *Fortunate Son*, my own firestorm of sorts was ignited and when a media circus took up camp in front of our house in Arkansas, I packed up my wife, newborn daughter, and mother-in-law and sent them off to the Jamie's home in Osage County, far removed from the harassment of the press.

Her country home was the perfect hideaway for my family from a door-bell pealing every ten minutes, our unlisted telephone ringing incessantly with calls from local newspapers and television stations to national and international media outlets.

In the Author's Note to the re-published soft cover edition of *Fortunate Son* by Soft Skull Press, Inc., I thanked Jamie for providing "safe harbor for a ship that was struggling in the dark recesses of the troubling waters." We had to be cryptic for obvious reasons during those trying times, but now I can thank her properly and publicly by being allowed the honor to pen the Foreword to *Unhappy Hunting Ground.*

Jamie S. Eccleston is a born storyteller and you will find this book difficult to put down. Her prose leaves no doubt that she is a kindred soul with the characters that inhabit these pages.

And when you close this book, you, too, will feel like you intimately know Jamie, an author who spent two years researching and writing this historical novel. But if there is anything I have learned from this adopted daughter of the Osage Indian tribe, it is this: That which does not destroy you, only makes you stronger.

J.H. Hatfield
October 2000

CHAPTER ONE

Jake Knupp chose to ignore the stench in the air as he watched the sun come up slowly in the east over Osage County. It was June 3, 1923. Grandfather Sun was bright to shine and slow to blister, as he hurriedly dried the dew from the long thin fingers of the county's fine bluestem grass. Nestled between the rocks and trees, the Queen Ann lace and the white yarrow were in full bloom, looking like summer snow, to impress the visitors. Jake kept a watchful eye on the eagle as the sacred bird of the tribe circled over the small village, more than once. Jake dismissed his gut feelings of doom and allowed himself to bask in the promised excitement of the day as it filled the wide open spaces of the Osage Nation.

Jake was no newcomer to the Osage. He was the best known of the wildcat drillers in these parts. He knew better than most that it was one of the four most important dates of the year; at least, in the Osage Indian town of Pawhuska, Oklahoma, appropriately named after Chief Whitehair. It was headright payment day for the Osages—now, the richest people, per capita in the world. Wah'-Kon-Tah had been good to the Little Osages. Unbeknownst to the white man or his government, he had lain sleeping under what appeared to be worthless scrub oaks and tons of rock—oil—lots of oil. Now, the Indians had it, the white men wanted it, and they were willing to pay anything for it—even over dead bodies, if that's what it took.

Watching the eagle circle, the khaki clad Irishman nudged his horse forward. The big bay was resisting. Unlike his rider, he didn't appreciate the masses of wildflowers or the beauty of the lush green pastures. They seemed to be interrupted every hundred feet by a string of countless wooden oil derricks. Jake Knupp stopped a moment and mopped the perspiration from his neck with his already wilted blue bandana. Refusing to take no for an answer, he prodded the horse on, again this time rather sharply. "Come on, Target! Let's move it!"

Reluctantly, the big bay started through the maze of oil derricks, rod lines, and powerhouses on the neighboring ranch. They stretched as far as the eye could see. Instantly, the man was aware of something strange—an uncanny noise. It was not the familiar thumping sound made by the barkers on the exhaust of the Bessemer single-cylinder gas engine from the power house a half-mile away. A sudden fear gripped his senses. The stench was getting stronger. Whatever it was, Target, didn't like it, either. His ears were laid back. He was snorting nervously.

The closer he got, the more it sounded like the wail of a hurt animal, he tried to tell himself. Perhaps it was a bawling calf that had been hurt by an oilfield jack. That often happened since derricks and cattle had become strange bedfellows.

He was just coming out of a gully by the creek into a clearing when he spied something. On the high bald hill above him, maybe, a half-mile away, he could see an Oklahoma pumpjack, nodding in the early morning's light. He squinted, shielding his eyes with his hand to get a better view. What was that flying into view over the thick grove of trees? Then, it was gone. No, there it was again! Then gone! It looked for all the world like a man flying up above the tree tops. "Oh, God!" He could feel the chills crawling up and down his spine. The wailing sounded more like a mournful, howling scream for help. He tried to move in that direction despite his and Target's better judgment.

He fought his way through the tall grass and brush, but the going was slow. Continuously, one piercing scream after another, penetrated the still morning, sounding like death, itself. Target tried to rear. Each wail gave Jake's goose bumps more momentum. Even though he was getting closer the pitiful cry seemed to be getting weaker.

When he reached the steep hilltop suddenly, there were no more cries. Had he imagined the whole thing? Then, he saw it. It was a figure of a man—an Indian—draped over the pumpjack. He jumped off Target and ran the last few feet. He slapped at the swarming blowflies trying to land on his sweaty neck. *God! What a stench!* He muttered under his breath. "Stay Target." Jake yanked on the reins of his nervous horse with one hand as he clutched the bandana over his mouth with the other. His eyes were watering as he looked at the hideous scene.

Sure enough, it was the doubled-over body of an Indian, tied to the jack. Together, they moved up and down in perfect rhythm. At first, he thought it was a gag. Someone had, no doubt, tied him on the thing when he was passed-out drunk. He knew the wells usually shut down at sundown.

Probably, long about daylight, when the well started up, the Indian had come to, to find himself hung over in more ways than one. One fast look and Jake knew that he was too late. *Another damn dead Indian*, he thought. That made how many? He'd lost count. All he knew was that the Osages were dying like flies.

He could see that the right side of his head had a big gash from a pipe wrench or some other oil field tool. Blood was dripping on the oil-baked ground. His hands were tied behind his back, but after a closer look, he realized that someone had tied a rope from the jack's base, up and around the Indian's neck. His makeshift noose was tied with a bolin knot, a popular twist in the oil patch. Poor devil! They'd rigged it, so that when the tail end of the jack went twelve feet in the air, the rope would pull tight, choking him. Then, the down stroke of the jack would plummet him to the ground, loosening the rope. He then, realized why the first of his cry was long. He had been in the down position, but as he went into the air, the rope pulled tight, clipping off his cry.

The rope burn was wretched. The jack was set for about twenty strokes a minute, and it had just worn through his neck. It looked as if he was wearing a necklace made of hunks of raw meat. He didn't look familiar. His long black hair, stiff and matted, just hung in his face. His stare was fixed at the ground going-no-where. Deprived of his last view of the sky, he had had a real close-up picture of the ground, as the jack and he dipped low, time after time.

Jake scratched his head. *It looks like another murder. No doubt about it.*

These murders are gettin' out of hand. Too damn much oil money floating around.

He'd holler at the sheriff and send him out. No use cutting him down, he guessed. Why give the screwworms and maggots a head start? Even the old red headed turkey buzzards would have to get in sync to pick at him.

He got back on Target, and headed for town. He couldn't be late for payment day. At the bottom of the hill, he looked back up at the Indian still riding high. The pumpjack couldn't care less about the extra burden, but then, why should it? This was the wild, untamed Osage where oil was the master, and the Indian was its paid victim.

Two hours later, standing in downtown Pawhuska, along Kihekah Street in sight of the new Triangle building and the Osage Mercantile Company Store, Jake could see it all. As he looked out onto the street, his heart began to race. Of course, there wasn't anyone living in those roaring twenties that hadn't felt his heart race. Life was just too good to be true. The American flags were flying. Model T. Fords were bumper to bumper. Horns were honking. A guy could get run-over just trying to get across the street. The Tin-Lizzies reminded him of black doodle bugs. They were in a hurry to get there, but they had no idea of the direction.

It was June 3, 1923, and everyone knew that the big cars were coming to town. Huge Packards, fine Cadillacs, and shiny Pierce Arrow roadsters, all filled with giant Indians. They'd be coming from Hominy, Fairfax, Barnsdall, and Grey Horse to get their quarterly payments. Since most of them had chauffeurs, the Osages would just sit in the back, clad in their Mackinaw blankets, bright silk shirts, and beaver hats.

And what a sight, it was. To add to the mass confusion of the early summer day, the Indian agency's town crier, old Ho-Lah-Go-Ne was circling the town with his bone-rattling cry. He was busy telling the Indian folk that they had better get themselves over to the west window of the council house. It wouldn't be long till the paymaster would begin to dole out the money.

Of course, there was still horse and wagon traffic. However, now that Kihekah Street had been paved, the horses didn't like it much. Keeping his eye on the crowd, Jake could see big goings-on up at the Red Store, operated by old man Hirt. His store was the oldest general store in town. There were a couple of other nice stores where the Indians liked to trade. One was the Osage Mercantile Company, and the other was the McLaughlin and Farrar Store. He could see them both from his vantage point a block away, and they all had more business than they could handle. He smiled. *Looks like summer ants streaming out of the molasses barrel*, he thought. Of course, these were all just looking customers now. There'd be no real buying till after the payment came in.

He leaned up against the old brick building that housed the meat market. *Be a good time for a smoke*, he thought as he fumbled around absent-mindedly in his shirt pocket. Most folks in the oil patch liked Jake. He fancied himself as a pretty fair wildcat driller. His gregarious personality had tagged him a regular guy. He had more friends then most and liked to entertain them with his notions on frequent occasions. He had a regular spiel to describe himself to newcomers. "I like big gushers," he claimed. "Good whiskey, fine looking women, hot deals, starched khakis, bullshit stories, and about six strong cigars a day." He'd be the first to slap a guy on the back that was down on his luck. "Hey man, never let 'em see ya sweat. Ever' day's a new day." Jake figured that he was nothing special, at least in the Osage. When he was pinned down, he was adamant about his pet peeves. "Well, let's see," he'd say, "I hate barb wire, second class whores, fishing tools, and mud, in that order." Then he would throw back his head and his boyish laugh would be heard for some distance.

He came to the Osage in the beginning from Pennsylvania as a boy. He'd done a little drilling for the army when they were looking for water in those parts about ten years ago. He stayed up at the Indian agent's house off and on, since both of his folks were dead. It was about this time when he got acquainted with the girl he later married. Her name was Maggie Lookout. Her daddy was going be chief again, as soon as old Chief Ne-Kah-Wah-She-Tun-Kah died. Jake owned a big drilling outfit in the Osage. He'd drill for whoever paid him the biggest bucks. He reckoned he'd drilled for more than his share of the big boys—Phillips and Sinclair, to name a couple.

Interrupting his thoughts, a familiar face caught his eye. *Well, look who's here, ol' Black Robes, himself,* he thought. He wandered over to the Catholic priest, just going into the meat market. They'd gotten friendly ever since he'd been here. Probably became life-long friends the night they finished off a secret jug or two of fine bootlegged whiskey, that Jake had brought over from Tulsey town.

The priest was a full-blooded Irishman. Everyone called him affectionately, "Father Jack". Jake guessed him to be about fifty-five, and husky built. There must have been some mighty square ancestors in his past. He had dark, curly auburn hair, with a bad scar over his eyebrow. "For character," he always said, but if the truth was known, he was the only priest in the world who had a knife fight in the seminary over the discovery of some well-hidden altar wine.

On a dare, he had crept down to the church's wine cellar only to be surprised by a wino that was more determined than he to escape successfully with the loot. The wino had wildly wielded his knife into Father Jack face before exiting the window. When the brother-in-charge found him lying on the floor, the repercussions were more severe than any knife wound. He always claimed that was when he became educated to that old time religion. His smile was friendly with more, than just a hint of onery in blue eyes that spoke bewitchingly of a time in his life, when God may not have been uppermost in his mind. But of course, they never discussed it.

"What do ya know, Father Jack?" Jake asked.

Father Jack shook his head, frantically. "Hey, Jake! Gotta hurry and get those women some more meat. It's our turn to cook for payment day."

It had long since, been the custom of the churches in town to cook for the big feast when the Indians came to town. The visitors might camp for two or three days. They liked to come and visit with the other clans, and to trade, and to rest.

"Hey, Father, got any new converts up at the church?" Jake asked.

Father hurriedly looked up, wiping the sweat with his bandana, looking for any excuse to rest. "I gotta blow a minute, Jake. Converts. Hell, I had 'em all, but since all this damn oil money, they don't listen to me or to God."

Jake slapped him not too gently on the back. "Better tighten up the reins, Jack. Hey are you missing one of the fold, by any chance?"

Father Jack didn't hear him and Jake decided to change the subject as he looked over the sea of honking cars, especially since they couldn't hear themselves think, anyway. It seemed the honking cars were causing the over two hundred dogs that were milling around to bark, all at different pitches. He guessed they sensed it was going to be payment day for them, too. He yelled at Father Jack. "Did you ever see so many folk? They're coming out of the woodwork."

"Yeah," Father said. "They've even let out school. I just saw Sister Olivia herding a whole bunch of girls down the hill from the St. Louis School. And the Osage Indian School turned everyone out till next week."

Jake began eyeing the crowd. "Father, who's that young guy walking this way?" Jake was sizing him up as he got closer. Jake stuck out his hand. "Howdy, you're not from around these parts, are ya?"

The startled young man looked to be about twenty-five, tall and lean with sandy hair slicked back under his derby. He wore a tight-fitting three-piece suit with a starched collar that looked hotter than hell. He looked like a sixteen-year-old pretending to be a middle-aged account-ant. He smiled, flashing even, white teeth. That meant that he didn't spend much time chewing.

Jake immediately liked his looks, "What's your name, young feller? I'm Jake Knupp, and this Catholic imposter here is Father Jack."

Father shot him a real unholy look.

"Glad to meet you. I'm Tom Fisher. I'm from back near Philadelphia, but I work for ol' man Phillips over in Bartlesville. He and I came over to see how the Indians like spending money."

Jake laughed. "Well, they like it just fine. Everyone's got a big house, a fancy car, a fine beaver hat, plenty of silk for shirts, and now, they've even got plenty left for drinkin' whiskey. You know, headrights are so big today, an Osage family of five, gets about forty grand a year; and it's going up."

"By the way, how's ol' Frank's company doin'?"

Tom laughed, "Well, Phillips Petroleum has made it to its fifth birth-day; so I guess he's doin' okay. You know, the stakes are gettin' kinda high, though. We heard last oil lease sale, that the Osages took in $11 million in one day."

"Yep!" Jake nodded and studied his toothpick, "Some fellow from Gypsey Oil paid $1.6 million for one lease last year."

Tom shook his head like he couldn't believe it. Jake looked at him over his toothpick. "Yeah, I've done a little drillin for ol' man Phillips a couple of months ago."

"Yeah, you're talking to the most famous jar head driller in the Osage." Father Jack announced in his official preacher voice. "Course, it don't hurt anything that he's a squaw man to one of the richest Osages."

Jake shoved him aside and Father Jack took that opportunity to head back in the meat market. Watching the bewilderment on his new found friend's face, Jake spoke, "You know, Tom, he's right. It just don't get any better than this, does it?"

The sheriff strolled by at that moment. He was nearly seven feet tall, and wore a long black coat, half concealing his revolver and holster. The holster hung down to his knee to house the ten-inch barrel on his Colt 45. Jake always mused to himself that if the local lawman could just get that piece out of his holster quick enough, he'd be damned dangerous. The middle-aged sheriff had black hair and steel blue eyes that made the steel of his gun look soft by comparison. Tight-fisted, thin-lipped and square-jawed, he made people wonder which side of the law he really belonged. Nevertheless, he always seemed to be a day late and a dollar short.

"Havin' a bad day, Sheriff? You look fit to be tied." Jake said knowing full well that his sense of humor was usually lacking.

The big man stopped short in his stride and grumbled. "Hell yes, it's a bad day. All hell's fixin' to break out at any minute. What's the government do but proclaim a damn holiday to give these fool Indians a freight train load of money so they can start drinkin' and fightin.' And it's my job to keep the killin's to a minimum. I've got every eligible man deputized. We're headquartered up at the courthouse. I just hope we can keep it peaceful." The big man began to relax.

"Sure thing, though, just as soon as those Indian bucks get paid, they'll high-tail it for Elgin's Rosie Saloon and get roarin' drunk. Lord, in the last six months, I've lost track of how many Indians been killed."

"Well, that reminds me," Jake said. "There's another one dead out by my place on the old Spencer ranch. I found him this morning on my way in. Someone tied him to a pumpjack after they bashed his head in with a pipe wrench. It was hideous. Made the jabberwockers crawl up my spine."

"Who was he?" Sheriff Cook suddenly looked tired and overworked.

Jake shook his head. "Don't know! Never seen him round these parts."

"Okay, Jake, I'll send someone out to get him." He took a deep breath, as if he was trying his best to put some of these worries aside. His gaze shifted to Tom, the newcomer. "You, one of them wildcattin' bunch?"

"Yes sir," Tom said, looking a little nervous as the big man towered over him.

The sheriff shifted his stance. He seemed to delight in ramming his broken toothpick between teeth held captive by chunks of forgotten tobacco. "Looks like quite a few of you oil fellers here today. Saw old Harry Sinclair talkin' to Frank Phillips over in front of the drug store a while ago. Guess they're here sizin' up the Indian's mood. Won't be long till the next lease sale."

Tom began to relax a little, and got the courage up to speak. "Where's the lease sale held?"

Jake watched the sheriff start to feel important, as his sagging body began to come to life.

"Oh, it's up yonder on the hill at the agency underneath the million dollar elm, weather permittin.' Shoot, they'll be this many or more folks here, that day."

Jake snickered. "Yeah, ol' Colonel Walters, the auctioneer, had better be warmin' up his oil boomin' voice. Boy, that sucker is smooth as corn silk. He just coaxes the bids right out of their mouths. He really earns that ten dollars a day."

Tom's interest was climbing. "Oh, really? I wonder who'll be top bidder this time?"

Jake thought about it a minute. "Well, I am goin' bet on old Bill Skelly. He's a cagey old devil."

All of a sudden, a loud crash broke up the conversation. It came from the street to the left.

"What's that?" Tom exclaimed as they all shifted their gaze to the disturbance down the block.

Sheriff Cook spoke in a terrible voice, dripping in sarcasm. "Sonsabitch, looks like Broke Arm just plowed his Cadillac into the back of Chief Bacon Rind's Pierce Arrow roadster. Hell fire. Ought to be a law. They've all got these cars, and not a one of them knows how to drive the damn thing."

The radiator on the Cadillac was steaming and hot water was running everywhere. As they bucked the crowd for a closer look, they could see that the wood-spoke wheels had collapsed and there was a terrible tent-like bulge in the hood. The Cadillac's emblem looked as if it was going to fly away in self-defense. Broke Arm was taking great pride in not moving a muscle. He was sitting right behind the wheel, arms crossed with the surliest of looks on his face. They could see he wasn't hurt, nor was he going to move. He had his wife in the other front seat, and in the back were Charley Whip and his pal, Hard Rope. They were all sitting with arms folded; and, blankets tightly stretched around their six foot-plus bodies. By now, two or three other on-lookers were trying to decide what to do. The horns of the backed-up, impatient traffic were blaring, continuously.

Sheriff Cook jerked open the door. "Broke Arm, what on earth were you thinking?"

No response came from the four sullen Indians. Frustrated, the sheriff hauled off and kicked the fender of the big car as they hurried to the front car where Chief Bacon Rind sat as if he was struck dead by lightning. Not even his otter hat was ajar. He wore tiny round spectacles, and his black eyes stared straight ahead.

Known by the tribe as Wah-She-Hah, he was one of the most important Osages. He was a very dignified specimen, well over six feet. He was looked upon as quite a character. He would show up in lots of nearby towns, clad in his buckskin leggings, moccasins, bright silk shirts, and expensive blankets. Today, however, his otter bandeau with the eagle feather sat snugly on his black braided hair. Positioned importantly on his chest was a large crucifix representing the new religion. Along side of the crucifix hung his Wah-sha-ske-skah, a disc gorget carved from some fresh water mussel, representing Grandfather Sun, of the old religious beliefs.

"Go get Father Jack!" Sheriff Cook thundered. "Maybe, he can talk some sense into them. Damn it. Hurry up!"

About that time Father Jack, black robes and all, came flying out of the meat market with five mongrel dogs, licking their chops and biting at his heels. "Father Jack!" The sheriff bellowed, "Talk some sense into these Indians, will ya? Damn fools!"

Father Jack was beyond harassed. He was yelling obscenities at the top of his Irish lungs. "Get these damn dogs out of here! Tell John Stink to call 'em off! They're all his, you know, Sheriff?"

The sheriff was waving him off, yelling like a mad man. "Do something with these Indians, will ya? They're just sittin' here like bumps on a log. I'll haul their blanket asses up to the jail. See how they like that." His foul mood was about to erupt.

"It won't do any good, Sheriff. What the hell can I do?"

"Well, do something, anyway. We don't want any more trouble today!"

Jake kicked the dogs out of the way and followed Father Jack up to the car, eager to hear what he'd say. It was only a couple of feet into the street, but in that length of time, Father Jack had reclaimed his composure. He spoke in a remarkably soft voice. "Bacon Rind, I know your car is hurt and it's a fine car, but we need to move it. Sheriff Cook needs to clear the street to get everyone together for the payment."

Bacon Rind looked straight ahead, not blinking an eye, and from a voice far beneath his Mackinaw blanket, he said, "Me no want 'wagon that runs by itself.' Wagon dead. Me get new one."

And the four Indians proceeded to get out of the car and disappear into the crowd, saying no more. The subject was closed. The men raced to the back car, but Broke Arm and his passengers had already disappeared. Silently, they had gotten the best of them. It was the sheriff's problem now. The Osages were halfway up the hill on foot to get new money and new wagon that ran by its self.

CHAPTER TWO

It was now half-past noon and Jake was getting hungry. His stomach had been pressuring him with blatant gurgles for some time. He decided to amble over in the vicinity of the council house on West Main Street. Ho Lah Go Ne, the town crier, had made his last swing on Kihekah Street crying his last reminder. His chore was over until it was time to call out each Indian's name as they stepped up for their annuity payment. Jake thought. *Damnation, maybe, even those confounded dogs'll lay down in front of the stores and nap for awhile.*

He made his way through the crowd toward the sandstone buildings and the trader stores of the agency. There was the council house, complete with bell tower, the doctor's house, and the government blacksmith shop. Interspersed between them were the Duncan Hotel and the Constantine Theatre.

At payment time, the Indians would camp for two or three days. Some of them camped on top of the hill back of the big three-story government school. The Big Hills clan from Greyhorse and the Upland-Forest people from Hominy camped in the bottoms down by the mill. The Little Osages and Heart-Stays people lived with the Thorny-Valley people in the village near the agency.

That day, since the weather was so celebration perfect, the agent had decided not to use the payment window on the west side of the council house. Instead, they would use the kiosk in the middle of the street. The kiosk used to be on Kihekah Street. However, in 1914, when the Triangle building was built—or the Osage skyscraper, as it was commonly called—it was moved it to West Main Street around the corner. When they built the building, they had paved the street, but it was not popular. The Indians' horses hated it because they were afraid of the hard, unfamiliar surface. Consequently, everyone was happier when it was moved to West Main Street where dirt and dust clouds still abound.

Jake knew he would find his wife, Maggie somewhere around her family clan, led by her parents, Fred and Julia Lookout. Wah-Na-Sha-She, Osage for "Little Eagle That Gets What He Wants," was Fred Lookout's tribal name.

He was a nice guy with a great trusting face. His black hair was parted down the middle with two long braids that hung on either side of his head. His bronze face was pitted and scarred. Fred, unlike the others, didn't wear an otter or beaver hat. He wore a big, black, straight brim felt hat. He seemed to like the white man's shoes better than the traditional moccasins, for some reason. He wore an expensive Mackinaw blanket over his shirt with a silk scarf tied around his neck. Resting on the scarf was his long colorful strand of Indian beads. Jake always mused that it was his eyes that were so unforgettable. They were kind, stern, and wise.

"Thick Hand," the Indian agent, better known to the government as Major Miles, had sent Fred away to Carlisle Indian School in Pennsylvania when he was a boy. He was smart, and he had learned farming from the Germans back east. When the allotment act of 1906 was enacted, Fred was one of the original Osage allotees. There were eight hundred and sixty full bloods and, leading that pack was, indeed, his father-in-law. He had been chief before, and he would be soon, again.

Jake found them. They were sitting with a large group of Indians under the big shade tree across from the council house. They wanted to be in earshot of the paymaster. The band on the kiosk was playing some post-war music, made popular about five years earlier. Oblivious to the band's music, the Osage drummer was beating out his territory to the important people—the Osages.

Jake thought how fetching Maggie looked today as he ambled toward her. She cleans up pretty good—dressed fit to kill today, he thought. He was right. Maggie was in full bloom. Her beauty was unmatched in the tribe. Her noble facial structure showed no signs of her ancestor's pain. She had transformed it all into a quiet, graceful elegance. Her shining hair was shoe polish black and her dark eyes held a sensitivity no white man would ever know. Jake thought to himself. How'd this ol' backwoods driller ever get so damn lucky? Um, um. Yes sir. She's a hum-dinger. She sure can purse those beautiful lips together when a pout seems appropriate.

She was not going to lose her looks like so many Indian women, because her Osage mama, Julia, was still a beautiful, graceful, majestic woman. Her name was Julia Pryor or "Sacred Arrow-Shaft" in Osage. She was of the Bear Clan, which lived with the family of Quiver. She was also a descendant of Baptiste Maugraine, but had little French blood. She had the Indian looks, but the French had definitely contributed greatly to her classic stature.

Julia had worn clothes of the fancy white women until she was invited to a dance where there was drinking and lots of white rednecks. The heavy eyebrows, as she referred to them, began shooting the place up. She became so indignant that she went home, put up her corset and bustle and went back to her old shrouding, leggings, and moccasins. If that was how civilized men acted, then she wanted no part of it.

Jake chuckled as he thought of Julia giving up her highfalutin ways. At that moment, Tom Fisher came running through the crowd. Jake grabbed him by the arm. "Hey, hold your horses there, Tom. Are the dogs still hot on your trail?"

"Gosh, Jake! I lost you after the car accident," Tom replied. He was out of breath and sweating profusely in his rumpled suit. "I had to find

Mr. Phillips and tell him I'd see him after the payment about four o'clock, down at the confectionery shop on West Main. He loves that sweet stuff. That reminds me, I'm starved. You know any of these Indians that we can con out of something to eat?"

Jake was really amused, as Tom seemed to have overlooked Maggie, standing by her husband's side. Out of the corner of his eye, he could see that she was not pleased. She had pulled her blanket just a little tighter, to show that she was miffed. "Tom, I'd like you to meet my wife, Maggie Lookout Knupp." Jake wondered just how nervous and pale the man could get before he regained himself.

Tom stammered feverishly. "Oh, Mrs. Knupp, how do you do? I am so sorry. I was rude about the food. I guess I've been spending too much time in the oil patch. Please forgive me."

He had turned on his back east Ivy League charm, as Jake explained to Maggie that this young man was from Philadelphia. He was there with Mr. Frank Phillips. She warmed up a trifle, but Jake knew it would take a while before she would come to like young Mr. Fisher. It was best just to pretend it hadn't happened.

"Come on over, Tom, and I'll introduce you to my father-in-law." Jake motioned, as Maggie followed them about a step behind.

"Oh Lord, Jake. I've stuck my foot in my mouth. I'm sorry, but my God she's beautiful, Jake. That's the blackest hair—and her eyes, damn, they're gorgeous."

"Thanks Tom." Jake laughed at the apologetic young man. "And she can pout pretty good, too. Don't worry, she'll get over it." They ambled over to Fred Lookout, and Jake shook his hand. "Howdy Fred!"

He seemed glad to see Jake, but he merely grunted his reply. Jake introduced him to a now very humble Tom Fisher. The Lookout lodge was close by and Fred motioned to the poles where the jerked meat was hanging and about a dozen women were attending huge boiling pots of stew.

"Want some?"

"We sure do, Fred. It smells wonderful." The Indian women provided them each with a wooded bowl and ladle, and Maggie brought them a cup of coffee. The three men wandered about the clan visiting. Fred would stop at each person, and they would laugh at a story or two. The Indians could sit for hours and visit with the other clan members.

Maggie stood by the lodge alone, watching Jake and Tom. *Another oilman*, she thought with more than a little agitation. Jake was already hooked. As she looked at Jake though, her heart softened. He was so good-looking. He had light brown wavy hair and blue eyes. He never bothered to wear a hat; and, his hair lay tousled like a boy's. His tall frame was nicely proportioned: broad shoulders, narrow hips, and long legs. He was the envy of all the women in the county, but he never seemed to know that. Brash and smart, he was always a winner. He had turned thirty that year. She was close to twenty-six. *Time sure flies*, she sighed. She wondered what she liked best about him. Probably it was his gentle, sensitive nature and the playful twinkle in his eye. He was just so damn Irish, always wheelin' and dealin'. *Oh, well.* She was over her mad, already. It was just too beautiful a day to stay miffed. She walked over to her husband and pulled on his shirt sleeve. "Lots of traders are here today, with good things, Jake. Traders from Ark City, Coffeyville, and Elgin."

Jake looked at her kiddingly. "See something you like, Maggie?"

She smiled, seemingly in a better mood over the prospect of shopping. "There was one or two things I saw that I'd like to have."

"Okay, Maggie, after the payment, we'll go see what you found."

She appeared to be happier as she moved to walk by her husband's side.

As Fred joined them, Tom was trying to fend off a dog that wanted his food as much as he did. "Fred, why do these Indians have to bring all their damn dogs?" Jake asked. The big Indian just laughed as he dropped a whole chunk of hot cooked meat between the chops of his favorite dog, "Bear".

Tom, who now had his belly full, was beginning to look around. "Who are those Indian guys over by the council house?"

Maggie bristled again. *This guy is batting a thousand. I hope he's luckier at finding oil wells.* Jake thought. "Those are Maggie's cousins."

Tom was determined. "What are they staring at?

Jake laughed at the young man's blatant curiosity. "They're just drooling over all the young lady clerks from up at the agency. They'd better lay off the whiskey tonight, though, while they're chasing them up at the dance at Elgin. Sheriff Cook says he's going to keep the peace, no matter what."

Maggie nodded her head in agreement. "My oldest cousin, Ben, want school teacher up at gov'munt school. He say, 'Her eyes green, like his new automobile, when rain falls on it.'"

The men all laughed. "Where is she?" Fred asked.

"She's over with other teacher at Osage Mercantile," Maggie quickly inserted. "She's very prissy—not good for having children."

"Hum," Jake said, deeply amused. "Tom, you married?"

"No, sir, I'm not."

"Well, you'd better look them over and land you one, if you can. These Indian men are pretty hard to beat out for the hand of one of these ladies. You can't believe what I had to do to get Fred here to let me have Maggie's hand."

Maggie and Fred both grunted in disgust.

Tom laughed and struck a match to light up the cigar he had just bummed from Jake. "Got any kids, Jake?"

"Yeah, one. A boy, just turning five. He's around here somewhere."

"What's his name?" Tom asked.

"Quinton Thomas Lookout Knupp," Jake said proudly. "He's a combination of his Irish driller daddy, and his Indian mama. He favors his mama, though. His Indian name is 'Wah She Ling Da' or 'Little Eagle That Sings'. He's a real corker, and I might add, my pride and joy."

"Where is he, now?" Tom asked.

Jake glanced around. "Oh, he was around here playing awhile ago with a couple of Iron Necklace's little nephews. Most of the time, Grandma Julia looks after him. He's most likely over in the Lookout lodge with her."

As Jake looked up and down West Main Street, he could see the bankers in their three-piece black vulture suits glad-handing everybody they met. They had on their little round-rimmed spectacles. "Look there, Tom. Those damn fool bankers struttin' around. I hate the bastards. Ever'one of those blood suckers has the words, trust me, written on his forehead." He said with utter distaste to Tom. "You know, It never fails to amaze me how the Indians seemed to rely on them—just bosom buddies." Tom nodded his head sympathetically.

In addition Jake pointed out several sleazy attorneys to Tom. "They're all a bunch of crooks. They're just here to try and swindle the Indians out of their money. See that tall white haired ol' boy over talking with them. That's the slickest of all. He's the Osage Indian attorney from up at the agency, ol' Pat Woodward. He has the inside seat on all the information. He's a sorry so-n-so. He just looks crooked. Hell, the only one I trust is T.J. Leahy. He's an Irishman, married to an Indian lady, Bertha Rogers." Jake scanned the crowd, but he didn't see him anywhere. "He's pretty low key—easy goin'." Jake looked at his timepiece. "Well, Tom, it's getting close to payment time."

Then suddenly, from out of nowhere, there came a series of gunshots. It was coming from the direction of the post office. Tom and Jake looked at each other and took off running the two blocks toward the government building at 7th and Kihekah. They had to dodge all the cars, buggies, and horses cramped in the packed street. Besides themselves, they had to keep from knocking down the other five hundred people, all running the two blocks with them.

There was a huge Pierce Arrow parked in front of the federal office with a crowd already gathered around it when they got there. The passenger door was open on the giant red car and there was a young Indian woman falling out of the seat. Her head had been thrust onto the street but her feet were still inside the car. She was elegantly dressed and Jake recognized her instantly. It was Mary Woodaxe. Her body was riddled, from what he could see, by at least five bullets. One in the head and at least four other bullets had found their ways into her white silk blouse, now a deep crimson as the blood from the bullet holes ran together. The driver of the car was trying to hold her head as the blood from her forehead, filled his hands. Of course, as rumor had it, he had to be James Martin, a full blood, and the dead woman's lover. Jake took one look at her fixed eyes and said to Tom. "Looks like it's a little to late for any romantic good-byes between them. Let's see how many dead Indians does that make today." Jake noticed the look on Tom's face was close to terror.

The sheriff was already there and he and the other deputies were trying to restrain another woman on the sidewalk. She was fighting and screaming, "Yes, I killed her! The whore! She took my husband! I warned her!"

The crowd stared as Sheriff Cook put the cuffs on the hysterical Mrytle Martin and took her away.

"What on earth is that all about?" Tom said in a low voice.

Jake shook his head. "I knew it was going to happen. That damn Indian, James Martin, left his wife Mrytle two weeks ago. She's that little seventeen-year old white gal they just handcuffed. James has been messing around with Mary forever. I knew Mrytle wasn't going to give up the money. She had been throwing a fit all over town that she was going to kill Mary. I guess James and Mary didn't believe her. Well, I reckon, they believe her now."

Tom nodded. "Guess she's going need one of them sleazy lawyers you were telling me about."

"Yeah, I reckon." Jake mopped the back of his neck with his plaid handkerchief. "Boy! These Indian murders are getting' out of hand."

Tom looked surprised, "Oh really. How many?"

"I bet there's been over twenty this year. Shoot, I found one dead, just this morning, coming to town." Tom raised his eyebrows as Jake went on. "You know, that Mrytle had some nerve now, killin' Mary right in front of the whole tribe, here on the busiest day of the year. Look! Everyone's leaving. Must be time for the payment. There ain't nothing going stop the Osages from getting their money." The whole crowd had disappeared into thin air. Money was important business. And murder was just an unfortunate sidelight in the little agency town.

Back at the council house, everyone sensed it was time. Activity was picking up. "Nothing like a little excitement, huh, Tom? But look at these Indians—they never moved one iota from their shade trees."

The Indian's rest period was over, and they were actually beginning to turn their gaze to the council house. Women were paying less attention to their cooking pots. White women in long fancy dresses were flirting openly with the young mixed-blood bucks. It was a game to see who was going to grab which Indian buck's brass ring and full money pockets, at least for the night.

"Tom, now, you'd better watch these women." Jake winked kiddingly at the younger man. "They love to flirt. They practice on those stoic faces that never change expression. Only their black eyes catch every feminine trick used on them."

Tom seemed impressed, and a little awed by their openness. "I don't think I'm quite ready for them." He laughed, almost self-consciously.

"Well, Tom, tonight will be great. Good whiskey and good women. That is, except for old James Martin and his wife. They've had their last rendezvous."

The two men looked up as they heard some honking in the background behind them. They turned to see that the Buick dealer, Joe Ferguson, had brought several of his new cars down to whet the appetite of the Indians, offering them the deals of the century.

"What was that?" Tom asked as his eyes searched the crowd.

"Oh, that's old Iron Necklace's grandson trying out the horn. He'll probably buy it. He wrecked his last four Caddys."

Tom's mouth dropped open. "Four Cadillacs?"

"Oh, sure, they only want the big powerful cars—room for all of them to ride."

Since the time was getting close, everyone was leaving the stores on Kihekah Street to come into earshot of the crier. The storekeepers and traders were taking that time to prepare for the Indian's return. They'd be back soon, with money to buy the items they'd been rummaging through all morning. They were getting their account books out to settle back accounts. "Wanta hear something interestin'? I can remember Fred telling me the stories about years ago, when they came to the agency town to trade. Each Osage would present his willow stick as a record for the amount owed to the storekeeper. He simply counted notches. Willow sticks are a symbol of long-life to the Osage. He used them for counting days, songs, debts, or whatever."

"That's a far cry from Wall Street, but I guess it'd work." Tom smiled. The clerks were busy preparing to cut bolts of silk and calico and the male clerks were ready to sell their ropes, harnesses, wagon implements, and other hardware needs.

"Listen—the tempo of the drum seems to have sped up. Good indication payment time's approaching." Jake motioned to his left.

Even the dogs noticed the increasing excitement and they all started to bark loudly. Simultaneously, the Indian children started to whimper as mothers ceased to pay close attention to them. Everyone was watching to see if Osage Indian agent and paymaster, old George Wright, was in sight. "Where is he, Jake? Point him out to me."

Jake scanned the crowd. "He's not here yet, but look, over there." He pointed over a ways, behind him. "There's the Federal Marshals on horseback. They're busy watchin' ever'thing that moves."

"Why are they here?" Tom asked as he looked around at the mounted figures sitting like statues.

"Oh, just in case of a chance robbery, I guess. The royalty payments have reached such proportions that the newspapers are making a big deal in the headlines. Never know when some murderers, thieves, or other crooks may decide to pay us a visit." Tom looked around even more nervous than before.

As if by magic, the crowd hushed as the Osage crier, Ho Lah Go Ne, announced in a long drawn-out call, that Agent Wright was in place. Over the heads of the crowd, Jake could see the agent standing on top of the kiosk. Then, ceremoniously, the crier called out the name of the first band chief. He would stand next to the crier to tell him his allotees names. Then the crier would begin the process of calling out each Indian's name as he walked to the kiosk. Agent Wright, a rather lean man of tall stature, thinning gray hair, and thick lens eye glasses, announced in a loud clear voice. "Now, is the time for the distribution of the second quarter annuity payment. The Department of Interior and the Bureau of Indian Affairs of the United States of America will be paying per headright this June 3, 1923, twelve thousand four hundred dollars."

The Indians all grunted approval, the white people cheered, and the band played three bars of "Happy Days Are Here, Again". Everyone watched as the chief of the first band walked to the kiosk.

"Wow, who's this?" Tom asked. "Lord, look how big he is. He's gotta be seven feet tall."

"Yeah, he's big. Hell, they're all big. This is the chief of the Big Chief band. He has allottees one through seventy-three. Here we go! Listen!"

The town crier began his slow dutiful cry. "Allottee number one, Paw-Hu-Ska, Tom Big Chief. Allottee number two, Me-To-Pee. Allottee number three—" The names rolled by with each Indian moving solemnly and slowly to the kiosk.

"The fourth band chief", Jake volunteered, "Is chief of the whole tribe. He is Chief Ne-Kah-Wah-She-Tun-Kah, allottee number one eighty-two. He's very old, and is about to die. He may not last the summer. If so, word around the Indians is that the next chief will be, Fred. He's of the Thorny Bush people of the Beaver band."

"What's his number?" Tom asked.

Jake thought a moment. "Fred is allottee, number five fifty four, I believe."

Tom was really taking it all in. "What about old Bacon Rind? I like him. He's a real character."

Jake nodded his head. "Yeah, he's one of the Wah-Ti-An-Kah Band of the Upland Forest Osages, with old Iron Necklace as chief. His Osage name is Wah-She-Hah, and I believe his number is seven forty-four. He's one of my favorites, too. His wife, Rose Chouteau Bacon Rind is number seven forty-five. This will go on awhile. Let's go get a cool drink. These are all full bloods till you get to number eight seventy-three. Then, the mixed bloods are called, ending with number two thousand two hundred twenty-nine."

"Why, that number, Jake?" Tom asked as he brushed a swarm of gnats away from his face.

History lessons sure are hard work, Jake thought. "Well, back in 1906, there was an old chief named Bigheart. He was cousin to my mother-in-law, Julia. He helped set up the Allotment Act, whereby each Indian would get about 650 acres of land for his own, plus a headright. Bigheart's the one that sought to keep all of the mineral rights as communal. He was one smart Indian. He could speak seven languages, and was real well educated. So anyway, when the roll was started, only two thousand two hundred twenty-nine Indians signed up."

"I see," Tom said, looking perplexed. "This is really complicated."

"Yeah," Jake laughed. "But now, the complications have paid off. Cause, these Indians are now, the richest in the world."

"Yeah." Tom grinned. "Thanks to all the wildcatters, like Frank Phillips, Bill Skelly, and old Harry Sinclair." He looked down at his pocket watch. "Oh, my gosh! I'd better go find Frank. Good to talk to you Jake, I'll see you, later." He ran off toward Kihekah Street.

Nice guy! Jake thought. He yawned as the allottee numbers drolled on, and the Indian drum was still keeping pace. He decided to find a shady place and catch a nap.

Maggie would find him after her name was called. So, he concluded that he'd catch a few winks, if those damn bugs and dogs would just leave him alone. No telling what kind of excitement would start up tonight. Course, Myrtle's killing spree at the post office would be a hard act to follow.

CHAPTER THREE

Jake had been asleep for over an hour when Maggie gently nudged his arm. Jake yawned lazily. "Have you gotten the money, sweetheart?"

"Yes. Come on Jake. Hurry!" She replied.

Jake sat up and straightened his not-so-pressed clothes. "So, where do you want to go, Maggie?"

"I want to go to McLaughlin's. They have new beautiful bolts of silk from Europe."

"I see. Where else?" He asked with a real lack of enthusiasm. "I show you," she said happily. They hurriedly moved in the direction of the general store.

Father Jack was talking to T.J. Leahy, the lawyer, as they approached the busy crowded store. They were deeply absorbed in conversation. As they motioned Jake into their huddle, he told Maggie to go on in and buy what she wanted. Jake didn't care. He had learned never to buck her, especially, if his drilling business ever got into a tight and he needed a little cash. He could always count on winning her over.

It was getting on late into the afternoon. The crier was about two-thirds through with the pay-off and the streets were bristling again with lots of eager full-pocketed Indians, ready to buy and trade. The late June afternoon was winding down. The dogs had worn themselves out, and the flies were getting renewed vigor. Kids were licking their dripping ice cream cones, outside on the sidewalks, while their parents shopped.

As Jake got closer to Father Jack, he could see from his demeanor that his words were serious. Father looked around and decided that too many other folks could overhear them, so he motioned Jake to follow him and Leahy up the narrow stairway to Leahy's office over the McLaughlin store. Once upstairs, they came to a big crinkled glass door with Leahy's name and the word "lawyer" in big black letters. They went inside and Leahy offered them a seat. His chairs were ox-blood red leather, and looked to be older than dirt. They had no doubt witnessed lots of nervous people, who had sat in their hard cushions for the last twenty years. It was a well-known fact that Leahy was a fairly decent lawyer. He was one hundred percent Irishman, but he was laid back. In fact, the phrase around town was that he'd have to perk up to die. His sandy hair was parted in the middle overlooking a full-freckled face. He was skinny and tall and everyone said he had a little money, but it was hard to tell from his clothes or the decor of his office. Leahy sat down at his huge oak desk across from Jake and Father Jack. It was a well-designed European style desk with carved legs and a smooth top, covered with glass. Under the glass were pieces of memorabilia that, evidently, meant a lot to him. Jake was busy appraising the contents. He could identify a picture of Bertha, Leahy's wife.

There were also a few stray receipts for services rendered for sizeable amounts of money. He was really working at reading them up side down, when Leahy took a plug of tobacco out of his vest pocket. He fished out his Remington pocketknife, and cut off about a half-dollar size piece. He offered the plug to the priest. Father Jack already had his old Case knife out of some mysterious pocket or the other of his black cassock, in anxious anticipation of the lawyer's high-priced plug. Jake declined the offer, as he was already unwrapping his cigar. He bit off the tip and spat it in the direction of the tarnished spittoon.

The three men, in silent agreement, could relax and think. There was nothing like a smoke to clear your mind. Leahy leaned back in his chair. He then put two of the biggest boots Osage County had ever seen squarely down on the desk. It was a little too hot and stuffy in the June heat, but circling overhead, was a four bladed ceiling fan humming and turning in slow motion.

"Now, what's this you've been hollering about, Father Jack?" Jake said breaking the smoke-filled silence.

That remark instantly brought the priest to his feet. His already red face was glistening with sweat. "You know what that sorry no-good banker, Clyde Baker, over at the Citizen National Bank, did to one of my staunch parishioners? He encouraged Claire Whitehorn to participate in a spending spree that made Cleopatra pale by comparison."

Leahy shifted his feet as his chair squeaked in reply. "Yeah, Clyde's rotten to the core. I'd never do business with the fat little worm. He really takes liberties."

"What did he talk her into?" Jake asked. His curiosity was suddenly aroused.

Father Jack took a deep breath. "Well, let me tell ya. Claire Whitehorn went to his office and told him she wanted him to handle some of her transactions. And boy, did they have a busy afternoon. She purchased a ten thousand-dollar fur blanket. You know a mink coat. A three-carat diamond ring, and a new Pierce Arrow convertible valued at four thousand dollars. Then, she bought two pieces of real estate—a down payment on a house in California for fifteen thousand dollars and two lots in Florida for five thousand dollars apiece. Can you believe that?" Father Jack was openly pacing, and the tone of his voice was loud. His face was blood red. "This is a sin! What's happening to my people? No telling how much kickback Clyde's making. He's fencing this stuff to unsuspecting Indians. We have to do something about this. It's a crime how people are coming in here and conning the Indians into spending money on stuff they don't want or need. They have no idea." He pounded his fist on Leahy's desk. "It simply would not have occurred to Claire Whitehorn to buy all of these things in one afternoon without someone putting ideas into her head. Besides, I'm getting more than a little concerned about all these murders. Someone is killing the Osages, right and left. Every day, it's another funeral. I can't figure it out. Why doesn't the damn agency do something about all this?"

"Like ol' man Woodward." Leahy said. "He's supposed to be the Indian's mentor. I trust George Wright, but Woodward's another matter."

"Oh yeah, that reminds me, I found a strange dead one up on the Spencer place this morning, hanging on a pumpjack. Pretty nasty deal. Obviously murder." Jake exclaimed suddenly remembering his early morning fiasco.

Father Jack hit the desk with his fist second time, rattling yesterday's coffee cups. "What is going on round here? They either con-'em or kill 'em, it looks like to me." Father Jack sat down, worn out from his flamboyant oratory, and looked for the spittoon sitting between his chair and Jake's.

"Father, you need a drink." Leahy suggested as he slammed his feet to the floor in a thunderous clamor and reached into another drawer. Below the tobacco stash drawer was a trap drawer neatly hidden by the heavy carving. He opened it and pulled out a half-pint of Irish whiskey. He pitched the bottle to Father Jack, who immediately tipped up the bottle and began to chug-a-lug a giant gulp. He then passed it to Jake, who followed his lead. Since the county was dry, and alcohol among the Indians was highly discouraged, the bootlegger was the only source of alcohol for the agency town. So, Jake made it a practice to never pass up a shot.

He wiped his mouth off on his sleeve and passed the bottle back to his host. "Maybe we should take this up with the agent. Something can surely be done about all of these con artists. You know the damn car dealers are no better. There's lots of those bastards making three times more money than the Indians."

Leahy nodded. "Jake, see if you can find out from Maggie and her father what's going on. Maybe they can give us names of some of these con-artists."

"Okay, I'll ask around tonight up at the camp, and see if I can find out anything. Hope all of this talk doesn't apply to me, when I talk Maggie into buying me a new string of tools." They all laughed. Father Jack seemed a little more relaxed as they all passed the well-traveled pint around, again.

Jake stood up reluctantly. "Well, I hate to leave such good company, but I left Maggie shopping and I promised to go with her. I just took a little side visit up here with you, guys." Father Jack and Leahy bid him good-bye, but they made no move to leave. Jake could tell old Black Robes and the Irish lawyer were going to spend some time with the rich tobacco and good whiskey. Jake let himself out the door. He tucked his shirt neatly back into his pants and smoothed down his hair. No use tipping Maggie off early that he'd had a little swig or two.

As he approached the bottom of the stairs, he was having difficulty getting used to the bright setting sun. He stood there for a moment watching the crowd roaming up and down the busy street. Since he was in no big hurry, he moved slowly toward the McLaughlin store. He spoke casually to a few Indians and entered the busy store. He couldn't find Maggie at any of the counters or by any of the racks where the brightly colored bolts of silk were located. He was beginning to think, he'd missed her somewhere. He walked back out onto the street and began a better search. As he walked, he became sidetracked by a couple of roustabouts from the oil patch who recognized him. "Hey, Jake, got any work for us with your outfit?" The roughest of the group yelled.

Jake stopped briefly and shook his head. "If you boys are lookin' for some well-site construction work, you might get a hold of old Al Evans. He's the one I am drilling for next. He might be able to use ya." They talked for a few minutes before he could ditch them and resume his search.

He attempted to cross the street, dodging cars. They were still driving helter-skelter up West Main. He watched several independent traders who had set up racks of their wares over by the Triangle building. It occurred to him that maybe Maggie had wandered over there to look at their merchandise. In the middle of the crowd, he spied Fred Lookout talking to Iron Necklace a few feet away. When he reached them, he asked them if they'd seen Maggie, but they both, said, "No." He had just gotten the words out of his mouth to them, when from the other direction came Maggie and her friend, Rose Whitehorn. His apprehension quickly faded when he looked at her face. She wasn't angry with him for leaving her at all. In fact, he could tell she was in good humor.

"Maggie, I've been looking everywhere for—."

"Oh, yeah, Jake? You've been drinking with some of your friends— probably those bad oil patch workers." She interrupted.

Jake let that go. "Well, let's go see what you want to buy."

"I already bought it." She said happily. She opened her hand, and in it was a tiny box. He took the box from her and opened it. There was a huge sparkling three-carat-plus diamond ring.

Jake's face went ashen and he thought he would hit the sidewalk in shock. "Oh, my God! Where did you get this?"

Maggie looked at him with beaming black eyes. "Claire Whitehorn took me and Rose to this man who sells big jewels. Isn't it beautiful?"

Jake felt himself getting sicker by the moment. Now, Maggie, too, was a victim of these same con men.

"What about my new string of tools? You know what bad shape they're in." Jake asked after finding his voice.

"No matter. We have plenty of money." She smiled happily. "Get whatever you want."

Jack and Fred looked at each other in bewilderment. Both of them were amazed that his people believed that there was no limit to the amount of money that gushed with the oil out of the Osage.

Suddenly, it had been a long day. The drum of the Osage was still keeping the pace of the fading day. It sounded now, more than ever like a loud wail of a dying animal as Grandfather Sun slipped beneath the horizon.

CHAPTER FOUR

Grandfather Sun's red light illuminated the tops of the trees as night approached. The Indian camps were well established on the hill north of the agency. The aroma in the new spring air was heavenly. Hot steaming pots of corn and potatoes, with huge slabs of buffalo meat, were cooked to perfection over the open fire. The smoke did nothing to interrupt the clearness of the night, except keeping away the army of June bugs. The old Indians were sitting on blankets under the elm trees. They were spinning yarns of how it was in the old days, when they had nothing but hardship and abuse. These Indians, now the world's richest, had gone through many generations' moons to reach their promise land.

Jake had found a tree to lean on, listening as the old Indians smoked and retold the stories of their beginnings. He knew their stories by heart. Yet, it seemed the Indians had to continually tell each story over and over in case their old minds tried to fail them.

The Osages were a branch of the southern Siouxs. They were giant Indians that had great endurance for walking, hunting, and fighting. Jake absent mindedly listened to the old Indian's conversation.

"Why did Father Marquette have to find our people along Mississippi River?" Joe Big Horse asked as if on cue. His long black braids framing his serious face. "That was beginning of our trouble.

Then, Louisiana Purchase move white man into Indian land. U.S. government make treaty. Say it legal for white man to possess land. Our people had no choice but to sign the documents. 1847 come. Osages forced to move from our homes in Missouri to land on the Neosho River in east central Kansas."

"Our people were poverty stricken—no game and no buffalo." Iron Necklace spoke in his monotone voice with a far away look in his eye. "Osages would return from spring and autumn hunt to find mean, vicious, white settlers had taken our dwellings and fields. White men organized claim clubs, stole horses, set up town sites, and enticed railroad. Indian's life was out of control. Our people had nothing left."

"Fighting was no option with sophisticated guns of white man." Joe Big Horse said regretfully.

"The government say they do Indians big favor. They would move Osages to protect us from trespassing white men." Tom Hard Rope hissed sarcastically. The fire in his eyes seemed to dart back and forth.

"Only because fewer Indians than white men. It was only trick." Iron Necklace spit disgustedly as he snapped a twig with his powerful fingers. "Then, Civil War come and our people had no military protection. Kansas want to get rid of Little Osages and sell land to white man for one dollar twenty-five cents 'n acre."

Jake watched as the Indian men smoked and passed the pipes as if they needed to rest their minds.

As the smoke slowly circled his head, Joe Big Horse continued. "I remember sad day when Little Osages sobbed and wailed at the graves of our people when we prepared to move again, for third time. Elders spend time wondering where our great leaders lay buried. Trail gone. They lay forgotten somewhere under snow and ice in silent, unmarked graves. Only the wind and Grandfather Sun remember whereabouts."

"When did our people get to Oklahoma, Joe?" Tom Hard Rope said on cue, knowing full well the answer.

"January of 1871. Federal government and the chiefs of the tribe decided on location in what's now northeastern Oklahoma on Silver Lake, close to the town of Bartlesville. Then, federal government say they make an error on location. Our people had to abandon homes once more. The government say they give us bigger better deal. Increase size of new reserve to one point seven million acres. Sell to Osages for seventy cents 'n acre. White man and government happy. 1872, we come to promise land here near Pawhuska."

As the talk drifted on Jake concluded that ironically, even without Moses, the promise land was worth much more than the milk and honey they had bargained for.

But always, as great and humble people do, the old men thanked Wah'-Kon-Tah and the heavy eyebrows God for at last, giving them the gifts of the earth. They prayed that Grandfather Sun would continue to watch over them. Chief Bigheart, Governor Joe, and Black Dog had all, been great leaders, dealing with the 'heavy eyebrows' in protecting the Osages.

Jake kept wondering, if indeed their suffering was really over now that money seemed to be no problem. However, It seemed to be only the old Indians whose day in the sun had passed, who were enjoying the summer camp get-together as the drum beat lazily continued at a relaxing pace.

Jake glanced around and noticed that the young bucks were already saddling up for the ride to Elgin. Young ladies and gentlemen were packing their Model T's for the twelve mile trek to the dance hall. Their wild war whoops already had a slightly drunken ring, as the excitement in their voices was building. Maggie was in a great mood after her little buying spree. She had been hounding Jake to take her dancing, too. Stretching his long, lanky body, he would lay low and see if she remembered. He took out a chaw of tobacco and let the cool night air soak in.

Thirty minutes later, Maggie came out of the Lookout lodge dressed and ready to go. "Are you ready, Jake? Let's hurry! Everyone else has left.

We'll be late." Jake opened one eye and looked her over, admiring the package.

"Okay," he mouthed. If she just wasn't so damn beautiful. The red silk of her blouse cast a glimmer of pink on her cheeks, and the moon used her black long hair as a reflecting pool. He uttered under his breath, *But I don't care how beautiful you look, sooner or later, we're going to have to discuss this ring.*

Jake and Maggie had to walk a ways to his car. He had left it in town the day before. On the way, Jake stopped behind the Red Store to hastily buy a half-pint of whiskey from his local bootlegger, old Henry Grammer. Things were looking up, now that he had a little something to wet his whistle. They finally came in sight of his car, a twelve cylinder bright yellow Packard—just what a successful driller should be driving in the Osage on a Saturday night. As badly as he wanted to talk about the diamond ring purchase, even he did not want to ruin the enchantment of the summer evening. Maggie could hardly talk in the car for just watching the ring, catching the glimmer of the stars. Disgust was crawling all over Jake and he fought to keep his mouth shut.

It would take them about an hour to make the trip. The traffic was slow as they left Pawhuska, heading north to the Kansas state line. It wasn't an easy dirt road to drive. Unannounced, horse drawn buggies, without any thoughts of lights, could appear from nowhere. It was not even unusual for an occasional deer to make an appearance. They would hide behind the huge blackjacks, ready to bound across the road, as if to rob you of your breath.

Jake and Maggie had the open air of the touring car to keep them alert, although Jake was getting mighty dry, he thought. It was always exciting to head out of town and let all twelve cylinders perform in his twin-six Packard. In honor of the moment, she floated down the road like the Osage's lady moon smoothly sliding across the sky. The Packard slipped into Elgin about eight-thirty p.m. Jake could see in a flash that the Osage County cowboys were in town, too.

They'd been drinking most of the evening, it looked like. He could just follow the trail of T-model Fords down Elgin's main street to the rough saloon.

As Jake helped Maggie out of the giant yellow car, he could tell by the string of countless horses at the hitching rail that no one was tending the ranches. It was obvious that every cowboy in Osage County was there. The horses were standing like a perfect chorus line waiting for the conductor's signal to dance. About fifty men were standing outside the saloon. They were leaning on the light posts, trees, or up against the building. It looked as if they were building up courage to make a move on some suspecting lady inside.

Jake and Maggie entered the saloon at the west side of the rather dilapidated building. It was a fairly small, wooden-planked room with a bar. The bar was a little meager, but then no one cared. Whiskey was whiskey. One kind would suit all. Couples were getting liquored up, or better yet sizing each other up for those late night formal invitations. Jake watched them, knowing all too well that at closing time, it wouldn't really matter what or who they had. He led Maggie through the room to the double doors in the back, toward the large dance hall. It had a wood plank floor and kerosene lamps hanging every dozen or so feet, casting a soft glow on the dance floor. A band called the Cowboy Fence Riders was playing at the far corner. They wore Levis and bright colored calico shirts. Each one of them wore a beard and a summer straw cowboy hat. Around their necks, they wore silk-like scarves tied to the side. The fiddle was already starting to whine to the whiskey-drinking songs and people were pairing up to dance. Maggie was eager to get inside. She was really in a partying mood.

As they entered the bar, she waved at several of the Indian gals she knew. Jake got them a couple of whiskey shots as they passed through the dance hall doors to the beckoning music, beyond. It took a few minutes to get used to the smoke. As it cleared, he could see another familiar group—the oil patch trash. They'd probably, been here since the day, before. They looked rough, but who knows, they might be 'fought out' by now.

Jake leaned over to whisper in his wife's ear. "Maggie, sure a lot men here tonight. I wonder how long it'll take to make all the ladies mad."

She smiled up at him. "All of the ladies under forty are here from the agency and the boarding school. There's Laura Van Estes, with her friend." Jake looked in her direction. She was red-headed and he looked her over—about twenty-six, high spirited, and pretty good looking. She appeared to be demure and shy, but she had already surveyed the entire crowd, at least once. "Whose the blond gal with her?" Maggie asked.

Jake leaned over for a better view. "Oh, that's Miss Lydia. She's the gun runner."

"Oh yeah! I recognize her now," Maggie whispered. "She works at the gun counter in Goodman's Hardware Store." The two ladies in question were standing in a group of about fifteen good-looking gals. Jake decided to keep that information to himself.

Suddenly, at that moment, the band fired up a lively boot stomping tune of "Take Me Back to Tulsa, I'm too Young to Marry." It was like a cannon exploding, shooting men into every direction. They all grabbed a gal and the dance was on. The Indian bucks were letting out war whoops and the cowboys were swinging gals with intricate maneuvers. It looked more like they were roping steers at the Pawhuska rodeo. The skirts were flying and the spurs were jingling. It evidently, had been too much trouble for the cowboys to remove them. The oil patch gang had some hard looking women with them, probably from the night before. It appeared that the oil patch had first dibs on the Elgin prostitutes.

Jake leaned over and moved the long black hair from his wife's ear, "Maggie, want to dance?"

She nodded as he attempted to muscle his way into the heavy traffic. It reminded him of a sea of ropers going down for the third time. All anyone could see was arms entangled as they tossed and turned, clamoring for space.

Elgin was a great place to come. Kansas wasn't dry, and the dance hall always drew a crowd. Elgin was in the heart of ranching country. It was the world's largest cow shipping point. The Santa Fe and Midland Railroads met there. Sometimes as many as ten thousand cows a day would be shipped out of the little one-horse town. It was really cowboy territory, but no doubt, before the night was over, there would have to be a contest to see who was the toughest—the cowboy, the mixed-bloods, or the oil patch trash.

Now that everyone had loosened up, one dance led into another. It was hot for June. Now and then, a guy just had to wipe his brow and toss down a couple. Of course, no one was drinking just beer. These guys were drinking hundred proof whiskey and chasing it with beer.

Jake couldn't help noticing Miss Lydia. Her long blond hair and fair skin made her a stand out in the crowd of dark skinned Indians. She was a real good dancer, but no one messed with her. She was Big Ed's personal property. No one ever robbed her guns or hassled her, because she was a crack shot. And besides Big Ed would kill them. Jake wondered where he was. He wasn't round those parts, much. Everyone believed that he was a big time gangster from Chicago. He always came around flashing a lot of money. He would make a few deals and leave. *Oh well, didn't look like she was missin' him too bad tonight,* he thought.

Jake had about finished his own half-pint. He was in deep conversation with Jones, a member of another drilling crew, when John Holburt came over. They shook hands. He was one of the biggest ranchers in the county. He had had a cattle lease with the Osages for better than twenty years. "Howdy, John, how's it going?" Jake asked.

"Oh, got a case of the gout, but I guess I really can't complain, Jake," he replied. "We've been busy. We're grazing about twelve thousand head of cattle up on the Chapman Barnard. These cowboys of mine are really over-worked. They haven't seen a woman for a little too long." They laughed as they enjoyed the joke.

"Yeah I can tell!" Maggie shot them a dirty look and wandered off to find her Indian lady friends.

John and Jake stood there talking about the current cattle prices. Despite the fact that cow men were not too hot on drillers, the two men were really pretty good friends. "Let's go out and get a little air, John." Jake indicated the door. He knew Maggie was tired of dancing for a spell. She was gossiping with her friends, and no doubt, flashing that damn ring.

The two men walked outside, and the goings-on in the front and on the side of the saloon were well worth the trip. About a dozen cowboys and the gals they'd lassoed were intertwined with two faces under the brim of every wide cowboy hat. They were feeling no pain, and the gals were giving hope to the cowboys, that tonight, they might get lucky. Lady moon was doing her part to make the June night a perfect setting for a memory. Too bad the alcohol would blur it all.

"How much land you got leased, John?" Jake asked.

"Oh, about forty-five thousand acres. The bluestem's really looking good this year, and the cattle market's stayin' pretty high. So it oughta be a pretty good year. Might even make a little money."

"Atta boy, John," Jake laughed. "Are you able to control the ticks?"

John nodded. "Yeah, you have to. Feds are really cracking down. Can't ship any on the Santa Fe without having 'em dipped ever eighteen days. Nonetheless, we're moving about ten thousand head a day on the cattle trains. Midland Valley's runnin' five trains a day, right now."

All at once, a loud commotion started from inside the building. It sounded like a fight. Just then, the mixed-blood body of Joe Cornsilk came flying out of the half-open window, and in a crash of flying glass, landed on a cactus bush. He was out cold, blood tricking down his chin. "Watch it," an unseen voice yelled, as out came two more bodies. "Someone go get the law! He's a couple of buildings away."

John and Jake ran inside and sure enough a brawl had erupted. About fifteen mixed-bloods and twenty-five cowboys were slamming each other into walls with fists flying. They could hear tables and bottles as they were thrown to the floor. The oil field trash was calmly leaning on the bar, jeering, and spurring them on. When someone passed close to them, they'd simply grab a bottle and crash the passerby's head. A whole pile of passed out men lay at their feet. The sound of bones and flesh parting directions was awful and the smell of blood, mixed with sweat, was overpowering. No one seemed to mind, however, except the band. They were hastily packing up their fiddles and guitars in old worn out black cases. The ladies were screaming encouragement to their particular favorite fighter from the sidelines. Jake ducked as a beer bottle sailed over his head. "You'd better do something, John, or you'll have no one to work the cattle. The cowboys are tired out. But those damn Indian bucks ain't done a lick of work and they're still fresh." He laughed as a body landed from out of nowhere on his boot. John just threw up his hands in disgust.

As the fight shifted to the right side of the hall, Jake saw Maggie make a run for it to where he was standing. She yelled, "Lets get out of here!" And just in the nick of time as some idiot Indian found a gun behind the bar and began shooting the lights out along the west side of the hall. Then the rest of his pals began yelling a war whoop that would wake the dead. As Jake and Maggie edged their way in the dark out the door, Jake could see the law coming. He knew it wouldn't be long till the party would be over.

"What happened in there to start the ruckus?" Jake yelled.

Maggie was out of breath as she related the story. "Bill WhiteOaks had one of the cowboy's sisters in that dark place over by the pool tables. She started to scream. He was real drunk, I think and he had her by the hair trying to throw her back down on top of the pool table."

"Whose sister is she?" Jake asked.

"I think it's Mike Hale's. He's the youngest son, isn't he, of old man Hale?"

Jake nodded. "Yeah, he is. He's a damn hothead. Gotta big chip on his shoulder. He just begs someone to knock it off. He never needs much provokin' for a fight, much less, some Indian tryin' to rape his kid sister. The whole family hates Indians. Anyway, what happened next?" Jake prompted.

"Mike was screaming obscenities, swearing to everyone, that he'll kill Bill WhiteOaks." Maggie's voice was high pitched and excited and her black eyes were shining. "Then, Miss Lydia got in to it, trying to protect the girl. She shielded her with her arm, and helped her down from the table. Her hair was tangled and all over her head. Her pretty dress was undone at the bodice with the sleeve torn away at the shoulder. She was crying like this." Maggie demonstrated with her face in her hands. "Miss Lydia was real mad. She said someone would have to pay for this." Maggie took a deep breath. "Bill had been making bad comments to her all evening. All the girls had heard him. Jake, he never meant to hurt her. It's the alcohol. It makes him crazy."

Uh-huh, Jake muttered, half under his breath. *Well, crazy or not, there would be trouble. The cowboys would not forgive or forget. Ol' man Hale would see to it.*

Sooner or later, there would be a show down. Maybe, if it had involved a lesser cowhand, but not two siblings of one of the most powerful ranchers in the Osage.

Jake and Maggie had been walking at a fast clip while they were talking. They were both completely out of breath when Jake finally spied the yellow Packard. They jumped in and Jake drove to a safe distance to hide and watch what happened. As the law stormed in, the Indians and the cowboys jumped out of every window and door. They had decided that they weren't going to jail. They ran to the horses and T-models— two Indians per horse jumping on them from the rear. Eight to ten cowboys were hanging in and out of the Tin-Lizzies. Some were running through the woods, gals and guys both. The whole scenario looked like a hornet's nest that had just been torched. Jake was laughing so hard he could hardly contain himself. Looked like the sheriff was going to have to arrest the out-cold crowd, because everybody else was out of there.

Jake put the car in slow gear, still laughing as they drove to a place on the hill, safe at the edge of Elgin. *What a night!* He thought. The moon was full and the wild lilacs were in bloom casting their scent across the prairie. He slid down in the soft leather seat a ways and put his arm around Maggie. He could hear a coyote or two howling at the moon, but it went unnoticed. Most of Osage County's animal kingdom was asleep.

"Maggie, it was a great day, wasn't it?" Jake whispered in her ear. She nodded, her head against his shoulder. She was still as a mouse. "You know, Maggie, I'm going to be pretty scarce for a week or two. Gotta start drilling a well Monday morning for old Al Evans, west of Pawhuska, a ways. Gotta round everybody up. You know, it takes awhile."

She nodded, and then raised up long enough to say. "Jake, you promised to let Quinn tag along with you for awhile. My mother's going to visit some of her relatives in Claremore, remember?"

He grinned. "Yeah, that'll be okay. There will be plenty of people to watch him."

Maggie glanced up at him through her long dark lashes. "Yes, but Jake, it's going to be dangerous out there, if you're building the rig."

Jake rubbed her shoulder. "Now, now Maggie. It'll be fine. I'll take good care of him." She nodded sleepily, again, and snuggled a little closer. Jake leaned over, kissed her. "I love you, Maggie! But one day, soon we're going to have to talk about that ring. This spending has got to stop. My drilling business is suffering with no new equipment. I'm so busy, that there's no time for repairs, and the rigs are getting worn out." There was no reply. Either she had fallen asleep or she was one beautiful Indian lady, playing a great game of opossum. He wondered. *I guess she doesn't need to know, just how strapped for money I am.* Instantly, his heart softened. She was so beautiful. He never get tired of looking at her.

She was like the seasons. She changed so with every mood like oak leaves progressing from spring to autumn. Her hair, so straight and black, was always captive to the wind with no will of its own. Her lips curved up at the end, always giving her face a happy wistful appearance. She pretended, usually, to be less than observant, but Jake had known her too long. She was in tune with even the most minute details. Her sensitive nature allowed her to miss nothing. She was as lyrical as the poetry she loved. Rather than seeing her beauty, he always seemed to feel it first. *Gosh, I love her, and that kid of ours is just like her.* He put the car in gear and begrudgingly pulled away from their hideaway. He found the open road and let the Packard have its way. Leaning back, he listened to her big catlike purr as she roared back to Pawhuska.

About six miles inside the state line, Jake could see two big cars, half-in and half-out of the ditch. He eased the Packard to a stop. He woke Maggie up and told her that he was getting out to check. He ran to the first car. It looked like it had flipped, more than once. The top was completely smashed. He raced to the driver's side of the upside-down car. He wondered if the two cars had hit each other. Behind the wheel, slumped over, was Charlie Tall Chief. Jake tipped back his head and felt of his neck. He was dead. It was only then that his eyes fell on the hole in the side of his head. It was a gaping hole, made by at least a forty-five bullet. Blood was pouring down his neck and on down the side of the car. Jake laid his head back on the steering wheel. He looked at the other car. Maybe he had been shot too. He ran to it. It was resting, practically, nose to nose with Charlie's car. It was Iron Necklace's grandson, Joe, with his new Caddy of a few hours. Jake looked around for a body, but as he got closer, he could hear a sleep-like snoring sound. It was coming from on top of the car's roof. Jake looked up just in time to see old Joe passed out on the roof. *Oh well,* he thought. *No sense disturbing his worry-free sleep. Even though he had probably slept right through a murder. Why worry,* Jake thought. *Neither of these two Indians was worried. He guessed there would be more money and more cars on Monday.*

Jake reported his findings to Maggie as they motored on toward town. "Why would anyone want to kill Charlie, Jake? He never hurt anybody."

Jake looked at her sympathetically. "I can't imagine. I liked him. I used to see him uptown a lot. We'd have coffee, together, once in awhile on Saturday morning. Wonder who'd want him dead? He didn't have any enemies. Maybe Father Jack was right. The bad guys just con you or kill you."

They passed several more cars on the sides of the road and a couple in a nearby pasture, as they neared town. He would have to find the sheriff and give him the unhappy tidings about Charlie Tall Chief. Too bad the day was over. It had been a good celebration day for the Osages, just a couple of major incidents. *Oh well!* he thought. *Finally, everyone was asleep. But soon, much before the Indians had revived, Grandfather Sun, the Earth and tribe's protectorate would make his way into a new day.*

CHAPTER FIVE

Daylight was just about a half-hour away as Jake made his way down the dirt road. The early morning dew had the dirt clouds, still under wraps, as he was the first that morning to leave his trail to the well site. The good old Dodge truck, built for dirt and mud, wasn't too fast, but it was dependable.

Quinn, in his charge for awhile, was still sound asleep. He was snuggled in his blanket between the tin cups, water jugs, coffee pot, and a whole mess of paper work. The other member of this early morning trio was Bear. He was Quinn's two year old, big, black, fifty-seven variety dog. He insisted on licking Quinn's face as he slept. But, in the deep sleep of a child, it went unnoticed. Quinn had turned five years old a couple of months ago. He was a dukes mixture of Jake and Maggie. His face, with his dark eyes and straight black hair, was all Maggie. But Jake had to claim his long, lean body. He was already strong and aggressive for his age.

Jake mind drifted back to the well. The site was sheer speculation. He wondered why old Evans had picked it out. It was about twenty miles west of Pawhuska. It was section 12, the lease sale description read. Evans was a real odd sort. He had no hair on his head, but his face always needed a shave. He needed spectacles, but seldom wore them, so he squinted, most of the time. In fact, it wasn't unusual to see his teeth and his glasses both in his pocket. He was overweight, twenty to thirty pounds. He looked like a Jewish horse-trader, by nature. He had a partner he referred to as "Lefty Kirk". Jake had never met him, though. Maybe he was the one pushing to wildcat that area. Jake was lost deep in thought. It sure seemed risky to drill there without another derrick in site. He was figuring out how much pipe it would take. There was no telling how much water they would hit out there. That could mean slow drilling and a lot of delays while the casing crew was rounded up.

Jake's tool dresser was already there. He'd been there since the day before. His name was Red Thompson. He'd been with him for years, even in the old water drilling days. His mind trailed off to some of Red's and his adventures, as the Dodge bounded over rock after rock. Even though some of those days had been danger-packed nightmares, they still brought a smile to his face. Probably because he had at least lived through them.

Red was quite a character—short, stocky, with a beer gut that protruded over his khaki pants. His top was his long underwear shirt. Cemented on it was a collage of the meals of the week, weaving their trail over his stomach like a jagged map of the oil fields. Despite the summer heat, long handles were the uniform of the day. They served more as protection than anything else, in case a red hot drilling bit would happen to graze your leg. He had learned that lesson early on. He had a long ugly scar on his leg that ran from his knee down his calf, to prove it. His strawberry red hair was thin on top, with an ever-growing bald spot. It was beet red from standing on the derrick floor in the hot sun for days on end. Even though Jake had never caught him, he still suspected from the heavy odor of petroleum products, that he plastered his hair down with grease. He could just about bet that he slicked it down in the dog house where he kept his personal stuff. "Your ol' head just looks slicker than snot on a door knob." Jake always kidded him.

Red was always laughing. You could hear him telling one of his new victims, usually a casing crew hand, one of his crude jokes. He was smart, though. As a "toolie", he was responsible for keeping the drill bits sharp. He was one of the best specialized blacksmiths in the business. He was an ace at the rig side with his forge and anvil. He dressed the bit in the fire to the proper gauge of pipe. Nearly, every time, Jake's success with the wells was due to Red's quality work with the drill bits. Heaven help them, though, if any unsuspecting newcomer was caught slacking off. As unpredictable as the weather, Red's good humor could turn to black thunder in one split second. Lodged in his barrel chest, his booming voice had been known to explode.

He kept telling Jake that he was worried about this string of tools. The wire lines of the baling equipment were worn out. Jake remembered that he'd told him he'd take care of it when Maggie got her check. Now he was going to have to tell Red, that they'd have to go one more time with that string of tools, cause his lovely Indian wife just had to have a new twelve thousand dollar diamond ring. Jake gripped the steering wheel and cringed at the very prospect of Red's reaction. He couldn't decide if he'd roll on the ground laughing, or scream like a banshee.

Jake was getting close to the site. The huge black jacks were getting closer together, as the Dodge forded the creek. The water was still clear at least for the moment, as it rushed over the sandstone rocks. Jake knew he was close, since water and wood was probably Evan's only criteria for choosing the site. Creekology was the term the old Pennsylvania drillers had used as a method of site selection. It was a simple theory—just drill in the bed of the creek. It may have been a great theory in Pennsylvania, but they'd found out the hard way. It just didn't hold true in the Osage. It was easier for crusty old devils like them to just smell it out, no matter if it was 3000 feet below the surface. Jake smiled as he thought, that it still beat the doodlebug theory of "x-raying" the land that some of them were trying.

The sounds of the cross-cut saws and sledges was getting louder. It was a big job cutting the timber and hammering planks in place. They sounded like they were still finishing up their construction. Jake left the low water crossing at the creek and turned to the left. Marking the way were white flags made from remnants of sheets. They were ceremoniously tied to branches of the oak trees along the parade route. The dog woke up, sniffing out his side of the truck, but Jake knew Quinn would stay asleep another couple of hours.

About a quarter of a mile in, the rig appeared. The wooden derrick looked like just one more oak tree in the grove, towering seventy-two feet toward the Osage sky. The laborers had cleared about an half acre, while the mule peelers had made room for the slush pit, well floor, belt house, boiler site, and engine house. The chain of men protruded like a wooly worm, heading south, away from the derrick. It was like an ant hill of workers going in twenty different directions. Jake could see in one glance from the unfinished state of the well that no drilling would take place that day. They were behind schedule. Several roustabouts in overalls were still building the engine-house walls. It looked like most of the equipment was in place. The wagon with the boiler sat about fifty feet from the well. There were a dozen or so men sawing the huge oaks and cutting them into planks.

Jake recognized Evans' four-wheel drive black "Jeffry Quad" truck, parked in the shade. He pulled up close, parked the truck, and let the dog out. Evans—who was running the show—and Red were walking toward Jake before he ever shut off the truck motor. Jake could see they were less than pleased. In fact, Evans looked really peeved. Red was rolling his eyes at him.

Jake thought to himself. *Well, I'll be damned. These ass holes ain't near ready.* But he managed to get a few decent words out. "Well, what's going on? Not ready to drill today, huh?"

Evans sneered. "Now, keep your shirt on, Jake. It's these damn oil patch idiots. I came out here Saturday and there wasn't one hand here. They'd all left to go into Elgin—some dance or the other. I've threatened to fire every damn one of them. I've docked their pay and put them on short rations."

Red and Jake snickered out of the corner of their mouths.

"Yeah, Evans, sometimes you have to get their attention," Jake winked at Red.

Red let out a big belly laugh. "Like hittin' the ol' mule in the head with a two-by-four." Everybody laughed, hoping that it would release a little of the tension.

Evans thought Jake would be mad as hell about not being ready to drill. "We liked to never got the mudsills cut for the derrick two weeks ago—dad blame rain."

"What do you lack?" Jake asked, surveying the construction.

"Well, the belt house is ready and the steam engine's in place."

"The derrick floor ready?" Jake questioned.

"Yeah," Red said. "And the bullwheel shed's finished. In fact, everything's ready, except finishing up the engine house, and settin' the boiler."

Jake pointed toward his left. "You got the water line and pump in the creek?"

Evans nodded. "Yep, that's all done."

Jake looked at the pipe rack to the right of the well-floor. "How much pipe you order?"

Evans counted out loud, motioning with his index finger in the direction of the pipe wagon. "I got two loads on the wagons. That's not much, but I guess it'll get us started. Each wagon load held three, twenty-foot joints of pipe, all ten inch. There's the other wagon load, now."

They heard the clattering of the big wagon slowly pulled by a team of big stocky mules. It was a pretty good grade and the mules were lathered up. One guy was hitching up the five teams to the boiler wagon. They'd be ready to set it before long. "Have you got the casing crew on alert?" Jake asked.

Evans spit on the ground and wiped his mouth with the sleeve of his long handles. "Yeah, old Rich Brewer's bunch—five of them, five hour notice. They'll be here."

Jake looked at Red. "How's his stabber?"

Red whistled. "Damn good and fast. He came up from the Drumwright field, and I think, he stabbed back in '12 for ol' Tom Slick."

As he finished this sentence, Evans rolled up his sleeves. "Now, Jake, we'll be ready by midnight at the latest, so make yourself at—". He stopped in mid-sentence, as some hand yelled at him, and he hurried away.

Red and Jake walked over to his truck and leaned on the back of the bed with his forearms. Red reached in his pocket for a chaw. "I need some of this good tobaccy. What a day!" Jake fished out a cigar from the shirt pocket of his khakis. Red wallowed the chaw around in his mouth, coaxing it to his favorite spot in among his yellowed teeth.

"Where's the string of tools, Red?" Jake asked.

"Still on the trucks, boss."

They were the best of the cable drillers, and they both knew it. "How many bits we got dressed?" Jake asked as he bit the tip off his cigar.

Red counted. "We got two twelve and a half inch bits. Two spuds with the rest of the iron ought to be in before we need it." He spit a big juicy glob at an ant hill and hit it square. "The sand line ain't in real good shape. It's showin' shabby, but I can cut it off, I reckon. Oh, by the way, did' ya get us some money?"

Jake let out a huge sigh. He looked down at the ground, avoiding Red's eyes, "No, we'll have to make do this time."

"Oh hell, Jake, you promised me you'd get some money when the payment came in—"

"Lay off, Red. It ain't goin' happen. You let me worry about it."

Red spit so hard, that he blew the ants right off the hill. He was disgusted. He ran his fingers over his slick-backed hair. Jake leaned back, took a big puff on his cigar, and closed his eyes. *This job is not going well, already—a big delay, a fired-up tool dresser, a hung over crew, worn-out tools, the kid under my feet plus his dog, hot weather, and a steady diet of beans and cornbread for the next two weeks.*

Red and he were both quiet for a minute or two, then, Jake decided to break the ice. "Gotta Shooter, Red?"

"Yeah, Blacky Morris. He'll be here about mid-way on, next week to look things over. He's ordered a hundred quarts from the nitro refinery over at the west edge of B'ville. Said, he'd carry it out in the soup wagon."

Jake nodded. "Is he a drunk?"

"Yeah, but he's better n' most. How deep you figure its going to go, Jake?" Red asked, trying hard to hide his fury.

"About three thousand, I reckon. I saw the tankies in town before I came out, and told them where we were drillin', in case we need them. So, I guess we're set." Jake turned as he heard a rustling in the seat of the truck. He looked to see Quinn, sitting up, rubbing the sleep from his eyes.

"You got the boy?" Red asked. "Well, why didn't you say so. Come on out here, Quinn. Quit lolly gaggin around and come see ol' Uncle Red. How's my boy?"

Quinn, delighted at seeing Red, jumped in his arms. "Howdy, Uncle Red. I'm hungry."

Red shifted him to one side. "Well, let's go to the dog house and see if we can find you a hot cup of coffee."

"Oh yuk! I want one of those big biscuits," the child said.

"What? No Jamoke coffee! Okay! Okay! You're just an ol 'good for nothin'—a worthless 'boll weevil'!"

Jake laughed, as the two went toward the dog house, hand in hand, in search of breakfast.

Jake found a spare cot and hauled it over in the shade by his truck. He stretched out. He would get a few winks, while he could. Wouldn't be long till midnight. Then it would be hard for a week or two to get any peace and quiet at all.

CHAPTER SIX

It was half-past one o'clock in the afternoon. Pawhuska's noon traffic had quieted down. Even the heavy summer air was ready for a nap. The town's mongrel dogs were all half-asleep. They were enjoying their newly dug holes from that morning. They seemed content to lie on the cool earth that had escaped the sun.

The Citizens National Bank had been busy cashing checks and depositing Osage money all morning. It was their busiest time, right after payment day. Clyde Baker, Senior Vice President, felt pretty good about himself, as he rearranged the stack of papers neatly on his desk. All things considered on the deals he'd made that morning, including kickbacks and all, his cut would be about three grand. *Not a bad half-day's work for a Monday morning.* In addition, the bank's President, Mr. Woods, was going to be out of the bank all day.

So, Clyde was in charge. He was built like a barrel with no neck and short legs. It was difficult to see anything past his round stomach. He couldn't seem to pass up those chocolate éclairs over at the hotel. In fact, the last button on his coat was just a memory to the far away button hole. The top coat buttons had bridged the gap, but were under severe strain. The two tellers hated him. They called him perverted behind his back, and his breath smelled like a dead animal as he lingered over their shoulders just a little too long. He looked around with his little beady eyes, magnified behind thick round lenses.

He would take this opportunity to throw a little weight around, among the tellers. *I have to keep them in line, especially that little snitty brunette, Liz Johnson. Yes, sir-ree! That's who I'll pick on this afternoon,* he thought. Surely he could find a mistake in her morning receipts, somewhere.

He was so absorbed in his malicious thoughts, he took no notice of the three inconspicuous men who were, now, standing at the tellers' windows. They'd entered the bank, separately, but, as if by signal, one, went to the front door, and dramatically pulled the shade, while the other two, pulled guns from out of their dusters.

"All right ladies, and excuse me, one fat gentleman." The one in charge looked at Mr. Baker, sitting as his desk. "We need you to just put all that good ol' Indian money in these bags. And be damn quick about it."

Liz, in the first cage, was pitifully crying while Charlotte stood at her post, middle-aged and ashen. They were both trembling with unmistakable fear. The ladies looked in the Vice President's direction for approval. Sam, dressed in blue overalls, was the tallest gunman. He waved his pistol in Charlotte's face. "Come on there missy! Hurry up! Or do you want to get hurt?" They began filling bags as Clyde feverishly tried to think of a plan.

The banker was sweating like a stuck hog. He knew his gun was in his drawer, but it was closed. He'd never get it opened, unnoticed. Curly, the second robber, dirty and reeking of leftover tobacco and whisky, ambled over to Clyde's desk. He cocked his shotgun two inches from Clyde's face. "Now, don't ya get no brainy ideas, you little fat worm. You wanta' stay alive, don't ya? So, you can keep on stealin' from a few more Indians, right? Huh, fat man?"

"Yes, sir! Okay!" Clyde stammered. He was desperately trying not to throw up.

Suddenly, Curly swung his leg around and boldly sat on Clyde's desk. He pointed to the third robber. "You know who that is, don't you?"

"No, sir!" Clyde said watching every move the robber made.

The robber laughed, "Well, that's ol' Al Spencer. Mighty fine specimen of a man, ain't he? We usually rob trains, but we figured, that beings it's today and all, you got so much Indian money, we'd just come pay you a little visit instead. We've robbed banks from one end of Oklahoma to another. Last big train job we did in this neck of the woods was over near the big town of Okesa, earlier this year. You know where that is, banker man?"

Clyde was nearly in tears. "Yes, sir, I do."

"It was so damn easy, just like falling off a log. The M. K. and T. Railroad was real good to us that day."

Clyde looked like he was going to faint. He knew exactly, who Al Spencer was, and he knew how ruthless his gang was. Al was obviously in charge and he threw Curly the bags. "Shut up, Curly. You talk to damn much. Okay! Fat boy! Open her up!"

"What, sir?" Clyde squeaked out.

"The vault! Mr. Banker, open her up!"

"It is open, sir!"

"Then, let's go see what we got. If anyone tries to come in the bank, let'em come on in. Hold the gun on 'em. Okay, banker man! Get the cash, and filler up." He threw him a big canvas bag in the air. "Hurry up! Or I'll shoot daylight into you!"

By that time several customers had entered the bank, including Tom Fisher and a couple of guys from Phillips Petroleum. Tom looked stunned, as he realized what was taking place. Joe, an old guy who'd worked in the oil business for Frank, had his deposit and money in his hand. "Give it here, old man!" The tall robber, Sam yelled. "We might as well have yours, too." The old man never flinched, he just closed his fist up with the money in it. That infuriated Sam as he reached up and hit the man's skull with the butt of his gun. The old man hit the floor as the gun accidentally discharged. Spencer came around the closest teller's cage. "Who in the hell, did that?" In the excitement, Clyde Baker took that precise moment to make a run for the gun in his desk. He had scooted the drawer open with the toe of his shoe earlier. Now all he had to do was to get it and shoot.

Clyde Baker never made it to the gun. He never even came close as Al Spencer nailed him dead, right in the heart with his sawed-off, twelve gauge shot gun. Old Clyde's heavy body landed on the floor with a giant thud, but not before the banker's guts sprayed a formidable mural on the wall behind him. The two women screamed and the other robbers threatened to give them some of the same. He motioned them into the vault. "Okay! All of you, in here, right now! Look I've already killed him, what do I have to lose by lettin' you have it?" They hustled Tom, the old Phillip's man, and the two tellers into the vault. "Now, git in there, all of you. Been real nice doing business with you all's bank." The heavy steel vault door clanged shut.

The gang ran to the back door, unlocked it, and threw bags and all into an old rusty red Marmon auto parked outside. They'd left it running in the alley. It was old, and anyway, they were planning to ditch it at the edge of town, where they'd hidden the horses. As the Marmon roared out of the alley full bore onto West Main Street, not even the pack of half-sleeping dogs lifted a paw to foil their getaway.

CHAPTER SEVEN

The Lookout ranch lay to the northeast of the agency town. About a mile on east of their house was Jake's and Maggie's place. The signs of late spring had manifested into full bloom. The green in the newborn leaves was invigorating. Maggie had decided to drive her buggy over to her mother's on that early Monday morning in June. Her mother was leaving about noon for Claremore to spend some time visiting her relatives of the Black Dog Clan.

Maggie's buggy made its way slowly down the narrow dirt lane. The flowers had never been more beautiful. The wild roses spilled over the fence rows like masses of red blood. They hid the wire's barbs with secret thorns all their own. The iron plant was tall. It stood over the fence with its purple multi-bloom heads, standing one after another. The bumble bees buzzed over them, as they promised to make their approach. She paused by the large pond about a half-mile from the house to let her horse drink his fill. But perhaps her main purpose was to admire the white lotus blooms of the water lilies floating gingerly on the cool water. The gentle splashing noise of the diving frogs made the symphony of the water garden complete. Harmony and peace had made it their home.

She had slowed the buggy down to a near crawl. What was that hidden in the trees? She could see something, big and shiny. She stopped and strained her eyes. *Oh, it's just a big black car. Looks like an old Marmon car! Someone just ditched it. Probably, ran out of gas,* she thought, as she dismissed it from her mind.

It was good to have Quinn spending some time with his father. She loved him with all her heart. However, it was nice to do some leisurely woman things like she was engaging in that beautiful morning. Her horse was busily chewing grass taking advantage of the unexpected stop. Maggie loved the singing sounds of summer. The birds her father had spent much of her life teaching her about were all there in rare voice. She had noticed a lot of meadowlarks and blue birds. Amazingly enough, the robins were still around, testing the soft ground close to the water for fat juicy worms.

She let the horse reins tangle as she walked along the rocks of the creek that fed the pond. The red cardinal flowers with their spiked heads looked like Greek soldiers, standing in the creek with red plumed helmets. She noticed the pink blossoms of the mypi flower along the creek was blooming. It would soon be time to harvest it to make Indian medicine. She would have to remember to tell her father, but then he probably already knew for he missed nothing.

She stopped and sat on one of the largest sandstone rocks. She removed her moccasins and slipped her feet into the cool creek's water. To the left of her resting place, her eyes fell on the wild blue ageratum. It was growing happily in the shade of the solid oak grove that bordered the creek.

The breeze ran through her mind as she silently remembered a few lines from her favorite poetry class in school.

O to the early morn of spring,
whispering to the forgotten flowers…some hint,
that the spirit flies on eagle's wings,
and with it, he takes their secrets,
claiming that age's time is spent.

Those were the wistful moments she wished she could share with Jake. But his mind moved quickly from one thing to another like a butterfly. He was never satisfied with just one flower because he had no family. He was orphaned early, and had lived with one strange family after another. He sure didn't have any trouble with indecisiveness. He had picked that up from somewhere in a grand manner. He knew exactly what he wanted and how to get it. He was a true wildcatter, and life with him had certainly proved to be exciting. She watched a big yellow butterfly with black tips on its wings land beside her. She laughed. "Yes, that's Jake all right, a yellow butterfly with his wings tipped in black oil."

The mid-morning's light playing tag in the trees caught the glimmer of her new diamond ring as she sat on her favorite rock. She looked at it and wondered why she had bought it. Yet, that curiosity was a far cry from her lips. She knew that Jake was unhappy with her and soon there would be words. She knew it would not stop with harsh words between man and wife. It would eventually turn into an Indian and white man's argument. She didn't need the ring, she thought. She had all she needed—a good husband and a wonderful child. But her Indian heritage had told stories down through the generations. Stories of Indians who had nothing. And what they did have, and tried to keep, had been taken away. Maybe the ring was important—something she could keep that meant the good news of change was happening for her people.

The young, slender Indian woman looked with a shielded had at the sun and decided, it was time to make her way on up to the senior Lookout house. She gathered up the horse's reins. "Time to go ol' fellow. Your breakfast is over." She climbed aboard the buggy, arranged her lighter weight blanket around her waist, and prodded the gray horse forward with a light tap on his rear.

The Lookout house was beautiful—big, white, and square. All Osage houses were the same shape, usually differing only in some degree of elegance. Fred's house was one of the most elegant. Two stories with big open windows in each room was the Osage customary design. The dark velvet curtains—half-inside and half-outside of the window—were blowing in the breeze. They spoke of a pretend world that everyone pictured as perfect. The Indians, however, could have cared less. The Osages had had nothing for so long, yet their dream had come true. It was a dream to obtain, but not to treasure. It was as if they had been given a catalog with a list of what every rich person should acquire. Then they were persuaded into buying the so-called items, even if they meant nothing to them. The front of the house was girded with a huge porch that fit the structure like an large white apron. Several big, high-backed wooden chairs sat on the porch waiting to ensure the Indians' rest. And rest was a sure thing to the Osage, now. The dining room was spacious with a long oak table and twelve chairs. The sideboard held a collection of fine European china. It was never used and seldom dusted. The crystal chandelier was rocking slightly in the spring breeze, and the crystal pendants tinkled like soft notes from the grand piano's treble clef.

The great room was elegant. It was filled with upholstered wing back chairs and twin sofas, in matching soft tapestries. In realty that was the last place any Indian would sit. The Persian rug with its vivid colors matched the ruby red velvet of the drapes. The richness of the red was the color, which always attracted the eye of every Osage. Huge globed kerosene lamps, with ruby red fringe hanging dramatically from the shade, were strategically placed on heavily carved English tables. The grand piano in the corner was shipped by rail from St. Louis. It was still waiting in silent anticipation for its first musician to visit the house and christen it with a maiden concert.

Three huge brown dogs slept on the bare wooden floor in the foyer while four more reclined in the giant kitchen. The breed was not important, while the size of the dogs seemed to be the Indians only criteria.

The kitchen was brand new, although the house was two years old. The Indians insisted on cooking outdoors. In fact, to the south of the porch in the shadiest part was the Lookout lodge, where the family slept. Almost all of the Indians felt that bad spirits haunted their houses at night; so consequently, the beautiful bedrooms remained closed-up for lack of use. The Indians had lots of fears at night, especially since the oil money had come in. Robbers and murderers canvassed the area, looking for the rich Indians. Therefore, Fred and many others had strung electric lights in the trees around the house. They hoped that would guard them against a silent attack.

As Maggie's buggy approached the big house, she saw her mother standing over the open fire by the lodge. From his porch chair, her father waved. She could see that he had on his new spectacles, which meant he was studying about something.

"Come on up here, Maggie girl," he shouted. At the sound of his voice, the four dogs ran out of the house at full speed to see who was here.

"Okay, Father! Is Mother ready to go?"

"Not quite," he yelled loudly to pitch his voice over the barking dogs. "She fixin' something for you to eat. Where's Quinn?"

"Jake took him with him to the well." Maggie yelled back. "He started drilling, first thing, this morning. He took Bear, too."

Julia came up the steps with a cup of hot steaming white bark tea, and a perturbed look on her face. "I don't like Quinn going with oil trash—too dangerous! He should stay here."

"But Mother, you are going to Claremore."

Julia grunted. "Only for few days—maybe a week. You and Jake better take good care of him, Maggie."

"He will, Mother. I just needed some time to myself. Jake's always on the warpath, looking for new drilling sites. He's never home. He has those old drinking buddies. One, of them is even Black Robes, himself."

"Yes, but he's a good white man." Fred said, motioning to a chair. "He take good care of you." Fred paused, looking at her with his dark penetrating eyes. "Now, tell me about big rock ring that you and Rosa Whitehorn buy. Who sell it to you?"

Maggie looked down at the porch floor and mumbled. "Oh, some white man I met downtown. He said it was finest quality."

"How much it cost?" Fred asked, breathing hard.

Maggie swallowed. "Only twelve thousand dollars. He said it's a great deal."

Fred couldn't swallow and with a mouth full of tea he coughed and spit in disgust. "What you mean, twelve thousand dollars? Are you loco? Are you like the rest of the tribe, who are letting white man con them into buying big things they don't need? You smart woman, Maggie Lookout. I raise you to use head like eagle. Our people are getting cheated everyday. Leahy tell Jake up town that more and more white men are coming here everyday to swindle us. I worry! Our people don't remember bad days when we walk the prairie with no home, and no buffalo. Now, they think money gush from ground forever. Maybe, Grandfather Sun punish us once more and dry up oil, like he dry up game and buffalo."

Maggie's eyes welled up with tears on her beautiful brown face. One by one, they fell onto her red calico shirt. Star, her favorite dog, sitting by her chair, licked her hand in sympathy. Several moments passed. The only noise seemed to be the irritatingly incessant licking of one dog to another. Finally, she sighed. "I'm sorry, Father. I want something that cost a lot of money to show others that we are important people. This money can make our people happy. Then our hearts, too, can sing with joy."

Fred's face softened just a bit. "Yes, but Maggie Lookout, our people's hearts always sing, just with Grandfather Sun bringing new day. Even rain, to grow flowers on prairie, make us happy, or new season of game to feed our people. Remember, Maggie girl, we have been brought to the land of milk and honey, as Black Robes tells us. We must take care of this land and of each other so we no lose it, again. Don't listen to the white man. He cons us and makes our people look as fools. You help me, Maggie Lookout. Warn our people to not fall in white man's trap."

Julia decided that the subject needed to be changed. "Come into lodge and help me gather belongings for road. Fred, you ride to neighbors and get John Lossin. He will drive automobile for me, as usual. Leave Maggie be. It's okay for her to have ring. No more, maybe, but this one, okay. I give her money, so there."

Fred shook his head as he left the porch on the way to Maggie's buggy. It was a short drive to the ranch to the north. Along the way, Fred grumbled, *I guess it's okay for woman to have one, big rock ring. I have two Pierce Arrows—fine cars that cost lots of money. I can't drive.* He chuckled. But there was always, someone around to drive when you wanted to go.

Back in the lodge, Julia spoke. "Maggie Lookout, don't cry. I give you money. Your father worry all the time about our people. He'll be chief, again, soon. Ne-Kah-Wah-She-Tun-Kah is very sick. This is his last summer."

"I know, Mother, I'm not angry." She sighed. "White man tell me and Rosa that we were beautiful and that we need, big rock ring. I just had payment money. I make big mistake. He showed us many jewels that he planned to sell to Osages."

"What his name, Maggie?" Julia asked.

Maggie thought a moment. "Rosa call him Henry, I think. He had on three-piece suit with ring, here." She pointed to her little finger. "Big rock! He talked real smooth—big words like undertaker speaks up at Johnson's funeral parlor. He smelled like ginger spice."

"Where was he?"

"He was up near Zorrow's Confectionery Store, but he walks around, not always in same place." Maggie replied.

"Well, you stay clear of him, hear me?" Julia Lookout hugged her daughter. "Time to go. I hear Fred and John," Julia said. "They have just pulled the big automobile to the front. Check in on your dad while I'm away. He sometimes drink whiskey a little, when I'm gone."

Maggie nodded. "I'll ride over every morning. I won't see Jake this week so I'll cook food for Father."

Together, they piled Julia's belongings in the car trunk, as John opened the massive back car door. Julia settled down in the luxury of the deep leather as John climbed in the driver's seat. Even the dogs had respect and perked their ears, as the purr of the magnificent car pulled away. Chances were, it would be nightfall before Julia would sit at the campfire of her cousins in Claremore.

After they could no longer see the car in sight, Fred busied himself with feeding the dogs. Maggie kissed him on the cheek. "I'll see you tomorrow, Father."

"When?"

"Oh, about noon, I suppose," Maggie answered still a little ill at ease in her father's presence.

"You going stay over at your house alone?"

Maggie relaxed a little and nodded. "Yeah. I'll be fine. I leave lights on and Spitfire will growl if he hears anything. I got the gun. Jake taught me to use it."

She climbed into the buggy and waved one more time to Fred as she started down the heavily rutted road past the gate. *Father's mad at me,* she thought. *Jake's mad, too. I'm in trouble, but I'll fix them, later.*

As the buggy bounced over the sharp rocks in the road, she was thinking about Mike Hale's sister, Betsy, the girl Bill WhiteOaks had tried to pin to the pool table at the dance in Elgin. She was a prissy girl. They had gone to school together up at the St. Louis School. She had never liked her, but Bill WhiteOaks was going to be in real trouble when old man Hale and his boys came after him. The Indians had nothing to do with Hale. The stories of long ago when the Hales were one of the first trader families were vivid in the Indians' memory. They stole furs from the Indians at ridiculous prices. Then they sold them for top money to other traders.

Turning the bend, the buggy picked up speed. She forgot about the Hale trouble. The horses knew where home was. Spitfire, her big black guard dog, was jumping at the fence. Spitfire was mean. Bear, Quinn's dog, was her pup. But then, Jake wanted her to be mean to take care of Maggie when he was away. The Knupp house was the same square shaped design, but a couple of thousand square feet smaller. It looked like a Lookout miniature doll house sitting by the creek. The dozen or so chickens scattered, squabbling loudly, as Maggie unhitched the horse. She fed him and put him inside the pasture. He was a fine looking horse. Jake had traded Sam Weatherby out of him a year or so ago.

The house wasn't locked and the porch made quick access to the living room. She opened all the windows and went from room to room, as Spitfire followed her. She had no intention of cooking. There was some cold meat in the well house and some blue corn and a biscuit she'd have later. Jake refused to sleep outside most nights so her outdoor lodge was fairly small. But she opened the flap for ventilation, anyway, more from habit than anything else.

She saw Quinn's toys scattered about the lodge, and it made her lonesome for him. The picture of him with his big brown eyes and wide smile flashed into her mind. He looked so cute with his black hair blowing in the breeze. Oh, well, there were chores to do. The chickens had to be fed and she would wash some of her clothes down at the creek. It would be a good drying day. Perhaps, Rosa would ride out later, or maybe, some of her other friends. They could catch up on the gossip after payment day.

The heat of the day had settled in on the Lookout ranch as Fred made his way over to the high-backed porch chair. Fred had watched her for as long as he could see her tiny form. He wondered if he'd been too hard on her. His anger at the white men was building. He would go to town tomorrow to the agency, and discuss these con men with old George

Wright, the superintendent. He shook his head, again. Maybe Sheriff Cook could help. He would see them both tomorrow. They needed a plan. He'd leave Maggie girl a note to tell her he'd gone to town. He'd leave in the early morning hours, long before the birds were on the wing. He felt better, already. Together, the three of them, and Black Robes, would take care of his people.

He took out his calico bandana, wiped the sweat from his face, and sat back down to rest. He could take off his spectacles. His thinking was finished. Now his nap would be worry free. The four dogs lay at his feet, as he tipped his porch chair back against the house wall. Now he would dream of how he and Grandfather Sun would protect the good-life for the Osages.

CHAPTER EIGHT

Excitement masked the stillness. Jake sensed it when he first opened his eyes. He knew by the level of activity that it was nearly time to drill. He had known that he had to get some sleep. He was going to have to drill all night and all day, until Red's and his relief came on the next tower. He shook the sleep off and stretched, wondering if he could get out of his makeshift cot without waking Quinn. *No such luck*, he thought. The boy knew it was time for the drillers too.

"Is it time, Daddy? Daddy! Hurry! We don't want to be late. Let's drill!" Quinn leaped up pulling on his hand.

They wandered rather briskly over to the doghouse for a cup of coffee. Everyone was gathered in there. They were all dead tired, hungry, and hollow eyed.

"These are the best damn hands I've ever seen." Evans yelled. "We made it, Jake. We got the walls on the engine house nailed down and got the boiler set in record time. Lord, what a job in this blessed heat. Red's got the string of tools ready to go. So I guess it's up to you now, Jake. Better have some of this grub. We saved you and the boy a plate."

Jake nodded, barely acknowledging him. "How's the weather look, Red?"

Red puffed on his cigarette. "Oh, partly cloudy tonight Boss, I reckon, but big patches of stars up there now, though."

The yellow dog kerosene lights were hung around in strategic places waiting for the bugs to find out that they meant business. Jake always insisted that they use them. They resembled a teakettle with two spouts and a wick out each spout. The bullshit stories were getting a little deep, Jake thought as he wandered outside. As always, Jake loved starting at midnight. Maybe, it was the excitement of the lights that reminded him of Christmas. The derrick was like a huge Christmas tree with electric lights, winding from the top all the way down its cross-armed branches, all made possible by the big steam-driven generator. The derrick was awesome, as its lights cast crisscrosses across the tin roof of the dog house. The crickets and katydids were all tuning up. The frogs along the creek were adding to the night's melodies. The yellow dog lights signaled that the oilman's midsummer's night dream had begun, one more time.

Jake jumped up on the derrick floor. He could see the lights on the old trucks leaving. For most of them, their job was finished. Their lights flickered in among the trees, as they snaked along toward town. He watched them creep along. In the moonlight, it looked like a huge worm slowly going for the creek.

He heard footsteps behind him and he waved at Quinn. "Come on up here, Quinn and help your Pa. What do we do, first?"

Quinn put his finger up to the side of his face, pondering. "Okay, Daddy, you tell me! Get me started!" The two were lost in deep thought.

"Okay, remember, first, screw the stem on the bit and hammer the tongs to tighten the joint."

Quinn was observing it all carefully. "Then, what's next, Daddy?"

Jake stopped to light his new cigar, and Quinn kept up the questions. "You pick up the stem and bit and get ready to drill?"

Jake shook his head. "No, not yet. Hold your horses! How are we going pick this up?"

Quinn shook his head. "I don't know, Daddy."

Jake puffed two or three times on his cigar. "Well, you've got to screw the swivel socket onto the stem and hammer them so the wire attaches to the stem."

Quinn happily jumped up and down. "Yeah! Yeah! Now, I've got it, Daddy."

"Uh-huh. Well then, what are these, Quinn?" Jake pointed to the coiled mass of cable.

"Bull ropes, Daddy!"

Quinn was grinning broadly and Jake smiled. "Right and where do they go?"

The kid wrinkled up his nose. "I don't know!"

"Okay, now think, Quinn, remember they go from the tug wheel which is attached to the band wheel to where?"

Quinn shook his head.

"Well then can you tell me what they do?" Jake couldn't help snickering again as he rubbed his chin just like Red, while he pretended to think. Jake continued on, seeing that he was stumped. "They run the drilling cable which is wrapped around the bull wheels. They go up over the crown block on the very top of the derrick. Then, they come down to the swivel socket, which attaches to the stem. Now, you see, from the tug wheel, right here, the rope goes to the bull wheel. This gives us power to lift these big ol' tools."

Quinn scratched his head. "You're dern tootin'!"

Red and Jake doubled over with laughter. Quinn had followed his explanation, not understanding any of it, but his acting was superb. Jake stood at the engine throttle with the reverse handle in his hand while Red was at the brake on the bull wheel. "See Quinn, things are beginning to happen!"

Jake opened the throttle slightly and pulled the handle into the reverse position. Red raised the brake handle and the steam engine began to chug. It turned the bull wheels which wrapped up the cable. That picked the tools up into the derrick where they hung like a giant plumb bob. Jake closed the throttle and Red lowered the brake handle to keep the bull wheels from swinging. At that point, the bit was suspended three feet from the rig floor. He kicked the bull ropes off the bull and tug wheel, and threw them out of the way. Quinn was taking it all in.

"See here! You take off the bull ropes and drop 'em here on the floor. Let the tools down to the ground in the hole here, in the derrick floor. Right?"

"Right, Daddy, you betcha!" Quinn agreed happily, as Jake winked at Red.

"Now, what's this, son?"

"The spuding shoe," Quinn answered with some difficulty.

"That's right. You remembered. It's attached to the jerk line. You have to hook the spuding shoe over the cable, that goes from the bull wheel up the derrick. The other end, here, of the jerkline is fastened on to an iron spool. Then, you slip the spool over the crank pin on the band wheel. Here see, Quinn, we put the washer and bolt through the hole in the crank pin to keep it from slipping off. Now, what's next?"

Quinn looked very serious and with his biggest pretend voice, he said, "Red, if you've got steam up, let's start to spud!"

They all laughed as the engine turned slowly. The jerk line pulled on the spuding shoe, and that, in turn, pulled on the drilling cable, which lifted the tool from the ground.

"Atta boy, Quinn, we did it! Look at the tools go down with a thud, up and down, pounding the ground. We have to pour a little water in, now and then. Don't let me forget," Jake reminded. "Okay, Quinn, we gotta let a little slack off the line to the bull wheel. That allows the tools to drop farther. We'll do this for about 300 feet, then we'll tie the cable to the beam, atop the Samson post. Remember, Quinn, what'd I always tell you—we drill with cable. But when we take tools out, we don't use cable. So, what do we use?"

"Ropes, Daddy!" he yelled, jumping up and down for all he was worth.

"That's right, son! Ever so often, we bale out the hole. We do it, ever how many feet?"

"Six, Uncle Red, isn't that right?"

"Yeah, yeah, you're quite a driller. You better go get yourself a drink. Now, that we're drillin' your Pa and I can handle it, thanks to you. This drillin's hard work for us ol' timers."

Quinn jumped down off the derrick floor, yelling, "You're dern tootin'" again, as he trailed off with Bear in search of a cool cup to whet his thirst. Red and Jake were left with the humdrum noise of the spudder as the drilling fell into a routine. As Jake ran the tools, he wondered which one of the crew Quinn had picked up his new phrase of the day. Must have been Evans. Anyway, it tickled his funny bone. Wonder how his mother would like it. Oh well, it could be worse.

After a couple of hours, Jake hollered at Red. "It's sure hot and muggy and slow going." He nodded, smoking every breath. Cable drilling was not known for speed, but it was still a great way to make a thousand bucks. "Hey Red, I think we're in luck here in this old creek bottom land. We're made about twenty feet."

"Good goin', Boss."

"Okay, Red let's pull the tools and run the baler. Get those damn bull ropes on." After some minutes had passed Jake yelled, "Hot dog, Red. Don't seem to be any rocks." They had a good supply of wood and plenty of water. Things were looking up.

"Hey, Boss, I'll get the well-log out of the knowledge box and log this in."

Red said as he jumped down off the derrick floor. The knowledge box sat in the dog house, usually unlocked so the log work could be kept up-to-date. Jake saw Red coming out of the dog house. He was trying to get his attention and his eyes followed Red's gaze. He was pointing over to a tree a couple of yards away. Close to the dog house,

Quinn was half-leaning, half-laying on Bear, as they watched the derrick lights. The monotonous pounding of the spudder had, through no fault of its own, caused Quinn to nod off with sleepiness.

Jake smiled as Red brought him a cup of coffee. "Where's Evans?"

Red laughed, "He's out cold. He's plum wore out from yellin' at the crew for a month."

"Well, where's his partner?" Jake inquired.

"Ol' Lefty? Haven't seen hide nor hair of him. He's back in St. Louie, somewhere, hustling money, I reckon!"

Lighting the cigar Jake had fished out of his shirt pocket, he spoke. "Tell me about him."

Red grunted. "Don't know much, Jake. Probably a crook. Never laid eyes on him, though. Hey Jake, we going to town when we get off at midnight, tomorrow? Take us a shower, grab us a bite to eat, and a stiff drink. I need a drink, now!"

"Yeah, Red. We'll be dead tired, so we can't fool around too long. And I don't want to leave Quinn here, unless Evans will watch him for a couple of hours. Not to change the subject, but you know, Red, I've been thinking. If I was Evans, I 'd be scared to death, wildcattin' out here in this new location. Glad I don't have any money in it. Good thing Lefty went out of these parts to get money, so they can't see what they're paying for. He'd better be a smooth talker."

They both laughed. "Jake, I'm going to find me a tree. I'll see you in a little while."

Jake nodded, already letting his mind wander.

Left alone on the derrick floor with only the pounding noise of the spudder, Jake was reminded of the slow, mournful beat of the Osage drums. That had all, become such a big part of his life. In turn, his thoughts moved to Maggie. He hadn't been gone from her but a couple of days, but he already missed her. He was sure that with him out of the house, she'd take advantage of the warm June evenings and sleep in the lodge. He always put his foot down when he was home and they slept in the house.

In his mind's eye, he could see her in the moonlight, dressed in her shift and combing her long silky black hair. Spitfire would be laying awake next to her, listening for any strange sounds that were not the summer's own. It was Tuesday. She would have checked on her father, then set about feeding her chickens. She probably spent the rest of the evening with her nose in one of her poetry books. Considering the diamond ring incident, it was probably good that they'd had a little time, apart. As long as, it wasn't too long. For some reason, from the derrick floor, she appeared in his mind to be even more beautiful than ever.

CHAPTER NINE

It was midnight. Grandfather Sun had long since journeyed to another part of the world. Maggie wasn't overly concerned about Grandfather Sun's return. Hope was easy. It was endurance for the Osages that was hard. The power of Wah'-Kon-Tah was evident to the Osages since the discovery of oil.

The moonlight was streaming through the yard as Maggie closed the screen door to the house on her way outside. She stood at the intricate porch railing, as she watched the stars flicker and dance. Her mind drifted to Jake. *Is he still mad at me? Is Quinn sound asleep in his Daddy's truck?* A lone tear ran down her brown face. She missed them both. Jake was a good man.

Wah'-Kon-Tah had truly blessed her. The slight breeze caught just a few strands of her long hair and brushed them across her face. They seemed trapped there, in the path of her tear's journey. She was not sad, just filled with longing for the moment. She remembered the spat concerning the ring and looked down at her finger. It was then that she realized she had laid the ring on the table by the door in the big hallway. She had last admired it under the warm elegant glow of the crystal chandelier.

Spitfire had followed her out on the porch. He could have cared less about the enchantment of the June night. He was full, content, and it was long past his bedtime. Even, the long mournful call of the whippoorwill was chanting the Indian's tale of his original journey from the stars to earth. Too bad the Osage drumbeat was silent. There was no accompaniment for the whippoorwill. The trees were luring him into an acappella concert. She closed her eyes and took a deep breath, catching the scent of wild honeysuckle as it misted her senses. Invigorated, her memory emerged with a few lines, belonging to an old familiar poet:

Tis said, in the midst of summer's tour, the rocks turn, the water rolls over; the butterflies seem less content; and the whippoorwill searches for a different key. While the trees ask the south wind for its destination.

Maggie smiled, wondering where had that piece come from. She wondered what the south wind had in store for her people. Perhaps Grandfather Sun knew the answer and maybe that was why that was the longest day of the year.

She left the porch light on and a couple of others lights in the house, but she wasn't afraid. She was too preoccupied with the season's intentions. She was glad the night was so beautiful, since Jake was not there. Now she could sleep like an Osage in her lodge. Spitfire slept outside close to the flap. She closed it and settled down inside. She wanted to hear the June bugs, but not feel them. She removed her moccasins and laid them, together, by the entrance. It was a small lodge, only eight poles. The skins had been aired sufficiently. She had placed them inside earlier that afternoon. As she laid down and arranged her ebony hair over the light tan of the skins, the contrasting picture was poetry, itself. The last thing she remembered was wondering why she needed the ring. The tangible scent of the skins served as a reminder to her of the security she felt with the Osage ways. She slept, filled with hope, that Wah'-Kon-Tah would bring Grandfather Sun around again, tomorrow.

It was nearly half fast four when she heard Spitfire barking ferociously. Her heart leaped and she sat bolt up. *Oh,* she thought, *Some coyote is after my chickens.* She felt around knowing full well that she had left the revolver in the house, but she was not overly concerned. Spitfire would run the coyote off.

As she started to turn over, suddenly, as if an attack from hell, she heard a thunderous single gunshot. It pierced the night like a cannon blast. Fear gripped every muscle in her body. She froze in place. When her ears cleared, she realized that Spitfire was no longer barking. She was now more terrified than ever. It was as if her heart was trying to beat the Osage warning in her one, last time. She knew she must have the courage to run from the lodge to hide, but where? She was a sitting duck, waiting for the devil to find her. The white man's evil spirit had escaped his inferno. She was driven by the 'Spirit of Goodness' to take courage and lift the flap. She took no time for her moccasins, as she slowly raised the flap, listening for footsteps, praying that the moon would shut off its light to protect her in its darkness. She was praying with all her strength that no gunshot would follow. She could feel the threat once more, the inevitability of harm, that was moving toward her.

All of this, plus a hundred other thoughts, were racing across her sensitive Osage mind. She reluctantly lifted the flap two hands length, but only silence greeted her. Had she dreamed it? The gunshot or the howling of the dog? It sounded like an animal caught in a trap? Had the dog been left silently to die? Why had she not been more careful? Jake! Jake! Her mind pressed on, though the fear was paralyzing its functions forever.

Suddenly in a surge of strength that was not her own, the flap was torn from her hands. There were light particles like two frozen icicles that crashed onto his ugly face—a whiskey crazed face, framing the entry like a portrait of a mad man on some museum wall. She saw a flash of crooked, yellow teeth and a blast of breath that filled the lodge with the scent of dead animals. One desperate scream after another escaped from Maggie's throat as she fought the man, half-in and half-out of the only canvas exit.

"Listen, you little savage darlin'! I've got your dog, your money, and looky here—a big ol' diamond ring!" He laughed wickedly. "A little something extra I found in your hallway. And now I've got you!" He slapped her with the other hand as she flew backwards dazed, nearly losing consciousness.

"Please let me go!" She begged. "Take the ring and the money, just leave me alone!" She tried to pull her body up, but he grabbed her by her long hair.

"And a fine horsetail, this is, my little filly." He dragged her around the lodge with one hand, slapping her with the other hand until the bruised face gave way to falling blood. The blood mixed with tears ran down her brown Osage face. He slammed her down and jumped on her from a standing position. Landing on her, he knocked the breath from her already aching body. He ripped the soft muslin cloth from her breasts, as she tried to kick him off with her failing legs. "Get off of me! Leave me alone! My husband will kill you! I w i l l k i l l y o u."

Her sensitive soul was losing consciousness. Her spirit was closing. It could take no more. The last gleam of light from the porch cast a pin point beam on the intruder's neck. There it was—a red jagged scar. It ran from his ear, clear down to his shoulder. It stood up like a river on a topographical map cutting its way south down the man's neck. Time only let her catch a glimpse before her mind and body lay quiet. "Oh, yes, my little Indian whore! Now, you'll be quiet while I finish my night's work." He shoved down his jeans and like a poisoned arrow he rammed his angry manhood into her silent, limp body. "Well, you'd done better if you had stayed awake, but that's all right! My little Indian china doll, you just feel so good!"

As he rolled off her sweat-soaked body, the light caught puddles of white on her legs. Her sadly beaten body was already bruising while she slept. "I need a bath darlin'! Don't smell too good in here. Guess it could be me or these damn old hides. No tellin' what. Oh well, I'm hittin' the road. Thanks little darlin'." He took his pocket knife out and cut a handful of her hair from over her ear. The knife got a little too close and nicked her. Blood trickled down her face, splashing on the remnants of her chemise. *Don't need all this hair. It's black. It's them blond hairs that means good luck, but I'll take a few, anyway. Don't need all this.* He threw most of the handful of long hair back on her face. She wasn't coming to. *Wonder if she's dead? Oh well! The boss says we got too many damn Indians round here, anyway. This one sure ain't no good. She's married. So, I can't marry her for the headright money.* His thunderous laugh echoed in the silence of the night.

He left the lodge and started toward the woods, when he saw the dead dog. There was blood gushing from the dog's chest. With one fell swoop, he picked up the heavy dog by the paws—two in each hand—and walked back to the lodge. He threw open the flap and heaved the dead dog onto the unconscious woman. "There, that'll save you from lookin' for him, darlin'!" He laughed again and ran for the woods.

In the silence the stars blinked as they watched below. They hurriedly traveled across the sky in search of Grandfather Sun. Perhaps the stars were fearful that if Grandfather Sun could see the thin bleeding half-naked body of this beautiful Osage girl he would decide not to return. They wondered if there was a chance that he might just let the forgotten flowers and the oak trees weep in the darkness and take the gentle wind away.

Chapter Ten

Fred Lookout rose early that morning—earlier than usual. He didn't know why exactly. He hadn't slept well at all. Rubbing the dog's ear nearest him, he spoke more or less to himself. *Oh, well, Julia wife gone. I have lots on my mind. I have to get to town, talk to Black Robes, the agent, Leahy, and maybe, Sheriff Cook. Have to settle this con man thing. I'm hungry. I'll write a note to Maggie and tell her I've gone to town. I'll have breakfast in town, first.*

He wouldn't worry about taking the automobile. He couldn't drive anyway. He'd just ride horseback the two and half miles to town. He went in the house with all the dogs behind him. It was strange not having Julia wife around. *No one to tell me what to do.* He smiled. *She call it, making helpful suggestions. Yeah! With meat cleaver!* He chuckled out loud. He loved Julia wife. *But, I think, I could do without her easy for another week or two.*

He changed into his red silk shirt, adjusted his braids, and slipped his new thinking spectacles, as Maggie called them, into his pocket. He was going on an important mission for his people. He hurriedly went down the stairs. The yelping dogs followed him out the front door as he slammed it shut. He climbed on his horse, Straight Arrow, which he had brought around earlier. He'd left the note to Maggie on the hall table telling her that he'd be back in late afternoon. He didn't want her to think that he was still mad at her about big rock ring.

He rode to the gate and yelled "Ky-we-ton-yip-hun-kih". The seven dogs knew that his piercing scream meant to quit following him. They turned around in mid-stride, stopped yapping, and high-tailed it for the porch. Fred patted Straight Arrow's neck and laughed. "They'll be fine. They'll wander over to Maggie girl's after they finish pouting! That's what Julia wife always do." He laughed again.

He closed the gate and noticed the patch of mipi plant growing in the low spot in the road. *Hum, nearly medicine-making time*, he thought. Medicine-making had been passed down in his family on his father's side for many generations. He was proud of his skill. *Never mind today—later*, he thought.

He picked up his pace as he urged the horse to town. The summer morning was so clear and beautiful. He had a hard time formulating in his mind his purpose for the trip that day, especially, when any self-respecting Indian would be fishing.

As he rode into town, he headed toward the Spurling's rooming house cafe, hoping he might catch the agent or Black Robes. He dismounted and tied the reins tightly on the rail. The skittish horses had never gotten used to their fear of the automobile humming past their rears. There were quite a few people in town that morning. Pawhuska was clear of the payment day activities, but for a lazy regular morning, business was moving right along on Kihekah Street.

He stepped onto the sidewalk, trying to size up who was inside by the buggies, horses, and cars parked outside. He could smell the coffee through the screen door, and the aroma of bacon caused him to walk faster. The cafe was fairly big. It sported a long counter with a row of round stools. There were about ten tables scattered out in random fashion over the wooded floor.

Behind the counter, through a fair size slit, was the kitchen. Joe presided there with authority, in his-once white undershirt and white cook's hat. His cohort in crime was Irma. She was short in stature with an red apron tied nonchalantly around her ample middle. Together, they provided all of the cafe's meals.

The tables all had cotton print pattern cloths. However, none of the cloths had ever seen another of the same pattern. Irma didn't like oil cloth table coverings. She said the grease from the kitchen just seemed to collect on them.

There was a big walnut hat tree near the door, that had had a fairly aristocratic notion at one time. The big brass cash register sat on the end of the counter with a small antique shot glass sitting beside it, filled with toothpicks. A box of cheap cigars sat nearby, and a customer could buy one for a nickel. The mismatched black and white squares of tile on the floor formed diamond patterns unsatisfactorily. The tiles seemed to wander to the area where the pine flooring took over. Nevertheless, it was down home cooking, and it was the morning place-to-be.

Satisfied customers yelled and waved at Fred. Most everybody knew him. The giant Indian liked to go there for coffee, often, and listen to the town's goings on. Fred held up his big hand in a half-wave and sauntered over to a table. "Agent Wright been in yet, Molly?" He asked the little Irish gal filling the coffee cups.

"No, Mr. Lookout," she replied. "He'll be here any moment, though."

"How bout Black Robes?"

"No", Molly said as she slung the dish towel over her shoulder. "It's too early for him. He's got to say Mass first up at the Immaculate Conception Catholic Church. But he'll be down after Mass, no doubt. He's trying to fix me up with a young gentleman from Philadelphia. He works big time oil with Frank Phillips. You know him?"

Fred nodded. "Yeah, I know him. Tom Fisher's his name. Better grab him, Molly," Molly blushed. Now her hair and face were both scarlet red.

"How old you, Molly?" Fred asked between his gulps of coffee.

She shifted her coffee pot to her other hand. "Nineteen."

"Well, you'd better hurry and get hitched, or old Black Robes'll have you up at the convent in St. Louie."

Just in the nick of time for Molly, Fred spied Leahy coming in the front door. "There's Leahy, Molly. Tell him to sit here with me. I buy!"

Molly met the tall lanky attorney at the door. She motioned to T. J. Leahy that Fred was sitting over there and he eagerly came over to shake Fred's hand. "Howdy, Fred. What's been going on? Haven't seen you since before payment day."

Fred smiled. "Yeah, I've been busy. All Osages busy, you know that!" Both men laughed heartily. "Let's have breakfast! I buy!"

"Okay, Fred."

"Seen George Wright?" Fred asked. "I need to talk with you, him, Black Robes, and Sheriff Cook."

"How come? What's bothering you?"

Fred put down his coffee mug. "It's about con-men swindling my people."

Leahy nodded. "Oh, you heard about Rosa Whitehorn and Clyde's little deal over at the bank."

Fred grunted. "Yeah, It get out of hand! Must do something."

"Yeah, Fred, I saw Sheriff Cook Saturday. He was upset about the car dealers. They're buying used cars out of state and bringin' em in here, and sellin' em for new to the Indians. Bacon Rind's nephew, Sam Charleyhorse, bought a new Packard, supposedly, for seven thousand dollars, and it was used. Shoot. I bet the damn thing was two years old."

Fred rattled the coffee cup into the saucer so hard, it rang throughout the café.

"Settle down, Fred! We'll figure out something." Leahy took a slow gulp of his coffee, "There's George Wright, coming in now. Hey, George! Come on over here, and sit down. Ol' Fred here's buying, even if he is ready to go on the warpath."

George, his long body looking tired and his hair blown awry, was clad in gray trousers, white shirt, rolled up sleeves, and no tie. "Molly, bring George some coffee," Fred yelled, waving both hands.

"Howdy, Fred, T. J. Lord! It's hot early today. I've been up the better part of the night. The entire Hale clan's been in my office, demanding to know what I'm going to do with Bill WhiteOaks for attackin' their sister. That damn Woodward refused to deal with the issue and left town. He's the s. o. b. attorney for this agency." George stopped and wiped his forehead with his handkerchief. "They're about ready to take the matter into their own hands. I called Sheriff Cook about midnight and he's been trying to talk some sense into them. Hotheaded rednecks. All they want is an excuse to fight and kill someone—and all the better, if it's an Indian. I tried to cool them off. Where in the hell do they think they'd be if it wasn't for the Indians leasing them all their damn land anyway? Damn, they've made a killin' off the Indians since back when they were traders. Hell, ol' man Hale thinks he's God anyway." He put his head in his hands. "Lord! Why did WhiteOaks have to pick a Hale to hammer on?"

Fred pushed his chair back, "Maggie girl told me there'd be trouble over that. She and Jake were up at Elgin that night. She went to school with the Hale girl. She's the apple of Daddy Hale's eye."

George took a breath. He was not to be deterred. He went right on, the words just spilling out. "On top of that, Chief Ne-Kah-Wah-She-Tun-Kah's getting sicker by the day. No way he's goin' make it through the summer. Fred, you're goin' run for chief, aren't you? I need a man with some experience with all this trouble goin' on from all the oil money, and everything else that's happenin'. For instance, Sheriff Cook told me a while ago, that there's some guy travelin' around and for a big fee, he'll get you a Indian wife along with her headright. So now, we're even sellin' Indians to white men."

"Yeah," Fred said. "I know. That why I want to see you. Con men like Clyde over at the bank and diamond hustlers are cheatin' Indians all over town. Maggie girl and Rosa Whitehorn are victims. Maggie girl got conned into buying a twelve thousand dollar big rock ring on payment day."

"Oh my God!" George uttered. "What next? Will Maggie cooperate and help us find this man?"

"Hum." Fred nodded. "I see to it. Jake's furious too, but he's out drillin' west of Pawhuska on section twelve for a couple of weeks."

"Molly", Leahy interrupted. "We want to order three house breakfasts. Sheriff Cook may not make it. He's tied up at the jail. Say, that reminds me, I guess you all heard about the big bank robbery."

The whole group hadn't heard as they all sat up straight in their chairs. Leahy puffed up. He had their attention. "Sheriff Cook says Al Spencer and two of his men walked in the Citizens National Bank and took all the money from the tellers and then cleaned out the vault. They shot Clyde Baker deader'n a doornail. He made a break for his gun and Al shot him right in the heart. Course, Sheriff Cook said, that'll be a little deal for the FBI boys. He won't have to do much in the investigation."

"How much did they get away with?" Fred asked.

"Somewheres around fifty thousand, I heard. Hey, don't you know that young oil man? I believe his name's Tom Fisher."

"Yeah, sure do," Fred offered.

"Well, he walked in on them," Leahy continued. "They put 'em all in the vault while they made their getaway. The gang went out the back door. Had an old Marmon parked out back and took off in it." The lawyer sat back, happy with himself that he had been the one to deliver the hot scoop.

"Boy, that's pretty big news," George Wright chimed in. "Even Al Spencer's gettin' bold. Wants his share of the oil money, I reckon."

About that time, Molly whizzed by filling coffee cups. "Hey. Molly, if Father Jack comes in, bring him over."

She nodded. "Fine, Mr. Leahy." She scurried away to the kitchen.

Leahy yelled, "And tell Joe easy on the eggs, and we need plenty of gravy for the biscuits."

Several minutes later, steaming' hot breakfast plates filled with eggs, bacon, grits, huge fluffy biscuits and lots of sausage gravy completely filled the table. Conversation slowed while the three men became preoccupied with the food. Molly would swing by now and then, filling the coffee cups with more of the hot steaming brew. "How the payment go, George?"

"Oh fine! We didn't get the money till the last minute. The federal marshals escorted the courier down from Kansas City. I was gettin' worried that someone had ambushed them, but they made it in all right. The horses were hot and tired. I guess they had to really push them."

The men were just pushing their chairs back from the table to relax and smoke when Father Jack came in, as always, in a big hurry. "Molly said, you, guys wanted to see me." He greeted the men.

"Sit down Black Robes. Take a load off." Fred motioned. "I want to talk to you. Where you been? You say Mass long time."

Father Jack shook his head and took a gulp of coffee, before he even pulled out his chair. "No. I got held up after Mass by Bill WhiteOaks' mother, Bessie. She was crying. Seems her son Bill's in a heap of trouble. The Hales are looking for him. They say he got drunk and attacked their sister. She thinks they're going to kill him. She wants me to talk to them."

"Yeah, that happened up at Elgin at the dance after payment day." Fred said. "I guess it was big fight. Maggie girl and Jake were there."

"Miss Lydia over at the hardware store was telling me." Leahy interjected. "She was the first one to help the girl off the pool table when the shooting started."

Fred could stand it no longer. "It's getting worse by the day. Black Robes, my people got big problems. They think money gush from ground with oil, forever. They're being conned by white men everywhere they go—from car dealers and diamond hustlers to booze hagglers. And the Indians don't care. You know my people. You have to talk to them from the big oak pulpit at Catholic Church. Tell them to stop spending money on things they don't need, before it's too late."

"Well, Leahy," Father Jack said immediately taking up the cause. "You damn professional men are no better. There's some doctor they've called in on the case from Tulsey town to just look at the chief and they sent the agency a bill for fifty-seven hundred dollars. Right, George?"

"Right!" George agreed from behind his cigar. Leahy shook his head. Fred continued. "If we can't run these guys out of town, we've at least got to educate the Indians to these crooks." Fred looked at Father Jack, "You tell my people at Catholic Church?"

"Yeah, Fred. We'll co-operate and tell everyone we see, but ask Sheriff Cook, George," Father Jack said, looking at the agent. "If we can't run these guys out, at least we need to make an example of them. Can't that attorney up at the agency do something. Or does he approve of it?"

George nodded in agreement. "I don't know what we can do with Woodward. He needs a kick in the ass. When I leave here, I'll go see Sheriff Cook, but we've got to crack down on the bootleggers in town, too. It's when all these damn Indians get drunk, what reason they got leaves. I got to swing up by St. Louis school too, today, see if any of the Indians are failing to show up for class. You know, I withhold their checks if they let their children skip school. Mother Katherine Drexel said that there'd been more absentees lately. But since they've got plenty of money, it's not such a hardship when I dock them as it was in the old days. Sister Jerome and Sister Olivia do a good job of teachin', if the kids would just stay put. Besides, I wanted to watch the girls' bow and arrow squad, practice. It's really somethin' to see. They're good!"

They all laughed and settled back for a smoke, happy that they had banded together to help the cause of the Osage.

CHAPTER ELEVEN

The afternoon was quickly fading into evening and Fred had made lots of stops in town since breakfast. He rode up the hill on Grand Street in the neighborhood of the agency. The huge white granite courthouse sat majestically on the hill over-looking Chief Pawhuska's little town. He noticed the massive white pillars in front. They somehow symbolized justice, or at least, law and order in that still untamed country. He had to laugh as he wondered if the courthouse really stood for justice. Or was it only a pretense to fool the Indians, again.

The jail was up at the courthouse and maybe Sheriff Cook was around. He seemed to be nowhere else in town. He was probably still working on Al Spencer's bank job. Fred had stopped at old man Flynn's, the blacksmith's, and the bank. He had to make sure they hadn't lost his money. After he left the bank, he dropped by at the Red Store where he ran into a couple of Chief Ne-Kah-Wah-She-Tun-Kah's grandsons, Tom and John. They had talked awhile, and Fred had asked them about the doctor episode and the fifty-seven hundred dollar bill.

"It's true, Fred Lookout," Tom said. "They didn't even touch him."

"They wanted to take him to Tulsey town to big hospital, but he was too weak," John quickly added. "He couldn't eat. He just lay on pallet and moan to spirit of death."

As Fred walked up the hundred steps to the front doors of the court house, he sighed. *I'm going to have the big job of chief of Little Osages again soon. Old chief will die before new moon*, he thought. Fred set his jaw and went inside, down the big wide corridor to Sheriff Cook's office. Fred knew he'd missed him again as he walked in the doorway. He saw the hat rack in the corner was missing the big white straw cowboy hat, as well as the big gun belt full of .45 caliber bullets. They were usually draped over one of the pegs when he was in his office. There was a stale cigar smell holding the fresh air captive. He quickly glanced at his desk. There were several, half-full coffee mugs. One, he noticed, had a fly floating dead in the cup's black liquid lagoon. The papers scattered around on his desk had coffee stains all over them, leaving the tell-tale signs that the sheriff hadn't been there for the better part of the day.

Fred closed the door and walked back into the hall, thinking, *Well, at least the day was not a complete loss, since Clyde Baker met with his demise. He won't pose a problem, any longer. His swindlin' days are over.* The courthouse seemed pretty empty. Court was over for the day and not even the judge or any stray lawyers were in the corridors. *Damn*, Fred thought. *I've got to go down the hundred steps to horse. I'm too old for this. Guess, I go home and sit on porch and rest.* He thought about getting a bite to eat as he climbed on his, patiently waiting horse. "Let's go home, Straight Arrow. Maggie Lookout will no doubt bring me some supper. She won't want me to be mad at her, still! Maybe, fried chicken."

The two and half mile ride to the Lookout Ranch was not too eventful. He did wave to Miss Lydia as she crossed the street in front of the hardware store. She was pretty for a white woman. She was blond, with Irish green eyes that seemed to dance when she talked. She was smart and full of life. She was the only female gun runner in the state of Oklahoma. *Hum! Maybe, I miss Julia wife more than I thought*, he thought. *No! What's the matter with me. I can hold out for a few more days. I better do a little fishing this evening after I rest on porch.* He and Straight Arrow noticed that the dogs were nowhere to be seen. They were probably cooling off at the pond or off to Maggie girl's. Evidently, they were still mad at him for making them stay at home that morning. He particularly noticed how quiet it was, really quiet with Julia wife gone. He put Straight Arrow in the pasture closest to the house and threw the saddle over the fence for the time being. His big porch chair was calling his name. He sat down, leaned his chair back, and mopped his brow with his bandana. In no time, he was dozing, too tired, for now, to think about the job of being chief again.

An hour earlier it had appeared that the afternoon was winding down. Wood bees boring their occasional holes in the wood of the Lookout porch furnished the only movement in the otherwise still summer day. The dogs awakened from the porch and from various other shady places in the yard. Refreshed, and with no sign of Fred, they started for Maggie's.

The dogs ran toward their usual dug out place under the fence. There was no welcoming bark from Spitfire, who usually thought their visits were the highlight of his day. They slowed down and began sniffing the air. The air did not smell right. Their ears were taut as they began cautiously to investigate.

The scent led them close to the house. No Spitfire. No Maggie. There was no one yelling at them to quit chasing the ducks and chickens. Even the two peacocks were acting strange. Star—Maggie's favorite tan dog, belonging to her father—began sniffing over by the lodge, and then she began barking. Instantly, as if on cue, all of the dogs, started barking. Star pushed her nose into the lodge.

The beautiful Indian princess was not moving. She was laying in a pool of her own blood while the dead still form of the black dog lay on top of her. The color of Maggie's light summer chemise was no longer distinguishable. It was soaked to a scarlet hue in Spitfire's blood. Star started to half-moan and half-cry. It was the descriptive sound of a grieving dog. She hunched low to the ground and began creeping toward Maggie. She soon began licking Maggie's brown beautiful face, but Maggie did not stir. Star began sniffing the motionless dog. Instantly Star began rolling in the blood on the floor of the lodge. It was already half-coagulated from the hours that had slipped by. The blood on the tan dog's hair was unmistakably gruesome.

The dog ran out of the lodge at full speed, barking with a message for anyone's listening ear. The other seven dogs ran in chase of Star toward the senior Lookout's place. They cleared the fence in the air, never minding their own entry under the barbwire.

Fred's finely tuned senses had awakened him when he heard the barking dogs a quarter of a mile away, as they left Maggie's. He wondered what all the commotion was about. *Maggie girl must be on her way over with supper. The dogs smell my fried chicken.*

Nothing could describe the workings of Fred's mind, as all seven dogs leaped on the porch. His eyes fell on Star's hair—a full coat of half-dried blood. He had lived too long and was too wise. He knew something was terribly wrong. He'd seen too many killings, and heard too many stories from his grandfather about Indian slaughters. He felt around all over Star's body. There was no wound. He smelled the blood on his hands. It was fresh, but not too fresh. No animal would roll in another animal's blood if it happened on it in the woods. This was a message. Star would not stop the insistent barking of a mad dog. She jumped on Fred continuously. As one dog would jump down, four more would take its place, jumping three-quarters of the way to his belt.

It had to be trouble at Maggie girl's. Where was Julia wife when he needed her? He whistled the scream of a fierce animal. Straight Arrow bolted from near the barn to the pasture gate. Fred and the seven dogs ran as fast as he could push his sixty-year-old-plus body. He swung open the gate and grabbed the dark mane of the big appaloosa. It was only Grandfather Sun himself that insured that he made it onto Straight Arrow's bare back safely.

The wind, the dogs, the appaloosa horse, and the Indian man with the wise eyes raced the distance to the little Lookout ranch. He had gone the back way through the tall green grass of the connecting pastures so he wouldn't have to dismount for the gates. His eyes were scanning the area of the house, missing nothing.

The picture looked all right. The chicken and ducks were pecking in the front yard. But no, the front door of the house was standing open and the porch light was still on. His fear mounted. Where was Spitfire? Where was Maggie girl? He leaned back within earshot of the front door and screamed like only a quiet Indian man can scream when his soul feels a piercing intrusion.

"Maggie! Maggie Lookout," he called. There was nothing except the silence. Then he spotted the dogs barking at the small lodge. The two peacocks were standing close by with their tail feathers in full strut. It was as if they were trying their best to protect something.

He jumped off Straight Arrow and crossed the few feet to the lodge in the blink of an eagle's eye. He threw open the flap. The nightmare's hell became real to his horror-filled heart, and he knelt beside his Maggie girl. Realizing the dog was dead, he grabbed the dogs paws and pulled him off the silent girl's body and laid him aside. Her body was covered with his blood. The blow flies were already swarming.

Later, he wouldn't remember what he had said to her; to Grandfather Sun, to Wah'-Kon-Tah or to the heavy eyebrow's God as he lifted her limp body into his arms. He suddenly realized that her body was still warm lying in his arms. She was still alive. "Maggie! Maggie girl! It's your father! Open your eyes, daughter! Open your eyes!"

And as he held her, she opened her beautiful tortured brown eyes, but her wounded spirit was not there. She only stared for a moment, and then, without any recognition she closed her eyes, again. Filled with hope, that her life might still be hanging in the balance, he lifted her up in his mighty arms and ran to the house. He laid her gently on the settee in the living room. "Stay with her, Star! I have to go get automobile!" He raced from the house, slamming the door. He jumped, once again, on the horse and rode to his house like the wind. *Where are you, Julia wife?*

She got big automobile and driver. I got two automobiles. I don't know how
to drive but I have to get Maggie girl to town.

After what seemed to be a lifetime, he arrived at the house. He took
the steps three at a time and ran to the back entry to a shelf with a glass
jar where the automobile keys were kept. He grabbed the only remain-
ing key and ran out of the house to the shed where the other Pierce
Arrow was parked. He knew from watching John, his chauffeur, how to
start the motor by stepping on the starter button located on the floor-
board. He kept trying to put the car's stick shift in reverse. He ground
through three different gears and finally rammed the rear of the shed
two or three times before he finally gave up and jammed the stick into
some forward low gear.

The entire length of the giant Pierce Arrow shot through the front of
the shed with the mighty roar of its belabored six-cylinder engine.
Boards were flying as the automobile crashed through to the other side,
leaving a huge gaping hole in the shed. Chicken and duck feathers filled
the air. Fred ducked and hung on as he tried to steer as best he could in
the dirt ruts of the road.

As the gate approached, he knew to kill the motor. He jumped out,
opened it, and ran the short distance to the house. He grabbed up
Maggie in his arms and ran to the car saying over and over, "Maggie
Lookout, don't die! Don't die, Maggie Lookout!" He carefully laid her in
the leather back seat, her long black hair hanging to the floor. Star
jumped into the front seat as the dog, the dying girl, and the sweat-
soaked Indian lurched down the road to town for help from the white
man's doctor.

They somehow made it to the main road by steering from one ditch
to the other, but now the on-coming traffic of the main road made
death a welcome sight. Horns of oncoming cars were blaring as they
attempted to dodge the giant Pierce Arrow, heading straight for them. It
was a trip only made possible by the strength of Wah'-Kon-Tah, the

spirits of many past generations of a proud people, and the ever watchful eye of Wah-Tze-Go, Grandfather Sun.

CHAPTER TWELVE

It was a little past eight o'clock in the evening at the well site. Jake was hot, tired, and dirty. His irritation was mounting by the moment, and it was still four hours before their relief crew was to show up. The drilling was going pretty well. They were down about a hundred feet. Evans was happy, at least. They still hadn't seen hide nor hair of Lefty Kirk, Evans so-called partner.

Red and Evans were really in good humor and Evans had even played with Quinn a good part of the day. He let him play in the creek. He'd made him a make-shift fishing pole to try his luck. Quinn thought that was heaven. All day, he'd chased katydids for bait, keeping them safe in an old pork and beans can, that Red had rounded up for him.

For the past hour he and Bear had been chasing fireflies, probably throwing them in the same can. Nobody told him the game worked better after dark. He was about worn out, though. Poor old Bear's tongue was hanging out a foot and a half. He'd crawled off by himself to get a drink at the creek. Evans was in such a good mood, that he'd volunteered to put Quinn to bed while Red and Jake went to town. That is, if those dirty suckers ever showed up to relieve them. Red couldn't figure why Jake was so irritated.

"Things just didn't seem right," Jake kept saying. But he couldn't put his finger on it. Jake's stomach, for one thing, was unsettled. Of course, he'd lost count of how many cheap cigars he'd smoked. The cigars were laying precariously on top of the pepper laden red beans and horse meat. Oh well! He'd feel better after his shower.

The spudder was pounding away but Jake's trained ear picked up another sound. It sounded like a truck coming in. He searched the trees for lights across the creek. Pretty soon, sure enough, an old black Ford truck came lumbering into sight. *Could it be?* Jake argued with himself. *Nah! Surely not. Only eight-thirty. Sure looks like Shorty.* "Hell!" Jake yelled at Red. "I believe our relief boys' felt sorry for us and came early!"

Red let out a war hoop. "Shoot fire, things are looking up!"

Jake had sent a message with Sy, one of the mule peelers, to tell Shorty about the shift change, but he never knew whether the ignorant fool would remember. Shorty and Chub ambled out of the truck. Shorty was chewing on the sandwich in his hand, wearing a half pint of rye whiskey in his shirt pocket, and grinning like he had just saved the day.

"Howdy, boys. You're a sight for sore eyes." Jake yelled. "Come on up, you old son of a gun! Let me give you the dope, so far."

They huddled together to look at the log, and surveyed the well's progress. "Things going pretty fair, I reckon. Pretty fair. Listen, we'll be back about mid-afternoon tomorrow. Be careful with the sand line, it's pretty worn. If it breaks, cut it off and take a fresh hitch on the baler."

Shorty and Chub started snickering. "Yeah, yeah, we know. Guess you didn't git no money, now did ja? Word in Pawhusky is that your squaw done spent the money on a big ol' diamond ring," Shorty leaned over and slapped his leg, trying to still his shaking belly, propelled into action by his uproarious laughter. His teeth were nasty—still had tobacco and remnants of his most recent sandwich lodged in the gaps.

Hell! Jake thought. *This damn fool's filthier than me and Red, and he just got here.* Instead, of mentioning this fact he just laughed with him. "Go ahead and laugh you sorry so-n-sos cause I'm out of here!"

After a few more moments of conversation with them, Red and Jake hugged Quinn good-bye. Evans was going to bed him and Bear down in his truck when they left. "Bye, Daddy! Goin' take bath and see Mama?" Quinn asked as he pulled on Bears ears.

"Yeah, we're going take a bath, but we're going about seven miles from here to Nellie's saloon, so I won't go on in to town tonight to see your mama."

"Okay!" Quinn said, trailing off with Evans. "See you t'morrow, Daddy."

"Okay, Quinn. You be a good boy for Evans."

Red and Jake damned near killed themselves jumping into the Dodge truck heading for Nellie's. Jake's bad mood had vanished. He could just taste the whiskey on the rocks, now, not that damn crap that they had been drinking for three days that burned like a gasoline torch down his throat. Of course, it didn't make much difference to Red. He was tipping up the last of his half-pint like it was ice cold. "Red, Golleee! How do you stand that shit?"

"Years of practice, Boss. Years of practice." He let his hearty laugh escape into the quiet night.

They drove to Nellie's, located in the middle of nowhere, getting there about ten o'clock. She had a couple of rooms in the back for rent. Most of the oil patch stopped in there. It was a big log cabin saloon with cracks between the logs wide enough to read a newspaper through. Scorpions, tarantulas, and spiders provided the entertainment for the drunks. Many a night, Jake had seen drunks, loaded to the gills, shoot right at the logs, thinking he'd spied something crawling. There were bullets still lodged in the logs and split wood chips all over the floor that nobody bothered to worry about.

Old Nellie was in her early seventies. She had been a pretty good looking woman fifty years ago. However, Jake's assessment of her was that she looked like she'd been ridden hard and put up wet, but Red didn't care. After a few shots, he'd be trying to load her in their old truck.

But Jake always said, "She was as nice a old gal as you'll ever meet—do anything for ya."

Their old Dodge truck pulled in, creating a whirlwind of dust. There were about a dozen other oil trucks parked out front. They could hear the piano playing from the truck. It sounded like drunken men singing, "If You knew Susie, like I knew Susie, Oh, Oh, Oh what a gal."

I don't think that was quite the way Al Jolson meant for it sound, Jake amusingly thought.

"Lord, smell that BBQ, Jake? I'm so damn hungry, I could chew the arm right off of Nellie!" Red barked.

"BBQ what?" Red waved him off.

"Hell, BBQed flies for all I care."

They went through the big barn door and about five old buddies yelled at them to come on over, but instead, Jake went on over to Nellie to get a room for himself and Red. Jake yelled to them from across the floor. "We'll be back for some supper after we get cleaned up."

After their baths, clad in clean under-shirts and jeans and smelling a whole lot better, Jake and Red reentered the saloon from the back door. Everybody was yelling and Miss Susie, the bar maid, was singing with the piano player as she whipped around the tables of horny men who were trying their damndest to grab her from behind. They were all laughing and yelling, since most of them had been there for hours, already, and were pretty full.

It was an ordinary looking saloon. The bar boasted about fifteen stools, all occupied by men, who looked like they were still pining away over some woman that had just dumped them. There were about ten wooden, bare-topped tables with a high gloss shine on them. Of course, underneath the shine, it looked like the wood had been pistol whipped every night for years.

Nellie was bartending so she could keep an eye on the money and Miss Susie. She had her old trusty twelve gauge leaning against the bar a quick arm's length away. There were no bottles in sight, but if she liked your looks, she'd come up with some pretty potent stuff that she kept in the back. That's why she was in the middle of nowhere in a dry county. She had slept with more sheriffs than anyone could count. It was a well known fact that no law ever bothered Nellie. She said on more than one occasion. "Don't 'llow no Indians. They're worse than rednecks for getting drunk and tearing the place up. Sides, I don't need no murders, out here."

Jake's buddies pulled up a couple of chairs for them, making eight at the big round table. There was old Doc Parker from over Foraker way, a driller. Another driller, Hamilton Sage sat on his far left. Bliss Jones, a rancher and his friend, Zeke Young sat across the table. No one knew what he did. On Jake's immediate left, there was George Simon, a Jew who had his own oil company over by Ponca. Next to him was some other guy Jake didn't recognize. Otis somebody—a weasel looking little man with a hawk-like nose. Jake didn't think much of him. Andy Donnelly pulled up a chair too. He had a big oil outfit, but Jake figured all he did, mostly was go around, promoting. He was about six and a half feet tall, red haired, real light skin and a drooping eye that led into a big birthmark that reached to his ear. It was a pretty congenial group.

"Did ya hear about the big bank job in town, Monday?" Doc Parker asked from out of the blue. The men stopped their conversation cold.

"Who robbed 'em?" Andy Donnelly asked. The men began to all talk at once throwing questions in the air.

"Al Spencer and his gang," Doc said finally getting a word in edge wise. "I reckon they got tired of trains. Walked in on the Citizens National after lunch and—."

"How much did they get, Doc?" Zeke Young interrupted anxiously.

"About fifty thousand, give or take a little, the way I hear it."

"Anybody get hurt?" Jake asked leaning forward in his chair.

"Yeah, they shot Clyde Baker, the banker, deader than a door nail. Stupid green horn made the mistake of trying to go for his gun."

Jake sat back in his chair. "Well, how 'bout that! Guess, ol' Clyde's learned his lesson the hard way. Looks like there's a little justice in the world after all. That's just such damn good news, I'll believe I'll just buy you ol' boys a round."

Miss Susie brought them all that was left of the night's meal—two plates of BBQ beef, a mound of mashed potatoes oozing with butter, two handfuls of fried okra, about a dozen tomato slices, four big sour dough hot rolls a piece, and two big hunks of chocolate layer cake. Then she brought them a big frosted pitcher of Nellie's home brew. Life was looking up once again. Red and Jake dug in with both hands while the group hashed over high oil prices and deep wells.

Andy was talking about Skelly and Harry Sinclair. "Those rich bastards are going to start coming to the lease sale by train from Tulsey town. They're fixing two fancy private train cars for 'em to eat on and ride up in comfort." That provoked some interest as Miss Susie brought another round of shots. "What's this I hear about that guy over Ponca way? Hear his name's Marland. Thinks he can out-wildcat the big boys—bigger and better than everybody else. Want to get in on a little of the action?" Doc asked. "I can put you in touch with some of his boys."

Hamilton shook his head. "I don't know. There might be something to it. Lotta crazy things happenin' round here."

"Sure going be wild at the next lease sale," George added. "Frank Phillips, we hear, says, that money ain't no damn object."

Everybody laughed as Red and Jake finished their meal.

"Hey, Jake," Hamilton asked. "Got a string of tools I'll sell you. Hear you're in the market for a string."

"Well, I am, but not this well. I ran into a deal and I'm a little short of money." Jake replied. The whole table laughed and Jake realized, instantly, that they all knew.

Hamilton was laughing the hardest. "Yeah, yeah Jake, we know your ol' lady got a wild hair and spent all the payment money." The laughter was deafening as the men enjoyed their private joke.

"Okay, okay." Jake waved them off. "You know how women can be." He tried his damndest to change the subject. They were all on a roll, now.

"Hey, have you all heard the joke about the ol' boy that came to town?" Bliss Jones asked in a tipsy voice. "He stopped by the shoe shine man in the hotel, and asked about where he could find him a woman 'to get him a little' for the evening. Have you guys heard it?"

They all said no and urged him on with loud drunken voices.

"Well, this here ol' shoe shine guy said, 'There's a good lookin' Indian gal that lives up on the hill. She'll do ya, but you got take her a present. Now, she's cold. All them Indian gals are real cold.'

The visitin' ol' boy said, 'Aw, that ain't no problem! There ain't never been a woman alive that I couldn't warm up.'

'I don't think so, sir'. The ol' shoe shine man went on. 'This gal will just lay there like stone.'

'Nah, ol' man, I got some moves, I can put on her that'll cause her to come to life. I'll show her what passion's all about.'

So anyways, he thanked the ol' man and got the directions to the Indian gal's house. He went in to the store and bought her a present. He was real happy with himself as he walked 'bout two miles up the hill to her place. He knocked on the door, 'Howdy Miss! I'm new, here in town, and they tell me, that you will let me have my way with you.' She looked at him through them narrow eyes, 'Where's present?' The ol' boy handed it over to her. She opened the box real careful like, and peered inside. 'Okay! Come in. Me agree'.

So, they went into her bedroom. The ol' boy was feelin' pretty confident by now. They both undressed, piled up in bed, and he started in. She laid there like a cold hard rock. He tried all his tricks—all his private moves that some New Orleans hooker had taught him. Nothing, no response. Finally, he gave it all he had. He was sweatin' like a big dog. But, all of a sudden, he felt one leg came up. Then, one arm got in motion, and he thought, 'O boy, finally!' Then the other leg came up, and then, the other arm. He knew it. He knew he could bring her to life. He opened his eyes, looked down at her and gulped, 'Oh, my Lord!' Right in the middle of ever'thing she was trying on the moccasins, he'd brought her as a present."

Everyone in the building was choking with laughter, and Jake really wanted to bust a few of them, but he was too worn out. So, he'd just let 'em have their fun.

Pretty soon, the air was blue from the cigar smoke and every eye in the room was blood-shot from smoke or whiskey. "Hey!" Jake asked trying to change the subject, "Anyone wanta bet on ol' Pete Lassiter's big well? It's ready to come in any day, now."

"Yeah", someone shouted. "How's it look?"

"Real good. Not much water and the samples look good, and smell oily."

Everybody started betting. They pulled Nellie over to take care of the money. Jake waited till the last. "Well, I'll bet ya five hundred dollars that the hole's dry as a bone."

The whole group looked up, wondering what Jake knew. But they were all drunk and no one cared. They were all in, at the high stakes. Payoff was to be next week. The well was to be in by then. *Here's where ol' Jake gets a new string of tools,* Jake thought. *I'll show you guys!* Red looked at him like he was as dumb as Maggie for blowing money.

Time was getting late and the room started thinning out. Even Miss Susie's rendition of "Hard Hearted Hannah" couldn't hold them. "Leather is tough", she sang. "But Hannah's heart is tougher. I'm a gal who loves to see men suffer. To tease' em and thrill'em. To torture and kill'em." She belted out a couple more verses of Ager and Yellen's new popular tune, but despite her enticing allurement, they said their good-byes.

"Come on, Red. Get your butt over here. Quit oglin' over Nellie." Jake maneuvered Red through the back door into their rented room. Jake opened the windows wide, but there wasn't much air. As he lay out on his bed, Red was already sawing logs, boots, clothes and all. Nellie was already forgotten for the time being.

The two men didn't wake up till about two o'clock the next afternoon. They grabbed the big box of lunch they'd ordered the night before and started back to the well. They were both lost in their own thoughts when Red asked, "Jake, how come you bet five hundred dollars on that dry hole? Have you gone plum nuts?"

Jake laughed out loud. "Cause Leahy told me in town that ol' Pete was hustlin' money, and that he oversold the shares of the well. So, he's only got two choices, now—either get killed or have a nice dry hole, no matter what." It was Red's turn to laugh. "That's pretty smart on your part, Jake."

"Yeah, Red, we'll get that new string of tools now, I figure."

The seven miles went all too quickly and they soon were back to the well. Shorty had picked up about another hundred feet and Quinn and Evans seemed to be better pals than ever. "What did you bring me and Bear, Daddy?" Quinn wanted to know.

Jake was used to that question as he hauled out another couple of pieces of chocolate cake—one for him and one for Evans. Quinn went over and sat down immediately under the tree, and started eating. They discussed the log with Shorty, and then he and Chub headed for his black truck. He waved good-bye, saying they'd see them about that time, tomorrow.

It didn't take long for Red and Jake to settle back into their jobs. It was lucky that they'd stopped in at Nellie's last night. The money would be good. Then, Maggie could have her ring and Jake wouldn't have to feel bad about it.

As late afternoon crept up on them, Jake's thoughts turned to Maggie, as the hum-drum sound of the spudding drilled on. If Shorty came at two o'clock the next day, he and Quinn could go home for a visit and surprise Maggie. He heard something that distracted him as the sun flickered behind a cloud. For just a minute, it got really dark. It was as if the clouds seemed to stop their summer play for some reason. Grandfather Sun hid his face behind the clouds, hoping that Jake would find it in his heart someday—to forgive a madman.

CHAPTER THIRTEEN

It seemed to Fred that the two and half miles to town was dragging on forever. He wondered if he would ever get there in time. His mind was racing. His driving concentration was losing the mental battle as he tried to figure out where to go. *I'll go to Black Robes! No, I'll go to gov't-ment doctor's house next to blacksmith's on Kihekah Street.* The idea of herding the giant Pierce Arrow down the narrow streets of town caused him to sweat even more. Star was still whining beside him, looking toward the back seat where Maggie lay.

The sight and sound of the huge automobile was creating a spectacle as it entered town. Fred had no idea that twenty-five miles an hour in second gear was causing the motor's roar. In fact, he couldn't even hear it, but heads were turning. People on the street watched the distraught Indian driving full-bore from one side of the street to the other.

As Fred passed the Catholic Church, he was tempted to stop and get help from his friend, Black Robes. But there was no time. He sped on by the church just as Miss Lydia was coming into view. She was locking the hardware store's door for the day. She placed the closed sign face up on the door hook. She heard the terrible roaring engine a block away and hurried out to the street. Fred saw her and lifted his huge foot off the gas. He began yelling at the top of his lungs. "Miss Lydia, Miss Lydia. It's Maggie Lookout! Help me! Help me! Jump in!"

Miss Lydia was smart. She had always prided herself that she could think fast on her feet. She knew instantly, that Fred was in real bad trouble. He couldn't stop the open-aired roadster completely. So in a split second, she dove, head first, over the door into the moving car, her skirt and petticoats still flying outside of the car. She landed up-side down on top of Star, who seemed more than a little indignant.

"Fred, what's the matter?" she said, half out of breath, fighting to push the billowing skirt down from around her head.

Fred once again attacked the gas pedal, racing the engine trying to pick up speed. "It's Maggie girl. In back. Hurt bad. Death coming!"

Miss Lydia climbed to her knees, wrestling the dog for position, and looked over the back seat at the blood-soaked girl. She screamed and at the same time climbed over the seat in a blast of skirt material. "My God, Fred! What's happened? What's happened?" Fred took his eyes off the road and looked back.

"I don't know! Oh God!" He looked back at the road, just in time to see that he was headed right for a tree. He managed to swerve in time. "I find her in lodge with dead dog on top of her! Does she still, have life in her?"

Lydia felt the girl's neck. She could feel a heartbeat. "Yes, Fred, but it's faint. Drive faster. We'll take her to Doc Lewis."

Fred nodded. "I can't stop the car, Miss Lydia. I never drive till today, till Maggie Lookout hurt!"

"I know, Fred! Well here, take your foot off the gas pedal. We'll have to turn this way." She pointed to the west. "Up on West Main Street." Then it dawned on her. "My God, Fred, you can't drive?" In a split second, she leaned over his shoulder from the back seat. Her long blond hair was falling in Fred's face, and her feet were dangling in thin air. From around his neck she grabbed the massive steering wheel, helping him turn in the direction of the doctor's house.

Fred yelled in her ear. "How we stop, Miss Lydia, when we get there?"

"I don't know! I'll think of something. Just keep that foot off the gas!"

When Doc's house came into sight, she scanned the front looking for some way to bring the big car to a stop. Thankfully, there was only one other car parked outside—probably Doc Lewis's car. It was going to have to be sacrificed. "Just roll into that car, Fred. No gas—no gas. Easy, easy now, Fred! You can buy Doc a new one later."

The crash could have been worse as the big Pierce scrunched the parked Studebaker, moving it backward about ten feet. Actually, it was a miracle that the lighter weight frame of the Studebaker succeeded in stopping the huge touring car. Wah'-Kon-Tah and Grandfather Sun shared the secret.

Fred opened the door and Miss Lydia flew out behind him with Star at her heels. "I'll go get Doc!" She was already running up the steps to the door. "Kill the motor, Fred, and bring her in!" She began banging on the door. "Doc Lewis! Open up!"

The door swung open and Ruby, Doc Lewis' black cook and house-keeper, stood at the door. "Ruby! Ruby! Fred Lookout's daughter, Maggie, has been nearly killed. Get Doc, please!"

Ruby, a big black woman and protector of the guard, took one look at the girl's face and let her in. "Hurry child! Come with me!" They both ran to the left side of the house to Doc's study. He was sitting in a faded old wing back chair with his feet up on a worn needlepoint covered footstool. He was pouring over some medical journal deep in thought, when the two women burst into his room, screaming. "Doc! Doc! Hurry! Maggie Lookout's hurt real bad!"

Doc looked up over his spectacles. "Now slow down just a cotton pickin' minute and keep your shirt on, Missy. Where is she?"

Miss Lydia took a breath. "Fred's bringing her in from the car." That was about all she could get out.

"Okay! Okay! I'll go have a look!" The gruff old man of about sixty-some years old said. "Bring her in to the examining room."

The three raced down the hall to Doc's office in another direction of the house. Fred was coming up the walk with Maggie Lookout's limp blood-soaked body in his arms. Lydia hurried over and held the door for him. "Follow me, Fred!"

Fred was trying to run, but he was about to give out. They made it to the room where Ruby and Doc were laying clean cloths down on the examination table. "Here, lay her down! Easy, Fred! What happened for God's sakes?" Doc asked as he quickly surveyed the situation.

Fred looked at him with a face sagging with exhaustion. "I don't know! I find her in lodge at ranch with dead dog on top of her!"

Doc looked up at Fred, and then back at the girl. "Okay, step back, Fred. We've got to get these clothes off, or as least, what's left of them. Lydia, get that bowl and some warm water and the disinfectant soap. Start sponging her off."

Lydia left the room with the bowl and Doc started checking her with his stethoscope, lifting her eyelids to study her pupils and checking her other reflexes. Ruby and Lydia set about, getting most of the blood off of her body, throwing the bloody rags in the corner.

Meanwhile, Fred silently paced, trying to think how was he going to get word to Julia wife that her Maggie girl was dying. Doc Lewis felt around over her body and looked at the bruises and cuts on her face and thighs. He noticed the jag of hair cut from her ear. There was a deep cut there, made unmistakably by a knife. The women had cleaned her face and her upper body and were moving to her thighs. "Leave that alone a minute!" Doc ran his finger over the dried white stains on her thigh. "This woman's been raped!"

Fred's head snapped around like he'd been shot. "What'd you say?"

Doc looked at Fred, "Look here, blood's still coming from her, up there! He's hurt her real bad, inside." Doc looked down. The fire in Fred's eyes was too, bright. "Her wounds don't look to bad on the out-side except for that one by her ear, but I'll have to take a look, inside—."

"Why, doesn't she wake up?"

"She's in deep shock, Fred. This was too much for her. Whoever's done this to her has closed her spirit. She's always been a real sensitive girl, and this has just been too much for her gentle nature." He paused. "She may or may not come out of it for awhile. You leave her with me and Ruby. I'll sew her up and get her on some medicine. I suggest you go find the sheriff and get him on this. Got any idea who did this to her?"

Fred shook his head like a mighty buffalo.

"Where's Jake, Fred?"

"He's at the well site."

Doc continued on, giving orders. "Well, you need to go fetch him, too. Give me a couple of hours and I'll know more."

Fred said something that sounded like he agreed as he went silently to Maggie's side. Only her pale face and long black hair was visible from under the sheet that was pulled up to her chin. Fred slightly bent his big frame toward her and whispered softly. "Maggie girl. You rest. I'll take care of things. I'll find who did this to you." He patted her arm through the sheet. He abruptly turned on his heels. "Come on, Miss Lydia. We go now. We'll be back soon." Fred and Miss Lydia left the house together.

"Sky has clouded up, probably due to God-awful heat." Fred said as they went into the yard. "We have to hurry, get sheriff out to Maggie girl's before storm wash away tracks." He quickly calculated the rain was about two hours off, if he was lucky. "I don't want to drive automobile." They looked at the radiator steaming on the Pierce, as it sat still snuggly hugging the Studebaker. "Miss Lydia, I go find sheriff. Wonder where he might be?"

She nodded. "Well, it's six o'clock. He's probably eatin' up at O'Grady's Café. Fred, tell me, where's Jake's drilling? I'll go find him and bring him back. That way, we'll be back about the same time."

Fred, looked at her, surprised at her courage. "He tell me, section 12, west of town 'bout twenty miles. Al Evans got a lease he's drillin' on. You can stop at ol' Nellie's saloon and ask his whereabouts. She keeps track of the oil patch hands. You know where that is?"

"Sure, Fred. Big Ed and I go out there, sometimes, when he's in town. Now, Fred don't worry. Maggie will be okay, and so will I." She pointed two doors down to the blacksmiths. "Let's run next door to Joe's. He'll loan us a couple of horses. He owes me a favor."

The old Indian and the blond lady cleared the yard in a hurry. She found Joe in the back of the building, and she quickly filled him in on the deal. "Sure, Miss Lydia, take my two best ones," he said. She took a deep breath after spilling out her story.

"Thanks, Joe." She stood on her tiptoes and kissed him on his cheek. He helped the two of them saddle up.

When he had finished, he spit his tobacco juice in the dirt and out of the corner of his mouth, he said, "You'd better tell the sheriff to find this guy. Too much bad stuff goin' on, right now." He shook his head and went back to his work.

Fred touched Lydia's arm. "You, be careful, Miss Lydia! Stay on main road. It is dangerous in the dark. And now, rain will come soon."

She patted his hand. "I know, Fred! That's why we've got to hurry. Giddy up, Bessie." She slapped the horse rump with the reins took off toward the west.

Fred rode off on his borrowed horse in the opposite direction past the Triangle Building and turned up Kihekah Street. He found O'Gradys in the middle of the block in the Leland Hotel. Dismounting, he threw the reins to a young boy. "Hold horse, son. I'll be right back!" The kid obediently took the reins as the tall Indian entered the restaurant.

"Where's Sheriff?" He fairly screamed at the lady in charge of seating.

"I'm sorry, Mr. Lookout, he's not here tonight. Can I help you?"

Fred looked around, frantically. "No, no, I'm not hungry. I must find him!"

A couple of the diners looked up, not being able to miss either the conversation or Fred's blood smeared clothes. It was Judge Worton and his wife, Grace. "Fred." The judge rose from his chair to talk to the Indian. "It's Wednesday night. Sheriff Cook usually eats over at the Duncan Hotel. They got their Wednesday night fried chicken special. What's wrong, Fred? You look awful."

Fred, at the sight of his old friend, just blurted it out. "Maggie Lookout's been attacked. She lay at Doc Lewis now in coma."

"Oh, Lord!" Mrs. Worton gasped. "Go, Jess! Take Fred over there or wherever, till you find the sheriff. I'll wait here. Hurry!"

Judge Worton wiped his mouth with his napkin on the run, and pitched it on the table in passing. "Let's go, Fred!" They raced by the rest of the horrified diners and the hostess, who still could not imagine what was going on. Finally, out in the street, Jess yelled, "Get in my buggy, Fred."

Fred ran past the boy holding the horse. "Stay here and tie horse up to rail. I'll be back!" They raced to West Main Street in front of the Constantine Theatre.

"There's the sheriff's horse. Looks like a couple of his deputies are eatin' with him, Fred," Jess yelled as they jumped out of the buggy. They ran together into the hotel dining room.

The place was packed. Each table had a platter of fried chicken and all the trimmings. Fred and the Judge hurriedly scanned the dining room. They both saw the sheriff, sitting near the back, sure enough, with his men, Bill Stokes, and Robert Newman. The sheriff had his napkin tucked in his shirt and chicken pieces in both hands. The sheriff saw the men running, nearly knocking the tables over as they came toward him. He was alarmed when he saw Judge Worton, but he took one look at Fred's face and knew it was serious.

"Sheriff, come quick to Maggie Lookout's before the rain! She's hurt, raped." Fred was struggling with the words. "Left for dead. At lodge!"

The sheriff had heard enough. The three men grabbed their hats and threw down some money on the table. "We'll meet you at the ranch, Fred. Now, take it easy. We'll find them. Where's Jake?"

"Miss Lydia gone to get him," Fred replied barely whispering the words.

"Where's the girl?"

"Doc Lewis!"

"Good!" the sheriff said, as they ran for their horses.

Judge Jess perspired heavily and gasped. "I'll drop you by your horse, Fred."

Quickly, they arrived back at O'Grady's Cafe. The kid was still holding the reins of the borrowed animal. Fred tossed him two bits. "Thanks, son."

"You bet, Mr. Lookout."

The judge looked at him. "Fred, be careful! Sheriff Cook'll find them." He stepped up on the sidewalk to reenter the restaurant where his wife was waiting. He looked at the dust from Fred's horse, and wondered if Fred had even heard him. "Times are bad", he said to his wife as he retold the story. He saw it everyday up at his court.

Fred was heading out of town, quite a ways behind the sheriff. He had to hurry. Storm clouds were gathering faster. Rain would come soon. As he was flying by the Catholic Church, for what seemed to be the tenth time that day, Father Jack was coming around the side to go in the front door of the church. Fred pulled the horse to a fast stop, causing the animal to rear, nearly throwing Fred to the ground. "Black Robes! Black Robes!" Fred yelled, as he rode right up on the church yard.

"My God, Fred! What's the matter with you? You been in a fight? You look awful."

Out of breath, Fred started in again. "Maggie Lookout in coma over at Doc Lewis—raped, left for dead at ranch. Go stay with her, Black Robes. Stay with her in case, she wakes up. Julia wife in Claremore. I don't want her to be afraid."

"Sure, sure, Fred. I saw Sheriff Cook and two of his men pass by a few mlnutes ago, riding fast. Does Jake know?"

"Miss Lydia's gone to get him."

"I'll go on over to Doc's." Black Robes yelled. Excitement had his adrenaline at a high pitch. "Fred, go on. I'll stay with her."

Fred rode back over the yard into the street at breakneck speed, heading for the ranch. He was deep in thought. *Where was Maggie girl's gun? Why didn't she shoot the guy? I need to go get Osage medicine man to pray over Maggie Lookout.*

The closer he rode to the ranch, the blacker the sky turned. It was as if Wah'-Kon-Tah's wrath was preparing to open the sky with all his vengeance. The air was still—too still. The clouds were tinged with green. *Ten minutes, no more before the storm hits,* he thought.

He did make it to the east edge of the ranch before the wind started up from nowhere, gusting for all it was worth. The wall of clouds was turning from black to gray as the old Indian prayed. *Please Wah'-Kon-Tah, do not send big wind that kills.* The rain started. First, a sprinkle of huge drops fell on his weary face, then a torrential downpour followed, coming from every direction at once. His heart was sinking. The tracks would be gone. He was close to the open gate, and in the driving rain, he could see the sheriff coming out of the lodge, and two other men entering the house.

Grandfather Sun was not in sight, but if he had been, he would have seen a pitiful sight. The old Indian was just sitting on his borrowed horse, water dripping off his face with no hat to break the water. The yard was beginning to flood. No chickens or ducks in sight. There were only a couple of the dogs on the porch, front paws on the railing, howling. Every now and then, when the thunder chose to hush, the loud, disturbed scream of a peacock could be heard.

Much like the rain, thoughts flooded Fred's mind as he sat there. Like the Osage Indian girl, maybe Grandfather Sun's sensitivity was enveloping them both, he thought. Fred knew that Grandfather Sun didn't care any longer about the tracks in the dirt. He was only interested in washing away the awful picture in his memory of his Osage girl, who had been robbed of her spirit. Fred knew that she would be forced to walk, maybe forever in the dark night of her soul.

CHAPTER FOURTEEN

Miss Lydia had taken off toward the west and had ridden fast out of town. People she knew waved at her, but she couldn't stop. Her blond hair, once tied in the back, was loose and flying behind her. She had her tiny derringer in her garter, but it was only a secondary gun. She wished she had her double barrel. It would be dark and raining soon. If she could make it to Nellie's by horseback, then maybe she could borrow Nellie's truck to go the rest of the way.

Her mind was flying as fast at the horse's hooves. *Who would do such a thing to Maggie? Was it robbery or just a sick sex thing?* She shuddered. She could feel Maggie's pain. *What if she never wakes up? What will Jake and Quinn do?* She wasn't close to Maggie, but she and Jake had been great friends for years. He spent a lot of time in her store, as most men did. She'd have to admit most of her closest friends were men, except for her best friend, Laura Van Estes. Her thoughts returned to the last customer she had had earlier today.

A small man with close set eyes and a big nose had come in late in the afternoon. In fact, she'd had most of the guns put up in the safe for the night. He had asked a few questions about her gun prices, but he had been very quiet. His eyes were moving constantly taking in everything, including her. She finally just let him look while she returned to her bullet order from her St. Louis distributor.

She forgot about him till some minutes later, when he came up to her. He had just stood there. She had asked him what else she could do for him. He had said in a low voice that he wanted a box of .380 auto bullets for a gun, he'd just bought. She had looked the gun over and had retrieved the bullets down from the shelf behind her. Then, she had asked him to sign his name by his purchase. He had seemed bit reluctant, but had signed it, "Henry" something. Looked like it started with a S. She couldn't help but notice he had a big diamond ring on his little finger.

Then, from out of the blue, he had asked her if she would sell him five blond hairs. That wasn't too unusual a request, as the Indians would come around and want to buy blond hairs for good luck. But she usually just laughed at them and sent them up to Elgin on the Kansas line. Diamond Lil ran a bar there, and sold blond hair on the side. "I am sorry, sir, but I don't sell my hair, even though I have been known to give a few away to my friends now and then." She had tried to laugh it off, but he just looked at her with his beady eyes. With no further conversation, he had turned his back and left the store.

Now she began to feel raindrops and she was forced to return to her current dilemma with the weather. She strained to see Nellie's lights in the log cabin saloon. She urged the horse faster as the downpour began. She was soaked by the time she got to the front door, but she ran in and up to the bar where Nellie was standing, tea towel in hand. "Nellie, help me! Help me! I've got to find Jake Knupp! Do you know where he's drillin'? His wife was raped and left for dead. She's in a coma at ol' Doc Lewis'. I've got to find him."

The older woman paled as she moaned. "Oh my God, not Maggie. He's drillin' for Al Evans, I think, isn't he guys?" All the while she was talking, Nellie was taking off her apron as the crowd of people left their seats to gather closer to hear the story. "They were in here last night and left about two o'clock today. Anybody hear where the well was?"

Sam, the old pumper spoke up. "He told me, section 12 'bout twenty miles west on the old Tucker spread. Do you know where that is, Miss Lydia?"

"No, not really."

Nellie came around the bar in a hurry. "Well, take my truck, Sam, and take Miss Lydia up there. There's a terrible storm in the works. She can't go by horseback. 'Sides it's not safe. Want me to go, too, Lydia?"

"No, that's okay, Nellie. Just let us take your truck. We'll find him." Nellie was fishing around in a drawer. "Here's the key, Sam. Bring it around while I get a sandwich for Miss Lydia, and a half-pint to take with her. Jake's going need it. You going take care of the boy?"

"Yeah." Lydia nodded. "I guess."

"Well, if you need me let me know." She was throwing the sandwich together, and barked at Miss Lydia to eat it. Then she ran to the back room, returning quickly with the bottle.

The stir of men's conversation was getting louder and more concerned, asking if they had any description of the guy.

"No! Sheriff Cook and his men are out at the ranch now," Lydia answered as she gulped down another bite. She heard the truck horn honk from out front. "Oh, there's the truck. I've got to go."

"Here, take this rain cloak," Nellie threw it over her shoulders. She ran out into the rain and jumped into the truck, thanking God for Nellie, and thinking how she dreaded getting to the end of their twenty mile destination.

Sam was a pretty good driver. He was an old pumper who was used to trucks, ruts, and storms. He didn't talk much as he kept his attention on the road. The trip took longer than she thought. A few tree limbs and small logs were across the road in some spots, and they had to dodge them. It was probably close to ten o'clock, and she wondered if the sheriff had found any clues. She wondered too, if Maggie had come out of her coma yet. Sam broke the silence of the ride. "Here's the turn, Miss Lydia." He veered across a series of big puddles.

"How much further, Sam?" Lydia asked over the loud roar of the storm.

"Bout a mile, I reckon, but this storm's gettin' worse. We have to cross a low water creek crossing down yonder, 'bout a quarter mile from the site. The road 'll be washed out. We'll have to leave the truck and walk in."

Lydia nodded. "Okay, Sam." She drew the cloak closer to her. The thunder and lightning were hitting simultaneously and they could hear trees cracking as the lightning made its hit. *O, Lord, what else can happen today? Big Ed's due back into town tonight from St. Louis. He'll wonder what's happened to me.* Then again, she thought. What the hell is happening to me?

After an eternity of inching the truck along, killing the motor in the deep water and re-starting it each time, she spied the creek in the dim head lights of the truck. "Yep, Miss Lydia, it's too high. We'll have to ford it. Can you swim?"

"Yeah, but I can't see a thing," she moaned. "I can hear the water. It sounds like it's running awful fast."

They got out of the truck, hoping for the best as the rain was torrential at that moment. She tried to hold on to the cloak with one hand as Sam held her other hand. She took a deep breath, praying no snakes would see her. They waded into the cool temperatured water. It was up to her waist with logs and limbs rushing by in front of her. She stumbled and fell. She lost Sam's hand and caught herself on a rock just before her face went completely under. She steadied herself and made a wild grab for Sam's shoulder. He was holding his hand toward her. Somehow a close flash of lightning allowed her to see it, and she grabbed it once again. The thunder was deafening. Sam kept half-swimming and half-dragging her along. The water was ominous sounding as it carried along tons of debris from miles back.

Across the creek the well site looked like a giant mud hole. The deep ruts of the trucks were rapidly filling with water. The bottom was falling out of the sky as the rain pelted the tin roofs of the temporary buildings.

The drilling continued despite the bad weather. On the floor of the derrick with a makeshift canvas tarp tied securely overhead, Red and Jake
stood watching the storm. "Lord, it's a bad one, Jake. Lightning's hittin'
close, everywhere."

"Yeah, long as it don't start a fire. Is Evans and Quinn both in the dog
house or in Evan's truck?" Jake asked as he tried to pigeon-hole the
whereabouts of everyone in his mind.

"He's in the dog house with Evans. He's studying the log. We're down
about two hundred and fifty feet, so he's in there drinkin' coffee and
speculatin' on whether to change to the beam." Red laughed as he tried
to dodge the rain. "Said he'd keep the youngin' in there on his cot."

"Okay," Jake nodded, trying to light his cigar in the wind. "Boy, I
could sure use some coffee, but its raining too damn hard, now."

Red nodded. "I'll go get us some, when it lets up. I don't know why
this dad burn storm didn't happen on Shorty's shift."

Jake looked out at the pouring sheets of rain coming off the roof of
the engine house. "Yeah!" He wondered that himself, but at least it broke
the heat. "I'll tell you what I'd give my eye teeth for—and that's another
big ol slab of Nellie's chocolate cake."

Red licked his chops. "Hm-hm, boy. That does sound good. Next
time, I'm just goin' buy the whole damn cake."

Jake moved his mouth to answer, but the thunder was too loud for
him to hear his reply. The wind was gusting. Jake couldn't even begin to
keep his cigar lit. He finally threw it down in disgust. They were both
pretty well soaked, but the sound of the spudder kept the pounding up
and so did the rain.

About twenty minutes later, Jake saw a flash of light through the
trees. He thought it might have been lightning on the other side of the
creek, but the light seemed too low for a lightning flash. *Bet that creek's
swollen. I can hear it clear from here,* he thought.

At precisely the same time from in the middle of the creek, Sam
yelled to the girl. "We've almost made it across, Miss Ly—." The mighty

roar of thunder and a crack of lightning sent a limb from the huge hickory tree overhead. It crashed down on Sam's shoulders, just missing his head. He went down like a ton of bricks with the limb holding him under the water.

Lydia screamed, terrified to death as she pulled on his shirt. She realized he was not only pinned by the limb, but over a rock. She kept screaming and with another flash, she twisted her body away and felt for the bank. She grabbed on to a small oak sapling nearby. She pulled and tugged Sam closer to the edge of the water, screaming louder and louder. It was a real contest as the storm tried to claim victory over her. "Oh, God!" she cried. "Is he dead? Sam! Sam!"

At least the limb had rolled off his shoulder, but Sam's feet were still tangled in its branches. The branches were snagged by the rock, so at least for the time being, they weren't washing on down the creek. "Sam! Sam! Can you hear me?" She kept screaming. Deciding he was knocked out or dead, she began screaming. "Jake! Jake!"

The rain was pounding the derrick floor and the tarp was trying to blow completely off when Bear started barking. Jake thought he was in the dog house, too, but he was under the wagon that had brought out the boiler. He was really getting upset and loud.

"What is it, boy?" Jake asked. "Whatta you see?"

"He sees rain." Red laughed, sarcastically.

"Shush, did you hear something? Sounds like a woman scream."

"Naw, I didn't hear nothing, Jake." A huge clap of thunder sounded.

There were no seconds to count between it and the lightning. "Boy, that was close."

"Yeah, it hit over there by the creek. That was some crack. Must have split a tree wide open."

The dog was barking louder, and he jumped on to the derrick floor with Jake. "He hears something, Red. There! There it is again! That's a woman's scream." At the same time, they jumped off the floor and Red grabbed the dad's lantern. They followed Bear, best as they could, in the driving rain. As he led them closer to the creek, Jake could see from the lightning flashes the swollen creek before them, looking more like a wild river. Then, another woman's scream pierced the air. "Oh, my God, Red!" Jake yelled. "Who's there?" Bear went wild.

"Jake! Jake! Help! Help me! It's Lydia! Hurry! I can't hang on much longer."

Red and Jake looked at each other at the same time, "Miss Lydia!" They both, jumped feet first into the rushing water.

As Jake reached her, she was crying, "It's Sam! He's dead, I think. A limb hit him."

Red grabbed Sam as Lydia grabbed Jake's neck like a desperate animal. He gathered the exhausted blond woman in his arms and laid her on the bank. Then he ran back to help Red drag the man out of the rushing water. They managed to untangle him and thrust him onto the bank, face-down. The storm had no intention of letting up so they could hardly hear one another. Lydia crawled closer to them as they worked on Sam. "Is he dead, Jake?"

"No," Red yelled, "He's still alive. But what the hell you doin' out here in the middle of nowhere in this storm, Miss Lydia?"

That seemed to break the dam on Lydia's nerves as she collapsed, crying hysterically. "Jake! Jake! It's Maggie! She's hurt, bad hurt!"

Jake could only get one or two of her words in between claps of thunder, but he knew it was bad. Red knew it too, and he started yelling. "Go on! I'll get Evans to help me with Sam. You get Quinn—."

"I've got Nellie's truck across the creek," Lydia yelled above the water's roar.

He nodded. "Red, can you and Evans handle the well?"

"Yeah, yeah, Boss. I'll go get Quinn."

"Hurry Red!"

For the moment, Sam was forgotten, but he was coming to slowly. Like a wild man, Jake grabbed Lydia in his arms, and started across the swollen creek. She was still crying on his shoulder, but at least she'd found him, as relief washed over her seeming to swallow her up.

It took a few minutes, but with the light of the dad's lantern sitting on the bank, Jake could see where to go to dodge the floating wood. He rolled her on to the bank. "Get in the truck. I've got to get Quinn." She obeyed and turned on the truck lights.

Red was standing on the other bank with Quinn in his arms. Quinn was rubbing the sleep and the rain out of his eyes with both fists. "Come on, ol' partner. Go to Daddy! I'll see you in a day or two," Red said softly to the boy as he handed him over to Jake. "Jake! I think we'd better throw Sam in the back. He's going need stitches, and I think his shoulder's broke."

"Okay, let me get Quinn to the truck, and I'll come back for Sam." Bear jumped in the water as Jake started across with Quinn.

Jake was to scared to even think about what was wrong with Maggie. He could only imagine, and his heart was dying a thousand times as he laid the boy in the seat next to Lydia. The sleepy boy laid his head in her lap, and with the innocent beauty of a child, he was instantly asleep. Jake jumped in the water one more time to reclaim Sam from the other side. Red and Jake managed to drag him through the water to the bank and hauled him to the truck. They lifted him onto the bed of the truck and threw the tarp over him, securing it with some rope in the back. Bear jumped on the back with Sam, while Jake jammed his tired, wet body behind the wheel. He put the truck in reverse, and they headed toward the main road.

Water pouring off of him, Jake cried, "My God, Lydia! What's happened?"

She was crying so hard he could hardly understand her. "Jake, Maggie's been raped, beaten, and left for dead at your ranch. She's in a coma at Doc Lewis."

"What?" Jake screamed. "No! No! It can't be! Is she going to die?"

Lydia shook her head. "I don't think so, but Doc says that she's in such shock that she may not come out of it."

Every muscle in his body was screaming. The truck crashed, lurched, dipped, and swerved as they recklessly drove to the main road. There were times that Bear and Sam both had to have been airborne.

"I rode the horse to Nellie's, Lydia said in between sobs. "I borrowed her truck, or I'd never made it. She sent Sam with me to drive." She continued to cry harder and harder as she looked in the back at the still form of her driver and friend, when the lightning flashes chose to give her a glimpse.

Finally, after Lydia had told Jake that Fred had gone to the ranch with the sheriff, and the rest of the story, they finally spotted the main road. Turning east, they could drive somewhat faster. "Who? Who would do this to her, Jake?" Lydia asked. "Could the motive be robbery?"

Jake stared straight ahead with a death's grip on the steering wheel. "I don't know. She had a gun and Spitfir—."

"Spitfire's dead. The dog's dead," she interrupted as she tried to relay Fred's gruesome story of the Indian girl's dog.

It was only the bumps in the road that kept Jake from losing his mind as he swore under his breath. *Don't let her die, God! Let me die, but oh God, don't let my Maggie die.* The storm's rage continued to build outside the truck and inside the man.

It was midnight or better when Lydia and Jake reached town. They drove down West Main Street to the doctor's place. There was a light still on in the study, and one small light in the examination room. "Lydia, get Quinn!" Jake shouted, already out of the truck. Bear started barking again and jumped out. Jake grabbed Sam's feet, tarp and all, and pulled him to the end of the truck bed. Sam was somewhat awake but moaning in terrible pain. Jake wrapped his arms around him as they started for the house. Lydia had grabbed Quinn up from her lap. He was beginning to cry from the rude disturbance of his night's sleep, but together they managed to run to the doctor's front door.

She pounded on it for the second time that day, as Ruby opened the door in her blue checkered gown and robe. "Oh, my God! Miss Lydia! You found him. Let me have the boy. I'll give him some milk and a cookie." She hustled him off to the kitchen.

Doc, hearing the door, wandered out of the study, just in time to see Jake with this limp man and Lydia looking like a drowned rat. "Not another one!" Doc cried.

"Yeah. Sam Smith, the pumper. He drove me to find Jake," Lydia blurted out.

"Lord help us! Bring." Doc was already moving in high gear.

"How's my wife, Doc? Do you know anyth—."

"She's about the same, Jake. Here, lay him down here on this leather couch. I'll tend to him in a moment. Come with me."

Lydia and Jake followed him to the bedroom off the examining room. A soft lamp light cast a warm glow on the damp night, and on the bed where the beautiful hurt Indian girl lay ever so still. "She hasn't woke up yet, Jake," Doc whispered. "I sewed her up, but she's got about a three inch tear inside of her female parts. Got her on some medicine, but it's just been too much for her. You know, it may take awhile. I'm trying to keep her from hemorrhaging. She's goin' live, providing no infection sets in, but her mind, Jake, I just can't say."

In the corner, Jake heard a slight noise, and moved his haggard gaze to a wing back chair, where Father Jack sat with his head hanging on his chest.

"He's been here all evening," Doc said. "Said he'd sit with her so she wouldn't be scared if she woke up."

Jake stood over Maggie's bed looking like the oldest man in Osage County. He knelt down by her bed and took her limp hand from under the sheet. "Maggie. It's Jake. It's Jake. Can you hear me?" There was no response. He could hear Lydia in the background standing by the door as she and the doctor left the room to tend to Sam.

The lightning was still illuminating the sky outside as the rain pelted against the window. The rain had the same haunting rhythm of the Osage drum. Every now and then, the whole room would light up like daytime. Jake had sat back on his heels when he heard a tiny whimpering behind him. He turned to see Quinn, holding Father Jack's hand. He had his other fingers in his mouth, and tears were running down his cheeks. *What did he see?* Jake wondered. *What did he think as he looked at the bed?*

"Mama! Mama!" Quinn cried, as he tore away from Father Jack and threw his little body across her, sobbing. "Don't die, Mama! Don't die!" Jake put his arms around him while Father Jack knelt by the bed, fingering the worn rosary beads of the heavy eyebrow's God. The storm raged outside, gathering momentum again, trying its best to energize the Indian woman and her Irish tempered oilman.

The lightning fought hard to remind them that Grandfather Sun would soon return to chase away the clouds. But for now, Grandfather Sun was nowhere to be seen and the whole Osage world wept.

CHAPTER FIFTEEN

Desolation from the rain had set in back at the Lookout ranch. The sheriff, his deputies, and Fred sat down to rest and talk on the porch. Sheriff Cook looked more than frustrated. "Fred, any tracks we might have found are gone. This damn rain's washed them all away. Bill, Robert, and I all feel that there was only one man, though. We've searched the house. Nothing much torn up. Evidently, he didn't want to make any noise to wake Maggie up. So it's my guess he knew all along she was here. He's ransacked the bureau drawers looking for jewelry, guns, or money. But I think he mainly came just for her."

"How'd he know Jake wasn't coming in, Sheriff Cook?" Bill asked.

The sheriff shook his head. "Don't know. He musta known Jake was drillin', I reckon. So it seems to me that he's a local person, not some transient whose read the papers about the oil money."

Fred nodded. "Did you find her gun?"

"No, we've looked, everywhere. Can you think where she might have kept it?"

"Well!" Fred said almost in slow motion. "She keeps it in her and Jake's room, upstairs. But now, that Jake's gone, she sleeps in lodge. She probably, forgot to take it out there."

Sheriff Cook agreed. "What kind of gun was it?"

Fred thought a moment. "Black six shooter—don't know the make."

Sheriff Cook looked at his deputy. "Bob, first thing in the morning you hunt around town for any guns that's been sold or traded lately. It isn't likely that he pitched it in the pond since he didn't use it on her. Go by Miss Lydia's at the hardware store and see if she knows anything."

"Okay, Sheriff." The deputy wrote down his instructions and stood up.

That reminded Fred of Miss Lydia. "I wonder if she found Jake? Terrible storm. How am I goin' locate Julia wife? She visitin' relatives in Claremore." Fred seemed to be talking more to himself than to anyone else. Sheriff Cook saw how weary Fred was. "I'll telegraph the sheriff over in that county and have him go tell her, Fred."

Fred was obviously relieved and his shoulders sagged slightly. "Oh, that'll be good, Sheriff."

"Fred, not to change the subject," Sheriff Cook asked. "But do you know if they had any money or jewelry that might be missing?"

"Money?" Fred thought back. "Kept in bank! Jake was careful about that, and no jewelry, except—. Oh, my God! Sheriff Cook, the big rock ring!"

"What big rock ring?" The sheriff's attention quickened.

Fred gasped. The words seemed to explode in his mind. "The one she bought from con man on payment day for twelve thousand dollars. Jake and I were mad. Con man get Rosa Whitehorn and Maggie girl. He get Claire Whitehorn, too. All victims!" Fred dropped his braided head in his hands. "It's terrible. My people. My people. Now, my Maggie girl," he said as a muffled wail came from his mouth.

Sheriff Cook touched him on the shoulder. "Now, Fred tell me about this ring."

Fred lifted his head. "It's a big diamond rock on gold band."

Sheriff nodded as he began writing a description of the ring. "Did she have it on when you took her to Doc Lewis?"

Fred looked puzzled. "I don't know. Too busy drivin'. No time to worry bout big rock ring."

"Okay," Sheriff Cook said, folding his note paper. "That's enough for now. We'll check on that too, Bill." He indicated to his other deputy. "Do you have the name of the guy who sold it to her?"

Fred moaned again. "No."

"Well, then, about the only thing we can do is to check on these couple of things, and wait till Maggie comes around. Maybe then she can give us a description."

Fred's eyes, full of worry, lifted. "She may not remember even if she does come around. Doc say, 'spirit closed', too much for her."

Sheriff Cook stood up. "Well, we'll wait and see, Fred. No need to go borrowin' trouble. I'll go by and talk to Doc Lewis about her wounds. You say she's got a knife cut on her face?"

Fred nodded. "He cut off hair by ear and he cut face, too."

Sheriff Cook looked at the deputies. "Okay. Well, that explains the loose hair in the lodge. Boys, we need to have that bullet dug out of the dog's head and get a caliber check on it. So you boys take care of that. Take the dog in with you. We'll look it over better in town. Let's take it over to the butcher shop and see if Hank can remove it. Looks like it's pretty well buried in its skull."

Bill and Bob got up and stood at the porch rail watching the steady rain as it continued its plummet to the ground. "Well," Bill said. "Lets look around some more, then get the dog and head for town."

Sheriff Cook added something to his notes, then refolded the paper and slipped into his shirt pocket. "Fred, I need to be getting' back to town, too. I'll go by Doc's and see what Maggie's condition is, and I'll get back with you. I need to talk to Jake, too." The sheriff started down the porch steps and then, as if he suddenly remembered, turned around. "Oh yeah. I'll get a hold of Claremore sheriff's department, and tell them to hightail it to find Julia, and get her headed back this way. You say it's the Quiver family of the Beaver Clan?"

Fred nodded. "Yes."

"She got a driver?"

Fred nodded again. "Yeah. John Lossin."

"Okay, Fred," the sheriff replied. "Now, you take it easy. Maybe Maggie's come around already, and we'll get this guy soon as we get a description from her." He turned, tipped his hat down, and continued on down the steps into the early morning rain.

Fred leaned back in his green tall-backed chair. He was exhausted, hungry, and his past day was beginning to catch up with him. His mind was racked with weariness and his whole body screamed for rest. His mind seemed to take advantage of the silence and Fred drifted into sleep. His sub-conscious state brought his dreams to another time and place, when another of his daughters had been taken from him by Wah'-Kon-Tah. His spirit led him to a place in his mind, long hidden away for many years, but now it seemed to be begging him to relive it, again.

Long ago Fred and Julia had fallen In love. It was a great Osage marriage between Sacred Arrow Shaft and Eagle That Get What He Wants. Wah'-Kon-Tah was pleased.

After some years had passed, Fred and Julia had lost many children. And now, their favorite daughter, Mi-Tse-Ge, lay dying on her pallet. The "White Chests"—the Indian's name for the Catholic nuns—had come to pray. But nothing could keep her spirit from leaving her tiny body. Suddenly, she opened her eyes. "Do not mourn, Father. Jesus is coming to get me. I am happy." And with that, the tiny girl died.

As her spirit traveled to the good place, Fred and Julia's deep mourning began. They gave away all of their clothes except for some of their worst. They gave away everything in the farm house. They hired a Delaware Indian girl to take care of the other two children. Then they donned the blue earth of mourning, and wandered down the creek fasting. After many days they came out of a clearing near the Red Eagle place. Red Eagle's wife took them in and seeing their deep despair began telling them of peyote.

She told them that Moonhead Wilson, a Caddo medicine man, had brought a new religion to the Osages. Through dreams and hallucinations he received from smoking the powerful peyote buttons, he had convinced the Osages that the Messiah was returning for the second coming in the body of an Indian. Mrs. Red Eagle explained to them that they had a peyote church to remove the evil. She further explained that it was the evil that had caused their daughter, Mi-Tse-Ge, to die. "You must go to the sweat lodge here. I have some buckeye root to make the tea. I will send for the Crow dancers, and they will paint their faces with red bud charcoal."

So Julia and Fred had gone to the sweat lodge. They had drank of the buckeye root, and they had vomited many times to rid themselves of the evil. Then they went into the peyote church to smoke. To the beat of the drum, the dancers began. The dance resembled a gobbler continually rising from a squatting position. That dance was to drive the sorrow and evil away from Eagle That Get What He Wants, and his wife, Sacred Arrow Shaft. Renewed in spirit, they returned to their farm on Bird Creek. They had an eight-sided peyote church built on their farm. Now, Wah'-Kon-Tah and the heavy eyebrows God were no longer enemies for the new translator was Chief Peyote.

Perhaps it was the pain of those past days creeping to the surface, or a worrisome fly's buzzing that awakened Fred. The pain he still felt for Mi-Tse-Ge poured over him like dam water into his current nightmare. *Wah'-Kon-Tah, you must save Maggie girl.* He had named her Wind In Her Heart long ago, and that wind must blow her spirit back to life. He would go to town to see Maggie girl, and then come home to his peyote church on his land. He would smoke and talk to Wah'-Kon-Tah about a second daughter, and how he must not lose her forever to the dark night of her soul. He would pray that the evil had not returned that had caused the death of Mi-Tse-Ge. He wondered when Julia wife would return. Suddenly, the big Indian man missed her. He needed her to share his grief.

CHAPTER SIXTEEN

Morning had dawned. Lucky for the little town of Pawhuska, Bird Creek seemed to be handling the deluge of rainwater from the night before. The Bird Creek flood of 1915 was still all too vivid to the residents of the agency town. Perhaps Grandfather Sun had decided to return and take control over his Osage people again.

It was about six o'clock that morning and Jake was still asleep in his chair when Father Jack touched his arm. "Jake, Sheriff Cook's here. He wants to talk to you. I'm leaving to go say Mass up at the church, but I'll be back."

"Okay." Jake nodded, looking over at Maggie's still face.

Ruby tiptoed into the room, and whispered. "Jake, here's ya a cup of coffee. I'm fixin' breakfast. Be about ten minutes." She patted Quinn's leg. He was curled up on the end of Maggie's bed, still asleep.

"Okay", Jake muttered. "Where's Lydia?"

"She's gone home to freshen up a bit, not that her stringy hair full of grass and debris looked too bad or anything mind ja." She laughed. "She had to open the hardware store for ol' Mr. Brown later this morning. She offered to take Quinn, but I said I'd watch him today till you decide what you want to do."

Jake watched her tiptoe out the door. *Ruby was some kind of woman,* he thought. Her mother had come with the Creek Indians from Mississippi across the big waters on the trail of tears.

Jake took his coffee to the window and stared out at the street. He thanked God the rain had stopped. As he stood there, trying to get his mind jump-started, he could hear Sheriff's Cook's giant footsteps coming down the hall. Jake turned to greet him. "Sheriff Cook!" He stuck out his hand.

The sheriff grabbed it. "Jake, sorry to hear 'bout all this trouble. Me and my men are all working on it."

"I know," Jake answered.

Sheriff Cook walked to Maggie's bedside and peered over her. "How's she doin'?"

Jake joined him. "No change since I've been here. Doc said, It may take awhile."

Interrupting his train of thought, Jake looked up to see Fred enter the room. He was obviously distraught, and in a great deal of mental anguish. He rushed up to Jake. "O' man! Am I ever glad to see you!" His shoulders caved in from exhaustion. Jake was there to carry some of his burden. "How Maggie girl?" He nodded to Sheriff Cook and walked over to the bed.

"About the same, Fred," Jake sighed. "Let's go out in the hall where we can talk."

Ruby met them in the hall. "Come on in, all of ya, and have some breakfast with Doc. He's already in the dining room. You can talk in there."

"Oh, thanks, Ruby," Fred mumbled. "I'm nearly starved."

The three men filed into the dining room where Doc sat enjoying his coffee and his copy of the Pawhuska Capital newspaper. He folded the paper up and tossed it over behind him on the china sideboard. "Howdy, gentlemen. Sit yourselves down and let Ruby fix you up with some of her fine cookin'. You know food's about the best medicine there is."

No argument there, Fred thought.

They all sat down as Ruby laid out eggs, hash browns, big slices of corn-fed ham, and biscuits with red-eye gravy. As Fred was piling his plate high, it dawned on him that it'd been twenty-four hours since he'd eaten.

"How she doin', Doc?" Sheriff Cook asked.

Doc took a swig of his coffee. "Well, I'm worried about her hemorrhaging inside. I'm giving her medicine and I've packed her up there with ice. Whoever it was really worked her over inside—bout a three-inch tear. I'm afraid of infection cause I figure it's already in her blood stream."

"I can't believe she hasn't come to, yet. What condition is her mind in, do you think, Doc?" The sheriff was having trouble shifting his thoughts from the honey on his hot dripping biscuit.

Doc shook his head. "Can't tell. May take her awhile to come around."

Sheriff Cook nodded. "I see. Well, my men and I were out with Fred at the scene, Jake, and, well frankly, the rain's washed away all of the tracks."

Jake raised his eyes. "Did you find any clues in the lodge or in the house?"

Sheriff Cook set his butter knife down. "Not really. I've about come to the conclusion that there was just one guy. Some things are messed up in the house, but not bad. We've taken the dog to the butcher to have the bullet removed, and then we can try and get a make on the gun. By the way, where'd Maggie keep the gun you gave her, Jake?"

"Up in our bedroom in that lamp stand by the bed", Jake replied, wiping his mouth clean with the edge of the napkin.

"Okay, I checked that drawer and all the rest of the drawers. It's gone. What was it?"

"It was a Colt .38 revolver with a six inch barrel and dark-handled stag horn grips," Jake pushed his coffee cup toward Ruby as she refilled it.

"Okay, and what about money? Did you have any there?"

"Naw!" Jake's voice was barely audible. "Maybe a couple a hundred in a blue and white sugar jar on the sideboard in the dining room."

Sheriff Cook kept prodding consistently along in-between bites. "Anything else? Jewelry of any kind?"

"Oh my God!" Fred and Jake bolted to their feet. "The big rock ring!" Jake yelled.

"Has she still got it on, Jake?" Fred asked. Dishes rattling, they jumped up from the table and raced to the back of the house to Maggie's bedside. Jake lifted her hands one at a time above the cover. All her fingers were bare.

They filed slowly back to the table, but no one resumed eating. After several minutes of silence, Sheriff Cook spoke. "Okay, so it looks like he got the ring, too."

"Did you see the knife wound by her ear?" Doc asked.

Sheriff Cook nodded. "Yeah!"

"It was pretty deep. They cut out some hair, it looks like."

"Yeah, we found a hunk of black hair in the lodge by the dog," Sheriff Cook said.

"Could it have been an Indian, Fred?" Jake asked.

"No, Indians want blond hairs for good luck, not black," Fred grunted in disgust.

Sheriff Cook wiped off the remains of his meal with his napkin. He slowly rose from the table, and picked up his hat. "Well, I'm going to talk to Miss Lydia over at the hardware store. See if she's seen anyone suspicious around." The sheriff said his good-byes and left the room. "Thank Ruby for me, Doc."

Jake threw down his napkin and went after him. He caught him on the porch. He was trying, but somehow he couldn't hide the absolute fury building inside his body. "Sheriff, are you going to find this guy, or am I? I'll kill him if I find out who it is that hurt her. She and Quinn's all I've got in the world. I can't live without her. Let me ride with you.

Deputize me! I'll find him. I'll kill him and bury him. You won't have to worry about a thing, Sheriff." Jake took a step toward him at the end of the porch when the giant arm of the sheriff stopped him.

"No, Jake. You'll just make it worse. And God knows things are bad enough in this town. Now, you just simmer down, and let me handle this. You've got a boy and a oil well to look after, besides Maggie. Now go on back inside. I mean it, Jake!" The sheriff walked down the walk to his horse. The horse was tied to the tree that shaded the tangled automobiles. But he and Jake were both to preoccupied, worrying about the current state of affairs.

Fred and Doc stepped out on the porch along side of Jake. "You know, I feel like a human being again, since I had a little food." Fred rubbed his belly. "Jake, I'm goin' to the ranch—goin' to peyote house. Go by and get Joe Blackbird, medicine man. We're goin' to have smoke and wait for Julia wife. I'll bring her back here to Maggie girl."

"Okay, Fred. I'll stay here till Quinn wakes up, then I'll go get cleaned up and stay around here till Julia comes. Red and Shorty can take care of the well for a couple of days. I don't want to leave her till she comes around."

Doc placed his hand on his shoulder. "Jake, don't count on that too soon." He walked back in to the house banging the screen door, mumbling something about a coffee refill.

"Well, look whose up and at 'em this morning!" Fred said as his grandson walked onto the porch with an orange juice glass in his hand.

The little boy beamed. "Howdy, Grandfather!" Jake caught the glass from him in mid-air as he ran to Fred. Fred scooped him up in his arms.

"Grandfather! Grandfather Fred! Mama hurt! Mama hurt! She won't talk to me or Daddy. I'm scared!" He started to pucker up and cry.

"Okay, Quinn child. It'll be okay. Your grandmother be back soon and you two and Doc here'll get her well in nothin' flat. You'll be back playin' with her at ranch in no time."

"Grandfather, can we go get Mama's dog? He can lay right by her bed."

Fred looked at Jake. "No, Quinn, not now. " Jake replied. "You and me'll stay here. We don't need Spitfire."

Quinn looked around, "Where's Bear?"

Doc spoke up over his coffee cup with his foot propped up on the porch railing. "He's over there. I tied him to a tree so he couldn't run off. Well, I gotta go check on Sam."

"Sam, who?" Fred asked.

"Sam Smith. Jake and Miss Lydia dragged him in here last night. He got hurt in the storm when they went to find Jake. His shoulder's broke, and he has a bad cut from the log. I've sewed him up. He'll be up and around later today. Course, there seems to be one thing that won't be up and around, today or ever."

"What's that, Doc?" Fred asked.

"My confounded Studebaker! There's some Pierce Arrow that needs to be surgically removed from it. I went out to tie up the dog and my Lord, looks like a freight train wreck in my front yard."

Fred looked sheepishly down at the ground. "I'll go to the bank, get the money, and have new automobile sent over. I never drive till yesterday. Miss Lydia say, 'Studebaker's the only way to stop giant Pierce Arrow'"

"Okay, okay, Fred. I know you'll take care of it." He laughed. "I just hope I don't have to make any calls to the country before you get one over here," he muttered as he went in the house, slamming the door once again behind him.

Quinn was down the steps over by the big maple tree playing with Bear. For the moment, he had forgotten about his mama. Fred and Jake leaned on the porch posts. "Well, Jake, got any ideas?"

Jake looked at him. "Well, one. It had to be somebody who knew I was gone, and two, he had to have known about the ring. Course, the whole damn town knows that." Jake took a deep breath. "What if she never wakes up, Fred? What if she never remembers anything?"

Jake watched the old Indian's eyes fill up with tears as he turned to go. "I don't know, Jake. I'm goin' to prepare the peyote church on the ranch. I must send message to worshippers. I want Charles Whitehorn to be Road Man. When Julia wife gets back, she'll pound peyote buttons. I'll ask his nephew to be drummer. I'll get three Firemen. We'll all go to sweat house. I must talk to Father Peyote and ask him to take message to Wah'-Kon-Tah about Maggie Lookout."

He was still making plans as he started down the steps lost in deep thought. That was all he knew to do. Jake waited a few minutes until he was gone, wondering if his peyote ways would help them. Jake yelled at Quinn, "Come on, Quinn. Let's go thank Ruby and kiss Mama. Then, we'll go get cleaned up."

As they entered her room, Grandfather Sun was casting rays across her bed and the rest of the room. Jake suddenly felt hopeful. Maybe Grandfather Sun would shine his rays of energy into her, and send her a message that would bring her silent spirit back to him. Quinn drew up a chair alongside the bed and climbed up on his knees, planting a big kiss on her good cheek. As his small five year old lips touched his Indian mama's beautiful face, her eyelids fluttered. Jake leaned over her. "Maggie! Maggie! It's Jake! Quinn is here! Come back to us!" The tears from his blood-shot eyes silently dripped on her hand.

From the dark night of her Indian soul, her two black eyes opened for just an instant. But in the warmth of the late June morning, she stared straight ahead with no sign of recognition. There were no soft eyes beckoning from her poetic being. There was no hint of the warm heart of a beautiful woman, no love springing toward her child or to him. Then, without even a silent whisper, she closed her eyes.

How can I let her go? His soul cried out to her. She had traveled back into the darkness where her mind was still locked in the inferno of a madman's crime.

CHAPTER SEVENTEEN

The day had slowly slipped away, and Fred was just finishing his chores at the ranch. He had planned to saddle up Straight Arrow after a bite of supper. His appetite for the cold corn and salt pork had been deteriorating. He had made up his mind earlier to ride over to Maggie girl's and feed the chickens. The dogs had all helped him eat. After all, invited guests were hard to come by.

All afternoon, he had stopped and looked up at Grandfather Sun to try to determine when Julia wife would be returning. He kept listening for the roar of the big Pierce Arrow announcing her return. She had been gone too long.

He wanted her back and by his side, now. It was twilight time, the most lonesome time of the day when no one was around. Heavy of heart, Fred mounted Straight Arrow and he and the dogs meandered slowly down the back way between the green pastures to the little Lookout ranch.

Fred was more than a little distraught. The medicine man couldn't come to the peyote church for another week. He and a large group of the tribe were still having prayer rites over the sick chief. Until then, Fred could only speculate with his humble heart and mind about what Wah'-Kon-Tah had in mind for Maggie girl. His head was low on his chest and the horse sensed, too, that it was a path of sadness. Straight

Arrow's hooves just seemed to ease into a pattern of plodding along through the tall grass and wild flowers. Their blooms, brightened by the previous day's rain, were striving for a taller stance, hoping to be admired by the old Indian man. But his eyes never saw them. They had no appeal for him. The beauty in his life was gone for the moment.

The dogs had even left him. They had picked up some scent and had headed toward the creek. He could just see the very tips of their white tails in the tall weeds as they ran through the forgotten wildflowers. Nevertheless, he sensed that he was getting close to the house, and he lifted up his proud head and peered through the trees in Maggie girl's yard. The twilight was dancing through the trees—perhaps an invitation to the stars to prepare them for their nightly appearance. Grandfather Setting Sun had not allowed him to see the big red automobile in the front yard. It was parked over in the late evening shade, provided willingly by Maggie girl's giant white oak tree.

The oak had long leafed-out arms that seemed to droop and shield the car and the man sitting inside. Fred came around from the back and Straight Arrow shuddered and perked up his ears. Fred didn't seem to notice until he was about twenty feet from the huge touring car, marked with an ornamental arrow pierced on the hood. There it was, parked there like a huge calling card. His adrenaline kicked in as he nudged the horse urgently toward the car. "John! John Lossin! Is that you?" Fred cried.

The man tipped back his hat. "Yeah, Fred. We just got back. Mrs. Lookout wanted me to drop her here first." John looked hot and weary from the feverish trip. "So you got message about Maggie girl?" Fred asked anxiously.

John looked at him strangely. "No, what message?"

Fred, suddenly alarmed, raised his voice. "About Maggie! Maggie Lookout. She was—Where Julia wife? Oh, no. Not the lodge." Fred jumped off his horse and started running toward the gate. A million thoughts plagued his already tired brain. From the vicinity of the blood-soaked lodge came a bone-rattling, blood-curdling scream that sent goose bumps racing up the quiet evening's nerves. It was first a scream, then a series of shrieks, then a woebegone wail. Fred stopped in his tracks. *Oh no! It's too late!* Fred raced around the yard to the battered lodge. Julia was lying in the doorway of the lodge unconscious. There was blood on both of her slender hands. Fred raced to her and sat her up in his arms. *Oh Wah'-Kon-Tah*, Fred cried to himself. *Why did she have to see this? Why didn't she get the telegram?*

John caught up with him yelling, "What is it, Fred?"

Out of breath, Fred gasped. "Maggie attacked and raped here."

"Oh my God!" John uttered as he stared at the lodge's interior. The ungodly odor of blood met his nasal cavities as his eyes fixed on the swarm of blowflies that had filled the lodge. He fell to his knees on the ground, trying to keep the vomit back that was coming up his throat. "Come on, John! Help me get Julia wife back over there out of this mess." Fred cried.

John pulled himself together, as they attempted to move her. But she was coming around too fast. She opened her eyes and looked at Fred. "There, there, Julia wife. I here," the giant Indian tried to whisper.

Then as her glazed-over eyes were brought into focus, she remembered the scene. "Where my Maggie?" Immediately without warning, she began screaming all over again. Fred tried to hold and comfort her, but she was so hysterical that he became fearful that her mind would go over the edge, too. He let her scream as he and John looked at each other, despairingly. Finally, after what seemed an eternity she tried to speak amongst her broken sobs. "Where's my Maggie? Dead?"

Fred tried again to speak, but only in disconnected phrases. "Maggie! Maggie girl raped, hurt. Doc Lewis. Still alive. I send telegram!"

Her black eyes stared at him incredulously. She could not lose another child, as her mind flashed back to the day when her Mi-Tse-Ge had lay dying. She simply couldn't take it. She sat up and shook Fred off. "Let me alone. I go sit by myself." She shakily got to her feet. She yanked herself away from Fred. Her red silk shirt was sopping wet with tears, and her Indian blanket was lying on the ground, thrown down in her panic. She stumbled toward the house.

John and Fred looked at one another and sighed. They were both glad to leave her alone for a moment. They needed to breathe again. She had scared them both to death. Fred looked at the chauffeur. He was near death from the look on his face, still fighting his urge to vomit. Fred put his hand on his shoulder. "You go on home, John Lossin. You take automobile home. I'll bring Julia wife."

"Okay, Fred." John said gratefully as he walked to the big automobile, still parked under the white oak tree.

Fred walked over to the car with him to thank him for bringing Julia wife home. John started the giant motor up, and the big car slowly pulled past Fred. Fred's heart was breaking into tiny pieces, for through the iron gate he could see his Julia wife. She was just sitting on the top step of Maggie girl's white porch. The climbing blue morning glories had trailed from the bed below clear to the top of the eaves almost encircling her like a picture frame. Her jet-black hair with just a hint of gray was just an older version of the beautiful face of Maggie girl.

Fred strained his eyes, but he couldn't tell where the morning glories ended and she began. Their blooms were closed for the day. Julia held two of the blue drooping blooms in her hand. She sensed their delicate sadness, and seemed to be trying to take some comfort from them. The curious peacock was perched on the rail swishing the blue and green eyes of his tail feathers all-knowingly in her direction. Perhaps it was his ploy to try and distract her from her pain.

Fred didn't say anything. He just opened the wooden gate and walked quietly up the sandstone rock walk. No words, especially white man's words, would help that moment. But she felt his presence and he felt hers. For now, that was enough for the two silent Indians.

Fred sat down close beside her. She leaned her head back on his arm. Apparently, her body had run out of steam. Her elegant, finely-etched face allowed only one more tear to fall. Fred took her hand and held it quietly for some time. "Julia wife," he finally whispered. "Glad you're home." She nodded ever so gently. As night fell down around them, they sat quietly. In the darkness Fred's silent heart thanked Wah'-Kon-Tah as the frogs on the creek announced to the Osage the news that Julia wife was home.

After an half hour or so, Fred gently touched her. "Julia wife, let's go to ranch."

"When can I see her, Fred?" Julia whispered.

"Tomorrow. She's at Doc Lewis'. But Julia wife, she sleeps. She won't wake up." Nothing Fred said seemed to penetrate her beautiful stately head.

"I will see for myself tomorrow." She rose to go, and Fred took her hand as they walked through the gate. He would let the horse or the new quarter Lady Moon lead them home. The forgotten flowers in the pasture would have one more chance to beckon them.

CHAPTER EIGHTEEN

Doc Lewis was checking Maggie over. She had been getting restless the better part of the afternoon, and he knew only too well the tell-tale signs of a fever coming on. He'd asked Jake to leave the room. He had been bathing her religiously with cold cloths, but Doc wanted to check to see if she had started bleeding.

As he moved the white sheet like cover aside, he could see fresh blood on the sheet. His fears had been confirmed. He had been mixing a poultice of herbs for her earlier, but he and Jake would need to bathe her in cool water all night to try to get the fever down.

Quinn had been asleep for a couple of hours. Earlier, Ruby had given him a bath and an oatmeal cookie. Jake was thankful for her help as he stood on Doc's porch and smoked. His mind was racing about things he should be doing, but he couldn't leave Maggie till Julia arrived. It was close to ten o' clock, and life in the agency town had slowed down to just an occasional buggy or car. There had been a few Indian children playing some game earlier up a couple of blocks, but even they had disappeared.

The crickets were loud after the thunder had gone away. Around the corner coming from Kihekah Street, Jake could see truck lights, as they turned west toward him. He watched a truck putt-putting along, even though his mind was far, far away. The truck, however, slowed down and parked in front of Doc's. He couldn't tell for sure, but it sort of looked like Red. The driver got out and Jake yelled out in recognition. "Red, it's Jake. Over here on the porch."

Jake met him at the truck. "Jake, how's Maggie? I came to town when Shorty came on. Hadn't heard nothin'."

Jake grasped his hand and filled him in or her condition and the sheriff's latest progress. "So you don't know nothin' either, huh? Well, dad blast it. I thought maybe Sheriff Cook would have him by now." They stood at the bed of his truck arms folded, looking at the array of oil field junk laying inside.

"Well, tell me, Red, how's the well?"

Red had stopped talking long enough to deeply inhale his cigar. "Oh, it's going pretty good. We're down about four hundred feet. We put it on the beam at three hundred and ten feet—still not many rocks and the water's not slowing us up much. Sand line's holding up. Shorty's trying to take care of it, all right. Say, ol' Evans' partner showed up today. Lefty—he's kinda of an odd duck, but he seems to get along with us all okay. Brags on my cookin' anyways." he laughed. "He must have gotten a little money in St. Louie cause Evans sure seems to be in a better mood."

Jake listened to him, smoking his third cigar for the day. "There's not much I can do out there, Red, until Julia gets back. She'll take good care of her, so I'll probably come out in a day or two to see what's going on."

"Oh, that's fine, Jake. Don't worry none about us. You just get Maggie on her feet. You know, Jake, I'm real sorry I got mad about no new tools, seeing how she spent the payment money and all. I feel real bad about that."

Jake shrugged it off. "That's okay, Red. Doesn't much matter anyway, now. The son of a bitch took the ring, too."

Red had turned around to go, but stopped dead in his tracks, "You're kiddin', man? Was that why he done it?"

Jake shook his head. "Oh hell! I don't know, but Sheriff Cook had better be finding out soon—real soon."

Red walked around to the door of the truck to get in. "Jake I gotta go. You keep in touch, hear, now? I heard over at O'Grady's that Sam's okay and that he left Doc's here earlier today. Reckon he's over at Nellie's by now, tossin' a few."

Jake laughed. "Probably. I haven't seen Miss Lydia but a minute when she stopped on her lunch time. I guess she survived the ordeal, alright."

Red nodded. "Yeah, look's like it. Wonder what Big Ed thought when he saw that blond head of hair full of sticks, grass, and a fish or two?"

Jake laughed again. "Well, if we ever get out of this mess, Miss Lydia's ordeal ought to grow into a pretty good story, especially the part about Fred at the wheel of the Pierce Arrow. Can you believe they smacked right in to Doc's car here to shut 'er down?"

Red was beginning to cough he was laughing so hard. "Hard t' believe." He opened the truck door and got in to leave. "Say, anybody heard about Bill WhiteOaks and the Hales'? What's ol' man Hale up to?"

"Jake shook his head. "Hell if I know. It's been real quiet uptown, but that's not necessarily a good sign, you know."

Red nodded. "Well, I got to be headin' back west toward Nellie's, or at least a big hardy slab of her chocolate cake. And I gotta check on our bet on old Lassiter's dry hole." He laughed and blew his nose in his faded bandana. "Sure hope ever' thing goes okay with Maggie." Smiling from ear to ear, he started the motor and slammed it into reverse. He waved to Jake as he headed on west out of town.

Jake watched him go. *Gosh, it was good to laugh and let off a little steam.* He was lost in thought about the details of the well as he wandered over to the Studebaker-Pierce Arrow entanglement. He was giving some thought to whether either could ever be fixed when Ruby yelled from Doc's doorway. "Jake! Come quick! It's Miss Maggie!"

Startled, Jake yelled. "What's wrong?" He bounded up the walk. He could see real fear in Ruby's black eyes, open as wide as she could get them.

She held the door as he passed her. "Doc says she's got the fever, and blood, lots of blood!"

"Oh God!" Jake uttered in mid-flight down the hall. He opened the door to see Doc busily bathing Maggie's face.

"Here, Jake!" Doc muttered without looking up. "You do this while Ruby puts cloths on the rest of her body. I've got to get some more medicine. This is what I been afraid of—" He trailed off. "Where's Julia? She back yet?"

Jake shook his head. "Not yet. Supposed to be in tonight sometime, Fred thought."

"What's all the commotion?" Father Jack said as he ran into Doc Lewis, hurrying around the corner.

"Maggie's taken a turn for the worse! Can you ride out to tell Fred and see if Julia's home? I need her and her herbal expertise."

"Sure." Father Jack nodded as he headed for the door. "I'll leave right now. I got my buggy outside."

"Great!" Doc mumbled as he continued on down the hall to his apothecary room.

Father Jack lost no time heading back the way he'd come. He grabbed up a handful of his black robes and stepped into the buggy. He tapped the horse with his quirt and hung on to the leather reins with a tight grip. *Oh, Lord! Don't let this happen! It'll drive Fred and those Indians back into peyote, again. And just when I was gettin' somewhere with them.* As the horse-drawn buggy jogged along, he was lost in thought. He understood their messenger concept of Grandfather Sun and Father Peyote. He could even see sweating and fasting to purge away the evil, but he had a hard time swallowing all those hallucinations brought on by smoking peyote buttons.

Father Jack made it out of town in short order. *Gosh, it's dark tonight!* He thought as he and the horse raced along the dirt road. That was his favorite part of the trip along the creek. In fact, many church picnics had been enjoyed right here along the water.

He was lost again in those thoughts when the horse tried to shy. His ears were laid back. "What is it, boy?" The horse was scared. He was snorting and shaking, and he refused to go one more step forward. "Okay! Let me get the light. Settle down, boy." He carefully climbed out of the buggy and lighted the lantern while he tried to calm his nerves. The spirit of fear was so thick he could cut it with a knife. He tried to take a deep breath. He just needed to trust in the Lord as he inched his way forward with the light in one hand and the horse reins in the other. It would have been a struggle to decide which was the most frightened—the snorting horse, or the shaking priest. The horse was frightened and Father Jack was scared to death. *Holy Shit!* The horse was trying to bolt. He could hear his own heart beating. He tried to remember his faith in scripture. *Lo, even though, I walk through the valley of darkness I will fear no evil. I—I—will not be afra—.* He started screaming, and the horse started jerking back trying to rear.

Straight in front of them there was a huge sandstone rock pile, mounded up like a bee hive, with what appeared to be an Indian's head resting on the top of the pile. He and the horse were absolutely terrified. With a death grip on the reins, he tried to tell himself that this used to be the burial custom among the Osages as he inched his way forward. As he came closer and closer, he could see that it was indeed an Indian buried in the pile with rocks up around his head. In the scant dim light, it was a horrifying sight. Then he saw the head move. "Oh, my God! Save me! Save me! He's alive!" He screamed as the head began to move, first nodding forward and then, backwards.

Father Jack, hiding behind the horse as if to use him as a shield, watched for a moment. *What the hell am I goin' do? I've got to do somethin' if he's still alive.* He stole closer until he was about three feet away. The head was grotesque. The stink was awful. The Indian's brown eyes were bulging. His tongue was hanging down the side of his mouth, and the dried path of blood had made many tracks down his face. Suddenly, it moved again. "Jesus, Mary and Joseph!" Father Jack's scream echoed through the night, as the head continued to move with its blank eyes staring at him. That was horror no holy man should ever experience.

He continued to watch as he caught sight of an animal's thin tail wrapping around the dead man's face. The priest couldn't believe his eyes. It was a opossum, chewing on the back of the dead man's neck, causing his head to bob. Father, covered with sweat, let out an yell, jumped in his buggy, and drove as fast as he and the scared horse could go.

Without looking back, he arrived at the ranch in about fifteen minutes. His black robes were covered with dust from his fast-paced, terrifying trip down the dirt roads. He was still out of breath, and sweat beads were dripping off his forehead. He could taste the mouthful of grime he'd collected, and he kept trying to conjure up spit from somewhere to get rid of it. He wondered why the rain hadn't settled the dust. He had trouble recognizing the turn off to the house. He was still preoccupied with the sight of the dead man's head. He even had to ask his guardian angel to lead him, and surprisingly enough, he found himself at the front gate. From out of no-where, all seven dogs began barking. He stood up trying to look for them in the dark. Something caused him to loose his balance. His feet became tangled up in his robes and in his long dangling corded rosary beads. He gasped, causing the horse and buggy to shift. He teetered back and forth, falling head first out of the buggy.

Instantly, four of the dogs were there licking his face. "That's what I get for tryin' to hurry!" he cried with all the exasperation he could muster. He jumped up, slapping his robes, and causing a sizable dust cloud to follow behind him as he ran up to the front door. "Fred! Julia!"

The Indian couple inside had heard the dogs and was on their way out to the porch. Fred could see Father Jack in the dim light of the yard.

"What is it, Black Robes?"

"Where's Julia? Is she back yet?"

"I'm here." Julia said as she stepped out into view.

Father started waving his hands. "Doc wants you to come, now. Maggie's bleeding and got a high fever."

She didn't wait till Father Jack had finished. She ran to the kitchen. She retrieved her medicine book from the shelf and flew down the porch steps. Fred and Father Jack were already at the buggy, and both men helped her in.

"I'll bring the horse." Fred ordered. "You go on!"

Black robes waved that he understood and the buggy lurched forward as they headed back toward town. He wondered silently what she would think if she saw the Indian's head, moving. Father Jack was leaning over the reins, doing his best to hurry the horse, but the proud elegant woman sat straight and still as a statue, never looking to the right or the left. Her blanket was pulled tightly around her, while she hugged to her breast the medicine book—a collection of secrets of a proud race—a race that relied on the wisdom of Grandfather Sun to heal his Osage people.

CHAPTER NINETEEN

The midnight hour was sneaking up on that whirlwind day when Father Jack and Julia arrived back in the agency town. The horse was lathered, but Father Jack pressed on the few blocks to Doc's. He jumped down, careful of his cassock this time. He tied the horse to the door handle of the Pierce Arrow, still embracing the Studebaker in Doc's front yard. Going around to Julia's side, he helped lift her straight Indian frame to the ground. With absolutely no emotion on her classic face, she adjusted her blanket and allowed him to lead her to the front door. They walked on in unannounced, and continued down the hall toward the lamp-lighted room.

Father Jack knocked on the bedroom door, and it was opened almost instantly. Ruby ushered them in, lowering her eyes and shaking her head in dismay. Jake was busy at the bedside, but he looked up to see Julia. His face softened as he went to greet her. "I'm so glad you're here, Julia."

She abruptly nodded and took the cloths out of his hand. "Go smoke!" She began methodically bathing Maggie's face and feeling her forehead. No one but Jake saw the faint movement in her eyes as she washed her child's bruised and swollen face. There was no sense of awareness of her mother's presence as Maggie moaned and thrashed from the fever.

Father Jack and Jake obediently stepped out for a minute. Jake wiped the sweat off his face and searched for a cigar. "Oh my God, Father Jack. She is so sick. Doc's worried. What am I going to do if I lose her?"

Father Jack looked at him sternly. "Come on, Jake. Cut that talk out. I've got all the nuns up at the school praying for her, and I prayed for her at Mass—her and Bill WhiteOaks' mother. Boy, that's a bad deal, too. She is so sure that Bill is goin' be killed by the Hale clan. Oh well, never mind. That's beside the point. Anyway, I'm going' on back to the rectory. Now listen, you've got to trust in the Lord, Jake. Hey, that's the least we Irish can do, right? It'll be all right" He pointed up toward heaven and smiled. "It's just a little test, you know."

Jake looked at him, and had to smile. The priest had been a good friend to him and to the Osages. Of course, bad times were his specialty, Jake reckoned. "Thanks, Father Jack. If we ever get through this, we'll celebrate with the biggest jug of the best Irish whiskey I can find, even if I have to go clear to Tulsey Town to get it."

"Where was that whiskey when I needed it earlier tonight? Damnation! I got myself scared to death on the way to get Julia. I ran up on another god-forsaken dead Indian under a pile of rocks up to here—" He pointed to his throat. "With some damn opossum eatin' on him. God, it was horrible."

Jake couldn't help laughing as Father Jack shuddered again. "Who was it?"

"Hell if I know. I didn't stick around long enough to find out." Father Jack swore.

They both laughed as a man coming up on horseback caught their attention. "That'll be Fred. I knew he'd be close behind us."

Fred rode up and dismounted. Fear was, once more etched on his face. "How Maggie girl?"

Jake dropped his head. "She's really sick, Fred. Now she's burnin' up with fever. She's bleedin' bad again, too. Did you get a message to the tribe for the peyote service?"

Fred nodded, obviously disgruntled. "Yes, but the dancers and medicine man are with the chief. He's nearly dead now."

"I saw George Wright in front of his office and told him to alert the Osages about what's happened." Father Jack spoke softly in his professional preacher voice. "Oh yeah, Jake. Maggie's good friend, Rosa Whitehorn, was at Mass today. She is really worried, but she's afraid to come by so soon."

"If you see her again," Jake said, "Tell her I want to talk to her."

Fred stuck out his hand to Father Jack. "Black Robes, thanks for coming to get us."

"Glad to." Father Jack smiled. His nightmare was all but forgotten now.

"I'll go in, Jake," Fred said as he walked toward the door.

"Julia's in there with Doc, Fred. She ran me out."

The front door had already closed on his words.

Father Jack stepped in his buggy and they said their good-byes. "Gotta find the sheriff and report the rock pile murder. Jake, you take care and keep the faith, hear?"

Jake waved as Father Jack headed out Kihekah Street on his way to the rectory. Jake sat down a minute on the dark porch chair. It was after midnight and he was suddenly exhausted. He had no idea what to do next to help Maggie.

Death was closer than ever, and he knew it. *Oh please, Lord, don't let her die!* Jake stubbed out his cigar and headed back inside. He peeked in the doorway of the bedroom. Julia was still sitting by the bed, painstakingly changing the cloths, one after another, to cool Maggie down. She said nothing. There was no expression on the Indian woman's face, but she knew he was there. Finally, after some time, she said, "I've got the medicine book, Jake. I'll find help for Maggie. Fred says we'll have peyote ceremony Friday, end of the week."

"Yeah," Jake nodded. "That's what he told me." Jake walked out of the room and found Fred and Doc in the kitchen.

Doc looked up. "Jake, I don't mind tellin' ya, she's pretty bad off. But Julia's got her medicine book from Fred's Grandmother, and she and I'll put our heads together and come up with some different treatment. We'd better find Dove Whitemoon, the old Osage woman, who knows where the best herbs grow. She has a surplus of medicine already dried." Jake nodded silently. There was nothing else to say.

It had been a long day. Jake had had many visitors come by, including Leahy, Miss Lydia and her friend, Laura Van Estes from up at the newspaper. Laura had wanted a detailed account of what had happened for the paper. Mother Drexell from up at the St. Louis School, Joe from the livery stable, and even Tom Fisher had dropped by. Tom had never said how he'd heard about Maggie. He had been busy giving Jake the details of the big bank robbery. He was on his way to meet "Miss Molly Somebody" at the cafe uptown.

Even Chief Bacon Rind had been going down the street in his big Pierce. He had ordered the car to stop and demanded his driver to honk till someone had come out to inquire about Maggie. In fact, six or seven car loads of Osages had come by during the day. None of them had gotten out of their cars, but each had been curious about what had happened to Maggie.

Jake rubbed his eyes and sat back a moment to rest. Doc had left them both to go check on Maggie. Fred sat down, too. He was so weary his eyes were nearly shut. They were just slits peering out at nightmares that refused to go away. Just before Jake dropped off, he mumbled. "Sheriff Cook had better have some information for me tomorrow."

"I have to gather up the peyote worshippers—" Fred sighed as they both surrendered, themselves to the day.

Two hours later in Doc's small, overcrowded apothecary room, piled high with a wide assortment of ancient jars of mysterious substances, Doc was searching through his medical reference books. Julia sat down at the crowded desk and opened her big medicine book. Together, they poured over the herbs, roots and flowers that would stop Maggie's bleeding and bring down the infection's hold on her. Julia realized that the Osage medicine men had little knowledge of cures, and that they were really only for show. It was the old women of the tribe that knew about the medicine from the powders, ground from plants. Fred's Grandmother had given her the verbal recipes, just before she died. Julia then had them transferred into a big book by Sister Katherine Drexell up at the school.

Doc spoke interrupting her thoughts, "What do you suggest for the hemorrhaging, Julia?"

She leafed through the book. "We can do no better than crushed sumac leaves mixed with dried bayberry leaves. We'll add a pinch of dove's foot plant, lady's mantle, and blessed thistle to make a poultice. I think tea from white willow bark and feverfew should bring down her fever, if we can get her to swallow it. I send Fred to Dove Whitemoon's. She'll have dried powders of these plants. She'll bring them to help, Maggie girl. I have her go get morning glory oil from blooms on Maggie girl's front porch. It will kill the pain when she wakes up. I also want Fred to ask Dove to start the chant at dawn each day to Morning Star. I'll start bathing her bruises with bayberry, too." She was talking mostly to herself. At last, finished with formulating her plan, she bowed her head and prayed. Grandfather Sun, that gives light to all plants and animals under Sun, tell me which plants will cure my Maggie girl.

CHAPTER TWENTY

A week had passed. Grandfather Sun had made seven full trips around the earth. He checked every day on his Indian princess. Julia had never left Maggie's side. Day after day, she had administered the poultices from the powders and leaves that Dove Whitemoon had sent. She had methodically spooned the white bark tea into Maggie's mouth many times a day, but still there was no response from her. The bleeding was better, but the infection was still raging.

Miss Lydia and her friend, Miss Laura, had taken Quinn home with them for a few days. Fred was preoccupied with the preparation of the peyote service out at his ranch and Jake had gone to check on the well a time or two. He had missed the sheriff on the couple of occasions he'd come by Doc's. But the word was that it was a fairly small but unidentified bullet that had killed the dog. There seemed to be no sign as yet of who was responsible. They still needed Maggie's description.

At the well site, Red had been excited. "We won! We won the bet, Jake! We got the thousand dollars. How bout that dry hole?" He shook Jake's hand with great vigor.

Jake laughed. "See there. I told you we'd get the new tools."

Still laughing, Red pulled him over to where Evans and some guy were talking. "Jake, I want you—."

"Jake, glad you're back," Evans interrupted. "Here's a guy I been wantin' you to meet. Come all the way in from St. Louie—the smart half of my operation. Lefty Kirk."

Jake had shaken his hand, while giving him the once over. He had seemed nice enough. He was about six feet tall and muscle-bound. Jake had come to the conclusion that he looked more like a redneck than a smooth talker from the city. He had only one interesting characteristic out of a rather ordinary face—light blue eyes. "Fish eyes." He later described to Red. He had on khaki work clothes and black oiled boots. After close scrutiny, Jake had smiled at him. "Glad to finally meet you. The well's making good footage, they tell me. Even the water's not a problem."

"Yeah," he said in a rather disinterested tone. "Seems so! Look's like we'll get a good one."

Jake hadn't spent much time out there bullshitting. He had just checked the log and returned to town.

The Lookout ranch set snuggly in the trees with the Osage hills circling it on three sides. The end of the week finally arrived. It was Friday, and Fred's peyote service was scheduled for dawn. There was no wind— only a promise of another hot day. Fred had greeted the other peyote worshippers and instructions had been given to the participants. George Wright's wife, Anna, from up at the agency, was attending Maggie at the Doc's house. Julia had left about noon the previous day to go make final preparations for the food for the service.

Jake had run into Tom Fisher the night before at the restaurant in the Duncan Hotel. He had filled him in on the latest on the robbery. He had told him that the getaway car had been discovered on the road to the Lookout ranch about three quarters of a mile from the house. "Guess they had horses tied up there waitin' on them."

Jake nodded. "Yeah, they're probably back deep in the hills by now or over the Kansas line—countin' the money. Did us a real favor shootin' ol Clyde Baker."

Their talk had shifted shortly to Maggie and the upcoming peyote service. Tom had asked if he could come along with Jake. Jake had agreed, glad for the company. He really liked Tom. He had made up his mind earlier that he was a smart young man. Jake had met him at the edge of town before even a hint of daylight.

They were now in sight of the ranch close to sunup. That was the designated time for the activities to begin. He could not be late. There was a haze hanging low in the valley, probably from the intense heat of the past week.

As they rode up to the house, the front yard, which encompassed about an acre, was filled with Osage worshippers. They had set up a couple of lodges, and there were empty meat racks standing by the fire pits, waiting for tomorrow's talk with Wah'-Kon-Tah. There were about fifty Indians around, many of them sitting on blankets under trees in close proximity of the peyote church.

They dismounted, and Tom was not missing anything. "Lotta people here. I had no idea. Where's the church?"

Jake pointed to a building around the house. "Over there."

"How big is it?" Tom asked as they headed in that direction.

"Oh let's see. It's about thirty feet in diameter and octagonal by design. It's a permanent building. They're always painted red with a white cross on the top."

Tom nodded. "You can't even see the cross for the haze hanging in the air. Boy, it gives you a real eerie feeling, doesn't it?"

Jake nodded. "Yeah, today more than others."

"How'd this religion ever get started, anyway?" Tom was busy making mental notes of his history lesson.

Jake lighted his half-smoked cigar. "Well, this is all part of Moonhead Wilson's peyote religion. They built sweat lodges due east of the churches. See it over there?" He pointed to an area beyond the house. He nodded as he went on. "He convinced them that sweating would rid them of the evil. He told them while they're in the sweat house, they have to drink buckeye tea. The tea will cause them to vomit, further purging them of the evil."

Tom shook his head in disbelief. "This is quite a ritual."

Jake puffed heartily on his cigar. "Yes, it is. All started yesterday afternoon. They got the pit dug and then erected the sweat lodge over it.

They use limestone rocks to hold in the heat. The logs were set up ready for it all to begin today at sun-up."

As his explanation wound down, Father Jack joined them, and they both greeted him. "I guess you're here, Black Robes, to protect your interest."

Father Jack laughed. "You're right, Jake for all the good it'll do."

To Jake's left, his eye caught Fred, motioning him to come to his lodge. "I gotta go. Take care of my friend here and tell him what's going on. Lord, I dread this. Wouldn't be so bad if you could keep your clothes on—" Jake mumbled, as he stubbed his cigar out again on the brick pedestal by the porch.

"You have to do what?" Tom said in utter astonishment.

Father Jack grabbed Tom's arm and steered him off in another direction.

Jake left them, and joined Fred in his lodge. "Hurry, Jake! Take off clothes! Here, loin cloth."

Jake scowled as he took the scant article reluctantly from Fred. "Is this part really necessary?" Fred ignored him as Jake unbuttoned his shirt.

By the time Jake finished getting ready, the Road Man who was in charge was just lighting the fire. About fifteen worshippers joined him, all naked except for the breechclouts. They entered the sweat lodge and all sat in a circle. The heated rocks were brought in and placed in the pit in the center of the circle. There were three buckets of water already inside the lodge with them, and as they sat there, the water was poured on the rocks. Steam quickly enveloped their senses and the entire lodge area. Out of the corner of Jake's eye, he could see Tom and Father Jack sitting on the side. He couldn't even begin to imagine what they were thinking. However, his time to think was cut short as his attention shifted to the business of the moment.

Fred had asked Paul Red Eagle to act as Road Man. He was a member of the Thorny Bush people and the Beaver Band. The Road Man took a cornhusk and rolled it with tobacco and lighted it. He began praying to Wah'-Kon-Tah. It was a prayer that the worshippers could all see rise with the smoke and steam. He then threw cedar on the coals for incense. Jake could already see the buckeye root being placed in a container, and hot water being poured over it to make the tea.

The Road Man passed it around and each of them took a drink. Jake knew it would be only a few minutes, until one by one, they would lift the side of the canvas lodge to go vomit. Jake was feeling bad already. The Indians each carried a crow feather to induce vomiting, but Jake needed no such thing, as he hurriedly lifted the side of the lodge. He wretched out what seemed to be everything he had eaten for the last month. He managed to crawl back in, but the traffic was heavy, as the Indians spilled in and out of the lodge to vomit in the grass.

The Road Man insisted each Indian must vomit four different times. The nausea, coupled with the dry heaves, racked Jake's sweat soaked body, and he held his stomach in pain. The heat had reached an intense unbearable state. He felt like he was fainting, but the violent sick feeling he was experiencing wouldn't allow it. His eyes, dripping with water, for some reason, kept fixing on a red, meaty-looking scar on the thigh of Ed Big Eagle next to him. He couldn't seem to pull his eyes from it, and he just got sicker and sicker. The scar just kept getting bigger and bigger and more and more grotesque. He couldn't die and let the Indians see his weakness, so he fought to stay conscious. He managed to glance at his father-in-law across the circle. Fred looked pale and his eyes were completely blood-shot, but Jake knew that Fred believed with his whole heart. It would remove the evil causing Maggie's fever. Jake guessed he needed to believe it, too.

After hours and hours and passed, it was time to leave the lodge and to bathe. Jake headed, as best he could, for the shower in Fred's house, but the Indians all headed for the creek. The rest of the day's activities went on, but for Jake, the day was over. He found a blanket under a tree and slept. Just before he dozed off, Tom Fisher jiggled him. "Man, you look awful." Jake grimaced.

"Jake, I'm leaving, but I'll be back, tomorrow. " Father Jack said. "Wow, this is a great experience. Tom and I really learned a—."

Jake nodded with his eyes rolling into the back of his head. Instantly, the tired Irishman was sound asleep, in spite of his sick stomach. At least the ordeal was over and Grandfather Sun could set for the day. Even Grandfather Sun felt it best to leave the miserable man alone.

Many hours later, Jake opened his eyes, slowly testing the day. From the looks of things, Grandfather Sun had been up for awhile. It had to be mid-morning on Saturday. Jake vaguely remembered having turned over in the night, and having found his way to a sofa in Fred's house. Forcing himself against his better judgment, he walked to the front porch, lit his two-day old cigar, and put it to his cracked lips. *Oh God!* It tasted bad. He stubbed it out and put it back in his shirt pocket.

There were twice as many Indians there as the day before, all milling around. Some were cooking and some were cleaning the peyote church. Julia and two of Hard Rope's nieces were pounding the peyote buttons, which had been previously dried. After they were finished pounding, they would pour water over the mixture and mix it like a bread dough.

As the day wore on, more and more people showed up. There were a few whites like Father Jack and Tom, but nearly a hundred Indians had gathered. Jake noticed that there were members of the Up-Land Forest's Big Chief band that lived in Bigheart\Barnsdall, several families from the Big Hill Band from over by Fairfax, and even a few of the Black Dog band from near Hominy. The majority of the crowd seemed to be a mixture of the Tall Chief band from Grey Horse, and the Thorny Bush people of the Beaver Band in Pawhuska.

It took the better part of the day for Jake to feel back to normal, but Father Jack and Tom were in good spirits. Tom grinned. "How do you feel, Jake?"

Father Jack laughed. "He needs a shot of whiskey."

Jake groaned and rubbed his sensitive stomach. "Boy, you're right about that. I do. God, that was an awful ordeal."

Tom rubbed his stomach in sympathy. "I can't believe a man would subject himself to such an ordeal, at least willfully."

"What's going on in the Frank Phillips Company, Tom?" Jake said trying to change the subject.

"Oh, lots of things, Jake. They've drilled in twelve different leases and brought in fifteen new wells, averaging about a hundred and ten barrels a day. Ol' Frank's really getting anxious for the next lease sell up at the agency. Of course, rumor has it that some other big shot over by Ponca City's really hitting it big. You know a place called Burbank?"

Jake nodded. "Yeah, it's not too far from where I'm drilling."

Excited, Tom continued. "He's really hitting some good deep wells. My guess is he's fixing to open up a brand new pool. There's big wells coming in at Lymon, Whizbang, and Webb City, too. That ol' boy knows how to wildcat, now. Frank doesn't share my opinion, but if this guy does open a new pool, he'll be a serious contender to ol' Frank at the sale."

Jake nodded, "Yeah, sounds like it. What's the big shot's name?"

Tom rubbed his chin and thought a minute. "Marland, I believe it is."

"What's his story, anyway?" Father Jack asked.

Tom had their attention as he launched into his story. "Well, he's a lawyer and self-taught geologist from back east. He wasn't a barber like ol' Uncle Frank." Tom laughed. "Hit it big though, on the Pettit number two. It's producing seven thousand barrels a day. Say, you want a hot tip? Frank just told me that last week he and L. E., his brother, negotiated a New York stock sale that raised nine million dollars just to invest here in the Osage. Can you believe that?"

The men all looked at each other in shock and shook their heads in disbelief.

"Skelly and Harry Sinclair's companies are both making tons and tons of money, too. This is the most exciting place to live in the world. Boy, am I ever glad I let Frank talk me into leaving Philadelphia. Shoot!" He waved his hands around. "I've even got plenty of money. Hell! Got myself a car. Frank gave it to me—one of his old Fords. Now, all I need is a woman."

Tom enthusiasm was contagious and Father Jack jumped in. "Yeah! I tried to fix him up with that cute little gal, Molly, up at the cafe, but they didn't take a shine to each other."

Tom blushed. "Well, she was okay, but she made it clear that she really liked the redneck cowboys from these ranches around here. And furthermore she said that she was going to let one of them find her. Fine with me!" Tom said with a twinkle in his eye. "So I'm still looking. In fact that reminds me, who is that good lookin' gal over by the meat rack next to Julia Lookout?" Father and Jake both turned around in that direction.

"Oh, that's Katherine Little Bear". Father Jack said smugly.

Tom's voice perked up. The oil wells of a moment ago were now forgotten. "Oh my gosh! She's beautiful!"

Father Jack smirked. "Want me to introduce you?"

"Sure, why not," Tom said.

Father winked at Jake. "There's only one hitch. You'd better hightail it to my church every Sunday, and bring her with you, savvy?"

Jake hit Father's sleeve. " Why, Father Jack, you're nothing but a black robed, bible totin', blackmailer!" Everybody laughed.

"Tell me about her," Tom said, obviously interested in every detail.

Father scratched his chin. "Well, she's about twenty, I guess. An upstanding Catholic, of course."

"Of course!" Tom and Jake chimed in together.

"Her dad was Thomas Little Bear, one of Chief Bigheart's relatives. She's real well-educated—real good stock. You know, old Chief Bigheart's been dead since 1908. But he could speak seven languages. He was one smart Indian. He served as interpreter for the tribe in Washington on the allotment deal. They just changed the name of his town from Bigheart to Barnsdall a couple of years ago, back in '21."

Father stopped to take a breath. "Oh well, anyway, pardon my transgressions. I got off-track. You know, she'd be quite a catch for you, Fisher."

Jake grinned, slapping Tom on the back. "You wouldn't need to work quite so hard. She's got about six headrights from her mother's side—the Tall Corns, and four, I think, from her father. They both died a couple of years ago."

Father Jack was in the process of hiking up his long black cassock, digging around in some pocket or the other, looking for his tobacco plug and knife as he winked at Jake. "But now, Tom, she's real particular. She don't like just everyone. You gotta play it smart with her, Tom."

"Yeah, I know. That's just the kind of girl I want," Tom said. "I'm already in love with her."

Father Jack laughed. "In that case, I've got a free day up at the church a week from Tuesday. You can get married then if you're a fast worker."

The men were still laughing a few minutes later when someone nudged Father Jack on the back. It was Miss Lydia. "Say, Miss Lydia," Father Jack turned around. "I hear you're giving drivin' lessons, now."

Miss Lydia's face flushed. "Father, you're awful!" She started hitting him on the arm.

Jake joined in, kiddingly. "How long did it take to get that mess of sticks out of your hair? And what did Big Ed have to say about you gallivantin' around the country all night?"

She put on her pouting act. "You gentlemen are not very nice. At least I found you, Jake Knupp." From under her thick eyelashes she caught a glimpse of the new face in the group. "And who is this fine looking gentleman?"

Tom puffed up and stuck out his hand. "I'm Tom Fisher, ma'am. How do you do?"

Lydia was turning on the charm, looking up at him from her suddenly turned, soft green eyes. "Well, how do you do?"

Father jumped in putting his hand on her arm. "Hey, Miss Lydia leave him alone. He's going to marry Katherine Little Bear a week from Tuesday at my Catholic Church."

They all laughed heartily. Soon the topic shifted to a more serious note as they discussed Maggie's condition. Jake asked Lydia, if she'd seen a gun or anyone suspicious.

"No, but I'm keeping my eyes open. That reminds me, I need to go check on your son, Jake." With that, she patted Tom on the arm and shot Father Jack an ornery look as she took off to hunt for Quinn. She left in the direction of the food, but Jake noticed that Quinn and Bear were running in the opposite direction with a whole gang of other Indian kids. They were trying to dodge people, meat racks, and boiling water pots. Jake turned his back. He couldn't bear to watch. Fred was everywhere talking to Indians in small groups. Jake figured they were talking about the dying chief, and about him taking over as the new tribal leader.

Jake wandered over to where Julia was turning meat over on the tall racks. She was hot and looked tired. She had been looking hollow-eyed lately from no sleep, and she was too thin. "How's it going, Julia?"

She wiped her brow with the tail of her apron. "Okay, I guess. I hope this is all over early Sunday. I need to get back to Maggie girl. Medicine seem to be working. Now, if Fred can just smoke and talk to Wah'-Kon-Tah."

Jake nodded sympathetically. "Yeah, I know, Julia. You look awful tired. Go sit down for awhile. I'll get Red Eagle's wife to finish here." She kissed Jake on the cheek and gratefully left to cool off.

The hot summer day wore on, and Saturday night finally arrived with no fanfare. Tom, Father, and Jake were sitting on Fred's porch, and Jake was explaining to Tom about the peyote service. "It's about ready to begin. The Road Man—Paul Red Eagle—will paint his face with peyote paint in jagged vertical marks like lightning—red on one cheek and blue on the other. He'll paint a big wide red line down his hair part to represent the road of Grandfather Sun. He'll let his hair hang long. In fact, Tom, It was only after peyote that the Osages had quit wearing roaches."

About that time Fred and Tom Red Corn came to get them. Jake invited Tom and Father Jack into the peyote church with him. Father declined on principle, but Tom agreed.

The whole church was full—about seventy-five Indians—Jake figured—and the rest of the crowd sat close by outside on multicolored Indian blankets. They entered the church. "Notice the cross. It is a symbol of Christianity and Road Man appoints two men to sit at each arm of the cross," Jake said to Tom. "They each represent a road to travel. To the right of the Road Man will sit the Drummer, and there will be three Firemen for tonight."

Tom was paying strict attention, and was wide-eyed as they found their seats. After everyone was settled, the Road Man began the meeting by telling the Fireman to get the water. He rolled a cigarette with the cornhusk and lighted it. He began to pray for Maggie Lookout to be healed of her sickness. He finished the prayer. "Please take this message to Wah'-Kon-Tah."

The Drummer then ceremoniously passed around the small round peyote balls. Each man took a piece and ate it. The Fireman left to get more wood and the ashes would be divided, symbolizing the opening up of Mother Earth. Each worshipper took some of the ashes and rubbed them on themselves as the sound of the drum penetrated the night's quiet.

Everyone sang in Osage together. Later, Road Man would sing the four songs that Moonhead had received from Father Peyote in his hallucinating dreams. But that wouldn't happen till in the wee hours of the morning.

At midnight, the door opened to Spiritland. No one sang then, and the drum was put away. Fred walked up before the Road Man and was given a corn husked cigarette to smoke. Fred lighted it and then he placed the cigarette in the Road Man's mouth. Road Man started praying for him. Fred began confessing all his bad deeds as the tears poured from his eyes. Grandfather Sun had to be convinced that his confession was sincere. The confession must come from the heart, and the tears helped to wash the evil away. It was a very somber moment in the peyote church as the old Indian humbled himself.

Now, after vomiting, sweating, and confessing he had been cleansed of all the evil. While he stood at the fireplace, the other Indians fanned him to keep the evil away. Then, as if on cue, the drum started up again. The Road Man sang, and they all started eating the peyote balls. As the ceremony proceeded, some people were experiencing nausea. Some were seeing red and yellow pictures in their hallucinations. Some were getting songs. Each worshipper was carrying an eagle feather to keep the evil away. Jake's face paled as he began to see animals, white and black animal-like dogs through red and yellow circles. Suddenly, of all things, a picture in purples and reds of Big Eagle's leg, and that ragged ugly scar, flashed into his mind. It kept intruding into his dreamland, but not into his stupor.

Shortly before dawn, they prayed for Maggie long and hard, again. Finally, as Grandfather Sun peeped over the eastern horizon, the worshipers followed the Road Man from the church, facing east to greet Grandfather Sun. They all stood praying to Grandfather Sun to be their messenger. The peyote participants kept singing, assuring Grandfather Sun that they were humble. At long last, they all prayed in Osage that they were helpless, pitiful men, and asked Grandfather Sun to heal Maggie Lookout.

After the short period of prayer was over, the purged group returned to the church while the women folk brought in wild honey for them to eat. It was a time of relaxation while everyone shared their visions or hallucinations. Then, as if they had been prompted by Grandfather Sun they began passing the peyote balls around once more.

Thankfully, Sunday noon arrived. The Road Man sang his four rising songs and he dismissed the meeting. The elaborate feast began. The women had prepared pork, beef, chicken, corn, squash, fried bread or costue, watermelon, and cake. Everyone was in great spirits, still feeling no pain from the peyote. After the feast the older people rested in the shade.

While they were eating, Father Jack spoke to Jake. "Well, that's over, and I hope Maggie's well, soon. I guess I'd better get back to town. Hey, by the way, ol' Tom does pretty fast work. Did you see him talking to Miss Little Bear awhile ago?"

Jake smiled. "That Tom's okay. He was eating peyote with us in the church. He's probably still high and that's how he got up his nerve to talk to her." Father Jack laughed. "Good for him! If that's the case, he may get married a week from Tuesday." The two friends laughed as Father Jack started down the steps.

After Father Jack left, Jake sat on the porch in Fred's tall-backed chair, and he surveyed the whole picture. The evil had been purged away. Fred had confessed his sins. Father Peyote had delivered the message to Wah'-Kon-Tah. Now it was up to Grandfather Sun to bring Maggie's spirit back to him.

The summer sun was still hot. The flies were still swarming. The dogs were still asleep in the shade, as usual. The children were still running and yelling, and the older Indians were still resting. Everything seemed normal as Jake sat and wondered. Maybe only the pastures of wild flowers knew the outcome. And maybe the bumblebees were their messengers as they landed on their soft delicate petals. And maybe the bumblebees knew. Maybe they all knew! But Jake didn't know and he wondered.

CHAPTER TWENTY-ONE

The summer night was finally relinquishing its hold on the day. Jake looked at his pocket watch. It was somewhere around nine o'clock, and the Indian women had almost finished cleaning up the food. The sweat lodge had been disassembled and taken away. Most of the Indians were thinking about returning to their homes. Jake looked at the twenty-five or more big cars parked in the field and wondered how on earth Indians who couldn't drive would ever unscramble the maze.

In a flurry of rustling skirts and petticoats, Miss Lydia ran around the corner of the house, bumping square into Jake. "Jake! I can't find Quinn anywhere!" Her blond hair was awry, and the perspiration on her face told him she'd been frantically looking for some time.

Jake hastily scanned the crowd. "I haven't seen him, either. He was with that bunch of Bacon Rind's grandkids the last time I saw him."

"No, no! He's gone. The kids said, they had been back in the woods by the creek behind the house. They were skipping rocks or something. They all left to come back, but Quinn didn't come with them." She put her head in her hands, moaning. "Oh God, Jake! I'm sorry! I shouldn't have let him out of my sight!"

Jake patted her shoulder. "It's okay, Lydia. Calm down. He's around here, somewhere. You look over there in the direction of the barn and shed. Maybe he fell asleep in the hay. I'll go in the back by the creek and look. Don't say anything to Fred or Julia. No use upsettin' them."

Miss Lydia searched everywhere—all over the barn, the chicken houses, the sheds, and found nothing. At the same time, Jake was looking across the creek. After neither of them turned up anything, they met back at the house.

Jake looked at her inquisitively. "No luck either, huh? Well, listen. Will you take Julia back to town, and stay with Maggie so Mrs. Wright can go back home? I'll find Quinn and bring him into your place, later."

"No!" Lydia stomped her feet. "I won't go! Do you hear me, Jake? I won't go."

She flashed a full blast of determination and Jake knew the argument was over. "Okay. Then go tell Fred to take Julia back. Tell him Quinn's asleep, and that you and I will bring him in when he wakes up. I'm going to the shed and get a kerosene lantern."

"Okay!" She nodded, blond hair flying. She took off wiping her tear-filled face on her fresh organdy sleeve.

In a few minutes, she returned. "I told them, Jake."

He nodded as he bent to light the lantern. "Do they suspect?"

She shook her head. "No."

"Good. Now, let's go back again by the creek. Where's Bear, anyway? Even if Quinn's fallin' asleep, Bear should be able to hear my whistle."

The searching couple had walked for what seemed to be hours. It had to be way after midnight, and Jake was getting over being aggravated, and was starting to become alarmed. Lydia was dead tired and worried to death. In that neck of the woods, there were no neighbors. Fred owned too much land. Jake didn't dare tell Lydia, who was by now bordering on hysteria, what his real fear was. He just kept trying to block out of his mind his fear of the dangerous deep ravine. Jake kept looking everywhere else but the picture of the ravine wouldn't go away. As the fear mounted, he knew he had to run out of other places to look sooner or later. They sat on a big flat sandstone rock to rest and Lydia started to sob. "Come on, Lydia. Don't cry," Jake whispered, but all the time he was praying he wouldn't find his son at the bottom of the ravine!

All of a sudden, the high spirited-young woman reached in back of her, and with a violent motion she pulled a dozen or so blond hairs out of her head. "Here, take these for good luck. I told that old Henry what-his-name that I wouldn't sell them, but I do give them to my friends." Jake just stared at her in disbelief as she jumped straight up in the air. "Oh my God! What was that?" she cried, as the howling of wild animals interrupted their train of thought.

"Wolves!" Jake said as his senses scanned the night. "It sounds like wolves. There's a pack or two of them around here. We'd better get movin'!"

Unconsciously, Jake tucked the blond hairs in his shirt pocket. He caught her hand as they started up again. The searchers were getting close to the deep draw when Jake heard a swishing sound from a rock ledge behind him. Quietly, Jake leaned over and whispered into Lydia's ear, "Watch it! There's a snake. A rattler. Hear it?" Despite his warning, she started to scream, but Jake put his hand over her mouth. "Quick!" he said. "Shine the light over here!"

There it was, coiled up on the sandstone ledge ready to strike. The five or six rattles on the snake's tail were causing enough noise to wake the dead. "I've got my knife here in this pocket," Jake cried searching frantically.

"Wait! Here, Jake! I know." Lydia scurried to a nearby boulder, hiked up her long gingham skirt and petticoats, and bent over to take the der-ringer out of her garter. "Here," she said. "Now, shoot. Dammit, shoot. It's a two shot."

Jake grabbed the gun and eased forward as close to the snake as he dared while she held the light. He pulled both triggers. The two shots found their mark simultaneously as the snake exploded, splattering his remains off the ledge in at least five different directions. "Good for you, Lydia! Let's go!"

"Thank God." She sighed a great sigh of relief. They gathered their wits together and trudged on another quarter mile or so.

Jake felt like he could have cut the fear in the air with a knife and it was beginning to get the upper hand. He could hear the wolves again, but the howling seemed to be farther away than before. He knew they had to be really close to the edge of the ravine by now, but it was dark.

"Listen! What's that?" Lydia whispered as she stopped dead in her tracks.

Jake listened and he seemed to hear a whimpering noise, too. "Quinn! Bear! Do you hear me?" the frenzied man yelled, ripping the silence as the rock canyon seemed to reverberate the sound to the earth's very core.

"There it is, again. Sounds like a dog crying," she whispered.

Yeah, Jake thought. *Or a little boy.*

Jake stood at the edge of the ledge and shined the light, but he couldn't see anything moving. Then, a faint sound. "Daddy, Daddy, is that you?"

A shot of adrenaline charged though his body like an electric current causing his heart to pound. "Quinn, my God! Where are you?"

"Over here, over here by this big tree. Bear's hurt. His leg—" the small frightened voice whimpered.

Lydia and Jake ran, half-stumbling over limbs and each other, swinging the lantern in wild circles. They found their way somehow down over the huge boulders to the very bottom. "Where, Quinn? I can't see you."

Once again, the tiny voice said, "Over here."

Jake swerved to the right and shined the light. There he was, huddled under a fallen tree. The big man enclosed him in his arms, as the little pitiful voice sobbed.

"Daddy, Daddy, I want my mama. Bear's leg's hurt! He couldn't go get you. We followed this old trail and got lost. Then, it got dark and Bear lost his footing and fell off that ledge. He couldn't get up so I climbed down here to stay with him!" He took a gulping breath. "Then, Daddy! Daddy!" His shoulders shook. "The wolves came!"

Lydia cried. "The wolves."

The exhausted child nodded as his sobbing hiccups got worse. "They heard me crying and found me. They howled from way up there at the top for a long time. Then they came down here, closer and closer. Bear tried to get up and he growled, but he couldn't move. They were right here." He pointed a few feet away. "They were ready to get me. Great big teeth! Then all at once I saw this white wolf—all white, come from way over there!" He pointed to the ridge to his left. "He looked real big— kinda like Spitfire, but white. He came right here and put his paw on my knee. Daddy, Bear wasn't afraid of him. The big white wolf started growl-ing and showing his teeth at the black wolves, and they turned around and went away. The big white wolf saved me, Daddy! He saved me!"

As Quinn finished, he collapsed in Jake's arms. He held him until Quinn could stop crying. And from the back of his mind, he remem-bered his dream in the peyote church. Had it been a warning to him from Grandfather Sun or Father Peyote? "Lydia, hold him while I try to see what's wrong with Bear's leg."

Lydia held Quinn on her lap, smoothing his hair, as an occasional hiccup raced through his tired little body. Jake shifted himself around to get to his knees and began to examine the whimpering dog. Jake tried to lift his leg, but Bear cried louder. "Oh great! I think his leg is broken," Jake said as he tried to gauge the hundred or so foot distance up to the top. "Lydia, can you and Quinn make it up if I carry Bear?"

"I think so," Lydia said reluctantly.

"Okay, you and Quinn go on first. Here, take the lantern. When you get up on top hold the light for me to see, okay?"

She nodded. "Okay." She gathered up Quinn's hand and they started up. The climb wasn't too bad. They took it slow over the rocks holding on to branches and each other till they finally made it to the top.

Filled with relief, Lydia yelled. "Okay, Jake! Hurry! Come on!"

"Alright, Lydia. Lay down on your stomach and hold the light down as far as you can." Jake turned to look at the sad eyes of the dog. "Now, boy! You won't bite me, will ya? It 'll be bad till we get to the top." Jake reached down and tied his big handkerchief around the dog's injured leg, and then tied his belt around Bear's body and leg to hold it taut. Jake took a deep breath. "Okay, Bear, here we go!" As he scooped up the fifty pound dog, the dog let out a piercing moan, but Jake continued to slowly climb to the top.

"Daddy! Daddy! He's crying! Bear's crying!"

Jake rolled his eyes as the thoughts kept coming, "I know he's crying, son." *Just what I wanted to do today, after throwin' up buckeye root tea a hundred times, smoking peyote till I'm high and weak, and then havin' to carry a fifty pound, overweight dog up the deepest ravine in Osage County.* He measured his progress up the hill wondering if he'd ever make it.

The rescue went pretty well until they were nearly to the top. Then Jake's boot caught in a tree root and the dog and he all but crashed to the ground. Something caught Jake and broke his fall. He had no idea what it was. He was so hot and exhausted and the dog was moaning and whimpering, louder than ever. Lydia and Quinn kept yelling words of encouragement, or he could not have made the last five feet. Lydia helped him haul the dog up on the grass, and Jake sprawled out beside him. Both bodies were heaving and gasping for air.

They laid there for a good ten minutes, while Jake tried to figure something to do to get the dog back to the house, besides carrying him. It was probably better than a mile back. Then, it suddenly struck him. "Lydia, take off your skirt and petticoats!"

She looked at like he was a mad man. "What! Are you still on peyote?" she cried.

He ignored her dirty look. "Come on! Take off your skirt and petticoats! I need them to lay the dog on to work as a travois."

She laughed maliciously. "Lord no! Not on your life, Jake Knupp!"

"Oh, come on, Lydia. I won't look!"

"Please Miss Lydia! Please help my dog!" Quinn was pulling on her sleeve with the saddest eyes she'd ever seen.

"Oh, all right!" She untied her skirt, and as it fell the white billowy petticoats came with it, landing in a pile. There, she stood in her long merry widow corset and bloomers. "Don't you stare, Jake Knupp. I'm warnin' you."

"I wouldn't think of it, Lydia." He laughed as he cut two oak sticks from a small sapling with his knife, each about eight feet long. He tied the material to them, one, on each side, to form Bear's hammock. He spread the massive yards of crinoline material out, and laid the dog in the middle. Bear let out a couple of yelps, but Jake thought Bear was probably relieved as much as he was that he wasn't carrying him. Lydia reached for Quinn's hand and their hunting party slowly returned to the house.

Quinn cried the last quarter mile from sheer fatigue, but at last, the rescued party arrived back at the ranch. Jake wasted no time putting Quinn, the dog, the petticoats, and the corseted girl in Lydia's buggy. He rode his horse behind them as Lydia headed for town. Jake concluded that Quinn was already asleep, probably laying on the dog's bad leg. That thought amused him, and he smiled. Then, he laughed out loud. *What's Doc Lewis goin' think this time in the middle of the night, when I bring in a hurt dog, a sleeping kid, and Miss Lydia in her underwear.* Even Grandfather Sun would have smiled at that if he had been anywhere around.

CHAPTER TWENTY-TWO

It was late Monday night. Jake was sitting half asleep by Maggie's bed. She seemed to be resting easier. Maybe that was a good sign. Doc had taken all of his deliveries of the night before in stride. He grumbled forever, but finally he had taken Bear to the back porch. He had given him a shot of something, and had put a splint on the leg. He said the dog wouldn't get well, but Quinn demanded to stand on a chair supervising Doc's handling of the patient. Now, Bear was asleep in the study. Quinn was staying with Jake to give Miss Lydia a breather. The high-spirited woman claimed she needed a rest.

Fred appeared to be a new man. He seemed no longer tired since Father Peyote had delivered the message to Wah'-Kon-Tah. Miss Lydia had given the Lookouts a much lighter version of Bear and Quinn's escapade in the woods. But Fred was positive that Wah'-Kon-Tah had sent the white wolf because he was pleased with the Indian's peyote service. Their pleas had been heard. Fred was sure of it.

Earlier that day, Tom Fisher had stopped to tell Jake that Katherine Little Bear had accepted his dinner invitation for the evening. His plans included dinner at the Duncan Hotel and a long ride home in the moonlight. Jake had mentioned to him that there wasn't going to be much moonlight, but he hadn't cared in the least. Tom had just given him a big old friendly grin. He was still spell-bound by Katherine Little

Bear's beauty and her gentle spirit. Jake had thought of Maggie suddenly and how much he missed her gentle spirit. Quinn needed her, too. The child had knelt by his mother's bed, begging her to wake up so that he could tell her about his encounter with the white wolf. They'd all been disappointed when they'd arrived at Doc's after the peyote service to find her better but still not awake.

The nuns from the St. Louis School had come down earlier in the day. They had prayed and sang the "Ave Marie" prayer in Latin. As they sang, Julia had knelt by her bed with tears running down her high cheek-boned face. Jake knew that she was remembering when the "White Chests" nuns had prayed unsuccessfully to their heavy eye brow God for her other daughter, Mi-Tse-Ge, many moons past.

About six o'clock Jake couldn't take being cooped up any longer. He just had to have some fresh air. He had decided to take Quinn and they had ridden to the ranch. He hadn't been there since her accident. He knew the Indian ladies had cleaned the lodge, removing any hideous reminders of that night.

They took the buggy and drove out to the ranch about dusk. He noticed the pile of rocks along the road. Father Jack's Indian had been removed. The square built house looked lonesome and empty as they drove up to the front door. Even Quinn had been strangely quiet. The chickens had been scratching in the front yard, and Jake scattered more corn out for them. The peacocks had been curiously glad to see them. They began to strut, flaunting their huge fan of feathers with poise and grace. It was if they wanted to impart their wisdom to Jake.

Quinn's salt lick had almost vanished at the edge of the woods. He and his father replaced it with a fresh one from the barn. The deer had the habit of coming up in the early evening to the salt lick on their routine trek to the wheat fields for their nightly dining pleasure. The house had seemed so quiet. Jake had heard nothing but his own footsteps as he'd visited each room. He'd stopped to wind the big mahogany grandfather clock. Its heavy brass weights laid on the floor and the pendulum stood still at the eleven o'clock hour. Jake looked at it tenderly. The antique clock was one of her favorite things. He'd bought it for her from an ad in the St. Louie paper. It had been shipped for her birthday, the first year they were married. She had loved it, and religiously wound it every week.

She had said, "Time is so short. For the spirit's character to be deeply etched, one must mark the hours."

Jake had walked over to the victrola and gently put the needle down on the record already on the machine. It was Tchaikovsky's concerto, "The Dance of the Swans". He had recognized it instantly, for she played it often and it filled the house with a peace. He'd sat for a moment in the big wing back upholstered chair, looking around at Maggie's and his life, and all the things she loved.

Quinn had gone upstairs someplace, probably to his room, digging around for some particular toy, no doubt. So Jake walked up the stairs to their bedroom. He turned the glass doorknob and pushed open the oak door. The windows on the south had been left open and the Battenburg lace curtains were slowly blowing in the breeze.

The room was filled with air that had been held captive with a hint of musty-lavender and delicate floral scents. They'd drifted in from the outside, kissed personally by Maggie's sensitive spirit. Jake had been nearly overcome by her presence, and he longed for her spirit to return. He had walked around the room. He'd looked at her books, all with colorful markers meant to remind her of her favorite verses of poetry. He'd picked up a book on their bed, turned upside-down with the pages open, like she had just left her bed a moment ago. He had folded and tucked it under his arm. His eyes glanced at her dresser where her Indian accessories were lying. He remembered the one red feathered and silver piece particularly as he'd picked it up. Her gold locket was laying next to it, overlooked by the robber. Jake opened it to see Quinn's picture on one side, and his on the other, both wearing smiles of a happier time. Her fine multi-colored satin ribbon dress had been abandoned on the back of her floral tapestry chair. He had felt in the dress pocket, wondering if she had, per chance, put the diamond ring inside. He'd felt something and his heart jumped, but it was her Indian beaded rosary with the silver crucifix. She must have worn the dress to church and slipped the rosary in her pocket for safekeeping.

Her presence had been so strong. Jake had hated to leave, but finally, he had closed the door behind him and walked down the hall to Quinn's room.

There was no sound as he opened the door. He hadn't seen him at first, but he peeked around the corner. There he was, asleep, curled up on his bed with his stuffed bears close around him. It was a room, trapped in the process of transformation—half-baby and half-boy. There were just some things the child had not been ready to give up.

Several miles away from the ranch, life in Pawhuska was preparing for the dinner hour. Romance had been promised a thrill. The evening temperature had dropped to a comfortable seventy-five degrees. A gentle breeze was catching the scent of the flowers nestled in the store fronts. Tom Fisher and Katherine Little Bear had just parked the automobile in front of the Duncan Hotel. Tom had scrubbed his hand-me-down Ford until it had shone. He had taken particular pains for a perfect evening. He had taken his blue suit to be pressed and his white shirt was starched stiff. He had even worn his grandfather's gold cuff links.

Katherine had been friendly enough when he invited her, especially since Fred Lookout had put in a good word for him. Tom's relationship with Frank Phillips' big oil company had, no doubt, helped his chances. He had parked the car and she'd stepped out with a smile and an attitude that only a beautiful girl in the roaring twenties could portray. When Tom swung open the door, every person in Pawhuska had been instantly alerted that the young good-looking oil man was escorting the Osage Tribe's most beautiful lady to dinner.

Katherine had the kind of beauty that made men gasp. She carried herself like a princess. Her tall graceful body moved like the wind, silent, but not unnoticed. Her lilting laugh sounded like crystal bells. Her unusual talent of talking sparingly, complimented her body language that seemed to say so much.

No one missed it. Her movements were musical. She was in a class all of her own.

The-not-too-subtle hostess had seated the attention gathering couple at a prearranged small table in the back of the fancy, sophisticated dining room. The starched white Irish linen cloth had been placed on the table with sparkling crystal water goblets, filled with water and a lemon crescent, floating graciously in its midst. Tom had earnestly searched for the Ivy League manners that he'd packed away in his oil patch trunk when he left Harvard. He fervently hoped he had relocated them.

He had ordered their four-course dinner earlier in the day. It consisted of a subtle pork tenderloin, lying in a bed of long grain rice pilaf with fresh asparagus, steamed to perfection. It was to be precluded by a fresh garden salad, and as a final touch, cheese cake petit-fours to be served with coffee.

She had been impressed and delighted with dinner. Perhaps Grandfather Sun had added a little something extra to spice up the evening's chemistry, working between them.

They had discussed colleges, automobiles, oil, friends, poetry, music, parents, and everything else. It was like they had needed to catch up on years of conversation in one special evening. The time had simply flown by, and the restaurant was nearly ready to close when he looked into her beautiful brown eyes. "Katherine, this has been wonderful. I've enjoyed your company so much!"

Katherine's perfect face blushed to a rosy hue. "Tom, I've enjoyed it, too. I feel like I've known you all my life." Later, they had walked to the car, and she had mentioned Maggie. "She's such a wonderful person. She just has to get well."

Tom nodded. "Jake is really hopeful. She does seem to be getting better."

Tom had started the Model T Ford's motor, and they had eased down Kihekah Street. It was about ten-thirty, and the night-life had wound down for a Monday evening. "Katherine, I need to leave a proposal with a guy over at the Pawhuska Vitrified Brick and Tile Company. Would it be all right with you if we stopped there for a moment on the way to your house?"

She smiled. "That would be fine." His request had sparked her interest. "Do you know much about the brick company?" Tom shook his head.

"Let's see. What can I tell you about it. Well, It's been here since 1900. Ed Hunter, one of the owners, says this is the best clay around anywhere, and with gas fuel from the oil wells, they maintain 2000 degrees of heat in the burners. That's what insures its real hard texture."

"Well, you're the expert." Tom said. "The only thing I know is that Hunter's the first guy to design a brick with holes in it."

She laughed. "Yes, and we're famous for the Pawhuska rugs. They've developed a machine that gives them the real rough surface, and that's what they call them."

"Oh, I see. You're a regular tour guide."

"I aim to please, sir." They both laughed, obviously enjoying each other's company.

Tom drove to the west side of town toward the site of the old brick company. They turned down Fifteenth Street, which led past the big cemetery. The big monuments of the Osages loomed in the shadows as they passed by, giving them both an eerie sensation. Katherine seemed to move a little closer in Tom's direction.

He knew that there would be a skeleton crew there just to maintain the burners. But he wanted to leave a proposal from Frank Phillips for a natural gas bid. Frank felt that they could undercut Liberty Oil and make a big profit now that they had the big gas well right outside of town.

After finding a place to park quite a ways from the buildings, Tom helped Katherine out of the car, and to his surprise, she took his arm as they walked toward the brickyard. He began to think that maybe this was not such a good idea. It was really deserted, and there were abandoned sections of high brick walls as they attempted to follow the path to the main area. There was only dim light provided by the natural gas lamps, and the flickering of the flames created a sinister feeling. He wasn't sure which way to go.

"Here, let's go this way," Katherine pointed to the left. "I've been down here before with my father when he was getting bricks for the house. Just follow me!" They weaved around brick walls and piles of discarded brick. It was kind of exciting to Tom as Katherine had held on to his arm the whole way. In fact, he was hardly able to keep his mind on bricks, at all.

After some distance, she said, "Let's go through here. The main office building is way over there, just beyond that high section of wall."

At precisely the same moment, she screamed bloody murder. Tom jumped backwards tripping over a pipe and falling down on the ground. She screamed and backed up so fast that the next thing Tom knew, she came tumbling down on top of him. They both looked up, not two inches above their heads swung two feet with moccasins. Terror gripped them, both. Tom, literally had to force his terrified being to stand up. Katherine continued to scream into the quiet night. He helped her to her feet and cuddled her close to him. She had hidden her eyes with her head buried in his shoulder. Tom peered over the top of her head. "Oh God, it's an Indian. A dead Indian. Someone's hung him." A tall thin, half nude Indian man was hanging from a rope wrapped around a brace, bridging the two brick walls. "Do you know him, Katherine?" Tom asked the trembling woman.

It was a difficult task to try to identify him with his eyes bulging toward them. His tongue, too, was protruding. His long black hair was hanging limp. His heavily tattooed body seemed to twist and turn in the gentle breeze like a giant wind chime. Katherine hurriedly looked at him, and screamed a wail-like sob. "It's—Oh, my God! It's Bill Whit—" Then she fainted.

Tom caught her in mid-fall. He looked at her and at the dead man and wondered where this date had gone wrong.

Miles away the sun was sinking rapidly over the roof line of Jake's ranch house but the glow was still illuminating the soft evening. Quinn and Jake had locked the massive front door behind them. The house looked even more forlorn with the setting sun behind it as they turned to leave. He had stopped by the gate and picked a handful of wild daisies for Quinn to take to his mother. He had been so relieved when Quinn had said, "Spitfire must be over at Grandfathers." Gratefully, Jake hadn't had to explain anything to him about his mother's dog.

Back in town, it was now a quarter to eleven. Quinn and Ruby had put the flowers in a blue vase by Maggie's bed before he had gone off to sleep. Jake was completely alone with Maggie. He sat there missing her, trying to feel her presence and take some comfort from her stillness. He remembered the book he'd brought from the ranch. He had laid it on the table near her bed. It fell open to the place that it had been turned to from laying so long on her bed. It startled him as he read. When he finished, he looked up at Maggie.

The night was quiet. Her fever was down and she was definitely resting easier. There was a shaft of dim light shining in the window. The crickets were singing more softly than on nights past. The breeze from the open window was cooling off her face, fanning her spirit. Jake touched her face with his hand as the gentle fragrance of the daisies filled his head with her presence. He seemed to sense that her spirit was returning, entering by the garden gate. He touched her face again tracing her lips with his finger tips.

As he leaned over and kissed her, he decided to re-read aloud to her, the time-marked place in her worn and favorite book. "Come my beloved, and frolic on my spirit's path. Where I search for freedom till the day I live. When my spirit's prison releases me from fears. You can choose then, my beloved, to come and live among my dreams. Come, my beloved, come."

As he finished, a tear slipped past him and innocently dropped onto the page. He sat and looked at the words wondering if she still held him in her dreams, or if she'd shut him out, too. Perhaps she had chosen to stay in this prison where fear couldn't enter, and life could not be lived.

He glanced up from the book, still pre-occupied with the stanza. And when he did there were two of the most beautiful brown eyes quietly looking at him that he had ever seen. "My God! Maggie!" He yelled.

She smiled, and said ever so softly. "Jake!"

He put his dizzy head down on her breast while his upside-down world strived to right itself once again. "Oh Maggie! Thank God! You've come back!"

Grandfather Sun had not missed this reunion of the spirits? Perhaps it was simply the end of the long dark night and he had recaptured her from the grip of darkness.

CHAPTER TWENTY-THREE

Tom Fisher had finally found the sheriff, and they had reported their hair-raising story. After the lengthy ordeal, it had been time to take Miss Katherine Little Bear home. At the door, she had said with a giggle, "Thank you for dinner, Tom, and for going over and beyond the call of duty to entertain me." He blushed. He had apologized to her again probably for the tenth time, but there seemed to be a strong bond growing between them. Consequently, they had agreed to dine again, soon— with no more visits to the brick company.

It was a typical summer noon the next day. Nothing was stirring around town, and the air was stagnant. Fred, Leahy, Agent Wright, and Jake were up at the café on their third round of iced tea when the sheriff came in with Father Jack. They relayed the story of Tom and Katherine walking up on poor dead Bill WhiteOaks. They all acted properly horrified, but none of them were really to surprised.

"Well, I guess you'll be arresting one or more of the Hale boys, huh, Sheriff?" Jake asked.

"Yeah, It looks like ol' Mike Hale's going need a good lawyer."

"Don't look at me." Leahy said dissolving the sugar in his tea glass.

Fred shook his head. "I think the whole damn town's gone to the dogs. Every day, another innocent Indian victim."

Sheriff Cook tipped his glass up and let the cold liquid slide down his throat. "Father Jack, you're going to have to go notify Mrs. WhiteOaks about her son. I don't envy you havin' to tell her. Better you than me."

"Yeah. Thanks a lot," Father Jack said sarcastically. "Especially, since she's been crying everyday up at Mass. She was expecting someone to kill him, poor woman. Every day it just gets worse. At least, Maggie is better, Jake. Any word on the guy who raped her, Sheriff?"

The sheriff shook his head. "No, I'm going to wait a couple of days till she's feeling better, then maybe, I can ask her about him."

The Osage agent, George Wright interrupted as he rattled the loose ice in his almost empty glass. "You know, every day I get reports about these damn guardians for the Indians. There's six hundred and some guardians I believe, and everyone of them is crooked. They've managed to spend over eight million dollars, given to them for their Indians clients. I personally, caught Lester Williams, charging Tom Big Horse twelve hundred dollars to oversee Tom's four thousand dollar a year income. And Nell Big Elk was worth one hundred thousand dollars two years ago. Now, she's broke, and twenty thousand dollars in debt, even with her twelve thousand dollar a year headright payment. It's terrible!"

"And what's that smooth talking son a bitch Pat Woodward up at the agency doing?" Leahy asked. "Some Osage attorney he is. He acts like he could care less. He's a guardian himself to several Osages. I'd like to know how that happened."

George just shook his head. "I know he's no damn good, but my hands are tied."

"Yeah, but the car dealers are the worst, George," Father Jack said. "They're still at it. Floyd Littleaxe was sold a two hundred dollar used car for twelve hundred and fifty dollars and the dealer pocketed the difference. But that's not the worst. I think old Clyde over at the bank pulled this off. Ned Running Bear still owes four hundred on a car that his guardian sold him for three-fifty cause the damn interest rates he charged him are so outrageous."

The tension was mounting. Jake could sense it as he laughed. "Well, thank God, Pawhuska's got the biggest jail in Oklahoma. And thanks to Al Spencer and his gang, we got rid of Clyde Baker."

George Wright was getting riled. "Listen, you guys, remember when I told you about 'em selling people for marriage? Well, last week, I got a letter from some idiot saying he was an upstanding citizen and all, and would I introduce him to an Osage woman. He said that if they get married, he'd pay me twenty-five dollars for every five thousand she's worth."

Father Jack choked, nearly spewing tea all over the table.

"Needless to say, I was furious," George stopped for a breath.

"Well, that's nothin'," Sheriff Cook exclaimed, shoving his chair back from the table. "Judge Worten and I were working on this case over at Ponca City. Pete Wildturkey fell in love with a white woman—name's Mary Johnson, I think. After a week-long courtship, they got married. Three days later, she left him, and then Pete had to pay her one hundred thousand dollars alimony. That just happened up at the court house last week."

"Yeah, Sheriff's right." Leahy put in his two cents worth. "I heard em' talking about it in the law library."

Father Jack pounded the table. "Well, I'll tell you one better 'an that! Last May, Ruby Blackhawk got hooked up with some old boxer. You know her, she's the richest of all the Osages—eight headrights, I think. Well, she and the boxer got drunk for three days in Kansas City and got married. Then, she got arrested. I found out that she was so drunk, she didn't even know what was happening at the wedding. Next thing I knew, we'd lost her again, and the sheriff up there tracked her down to Colorado Springs. This boxer husband had her locked up in a hotel room and kept her in a stupor with drugs and alcohol. The police busted in and got her out, and we annulled the marriage. It beats all I've ever seen."

Sheriff Cook shook his head. " By the way, Father Jack, your opossum eating Indian friend in the rock pile turned out to be Ed Tall Corn."

"Oh really, I've heard the name, but I can't place him." Father Jack mused.

"Well, boys," Sheriff Cook stood up. He took particular pains to put his straw cowboy hat on with just the right tilt. "I guess we could sit here and tell each other these kinds of stories all day, but I guess I've got to get out to the Hales and arrest Mike and Tom for Bill's murder. Ol' man Hale'll love this. Maybe he'll think twice the next time about bad mouthin' the Indians all over town."

The rest of the table of men grunted in agreement. The big lawman replaced his chair under the table, and left. Father Jack said regretfully that he had to leave too, to give Mrs. WhiteOaks the bad news. "Glad Maggie's better, Jake."

"Thanks, Father Jack. Me, too."

Sheriff Cook picked up the boys at the jail and rode to the big ranch south of town. Osage County was well known for its big grass and range land. About three quarters of its million and a half acres were lush native bluestem grass that grew as tall as a horse's back. In the spring, bluestem had the protein content equal to corn for fattening cattle. Texan cattle drivers had been bringing cattle across the lush bluestem grass of the Osage to the Elgin, Kansas shipping point for years. After the allotment, some Indians chose to lease their land to large operators. They, in turn, put together large ranches. William Hale was one of the most influential of those ranchers. He had two sons and his little gal, Betsy, who had gotten herself nearly raped up in Elgin. In the beginning, he had been one of the few traders allowed into the agency by the government. They made lots of money by over-pricing staples.

A common story had been told for years around town—that on more than one occasion, Hale had offered to trade furs from the Indians for fifty-thousand dollars, and then resold the same furs in excess of a hundred-fifty-thousand dollars. The old man had moved fast from that form of trading into the mercantile store business. At the same time he was building a huge cattle empire in the Osage, and acquiring most of the Citizens National Bank, as well. His two sons were big bull riders and steer ropers. They performed at most of the rodeos around. They had taken top honors at the Osage County fair grounds many times over the years. Rodeos and women were all they had to think about.

Sheriff Cook wondered as he rode up onto the ranch why the Hale boys would give up all they had. Were they willing to risk going to jail for killing an Indian who really hadn't even gotten the job done on Betsy Hale before the law broke it up. Sheriff Cook and his men quickly dismounted and tied the horses at the rail. They represented a small but formidable group as they walked to the house and up on the big grand porch. Old man Hale met them at the screen door. He threw it wide open as he shoved his foot against it to keep it open. "What's goin' on, Sheriff? What's brought you out here to this neck of the woods?"

Sheriff Cook shook his hand. "Well, I'm here to see your boys on a little business. Seems there's been a killin' up at the brick company, and we think your boys may have had a little something to do with it."

Hale narrowed his steel blue eyes down to just slits behind his black horn-rimmed spectacles. "Look, Cook, you new in town or what?" He twisted his cigar in his mouth. "Don't you know? My boys ain't going to kill nobody, especially no Indian. Ain't worth our time."

Sheriff Cook looked at him. "How'd you know it was an Indian?"

Billy Hale looked him right in the eye without flinching. "Heard it in town up at the bank this morning. By the way, Sheriff, you got a warrant?"

"Yeah," Sheriff Cook said. "Yeah, I do, but right now all I want is to question them."

Hale puffed on his fat cigar blowing smoke deliberately into the sheriff's face. Nonchalantly, he waved them to the back of the house. "Okay, Cook. They're around back cuttin' a bunch of calves. Go on around there, but you'd better be careful and not go round accusin' my boys, Sheriff. Ya hear?"

Sheriff Cook and his men hastily retreated down the porch steps and headed around to the back. They found Mike and Tom together, working with a half dozen hands on the calves. "Hi, Sheriff Cook!" Mike waved. "Gonna have a big calf fries party this weekend. We got us a good crop here, if we can get em' skinned." He reached in the bucket and picked up a bloody handful of the castrated testicles to show him.

Sheriff Cook waved him off. "I need to talk to you boys about your feud with Bill WhiteOaks."

Mike, the older brother, took the offensive quickly. "Yeah! That dirty rotten sucker tried to rape Betsy up at the Elgin dance. Ain't none of these damn Indians around here goin' grab her like that—"

"Well, he's dead, boys, so you might as well simmer down. Somebody hung him last night up at the brick company."

"Yeah!" Tom nodded. "We heard. Dad told us this morning."

Sheriff Cook moved the dirt around in little circles with his boot. "Well, so did you boys do it?"

Tom and Mike looked at each other. "Heck no," Mike said. "We've been up practicing ropin' at the arena."

"Got anybody who can prove your alibi?" Bill, the senior deputy, inquired.

"Well, sure! We'll get right on that list, Deputy," Tom said with his voice dripping in sarcasm.

Sheriff Cook's anger rose. "Okay, boys! Let's take 'em in, and they can give us their long alibi list up at the jail. We'll be the judge of how good it is."

The Hale boys wanted to fight, but they just couldn't believe, that he was actually going to arrest them—especially for hanging an Indian. The Hale boys exchanged looks as the deputies moved toward them. Tom walked away toward the fence, kicking a water bucket twenty feet in the opposite direction. "You ain't goin' put no cuffs on us. You're fixin' on openin' a can of worms you boys can't handle. You'd better be leaving us alone. My old man'll clean your plow."

Mike squared his jaw. "Look you stupid ol' bastard. Have you forgotten who we are? You're as big a fool as these Indians around here."

"You're just wasting our time. Our ol' man'll have us out before supper." Tom shook his fist in the face of the closest deputy.

"He'll git you for this. You wait and see. He's god in these parts." Mike yelled.

"Bring 'em in boys. I'll meet you at the jail, Bill," Sheriff Cook said, as he turned and walked on back to the house.

The lawman still had to deal with the old man as his big framed body went through the screen door unannounced into the living room. "Hale, better get your boys a good lawyer. I'm takin' 'em in. They ain't got no alibi and plenty of motive, and I've got a real dead Indian to contend with."

Hale sat in his overstuffed chair, never flinching a muscle. The only visible sign of his fury was the deep prints in his clinched cigar. He finally worked the cigar out if the way as he forced the words through his lips. "Cook, you'd better be looking for another job. Cause when I get through with you, you'll be history in Osage County. You don't seem to know when to butt out of my business."

He picked up the phone and called Jeffrey Samuels, his well-known crooked lawyer in Pawhuska. "Samuels, Billy Hale here. Seems to be a little mistake up at the jail concerning my boys and a dead Indian. Can you get right up there? Thanks, Samuels."

Sheriff Cook didn't even listen as Hale hung up the phone and shouted a few more obscenities in his direction. He just slammed the screen door and headed back to town.

It was about noon in Pawhuska and the temperature had already reached ninety-five degrees. The cafes were filling up and you could smell chicken fried steak from every direction. Father Jack's mind was not on food. He was having problems of his own. He had to find Bessie

WhiteOaks to tell her that her worse fears had come true. She hadn't been at Mass that morning. That would have been too easy.

Bessie was a spry, tall framed Indian lady. She was quiet and kept to herself. She had black eyes and her once blue-black hair was rippled with gray. Father had always liked her. And she was known to be one of the church's biggest supporters.

He drove his buggy to her house, which was only a short distance from the church. As he urged the horse on, he prayed that the Lord would tell him what to say and how to console her. *Damn this heat.* He thought as he knocked on the door of the modest red brick house. It was elegant, but fairly small.

Bessie had moved into town off of her land when her husband died. Besides Bill, she had had four daughters—Rita and Mollie were the only two still alive. Rita was a bad alcoholic. Bessie had told him sometime ago after Mass that Rita had married some guy named Henry and had left the church. Bessie had disowned her but she had paid the price of a broken heart. She hadn't seen Mollie, her other daughter, for five years. She'd run off several years ago to get away from the confines of the little agency town. The last Bessie had heard, Mollie had ended up in St. Louie married to some no-good.

Bill had stayed out on the land over by Bird Creek in a lodge next to the unoccupied farm house. On the few occasions Father Jack had been at the ranch, he remembered that it was modeled after the Lookouts' ranch house. He had to smile, as he had never forgotten the grand piano sitting in the front yard with a half dozen chickens scratching under it, and two roosters perched on the top like saucy saloon torch singers. They had a large black Packard touring car, and it was nothing to see them riding to town past the church with a calf or a hog in the back seat of the fancy car.

All of these thoughts served to try to get his mind off his mission and the heat. He knocked a second time—still no answer. He walked around to the back. The big back porch was empty but he could see the back door was ajar. He crossed the porch and walked to the doorway and pushed open the door. He called her name. "Bessie! Bessie WhiteOaks! Are you home?" He took a few more steps into the kitchen. He noticed that there was jug of milk on the counter and the flies were swarming around it. He looked around. Nothing else was left out. He felt the milk jug—it was warm. It had been out for a long time. It was already curdled. He went on into the living room. There was nothing amiss there among the crucifixes and statues. He kept calling her name. He was getting increasingly upset.

He went upstairs and knocked on her bedroom door. No answer. It was just cracked open so he opened it wider. He could see someone lying on the bed. He called again. His heart was beating a hundred miles a hour, as he entered the room. His voice was trapped inside his body by his racing heart. He couldn't even scream as his eyes rested on Bessie WhiteOaks. She lay face down, nude on the bed, soaked in blood. Her long black hair had been tied in a big ugly knot, revealing the tattoos covering her back—all in the image of the huge Osage spider design. Her head was tilted to the side with her mouth open as in a half scream. Her black eyes were fixed. Father gasped again for air, fighting the urge to run, but yet he had to find her wound. There were deep gashes in her head, which had caused the blood, but on a closer look, he saw the murder weapon. He started to wretch. "Jesus! Mary and Joseph!" he cried. The killer had choked the poor woman to death by winding around and around her neck, Bessie WhiteOak's own scarlet rosary beads.

Father Jack tried not to touch anything as he turned tail and fled the house. He ran to his buggy and whipped the horse into motion. He had to find Sheriff Cook.

Fred and Jake were just walking back to Doc's to see Maggie when Father Jack's buggy came around the corner like gangbusters. They didn't see him in time, and the horse reared up nearly causing the buggy to overturn. Fred grabbed the bridle to settle down the horse.

"Good Lord! Father Jack, what's wrong?" Jake yelled at the distraught priest.

"Jake! Fred! I'm goin' to find Sheriff Cook," Father Jack stammered. "Bessie WhiteOaks' dead! 105 Purdom Street! Backdoor! Hurry!" He gave the horse a lick with his quirt and took off again.

Without a moment's hesitation, Fred and Jake raced to their horses, riding as fast as they could to the WhiteOaks' home. It was no trick to get in the house as Father Jake had left the door wide open. They raced up the stairs and quickly found Bessie in the bedroom.

"Yep, she's dead, all right," Fred muttered, touching her on the neck.

Jake finally found his voice. "My God, Fred! She's been choked with her rosary beads. Hit in the head, too." Jake had forgotten that some of the older Osage women had full-body tattoos. But it still got to him as his eyes seemed unable to leave the huge black spider. "Fred, why on earth the tattoos?"

"Tattoos were done by husbands. The more money, the more tattoos."

Jake nodded. "But, why the spider?"

"Custom started from old story," Fred talked as he paced. "It means, 'all good things come to him like to the web of spider.' Bessie WhiteOaks was one of few women left with spider tattoo on back. Most Osage women have spider on back of hand."

Jake looked over at Bessie's hand, limply hanging off the bed. Sure enough, the spider was visible on her hand. It looked so real Jake half expected it to jump onto his leg. It was only then that his eyes caught something, and he grabbed Fred's sleeve. "Does Bessie have any jewelry?"

Fred shook his head. "No, she lived modestly. Gives all her money to church."

Jake looked like he had been struck dumb. "Then, why Fred, has Bessie WhiteOaks got on Maggie Lookout's big rock ring?" They both stared in silence at the ring on the dead woman's finger.

CHAPTER TWENTY-FOUR

The crime picture was about as clear as mud, and several days passed. The little agency town was still in heavy turmoil over the most recent murders. Sheriff Cook was beside himself. The murder count was up to forty, and he could not untangle the maze of killings by himself. He was seriously considering calling in the FBI. Agent George Wright was going to contact Washington D.C. and talk to the U.S. Attorney General's office. Pat Woodward, the Osage Indian attorney, was spending a lot of time out of town, too.

The sheriff was upset that he appeared to be such a fool over the arrest of the Hale boys. It was obvious after the killing of Bill's mother, Bessie WhiteOaks, that there was more there than just a grudge match between the Hale boys and Bill over Betsy's attempted rape. He was really unhappy, and he took it personally when he had to free the Hale boys.

Old man Hale had just smiled as Samuels, his attorney, said that they would probably sue everyone concerned for maligning the Hale family's character. Sheriff Cook needed some time off. The worst part of the whole deal was that he had no leads on who killed Bill or his mother.

Pawhuska was experiencing nearly perfect weather. Everyone was talking about it. But it was truly a day of celebration for the Lookout family. Jake was going to take Maggie home. Her recovery was nearly complete, but Sheriff Cook wanted to ask her a few questions before they left Doc's. As the sheriff and Jake walked into her sunny room, she was sitting up in bed with the pink satin bed jacket her mother had bought over at the Mercantile Store. Quinn was sitting on the bed with her as she read him a story about trains, his favorite topic. She looked so beautiful with the pink color quickly returning to her cheeks.

"Hi, Maggie," Jake said as he bent over and kissed her. "Sheriff Cook is here to see you before you leave today. He wants to know if you remember anything about the guy who attacked you."

Maggie nodded, as Sheriff Cook took her hand and held it for a moment. "Boy, I'm sure glad to see you up and around, Miss Maggie. You gave us all quite a scare."

Maggie smiled. "Sit down, Sheriff. I'm glad, too. I'm feeling better each day." Sheriff and Jake each pulled up a chair by the bed.

Ruby was fluffing up her pillows. She stopped and grabbed Quinn by the hand. "Come on, Quinn. I'll get you a sugar cookie and we'll see what old Doc's doing in his study."

"Okay, Aunt Ruby. Let's go. I'll help you." The five year old clamored after her.

"Now, Miss Maggie," Sheriff Cook began. "I know this is difficult—but. Well, can you try to tell me what happened from the beginning?"

Maggie took a deep breath and began recounting the story in slow, deliberate sentences. It was as If she was having to unwrap every event in her mind since her memory had been packed away so long. The young sensitive woman finally got to the part about hearing the gun shot and how she knew someone had killed Spitfire. She told them how afraid she was when she realized she had forgotten the gun in the house. She slowly began her nightmarish ordeal with the madman. She stopped a couple of times as her shoulders shook with sobs. Jake moved to the bed and held her as they waited for her pain to subside.

She seemed to feel a release by getting the story out, and by forcing her mind to focus on the horror, yet, all her conscious brain wanted to do was to retreat. However, as she became more and more relieved, her pent up energy poured into Jake, and he got madder and madder. He shot the sheriff a few piercing glances as the story of that night unfolded. She spoke of how she'd left the ring on the hall table. She went into detail about him finding her, and about him hitting her again and again as she attempted to fight him off.

"The last thing I remember seeing, just before I passed out, was a huge, ugly, red scar on the man's neck. It started up here." She pointed to her ear. "And it went all the way down to his shoulder." She shuddered as the sheriff concentrated on his notes.

"Did you know about Spitfire being put in the lodge with you?" Jake asked as he stroked her hand.

"No." She shook her downcast head. "The man was drunk and crazy. He was a madman, Sheriff. He was tall and muscular. He had dark hair and light blue eyes like shallow blue pond water."

The sheriff nodded. "Anything else that you can remember?"

She thought a moment wiping her eyes. "No, except he showed me the ring. Said he'd found it on the hall table in the house."

"Oh yeah, about the ring. Can you remember the guy's name that sold it to you?"

She thought for a minute. "Henry. Henry something. Oh I can't remember, but he was a small man in a three-piece suit. He had blue beady eyes and a big nose. He said the ring was worth eighteen thousand dollars and he would sell it to us for twelve thousand. He had a paper of proof, he showed me."

Sheriff Cook looked up. "Did he give it to you?"

"No." She shook her head quietly.

"I see! Well, Maggie, you go on home now. You've helped us a lot."

She nodded, and hugged Jake's arm.

"Jake, I'll talk to you, later. I gotta get back to the office."

Jake shook his hand and Sheriff Cook left the room quietly closing the door behind him.

Three hours later, It was a happy trio saying their good-byes at Doc's. Ruby helped Jake tuck Maggie in the yellow Packard's front seat and she placed the poetry book in her lap. "Better not forget this, Miss Maggie!"

Maggie hugged her good-bye while Doc Lewis gave her his last minute instructions. He leaned in the window of the front seat as she hugged him and planted a big kiss on his cheek. He looked over her head and winked at Jake. "Now Jake, you and Julia take good care of my patient."

"Oh, we will, Doc. Julia and Fred's already out at the ranch getting her room ready."

Quinn was so happy. He had his mama back. At long last, he was going home with her, Bear, and his big sack of cookies. Ruby had baked them especially for his trip home. He and Bear were in the back seat. He resembled King Tut in his golden chariot.

"Thanks, for everything, Doc." Jake said as he started up the big motor.

Doc waved. "You bet. Hey! Look out! Here comes a car."

Jake looked up just in time to see a big shiny red Studebaker coming toward them. At the last moment, it swerved somehow missing the yellow Packard.

"Hi, Doc," the driver yelled. Jake recognized him from the car dealership uptown. "This here's for you. Ain't it a beaut? Fred Lookout told me to deliver it to you. Where do ya want it?"

Jake laughed. "Well, Doc, guess old Fred's a pretty good man of his word."

Doc grunted. "Might know a Indian'd bring me a dang red car. I'm the Doc, not a damn fireman." But he was quick to tell him to park it. Doc was still happily eyeing his new automobile like a kid with a new toy, as Jake and Maggie pulled away from the house on their way to the ranch.

The drive to the ranch was uneventful and Fred met them at the gate with a big old wave. "Welcome home, my Maggie girl!" Jake unloaded the two wild ones from the back seat. The happy dog and boy immediately ran as fast as they could to the house. Bear and the kid were back. The chickens' and ducks' vacation was over. Jake lifted Maggie into his arms and kissed her.

"I'm so glad to be home, Jake. With you and Quinn." Her brown dewy eyes were full of tears as she tried not to look in the direction of the lodge. Jake carried her up the porch steps, and the scent of the morning glories nearly took their breath away. It seemed as if they had been saving up all of their summer's fragrance to welcome them home.

Fred opened the door. "Hello Maggie girl!"

"Hello, Father." She lovingly hugged his neck. She was looking at her home as if she'd never seen it before. "Now, go slow, Jake, so I can see everything. Oh, look! Someone's started my clock."

Jake smiled. "Of course I did. Time has started all over again for us now that you're back home."

Jake carried her upstairs to her room, and Julia was there already turning down the bed covers. Jake gently put her down in the middle of the big feather bed. She looked tired even though the trip had been fairly short. Julia pulled the covers up to her chin. "Welcome home, Maggie girl. I get you cup of tea. Then, you take nap while I cook."

Maggie leaned back on the pillows and thankfully closed her eyes. They pulled the door shut, as Julia went in search of the tea and Jake joined Fred on the porch. Fred was in the lap of luxury. He was content and all seven dogs were sound asleep around his chair.

Jake took a deep breath. "Well, Fred! The guy's got a big scar!"

Fred's mouth fell open. "Who? Maggie girl's attacker?"

"Yeah. She says he's tall and muscular with real light eyes." Jake continued. "But she couldn't identify him. He found the ring on the hall table." Jake recounted her story to Sheriff Cook. "Oh, yeah! The guy that sold the ring to her was named Henry. Different guy altogether. Sheriff said he was going check out the Henry deal and look for a guy with a nasty scar. Henry's really the only clue he has, especially since the ring has showed up on Bessie's WhiteOak's finger."

Fred looked perplexed. "Hum! Well, if my name was Henry, I leave town on a fast train especially, before you and I catch him."

Jake nodded. "That's right."

The two of them leaned back in their chairs. Jake handed Fred one of his cigars, and they both lighted them and puffed away. Jake knew it was going through both of their minds that even though the little town of Pawhuska was full of murdered bodies, at least for the moment, Grandfather Sun had smiled down on the Lookout family.

CHAPTER TWENTY-FIVE

War had been declared between reason and fear, and fear was winning. A month had passed. The town was knee-deep in worry about the murders. Even old man Hale had put up a one hundred thousand dollar reward from the Citizens National Bank, which he owned. The sizable reward no doubt reflected his gratitude that his boys were off the hook.

Sheriff Cook and George Wright had talked to Patrick Woodward, the Osage Indians' attorney. He had offered no help so they'd sent word to Washington for help, and the U.S. Attorney was sending down a team from the crime commission to investigate the murders. However, it might be fall before they got here. The government wasn't in the habit of moving quickly.

During the past month, Jake's well had turned into a nightmare. Progress had been slow. They should have been out of there two weeks earlier. They had run into water problems, and then a bailer had given out. Red had been trying to hustle one up, but so far the hunt had proved futile. Actually, the hold-up didn't bother Jake, since he could spend more time with Maggie at the ranch. But Evan's good humor was on the down and outs.

It was Sunday, August 3, 1923, and a calm, lazy day had been promised. Fred and Julia had left Jake in charge of Maggie's care while they went to town to attend Mass at the Catholic Church.

The Catholic Church built in 1910 was big, bold and beautiful. It's ornate marble altar was reminiscent of the bigger European Cathedrals. Nine stain glass windows made in Germany depicted images of various saints. The brightly colored saints formed a semi-circle in the huge dome, and stared at the crowd from high above the altar. The sanctuary lamp had been ordered from Europe. It was another sign of the Indian's affluence. It was heavy, gold, and ornate. It hung in the middle of the sanctuary, announcing to the Osage Catholics that the Lord was present.

Everyone was gathering for the nine o'clock Mass as Fred and Julia came around the corner to the front doors. They were wrapped in their best Sunday Hudson Bay blankets. They made a striking couple as they came up the steps of the red brick church. Father Jack was standing out front with the long skirt of his cassock flapping in the breeze. He liked greeting the mainly Osage congregation as they filed into the church of the Immaculate Conception. Fred shook Father's hand. "Howdy, Father Jack!"

"Hello to you too, Fred, Julia! Fine morning isn't it?"

Fred leaned over in a low voice. "I hear Chief Ne-Kah-Wah-She-Tun-Kah is near death." Father Jack nodded. "Yeah, the Tall Chiefs went in a few minutes ago, and they told me he was bad. I'll go out to his place this afternoon and give him the Last Rites of the church."

Fred and Julia walked on into the foyer. The Church held about five hundred people, and it was about half-full. The organ music started and Grandfather Sun was shining through the stain glass windows, making the colorfully robed stain glass saints even brighter than usual. Grandfather Sun, the glass Saints, and Wah-Kon-Tah watched over the kneeling Osages with their brightly colored rosary beads, as they prayed to heavy eyebrows God to stop the Osage murders. It made a humble picture to see them pouring out their petitions for God's mercy to spare themselves and the rest of their kinfolk.

Father Jack was mid-way through Mass and halfway into preaching his homily when the side door closest to him opened. An Indian man

briskly walked up the middle aisle, genuflected, and stepped up to
Father Jack. Father stopped in mid-sentence as the man whispered to
him. Father Jack nodded, then he closed his Bible and folded his hands
silently praying. After a few moments, he spoke in a soft voice. "Ladies
and Gentlemen. My dear friends in the Lord. I have just been informed.
Your Osage Chief, Ne-Kah-Wah-She-Tun-Kah is dead."

There was astonishment and excited whispering among the people,
although the news had been expected. Grandfather Sun ducked behind
a cloud, for death of the Chief meant change, and change was not a welcome thing—especially when one had to constantly look over his
shoulder to see if another Indian was being murdered. Fred's eyes
searched Julia's face. *"O God!" he thought. "Now if I'm elected, the burden
of this tribe will be mine."* He looked down, closed his eyes, and prayed
harder as the Mass continued.

Later, Fred, Father Jack, and Jake met to ride out to the Chief's. It was
about one o'clock when they arrived. The Chief had two wives. He-Ah-
to-Me, his first wife, met them at the lodge. They entered. There on his
pallet lay the dead chief with his other wife, Wah-Hrah-Lum-Pah by his
side.

As were their customs for the dead, some things had to be done
according to the peyote religion before the heavy eyebrows God and the
Catholic Church could take over. Fred had been asked to perform the
duties of the Road Man. It was his duty to paint the dead chief's face for
the journey into the Spirit land. The Osages believed that if the chief
was to reach Spirit land, his face must be painted for identification,
there. He must be ready to follow Grandfather Sun to the west. Fred
greeted the chief's family, as did Father Jack. The priest held their hands
as he offered his condolences to each of the family members. Jake
watched George Little Star, the Chief's son, as he asked Fred to perform
the task of painting his father's face.

"When do you wish to have the funeral?" Father Jack said.

"Tomorrow," George said. "Ten o'clock. Bury him at cemetery on sand stone hill above town. Feast here at high noon. Agent Wright just left. He send Johnson out with big bronze expensive casket. Fred, you paint?"

Fred nodded. "Yes, George, tomorrow at sun-up." Father Jack nodded. "George, there'll be a lot of dignitaries and reporters here in town for the funeral. Your father was a great man." George nodded silently. Father Jack went over to the chief's body and laid his hand on the chief's head. He opened his book of prayers and prayed in Latin for the dead chief's sins to be forgiven, and to allow his soul to be taken up to heaven. Soon after, the trio left to return to town. They would return early the next morning to prepare the chief for his final journey.

Next morning dawned early and the trio arrived at the chief's before sunrise. They entered the lodge. The chief had been placed in the expensive casket, facing west. He was dressed in all of his ceremonial robes and his finest otter bandeau. There were white candles burning at his head. The chief was ready to be painted for the journey. Fred began the prayers for the Rite of Vigil. Then he took the red paint and painted a vertical line on one cheek and with the blue paint, he painted the other cheek. A horizontal line just below the hairline was drawn across the forehead to connect the vertical lines.

The lines formed the Ho-e-ka, or snare, the purpose of which was to draw all life into a trap. The Ho-e-ka was also a symbol of the earth. Next, Fred painted four vertical lines from the horizontal line to a point a little above the eyebrows. Those lines represented the four winds, symbolic for the breath of life and the voice of spirits.

After Fred finished, the hundred or so relatives and friends were invited into the lodge by George Little Star. Each person filed by the casket and touched the chief's forehead, his hand, and his chest. Then each one touched himself in those same places. The family and friends would use that private time to mourn before leaving for the church. Once in a while, in the still early morning, a mournful wail would escape the lips of one of the wives, but more often than not the crowd of Indians was silent.

Two hours later the Immaculate Conception Catholic Church was filled to capacity. There were people in the loft, and the aisles were standing room only. The nuns from up at the school had brought all the children down the hill for the event. The first three rows of children resembled an unruly bucket of worms as they fidgeted waiting for the funeral to begin.

Father Jack was sitting on his white marble altar chair and Fred was standing at the podium. They both watched the crowd, noticing all the dignitaries and political figures scattered among the Indians. The blanket-covered casket rested on its pall in the center aisle as Father Jack rose from his chair. The young altar boys carried the incense as Father Jack filled the aspergillum to bless the casket. Then, in the quiet of the August morning he prayed for the chief's soul to rest in peace as the majestic organ played in the background. Father Jack, clad in his white satin robes, walked to the podium. He proudly spoke of the life of Chief Ne-Kah-Wah-She-Tun-Kah, or "Big Impulse Man". "He was born January 1, 1840 and died August 3, 1923 at the age of eighty-three. He is survived by his wives and son. He served two terms as chief—from 1906 to 1908 and from 1922 to the present. He was a wise and great man. His sole aim in life was the welfare of his people. He recognized the need for change, and the need to retain the old, as well. He was a good man, a good leader of your tribe. We must allow him to go to heaven, even though he will be greatly missed. Let us pray that God will help you choose a new chief, who will protect the Osages from harm. Lord, please stop these senseless killings. Please stop the abuse the Osages have endured since the beginning of time. We ask this in Jesus' name, amen."

After the funeral Mass, the entourage of fine automobiles filed up fifteenth street to the top of the sandstone hill cemetery. The Pierce Arrows, Packards, Buicks, and Cadillacs formed an expensive-looking worm as it crawled through the streets from the church. It was like taking a journey into Osage history, as the automobiles filed past the huge monuments of other great leaders. Bigger-than-life statues of guardian angels and crucifixes stood at attention to greet the newest leader. As the crowd gathered at the grave site, they could still hear the tolling bells of the church, announcing the arrival of the chief to his final resting place. Fred had been chosen by the family to say the formal good-bye. Majestically, he stood at the foot of the grave facing the chief. He shoved a four-sided cedar stick, three feet long into the ground, and looked into the grave.

"Now, Mother Earth is open to receive back our brother." Then, as tradition would have it, as the noon sun was directly overhead, Fred spoke. "Grandfather Sun, we ask you to take our chief with you on your journey."

Standing close by, Chief Bacon Rind placed a lunchbox on the foot of the casket. It was filled with food of the feast, so that the chief would have food on the long journey to Spiritland. As Fred stepped back, Father Jack prayed in Latin for the soul of the departed Chief to be received into heaven as he waved the aspergillum, full of smoky incense, over the casket in a final blessing. Nearly every clan seemed to be represented, and as Jake looked at the faces of the Osages standing there in their wool blankets on that August day, he wondered how their faces could show so little expression of grief. Yet, he knew they were grieving in their spirits, where no one else could see or judge them. They had developed the fine art of suffering within. Jake looked around at the other faces in the crowd. There were nearly two hundred people at the grave site. Frank Phillips was standing there with Tom Fisher and Katherine Little Bear. Skelly and Sinclair were off to the side with a sizable group of oilmen. They'd come up on the morning train from Tulsa with a large group of reporters from various newspapers. The agency was closed all day and all the employees seemed to be here.

Sheriff Cook was standing by Agent Wright and a tall, white haired man that Jake recognized to be the Osage Attorney, Patrick Woodward. Another man was standing close-by. Jake didn't know him, but maybe he was from the Oklahoma crime commission. "Good," he said under his breath. "Now, maybe we'll get some answers."

Julia, Maggie, Quinn, and Jake were in a group with Leahy, Doc Lewis, and a banker or two—mostly professional men. Everyone was hot. The temperature was dangerously close to a hundred degrees in the shade. As the heat was breaking up the crowd, they filed to their big automobiles to travel to the chief's ranch for the feast.

By the time Jake's party arrived at the feast, everyone else was there. The huge racks of meat were sizzling, and the aroma was almost too much in the intense heat of the day. Father Jack and Jake found a tree to lean on. Father Jack was mopping his head with a big white handkerchief, and lamenting about the heat from his robes. "Damn. You know, Jake, this is the twelfth funeral I've had this summer up at the church— two by natural causes and ten murders."

Jake nodded. "Yeah, I know, but did you see Pat Woodward at the cemetery talking to George Wright and Sheriff Cook? I think the U.S. Attorney has sent the new guy here. I think he was there, too."

Father Jack motioned for Jake to give him a cigar. "Yeah, his name is Vaughn, I think."

"Bet ol man Woodward didn't appreciate it when George went over his head." Jake said.

Father Jack laughed.

Jake bit the tip off his cigar. "Hey, did you see Tom Fisher's date?"

Father laughed. "Yeah, that cheap sucker. Some date. Oh well. I guess a date to a funeral beats a date to the brickyard."

They both laughed.

"Well, it's all over town. I think they're a item."

Father Jack nodded. "Well, that may be, but I haven't got time to marry 'em cause I 'm too busy burying people. You know, Jake, what we both need is a stiff drink."

"I agree," Jake said as Maggie and Quinn came walking up with Miss Lydia.

"Well, how'd ya feel, Miss Maggie?" Father said.

"Fine, Father Jack. It's good to be up and around again."

Father turned his head toward Lydia. "And look who's here, looking for adventure, no doubt. It's Miss Lydia, our local driving instructor."

Lydia gave him a dirty look. "Howdy, Father Jack. Jake. Listen, I've been real good lately. But I've been lookin' for you. We need to talk. Maggie was telling me over there at the lodge about her ring and the attack and all. She said the guy's name was Henry that sold her the ring. Well, there was this seedy guy who came into the hardware store to buy some 380 auto bullets the day after the rape. He signed for them—signed it Henry—and the last name started with a S or something. I couldn't make out the last name. I'd never seen him before, but Maggie and I would both recognize him if we saw him again."

"Hum, that's interesting." Jake said. "We need to tell Sheriff Cook. Bet he'll be happy to hear that."

The topic of conversation changed as Tom Fisher walked up, and they all started razzing him. "Well, Tom. How's the oil business or would you know?"

Father Jack said. "Or are you thinking of acquiring your own Indian land to drill on?"

Tom blushed beat red. "Now, gentlemen, things are going real well for me and Miss Little Bear. Mr. Phillips told me today that I need to get married just before the big lease sale, cause he's going have the biggest reason to celebrate after it's all over. He thinks we should combine the two events. He says it's going be the biggest sale ever, and he's going get it all—goin' beat out Marland, Skelly, Sinclair, and all the rest of 'em. Frank said, if you think it was exciting' last year when he stood under the million dollar elm and bid four million bucks, you ain't seen nothing, yet."

Everyone laughed and slapped him on the back as Sheriff Cook strolled by. "Well gentlemen" he said. "The new crime commission investigator's here. He's talking to Pat Woodward, and they going to get to the bottom of all this."

"Lydia, tell Sheriff Cook about the guy that came in the store." Jake said.

Lydia related the story again. "Oh, yes. He wanted to buy some blond hairs, too."

Sheriff Cook nodded and spoke in a rather confidential tone. "Well, I think we know who he is. His name is Henry B. Smith and he's married to a real interesting person.

"Who?" Lydia cried.

The sheriff took a breath. "You'll never believe it in a million years. He's Bessie WhiteOak's son-in-law. He's Rita WhiteOak's husband. She's the alcoholic daughter who—"

"Hey, that's right," Father Jack said. "Bessie told me that Rita had gone off and married some guy after they'd only met three days before. She disowned her over it."

The sheriff went on. "That's right. They're living over by Fairfax, now. I had to locate her when I found her mother and brother both dead. That's when I happened up on Henry downtown. I'd gotten a hot tip from Claire Whitehorn about him, too. So I asked him about the ring. He said he had sold a ring to an Indian lady and her friend, but it was an honest deal. He had no idea however, how it got on his mother-in-law's hand at the time of her death. Rita was half-on and half-off the wagon then, but I guess she really went on a binge after I told her about her mother."

"Yeah, neither daughter came to the funeral." Father Jake said. "Where's the other one?"

Sheriff Cook carefully tilted his hat toward the sun. "Mollie's her name and she lives in St. Louie, married to some other no-good. I haven't located her, yet. I can't even find out her married name."

"That Henry guy definitely wasn't the man who attacked me." Maggie said in a shaky voice. Her face paled as the memory surfaced. "The guy who sold me the ring was small and mousy."

"Let's change the subject." Jake said seeing Maggie's pale face. "It's too soon for Maggie. I don't want her to dwell on it."

"I agree. Sorry Miss Maggie." He turned to leave. "Oh yes, one more thing, then I gotta go," Sheriff Cook said. "My old buddy Hale says he's upped the ante on the murder reward another twenty-five thousand, just so he can prove to me how wrong I was. Guess he wants me to eat a little more dirt. He'd better keep his nose clean. I'm watching him and his boys like a hawk. I'd sure like to know how that no-good humanitarian crook figures in all this. What's his angle. Oh well, gotta go. See you all later."

Sheriff Cook walked away, and everyone else seemed compelled to go about his own agenda. The afternoon passed pleasantly with groups of Indians huddled together, no doubt, talking Osage politics. The women were in attendance to the Chief's wives, and the Osages seemed reconciled to the unhappy fact that the old Chief was indeed gone.

Jake knew he needed to gather up Quinn and take Maggie back to the ranch. She wasn't strong enough to take a lengthy outing. He tried to find the energy to look for Quinn, but Maggie was sitting by him under the big sycamore tree, and he just kept putting off his departure.

He sat there, next to Maggie. " I keep wonderin' why did Henry Smith want the blond hair? And how did the ring get from our house to Bessie WhiteOak's hand?"

Maggie smiled and inched closer to Jake. "I wondered that, too, but who cares about the ring? At least we have each other."

Jake put his arm around her and drew her closer, nodding. She leaned back in his arms. "Isn't this a beautiful late summer day? So different to the terrible blood bath we're all experiencing. I read once, somewhere:

'The summer's sun blots out life's pain, and autumn's rain washes it away without a trace.

To take control over evil's purpose. For someday God's victory will transform this place.

Jake sighed. "How do you remember all those verses?"

She giggled. "I'm just your resident cultural expert, Jake."

"I guess," he muttered.

The hot, dry, dog days of summer had settled in for the duration in the Osage. Jake thought. The tide had changed. The chief was on his way to Spirit land, the little agency town was dripping in a blood bath, and the Osages, rich as they appeared, were still suffering. For the Osages, it was the worse persecution ever. It was worse than losing the buffalo, the game, and even the land. Now they were losing each other. Darkness continued to fall on the Little Osages because Grandfather Sun couldn't bear to watch the holocaust any longer?

CHAPTER TWENTY-SIX

Autumn is definitely in the air, Jake thought as he rode to the well site. Quinn and Bear had tagged along with him. He had taken Maggie over to Julia's for a few days of recuperation. Red had sent him a message to get his ass out to the well, pronto. The casing crew had been called. They were down about twenty-seven hundred feet, and Red had the string of tools repaired along with the baler. It would be time to shoot the well in a day or two, if things continued to look good from the samples. Even though the well was looking promising, Evans was having a heart attack at the delays.

Nevertheless, the ride was pleasant that morning. The golden rod was standing in a line along the road like a golden army. They were proud of themselves with the over-abundance of rain. The sumac was advertising autumn's reds. It was if they were personally responsible for the Osage Indian summer. The squirrels were working diligently. Their lean brown bodies were darting up and down trees in search of hickory nuts. Maybe it would be an early winter.

Quinn and Bear were on guard watching for squirrels. Bear had evidently seen a few as he had his head hanging out of the truck, canvassing the area with his razor sharp senses. He barked for all he was worth. Jake put the Dodge in low gear as he preceded to cross the creek, when the memory of that awful night with Lydia appeared in his mind. As he listened, he could hear the familiar sounds of the well across the way. Quinn broke up his thought suddenly.

"Daddy! Daddy! Let me and Bear off here at the creek. We want to look for tadpoles."

"Okay, Quinn. But it's too late for tadpoles. Now you be careful."

Quinn didn't care as he and Bear jumped out. Jake drove on and parked in the shade.

Red was coming over to the car. He resembled a sweating hog. "Lord, I'm glad you're here, Boss. The casing crew's nearly through. We're down close t' twenty-seven hundred feet. Looks like we're nearly into the sand. The soup needs to be ordered, if we're goin' to shoot it, but the Bartlesville Nitro Company is way behind on nitro deliveries. They say they can't get any up here for God knows how long. And Evans is fit to be tied. He needs to be drilling another well, and claims it's our fault. He flat told me to tell you we could both go to hell." The grease on his hair just seemed to glisten and bead up in the sunlight.

"Now simmer down, Red. Jake patted him on the shoulder, "I'll take care of Evans."

"Well, you'd better watch it. He's been drinking a lot here lately."

"Where's his partner?"

Red shook his head. "Hell, I don't know. Ain't seen him for a couple of days."

Jake narrowed his eyes. "You know, Red, Evans knows we've had a couple of emergencies come up like with Maggie and all. He just needs to calm down."

"Yeah, I know. Those two have really been rubbing me the wrong way. Course, I guess if they get a big one, they'll get over the burr up their ass."

Jake laughed. "Yeah, now all I got to do is find some soup."

"I reckon so. The casing crew's been here awhile—five of them. They're pretty good. They're the worse-lookin' crew I ever saw, but

Lord, can they screw that pipe. The stabber, Joe Thomas, did work for Tom Slick over at Drumwright. Boy, does he ever tell some wild stories."

They both laughed. Red was starting to calm down, and Jake gave him a cigar to put him in a better mood. "Let's go look at the log. Then, I'll go high-tail it to town, and see if I can come up with some soup."

They walked to the dog house, and Evans met them at the door. "Well, it's about time. I've about had it with you, Jake. I need this well completed. I need to be on another site already. In fact, I've got the mule skinners deliverin', and the rig builders workin' on another site on the next quarter right now. Now they tell me we can't get any soup. It's the damnedest business I've ever seen round here. Lefty's on my ass—just one delay after another."

Jake listened to him rant and rave. He could have cared less. "Yeah, I know it's been a tough one, Evans, but it looks pretty good to me. I bet that if you'll just keep your shirt on, I can get ya the soup. So just hold your horses."

His voice rose about an octave. "No, damn it! Don't you see? There's not one damn drop of nitro in this whole damn county, unless your name's Phillips or Marland."

Jake rubbed his day-old beard. "How about you tossin' me a little part of the well, say about an eighth, if I can get the nitro here by Friday?"

Evans thought about it long and hard in his slightly tipsy state, trying to figure the odds. "Okay! Okay! You're on! It may have to come out of my half when Lefty finds out, but it's a deal!" Jake made him go sign a paper stating their agreement, and he folded it and put in his truck. Red offered to keep Quinn so Jake started to town.

Jake knew he could find Tom Fisher and have him make a phone call and get the soup by using Phillip's big name. Jake knew the well looked real good, and he also knew that it was an even easier way to make money than drilling. It was called being in the right spot at the right time.

An hour later Jake arrived in town. It was lunch time. He parked his truck and stepped over two dogs lying on the sidewalk. The fleas were giving the dogs fits this summer, making it difficult for them to resume their nap. Jake walked into the Duncan Hotel where Tom was living. He knew he'd be eating lunch there about that time, and he could probably catch him. He asked Pricilla, the hostess, if he was there. "Yes, Mr. Knupp, but he's with a lady."

"Well, that's okay. Tell him I'll just have a glass of tea and stay for a minute." She gave him the message, and Tom waved him back to his table. "Tom, Katherine, how are you?" Jake said tipping his hat to Katherine.

"Fine. Sit down here, stranger. We were just talking about how great Maggie was lookin' at the chief's funeral."

Jake pulled out the chair. "Yeah. I'm so happy with her progress. It's great to have her back home. Quinn really missed her. Forgive me you all for interruptin' your lunch, but Tom, listen I need a favor. They won't send me any soup and I need to shoot this well at the end of this week. Can you call them in your official Phillips Petroleum voice and tell them to send it? I need a hundred quarts, and here's the money." Jake pulled out the bills and laid them on the table.

"Sure Jake, no problem. In fact, Katherine and I are going over to Bartlesville tonight to have dinner with Uncle Frank and Aunt Jane and spend the evening. So I'll stop by the nitro plant and order it and I'll tell them I've got to have the soup wagon on site, no later than Friday noon."

Jake grinned and shook his hand. "Hey! Thanks, Tom! I really appreciate it. I owe you one."

Tom grinned back. "No sweat, Jake. Glad to help."

Jake stood up. "Well, I've got to get out of here and let you two lovebirds enjoy each other."

Katherine blushed. "Tell Maggie, I'll be over to see her one day real soon."

"I will. Take it easy, you two."

Jake left the dining room and walked on up to the cafe for a bowl of stew and crackers. He sure was relieved about the soup. It sure did pay to have friends. George Wright, Pat Woodward, and a third man were eating at a table, and after seeing he was alone, invited him over. "Jake, want you to meet Bill Vaughn out of Oklahoma City." Wright said. "He's here to solve these murders, and we're mighty glad to have him."

Jake shook his hand. Vaughn had a medium build and a receding hairline. What was left of it he parted precariously down the middle. His eyes moved about like darts missing nothing. His clothes were ordinary. He wore a once-white shirt with rolled up sleeves, rumpled trousers, and cowboy boots that had seen better days. They made small talk and visited about his work.

After they'd gotten their food, George spoke. "Now Jake, this is just between you and us. I don't want it to go no further, alright?"

"Yeah sure." Jake nodded agreeably. "Go on Mr. Vaughn, tell me."

"Okay, Jake. I was just tellin' them that I want to let Blackie Thompson out of the pen on the condition he starts ratting on the crooks around here. He's the best snitch we got round these part, and his mouth's just droolin' for early parole. I especially want to know who's the mastermind behind these murders."

"Well, it's got to be somebody with some real smarts," George said. "But I just can't come up yet, with a common link. I've even given a little thought to our number one citizen."

Jake swallowed his spoonful of stew. "Who's that?"

George looked to his right and left and whispered in a barely audible voice. "Ol' Bill Hale. Why is he so interested in a reward? He hates Indians. This conversation had better not leave this table. If it does, I'll swear it's a lie." Sweat was beading up on George's head.

"You're not the only one that is suspicious of Hale's motives, George. The sheriff and I both have been givin' it some thought." Jake's words escaped out of the side of his mouth.

Pat Woodward was sipping his ice tea slowly and not saying too much. Jake wondered what he was thinking. Woodward was hard to read. He prided himself in being non-committal. *I don't trust this guy as far as I can throw him. This guy knows somethin'.*

Vaughn broke Jake's thought pattern in mid-stream. "Mr. Woodward, I need to come up to the agency and your office and start through the records."

Jake thought that Pat Woodward didn't seem overly pleased about the idea, but it was only a little shift in his body that was noticeable.

George answered for him. "That'll be fine, Mr. Vaughn. Our door is open to you at your convenience. If this works, when will Blackie be out on the streets?"

Vaughn took a drink of his tea. 'In a couple of weeks."

Jake looked Vaughn straight in the eye. "Not to change the subject. Seen anyone with a big ugly scar on his neck? That's who I'm looking for. Sheriff Cook's looking for him, too. I guess he's not through with that weasel Henry Smith yet."

The men were both non-committal. They ate their lunch and Jake mostly listened while they went over the murders. Jake had forgotten the buried Indian that Father Jack had reported. He had been identified as Ed Tall Corn. It had turned out that he was a cousin of Katherine Little Bear's, which was news to Jake. He was a recluse who lived out by John Stink. Stink was the one who had reported him missing. He was one of John's drinking buddies. He helped him feed that pack of mongrel dogs. Ed was well educated back east, but no one knew it. He had kept it a big secret. Ed never cared about doing anything—not even taking a wife. So, why in the world, would someone kill him? It hadn't made sense to any of the men. The conversation wound down, and everyone paid their checks and hurried on their way.

After he left the café, Jake dropped by Bill Grammer's place. He thought he'd pick up a couple of half-pints from the bootlegger for

Evans and Red as a peace offering. ""Bill, I need a couple of half-pints of Wild Turkey."

"Okay, Jake. Hear the well's got some hitches."

"Yeah, we can't get any soup. Too much demand and not enough supply, I reckon. How'd you know?" Jake asked.

"Oh, Lefty Kirk was in last night. I told him I could fix him up with a couple of quarts, but he said he needed a hundred."

Jake snickered. "I didn't know you kept any soup, Bill, or is that just what you call the real hard stuff?" They both laughed as the bootlegger dusted off the bottle. "How's business, anyway?"

"Pretty good, with all these murders. Damn Indians are drinking themselves silly."

"Got any suspicions about whose doin' the killin'?"

Bill was busy sacking up the whiskey. "No tellin', but I keep my eyes open here and up at the ropin' arena."

Jake smiled. "Yeah. You doing any ropin'?"

"Oh, a little, I reckon," Grammer replied. "Gotta keep in shape, you know."

"Yeah. I guess you still have to go out and show the young punks how a world champ does it."

He laughed. "Yeah, I reckon."

Conversation slowed down as a man entered the building. Jake didn't pay much attention to him as he was just hanging around until he walked up to Grammer. Grammer seemed to know him. Jake was ready to leave when he heard him ask Grammer if he knew where he could buy some blond hairs. Jake stopped dead in tracks. Somehow, he made it out to his car, and waited for him to come out. A couple of minutes later, he came out of the building. Sure enough, he had beady eyes, a small frame and hawk nose. It had to be Henry Smith.

"Well, Henry, how's it going?" Jake asked. "I hear you're lookin' to buy some blond hairs."

Henry looked at Jake and walked to about ten feet of him. "Yes, sir, I would. Do you know where I can get any?"

Jake lit up a cigar. "Maybe. Say, I heard you bought a gun the other day—a 380 automatic."

Henry shifted his beady eyes to the ground. "Yeah, so?"

"Well, I was looking for one to buy. Would you want to sell it?"

Henry took a deep breath. "No, sir. I need a gun with all these killings going on round here."

"Yes, but Mr. Smith, they seem to be killin' just Indians."

Henry looked around. "Well, I have an Indian wife of sorts. She's a big customer of Mr. Grammer's intoxicating beverages."

Jake nonchalantly puffed away on his cigar. "Oh yeah! You're married to Bessie WhiteOaks' daughter Rita, aren't ya? Say, where's her other daughter, Mollie? I heard she wasn't at the funeral."

Henry fidgeted with the ring on his pinky finger, turning it around and around. "I haven't made her acquaintance." He cleared his throat nervously. "You see, my wife and I have only been married a short time—. Well—I—believe her sister lives in St. Louis. I have to go now. Nice to make your acquaintance, sir."

Henry started to leave, but Jake refused to give up. "Who's she married to?"

Henry focused his eyes on something invisible about three feet away from Jake, missing his eyes. "I'm not sure, sir. She was here not to long ago to see her mother, but I didn't see her." He took a deep breath and spoke slowly. "And who might you be, sir?"

Jake stopped leaning on the car fender and he stopped chewing on his four day old toothpick. He stood straight and looked Henry right in the eye. "I'm Jake Knupp—Maggie Lookout's my wife and you're the guy who sold her the ring."

Henry started backing up like Jake was going to hit him. "It was an honest deal, Mr. Knupp. I gotta go." He quickly ducked around the corner and down the alley.

Jake walked back into the bootlegger's building. "Hey Grammer, you know that guy?"

"Yeah Jake, his wife's Rita WhiteOaks—a pretty good customer. She drinks a jug of my best a week. He don't mean no harm. Ol' Henry's just a little shrimpy weasel kind of a guy."

Jake nodded. "Say Bill, what happened to Rita's sister, Mollie?"

"She's in St. Louis, I think. She came in a few weeks ago and bought some of my good stuff."

Jake nodded. "Oh yeah! Who's she married to?"

"Why, your boss's partner, Jake."

"Who?" Jake looked astonished as Grammer handed him the sack he'd left there earlier. "You know, Kirk. Lefty Kirk."

Jake couldn't believe his ears. "Why—did—I—I have the idea he was new in town?"

"Well, he is kinda. She met him in St. Louis, I think. He's got a little money, I figure, or else she's got plenty for both of them."

Jake thanked him and he hastily made his departure. As he drove back to the well, he couldn't believe the day's good fortune with all his choice tidbits of news. He drove the old Dodge by rote deep in thought while he considered his new puzzle pieces.

It was a perfect evening for a drive. There was just a hint of rain in the air under the party cloudy sky. Grandfather Sun was doing some acrobatic tricks through the clouds for entertainment. Tom Fisher and Katherine were enjoying the sunset as they motored to Bartlesville in her father's Pierce Arrow. They had been invited to dine with Mr. and Mrs. Frank Phillips at seven o'clock. "Now, tell me about Aunt Jane before we get there, Tom," Katherine said nervously.

"Oh, you'll like her. She loves the piano and card games. She's real social, but she's used to Frank's wildcattin' stories and the smoke from his big ol' expensive cigars. You know, he has a girlfriend in New York. Fern. She's quite a gal, but I guess Aunt Jane either doesn't know or doesn't care."

Katherine was so overcome by surprise that she was speechless. "What! Who! I—I'm horrified," she finally said. "I can't imagine—She has everything and yet—nothing." She became lost in thought. *These rich oil folk were certainly different.*

The trip took over an hour, but true to his word, Tom stopped at the Bartlesville Nitro Company at the edge of town and ordered the nitro.

"No problem, Mr. Fisher. You tell, Mr. Phillips we'll have the soup wagon there by Friday." The order clerk happily replied. Tom thanked him, gave him the lease location, and left.

Tom and Katherine motored on into town to Cherokee Street, right off of Seventh Street, several blocks from the boom town's main street. Tom parked the car out front of the Phillips' city home, and he and Katherine walked to the front door. The Japanese butler and valet, Dan Mitani, greeted them at the door. He was a small but gracious oriental man. He grinned at them with a set of oversized white teeth. "Come in, ma'am, Mr. Fisher, let me take your hats and coats."

"Thanks, Dan."

He led them to the big luxurious parlor where Frank was standing next to the large mantled fireplace. He was dressed in his red silk smoking jacket, and the smoke rings from his cigar were circling his head. "Welcome Tom! Katherine! Come in, my dear, and meet Aunt Jane."

Katherine and Aunt Jane liked each other instantly. Aunt Jane was dressed in a long pink gown adorned at the sleeves with matching pink feathers. She graciously took Katherine's hand and led her to the chic floral settee. "Well, my dear. How to you do? I hear you're a Vanderbilt girl."

Katherine smiled and nodded. "Yes, Mrs. Phillips."

"Well, my, my! It's been a long time in this god-forsaken town since I've had the chance to talk to someone with a little class. I usually have to go to New York to do that. Come dear. " She patted the cushion next to her. "Sit by me and tell me all about yourself."

Before long, Tom and Frank were lost in oil business talk and the new prospective drilling sites. "I'm sure happy with your work over in the Osage, Tom. We're going to do big things—or bigger things, I should say. You know in twenty-one, just two short years ago, Oklahoma produced twenty million barrels of oil, and this year's going to be the greatest ever. We are going to be the biggest single operator in Burbank—one hundred and twenty-five thousand barrels a day."

Tom nodded enthusiastically. "I know, it's great Uncle Frank. I love every minute of it."

Uncle Frank puffed on his expensive cigar. "You know, Tom, I'm so proud of all my employees, I'm even going start a group-plan to cover each one of my employees with life insurance. Son—it is alright if I call you, son, isn't it?" Tom laughed as Frank went on ahead. "With your help, we're going to be the biggest supplier of natural gasoline in the nation."

Some thirty minutes later, Dan Mitani announced that dinner was served. They were ushered into the dining room lavished with silver, hand-cut lead crystal, and fine European china. An epergne of fresh autumn flowers and ecru candles served graciously as a masterful centerpiece. Soft, peach-upholstered chairs lined a table, that comfortably could sit twelve or more guests. The black maid and butler served the formal dinner. One tasteful course after another followed. Frank even brought up in the conversation about their first date to the Pawhuska brickyard on his official errand of company business.

Katherine spoke in her most demure voice. "Oh, Mr. Phillips, it was so terrible seeing the Indian's swinging moccasins grazing my head, and to think that will always be my memory of our first date. I was frightened to death."

They all laughed. Frank liked her. She was very witty.

"Have they found the culprit, Tom?" Frank asked.

"No. Nor any of the culprits for the last twenty-five murders in Osage County. The U.S. Attorney General is in on it now, along with the FBI

Special Investigator. They're calling it the 'Osage Reign of Terror' in the newspapers."

Frank nodded. "Yeah, I've been reading about it. Even the New York times had an article. And what's this I hear about you being in the middle of a bank robbery?"

Tom blushed. "Well, if anybody wants an identification made on Al Spencer, I'm the guy who can do it. Course, I was shaking so hard, my vision might have been blurred."

Frank doubled over laughing causing the dishes to rattle. "Well, son, just do me a favor. Just stay out of my banks over here. I don't want Al Spencer following you. I can just see it all, now." They all joined in the laughter.

After dinner, they moved back into the parlor for after-dinner coffee and brandy. They all enjoyed their contented state and relaxed. Frank was intent on lighting his fine cigar. The smoke spirals rose toward the tall ornate ceiling. Suddenly Frank looked over his spectacles. "Now son—just—when are you two getting married?"

Tom and Katherine nearly fell out of their chairs. "Gosh, Frank," Tom exclaimed. "We haven't even talked about it."

Frank winked at Katherine. "Well, Tom, you'd better hurry up. Things move fast in the Osage. How about if I give you a bachelor party? We can get Ruby Darby to ah—er—to entertain us." They both laughed. Frank laughed because it was funny and Tom laughed because he was a nervous wreck. Frank eagerly continued on. "No use wasting time. You love her, don't you?"

"Frank, that's quite enough." Aunt Jane interrupted with a definite tone to her voice. "You're embarrassing them."

They all put every effort into changing the subject and it seemed to work. "You know. I've been thinking." Frank said off on a different vain. "I've got about thirty-six hundred acres out near lease one eighty-five. I'm going to put a big lodge out there, Tom. It's full of lakes, woods, and rocks. When I get it done, we'll have us a real party—invite the Osages, the outlaws, and everybody, even Ruby. Well, what do you think, son?"

"Sounds great, Frank." Tom smiled while he wondered what on earth Frank would do next.

They announced their departure soon after. Aunt Jane hugged Katherine, while Frank took Tom aside for a moment and slipped him a sack. "Here's a little something romantic, Tom. It's a bottle of my finest. There's two glasses, too. Now, go propose to that girl. Tell her you love 'er and sing a few bars of let's see, how about 'Let me Call You Sweetheart'. They all love that. Now hurry up. So you can get your mind back on oil."

Frank concentrated on his cigar intently and never bothered to notice that Tom was aghast. He just wheeled him to the front porch where they rejoined the ladies. "Nice automobile, Fisher. Must be paying you too much." Tom laughed.

"It belonged to Katherine's father. Thanks again, Mrs. Phillips. Frank." They both said their good-byes and hurried away to the Pierce.

They had a lot to think about as they eased out into the light traffic. It had been a delightful evening. "I told you that Jane and you would hit it off." Tom said with a twinkle in his eye.

"Yes," Katherine replied. "But you forgot to warn me about Uncle Frank. He's a real mess."

They both laughed. "You're right. There's not much tellin' what'll he do next. Never a dull moment. I've always liked that about Frank till he decided to concentrate on my love-life."

As they sped back to Pawhuska, there appeared to be a barrier in the road about five miles inside the Osage County line. The guy stopping traffic filled them in on what was happening. "Sorry to bother you and the lady, sir. Been a bad wreck up ahead. Joe Jones, a Paw-huskee taxi driver, was asked by a bunch of them wild Osages to drive 'em to B'ville in their ol' big tourin' car to get 'em some whiskey. " He hesitated just long enough to shift his chewing tobacco and spit a spray of juice along side the car. "They was already pretty well tanked up and ol' Joe must'a really had his hands full with them in the back seat. Just before they started down the hill here, one of them Osages hollered, 'Wanna see what it's like to be an Indian?' They let out a god-forsaken war whoop and them Indians threw their blankets plum over Joe's head. Couldn't see a thing. Ol' Joe lost control and the car went over the cliff. It rolled four or five times. Ain't nobody hurt too bad, 'cept maybe the Pierce." The man's spiel ended as abruptly as it had begun. He tipped his hat and began encouraging traffic along.

Katherine laughed. "Okay, is this another one of your entertainment ideas to spice up our dates?"

Tom laughed. "I aim to please, madam."

They continued to laugh and enjoy each other's company with the Osage's Lady Moon casting a happy glow on them both. At last they drove up to the Little Bear Ranch about a mile out of town. He stopped the car just in sight of the house. "Let's get out for a moment, shall we? The moon is so beautiful." He lifted her up on the big car's fender. "Wait just a minute." He went to the car trunk and brought out the two wine glasses and the still cool bottle of champagne. "Frank gave this to me. It would have been colder, but we had to stop to get the news of the Indians' joy ride". He uncorked the bottle and poured a glass and handed it to her. After filling his own, he toasted. "Here's to oil, the Osages, and you, Katherine, my new wife-to-be." As the glasses clinked in the moonlight, he could see that she was really pleased, and his heart swelled with pride.

"Oh, Tom! How wonderful," she whispered as she put her hand up to his face, out-lining it with her fingers. She was so beautiful. Her dark hair and her dewy pansy-like eyes made him simply gasp for breath.

"I got this for you awhile back, but tonight I want to give it to you, if you'll promise to marry me." He handed her a small green box. She giggled as she opened it. It was a beautiful diamond solitaire mounted in gold. "It's not the biggest diamond ring yet, but one day I'll get you one that will compare with your beauty."

She looked at him as one tiny tear escaped her soulful eyes. "Oh Tom! It's beautiful! I love you. I do love you. Yes, I'll marry you." She hesitated.

"But promise me you won't come up with any extraordinary ideas for our wedding to shock me."

They both laughed and hugged each other in the magic of the special moment.

"Okay! Okay! I promise! Well, let's get married in March just before the big lease sale. What do you think? That'll give you time to plan the Osage wedding and Father Jack's ceremony, too."

"Oh, that would be lovely, Tom." She wrapped her arms around his neck as he bent his head to kiss her. It was a perfect autumn night. The girl he loved from the first moment he'd seen her had promised to be his wife. Thank goodness, God's path had brought him to the Osage, where that sensitive, beautiful woman had been waiting for him.

CHAPTER TWENTY-SEVEN

Jake was up waiting for the dawn Friday morning. It was the day they needed to shoot the well, and they needed nitro badly. Yesterday they'd drilled into the sand about sixty feet with a good show of gas and nearly a thousand feet of oil. The lease had real promise. Word was that Marland's pool at Burbank would bring in about thirty-one million barrels of crude this year, about nineteen percent of the state's intake. Rumor had it that Marland's big boy oil company was everywhere. Consequently, there was a shortage of everything—lumber, pipe, and cement, not to mention nitro. There were cot houses everywhere. These were the wildest times Jake had ever seen, and they were getting wilder by the day. Tulsa Rig and Reel Lumber Yard at Barnsdall was working round the clock. The trains unloaded the supplies just anywhere in the fields.

"Hey Boss."

Jake's deep thoughts were broken.

"When this well comes in, Evans wants to take us up to Burbank to see Ruby Darby."

"Oh yeah," Jake answered rather absent mindedly.

"I ain't seen her, but once, and I want to again real bad. " Red continued on. "They say she drove into Pawhuska on her way to Burbank. She got caught speedin' in that fancy car down on Main Street, and just like usual with nothing on under that expensive fur coat but a smile."

Jake laughed as he searched for a straw weed to chew on. "Yeah. That'll be great. Say, Red, there's a brand new whorehouse opened up, too. That makes four now, and two a day settin' up shop in Burbank." They both laughed.

"Hey Boss, is that little tidbit for my needs or my information?"

The hours dragged by slowly until It was finally late afternoon. Jake was still waiting for the soup. Evans was just coming out of the dog house as Bear started barking. Quinn was hot on his trail as they headed in Jake's direction. Jake scooped him up in mid-stride. "Hold on partner. It may be the soup wagon that Bear hears. So, you need to stay right here by me."

Sure enough, moving one mile an hour, the soup wagon came through the creek. "Hot dog, Red! I owe that Tom a big one!" Jake cried.

Red nodded. "God, I hope he's got extra paddin' on that stuff. Now'd be a heck of a time for her to blow. I can still hear those stories from over at Barnsdall when that nitro truck blew. There ain't enough whiskey in the world to get me to drive that wagon."

Jake made an ugly face and laughed. "You mean you wouldn't jump at the chance to do his job for eighty dollars a month plus all the whiskey you could secretly drink?"

Red didn't even grace his remark with an answer.

They all held their breath as the wagon pulled to a stop. The poor driver got down, and tied the horses. His whole body was in a wash of sweat and the water was dripping off his face like he'd just come out of a downpour. "Get him a drink, Red." Jake yelled, as they prepared the well for its dose of the hard stuff.

The shooter had brought an even hundred quarts in square copper cans, each holding ten quarts. Each can was nestled in individual rubber compartments in the wagon. The shooter's name was Blackie Hampton. Jake always insisted on getting their names, in case, he'd have to notify the next of kin. Blackie was really amusing in a bazaar kind of way. He was dressed in dark pants and a once fancy white long sleeve shirt with a black vest. He wore a black felt hat with an inch wide brim. The poor devil looked like he was trying his best to be dressed properly to die at any moment.

On the platform, Red slipped the 'go-devil' over the wire line while the shooter got all the canisters out of the wagon. Laboriously, he started to pour them in, one by one. Everyone was holding his breath as the liquid went into the sleeve. It resembled a stove pipe with a pointed bottom. The bottom had a hook on it, and a bale at the top. The cans were all hooked together in a string, and as each one was partially lowered in the well, the next can was filled, and the next can, lowering the whole string and on and on till they were all filled.

When the last can was full, the percussion explosive device was put in the top. The cans were lowered with a wire line by the use of a hand winch, called a shooters reel. It took about a half an hour to get the canisters slowly emptied, one at a time. He added pea gravel for a couple of hundred feet above the shot. It had to be packed good, so the force would go out to the sides, down, and up at an angle. They wanted the hole to be biggest at the bottom. The bigger the hole, the more oil they'd recover.

It was nearly dusk. The air was hazy, but it was beginning to cool down. Everything was dirty. The men were filthy, and so were Quinn and Bear. They were all thinking how good it would be to go home and soak in a tub of hot water. Despite the long, drawn out drilling ordeal, the time had finally come. Excitement was in the air. Evans and Lefty were drinking coffee and pacing while they anxiously awaiting the well's verdict. Quinn and Bear were excited. They'd never seen a well come in. Adding to the confusion, he and Bear were wrestling each other under the men's feet. Bear was playfully growling as he pulled Quinn along by his shirt-tail.

Red seemed to be particularly anxious, but then he just wanted to see Ruby Darby. "Jake, can't you just taste Nellie's chocolate cake? And beer, and steak, and mashed potatoes, and gravy, and biscuits?"

Jake laughed. "Yeah, and I'm glad to hear you'd rather go fill your gut than go see Ruby Darby."

Red feigned indignation. "Oh, yeah, like hell, Jake. Course, it'll take me a whole week to get cleaned up and presentable."

From the floor of the well the shooter motioned it was time. "Hey Red. Blackie's ready. Everyone! Get your fat asses under somethin'!"

Everyone took cover up-wind from the well. Blackie looked around to see if everyone was clear of the derrick. Then he turned the "go-devil" loose to slide down the wire as he baled off the derrick floor to find cover himself. The impact of the go'devil hitting the firing device would get action. "Hold your ears, Quinn!" Jake hollered as he held a death's grip on the boy and the dog. "Goin' be a big noise! Get ready!"

Each crashing nitro boom Jake had ever heard seemed louder than the last. In the middle of the woods, it sounded like the top was blowing off the earth as the ground tremored, growled, and wretched up from its dregs. Everyone and everything was still deaf from the blast.

"Here's she comes!" Evans yelled as an explosive show of violence thundered forth.

The magnificent fountain of oil spewed forth, followed by a flamboyant parade of gravel, rocks, and more oil. It blew straight up in the air, at least twenty-five feet above the derrick. They were instantly covered with oil and dirt. It was all over them—sticky, gummy, and black—that colossal magnificent scum that could only spell one thing—money! They started dancing around, yelling and screaming and slapping each other on the backs. They looked like a happy bunch of school kids playing ring around the rosy. Instantly, everyone had whiskey bottles tipped up and were passing them around. Bear looked like a giant chocolate-covered grizzly bear. All Jake could see of Quinn's face was two big brown eyes glistening in his oil-covered face. The ground was so slick it was impossible to walk. The tools were so oily they couldn't pick them up. Even the shooter was happy. Of course, he was just happy to still be alive.

Evans and Kirk were delirious. Jake motioned to Red. "Come on! Fun's over. We need to get this baby capped and stop the flow. We need the oil in the tanks, not on the ground."

The capping procedure took them the better part of a couple hours. Quinn was under his favorite tree just about to fall asleep by the time they finished it up. Evans and Lefty had barricaded themselves in the dog house doing some serious drinking. "Well, looks like we got 'er put to bed, Red," Jake said to the black oily man next to him.

"Hell yes, I reckon we did." Red nodded. "Boy, that's the biggest gusher I've ever seen, or tasted." He laughed as he licked his black lips again.

Jake wiped his mouth off on his already black sleeve. "Me, too. I figure this is right on the edge of the big Burbank pool. Phillips and Marland's in the middle. I can't imagine how Evan's managed to steal this lease."

Red laughed. "No tellin', but he's hit 'er big this time."

"I reckon." Jake agreed. "And I didn't do too bad, either. You know, I talked 'em out of an eighth. Wonder when Lefty's going get that bit of news?"

Red coughed and spit his coffee on the ground. "You did what?"

Jake laughed and slapped him on his wet slick back. "I talked Evans out of an eighth when I bet him I could find the nitro."

Instantly, Red looked worried. "Oh, Lordy, Jake. There's going to be trouble over that—liable to be a killin.'"

Jake slapped him on the back again. "Naw, I doubt it. Lighten up, Red. Hell, I had it coming for just puttin' up with the son of a bitch."

Red and Jake walked over to Quinn's tree and stretched out on the ground. Jake was as exhausted as he looked. But at least it wouldn't be long till he and Quinn could go home and see Maggie—and Ruby Darby, as Red put it.

About a half hour went by and Jake was just about asleep. Red was snoring out loud, and Quinn was sprawled out on Bear's neck. Jake was just half-in and half-out of his conscious state when he heard loud arguing from the dog house. A gun shot ripped through the night. Red and Jake jumped straight up and headed in the direction of the ruckus. When they ran to the door, they stopped short. Evans lay on the floor with a bullet hole in the shoulder. Lefty was standing there with the gun in his hand. As they ran in, Lefty instantly turned the pistol on them. "Now look here, you low life oil bums. I gave Evans what he had comin', the no-good bastard." He waved the gun around toward Jake and his drunken oil-covered face was ablaze with fury. "So he gave you, Mr. Hot Shot driller, an eighth of my oil well, did he? I don't think so. Now I've got his half, and I'm fixing to reclaim your eighth."

At that instant, Quinn burst in the door. "Daddy! Daddy! I heard a gun go off!"

"Get Quinn out of here, Red," Jake screamed. Jake took that split second to kick the gun out of Lefty's hand. The gun went off as Jake landed a left hook and hit Lefty in the jaw. Jake heard a piercing scream from behind him. It was Quinn. The bullet had struck him in the leg somehow. Quinn screamed. Then he lay silently, unconscious.

The fight now became more fierce. The two men landed blows to each other's heads as they stumbled over Evan's body. Kirk crashed into the table and roared back at Jake from across the room. They exchanged punches as he pulled a knife from his boot. Red decided then that the fight was less than fair. He jumped him from behind, and together they wrestled Lefty to the floor trying to get the knife away. Lefty's clothes were so slick, he got away from Jake.

Lefty was like a wild man as he lurched forward, but Jake dodged at the last second. As Lefty lunged, he tripped over Evan's foot and fell to the floor, dropping the knife. Lefty landed face down as Red hit him from behind with a frying pan full of day-old fried greasy potatoes. Lefty stopped moving. Jake grabbed his hair in one hand and his shirt collar with the other to tie him up before he came to. Lefty's shirt tore away from his body. Jake stared in absolute horror.

There it was—a hideous, ugly, raised scar from his ear to his shoulder. "My God! It's the son of a bitch who raped Maggie! Red, tie him up before I kill him!".

The only thing that saved Lefty Kirk's life was that Jake had to get Quinn to the doctor. He picked the boy up in his arms. His little black oil-covered body was now paling as the blood washed the oil away. *Oh, God, not Quinn! What else can happen?* Jake picked him up and ran out into the night looking for the truck. "Red," Jake yelled. "I'll send the sheriff. Tie him up good! Bear, you stand guard!"

Jake's sense of direction in the dark proved to be accurate as he opened the truck door and laid Quinn in the seat. He tore apart everything in the truck looking for anything clean to wrap his leg. There was nothing. Everything was soaked with oil. Finally he pulled a filthy rag out from underneath the seat, and tied the tourniquet around Quinn's little thigh.

Jake headed for town again. He wondered if the nightmares would ever end? Finally, after what seemed to be hours, they arrived at Doc's just as Ruby was serving him supper. Jake yelled from the back door into the kitchen. "Ruby, let me in! Quinn's been shot!"

"Oh, my God!" she screamed, nearly knocking over the dinner table.

Doc jumped up. "In here, quick!"

Jake followed him down the familiar narrow hall. "Doc, Evans is still out at the well. Can you send Doc Walker out there? He's hit in the shoulder."

Doc walked to the phone and spoke briefly to the other doctor. "He says he's got someone he can send out there to pick him up, and then he'll meet him at his office. Here, Jake! Give him the location." Jake grabbed the phone and gave the other doctor the information.

Doc Lewis examined Quinn's wound. "I'll have to operate! Prepare the room! Ride, Jake! Go get Maggie!" He screamed orders to everyone.

Jake took off without another word. He drove the old Dodge for all it was worth downtown past the church toward the ranch.

Several miles later, Jake finally saw the ranch house. He parked the truck in front of the gate and ran up the steps two at a time through the front door yelling. "Maggie! Maggie!" She was in the kitchen with Fred and Julia.

"What's wrong? It's not Quinn, is it? Tell me! It's not Quinn—"

Jake grabbed her shoulders and shook her. "Maggie! Listen! I found the guy who raped you. And he shot Quinn in the leg. He's at the Doc's. Hurry!"

"We'll be in right behind you, Fred cried. "Go on!" The four frantic people were going in ten different circles at once.

Jake nodded as he and Maggie headed for the door. "Fred, go get Sheriff Cook! Hurry! Tell him to get out to the well. Evan's shot, and Red's holding Lefty Kirk at gun point."

For a moment Maggie looked like she was going to faint. She paled to a ghostly white, but she bit her lip, and with tears running down her face, hurried to the truck with Jake. The dirt road to town was usually short, but that night it was a million miles long. Maggie huddled as close as she could get to Jake as she prayed one Ave Maria after another for their only child. Maggie knew in her heart that It was quite possible that Grandfather Sun would have to personally talk to Wah'-Kon-Tah to keep Jake from killing Lefty Kirk.

Chapter Twenty-eight

The wee hours of the morning were really a blur. Maggie and Jake had sat by Quinn's bed for several hours after his operation. He was still unconscious from the effects of the pain killers that Doc had given him. Julia was sitting on the other side of the bed. Quinn looked so pale with a huge bandage wrapping his leg. Maggie sat still as a mouse, holding Quinn's tiny hand and crying softly. The sight of seeing Quinn covered with oil and blood had nearly caused his mother to faint. Jake guessed Quinn wouldn't be going to any more oil well sites for awhile.

At about a quarter of five, Quinn's condition reached the critical stage. His blood pressure dipped and his body got cold to the touch. His heart beat was not stable. Father Jack had been called to come and pray for him and to give him the Last Rites of the church, just in case.

Soon after six, Father Jack arrived flying down the hall. He didn't even take time to ask what had happened. He prayed over Quinn and blessed him as they just sat huddled around him and waited.

It was dawn and the sun's first light was barely visible. First, one tiny eye opened, then, the other. Maggie looked up. "Quinn! Quinn! It's your mother, honey! You're going to be alright!" Jake looked around the room. He could feel the tension, escaping from the burdened bodies as everyone sighed.

"Mama! Mama! I was so cold! I felt like I was in a deep, dark hole. I couldn't get out." His eyes got bigger and bigger as he relived his dream. "Then, I saw Jesus, and he had my white wolf with him. I was so glad to see the wolf. Jesus told the wolf to lay on top of me to keep me warm, and I could feel myself get warmer and warmer. Then, I opened my eyes and there you were. Daddy! Daddy! My leg hurts!"

Jake reached over and brushed the hair from his forehead and hugged him. "It's okay, Quinn. You'll be fine. It'll be better. Just lay quiet."

With a sigh of relief, Father Jack and Jake walked out of the room. Doc and the women would take care of Quinn. The crisis was over. Father and he walked out onto the porch. "Wow! That was a close one! So, what the hell's going on, Jake?"

Jake filled him in quickly without too many details. "I can't believe Mollie WhiteOaks' husband is Al Evan's partner, but I'm horrified that he's the guy who raped Maggie."

"You and me, both. I 'bout died when I saw that scar. I can't believe I didn't kill him, Father." Jake lighted his cigar and passed one to Father Jack. Jake inhaled as he tried to relax. "Sheriff Cook had better take care of him."

Father looked pensively. "So now, it's becoming clearer that Lefty Kirk and Henry Smith were more than brothers-in-law—in cahoots as well."

"Yeah, and the ring ending up on Bessie WhiteOaks cinches it. I figure that they were both in on it. But how, exactly, I don't know."

Father Jack rubbed the back of his neck thoughtfully, "What do you think of this new investigator, Jake?"

"Who? Vaughn?" The priest nodded. "I like him, but I bet Pat Woodward isn't going to be too cooperative."

Father flicked the ashes from his cigar into the flower bed. "What's his deal anyway, Jake?"

Jake puffed hard on his cigar. " Hell, I don't know. Maybe he knows some stuff. You know he has access to a lot of guardian information and all the personal documents of the Osages. Hell, he's a guardian himself for several Osages."

Father rubbed his chin. "Well maybe he's being greedy—wantin' a little extra money."

"Could be. Well, someone's masterminded this murder scheme. I wouldn't be surprised if Woodward wasn't in on it."

Sheriff Cook arrived at Doc's about a half-hour later. The sun was up and the October day was brisk. Ruby had brought them each a cup of coffee while they talked on the porch. "Howdy Jake. Father Jack." He tied his horse to the rail.

"Come on up and join us, Sheriff," Father yelled.

"Well, we got Evans up to Doc Walkers. He's going to live, I reckon. We arrested Kirk and have him up at the jail. But, he's going to be out on bond by late this afternoon. Attemptin' to kill don't warrant you too long a stay in the Osage County boardin' house. Course you know he's denied the whole damn rape thing, too. We need Maggie to come identify him."

Jake looked at him eye to eye. The pent up tension was taking it's toll. Jake's voice was angry. "Listen, Sheriff, you'd better keep him in jail or I'll kill the no-good s-o-b. I've had it. How many more members of my family do you think he's goin' hurt before I kill him deader than a door nail?"

Sheriff Cook looked Jake back, eye to eye. The big man seemed to grow even taller. He was striving for patience. "Now, Jake, you can't take the law in your hands, too."

Jake laughed sarcastically. "Why not? Hell, everybody else does."

"Now look here, Jake. I have real confidence in this investigator, Vaughn," the sheriff said trying to change the subject.

"Well, we'll see! What about Pat Woodward?" Father Jack asked. "He doesn't act too thrilled about Vaughn being here, snoopin' in his files. I wonder just how good a care ol' Pat really takes of the Indians. Affairs that no one knows about. Me and Jake don't trust him."

The sheriff chose to ignore the remark as he turned to leave the porch.

"Well, I just came by to see how your son was, Jake."

"The crisis passed about an hour ago," Jake answered in a somewhat cooler tone of voice. "Doc says he's out of the woods."

Sheriff looked relieved. "Good, glad to hear it. Well, I've got to get back to work. Saw you out here and thought I stop and give you an update. No offense, Jake." The lawman stepped off the porch to leave, and then as if by a second thought, he wheeled around. "Lefty said you started the fight, Jake. Cause Evans gave you an eighth of the well. Is that right?"

Jake smiled for the first time. "Yeah, he did. Tough luck, but I've got the note he signed to prove it. You think I care after what Kirk did to Maggie?"

The sheriff shook his head. "No, I reckon not."

"Can you get Lefty to tell you how to get in touch with his wife, Mollie?" Father Jack asked. "I'd sure like to find out how Bessie got the ring. Mollie'll tell me if she knows."

The sheriff mounted up. "Sure. I'll see what I can find out. Oh, by the way, guess the federal boys got their man. They killed old Al Spencer 'bout a week ago. They found him up near the Washington-Osage county line. He was running down the road. He fired one shot at the posse in pursuit and fell dead. Had ten grand in liberty bonds on him. I guess they'd been staking him out in the woods for awhile. He was nearly starved, down to a hundred and fifteen pounds. They had him laid out over in Bartlesville and witnesses clear from Arkansas and all over Oklahoma came to identify him. Even the bank tellers over at the Citizens National identified him as the one who killed your buddy, Clyde Baker. Mrs. Spencer let nearly fifteen thousand people view the corpse before she shut 'er down."

Jake took great pains stubbing out his cigar. "Well, it's nice to see the feds can catch some murderers, isn't it?"

"I'm just givin' you your news update, Jake. I'll see you all later."

Father Jack stood up. "I gotta go too, Jake. I'm just glad I don't have to bury the scoundrel. There's at least some good news." Father Jack laughed. "Glad Quinn's out of the woods, Jake." He looked up at the heavens, folded his hands. "Thank you, Jesus, for the white wolf!"

Jake laughed. "Yeah, you know, Father Jack, that reminds me. I had that vision in the peyote church about the white and black wolves. And then when Quinn was lost that day in the ravine, it was the white wolf that paid him the visit."

Father Jack's jaw dropped open. "Lord, Jake, maybe the Lord does give messages through that peyote stuff." He thought for a moment then he shook his head. "Naw, I doubt it. What can I be thinking?" He wandered off Doc's porch in the direction of his buggy.

Life in Pawhuska crawled by slowly and uneventfully. Autumn was deep in its last throes, and Osage Indian summer was giving its last curtain call. The early mornings were even crisp. There was an energy in the air. Winter was not far away or so the old timers were predicting.

Father Jack was up at dawn as usual. He went over to the church, as was his daily routine to unlock the mammoth front doors. He set up everything for seven o'clock Mass. He found the Bible readings for that day, filled the cruets with wine and water, and turned on the huge sanctuary lights. He puttered around straightening hymnals and returning the kneelers to their up position. He looked at his watch. It was about six-thirty—time for him to hear confessions. He put on his white robe and his purple stole, and went into the confessional to wait for any stray penitents who might venture in. He had been reading his breviary of prayers for several minutes when he heard the other compartment door open. He heard the kneeler squeak as the person knees pressed on it. He slid the small door open between them. It was a woman with a small timid voice. She spoke reluctantly. "Bless me, Father, for I have sinned.

It's been two years since my last confession. Father—I—" She started to cry.

Father shut his breviary and sat up attentively. "Yes, my child! What is it?"

There was a huge sob on the other side. "I—I think my—my husband is an Indian killer. I—think—he's—planning to kill my sister for the headright money. I think he killed my—my mother, too!" She was openly sobbing now.

"There, there. Don't cry." Father Jack said, trying hard not to fall off his chair. "Did you have any part in these murders?"

"No, no, but I'm afraid—afraid he'll kill—me—me, too. Please, God. Help—me."

Father Jack thought for a second. "My child, listen! You need to go to the sheriff and tell him."

There was a terrible gasp from the other side. "No! No! I can't tell anyone. And you can't tell anyone either, Father. You have taken the vow of silence!"

"Yes, yes. That's true. You need to pray for guidance and safety, my child. You need to pray for someone you can confide in to help you. Come to me outside the confessional. I will help you."

Her whole body shook. "I can't, Father! I can't." She abruptly rose and left the small hot room. Nothing remained but words—words that would haunt him till the day he died. He was trapped by the vows of the Catholic Church forever in his mind.

The remainder of the time sped by, and Father Jack heard only two other confessions. The priest wondered later what he had told them. His mind was on only one thing—Indian killers.

It was nearly seven as he started Mass. Only about a dozen people were there. As Tom Big Horse read the readings, he looked out at the small gathering. Where was the lady? He scanned them all. Which one was she? He couldn't decide in the brief time of the reading. As Mass was over, he stood outside as usual and spoke to the Indians as they filed out of the church.

He went about the next week with the heavy burden of silence weighing him down, as he prayed harder than ever that the senseless killings would stop. At night, he tossed and turned in his bed. He couldn't sleep. The memory of the woman's voice was driving him crazy with worry. But, what could he do? On the seventh night, he finally got up from his tangled bed covers and wandered down to the kitchen to heat up some milk.

Twenty-eight miles away as the crow flies, Henry and Rita Smith were in bed in the upstairs bedroom of their fashionable house on the outskirts of Fairfax. There was a hush in the air. There was no moon and there was a chill on the window panes. Henry was awake. It was three a.m. by the clock on the dresser. He could hear the frogs and the crickets outside making a louder chorus than usual. *Must be gonna rain,* he thought.

He was lying there, thinking. *Lefty is in big trouble now, and he's liable to squeal on me and everyone else to make a deal with the sheriff. Maybe I should talk first. I could go to Investigator Vaughn. The killings are getting too close together. And that Jake Knupp upset me immensely, questioning me about that ring I sold his Indian wife.*

It's that damn Lefty's fault. Lefty was mad cause I'd sold the ring. He said he was going to get the damn thing back and forced me to tell him who had bought it. Lefty said his wife, Mollie had wanted it back.

Rita let me sell it after she inherited it from her Grandmother, but Mollie found out about it. Evidently, Lefty stole it from Maggie Knupp and raped her while he was at it, leaving her for dead. Lefty took the ring to Mollie. Mollie came back to town from St. Louis about that time to visit her mother, Bessie. She gave the ring to her for safekeeping, unbeknownst to Lefty. But he had already paid to have the old lady killed ahead of time for the boss. So now Lefty and I share another headright. He looked at the clock again—three-ten. *Lefty is such a blood-thirsty idiot and he's going to*

*get us, both, killed by our fearless 'big shot' leader. The big boss is the greed-
iest of all. Makes Lefty look like an angel. But if that damn Lefty 'd just
keep his shirt on, we've 'bout got 'em all killed. I wonder when he'll decide
to knock me and Rita off to get our share. Hope it's not too late.*

That was the last thought Bill Smith ever had, as the blast heard five
miles away ignited his house, and sent him and his sleeping wife airborne through the roof of their two-story house. For the better part of
an hour, the body pieces drifted like confetti all over the yard.

Wednesday afternoon was beautiful. Father Jack was taking advantage of the mild windless day to work outside on a church window that
wouldn't open properly when Miss Lydia yelled at him from across the
street. "Father Jack! Father Jack!"

He looked her way and waved to her from his ladder. Lydia came
quickly up to him. "What are you doing on that ladder, trying to kill
yourself? He ignored her.

"Did you hear the news?" she asked. "Sheriff Cook was in this morning at the hardware store to see if I had sold any dynamite caps. I asked
him why he wanted to know. He said that somebody blew up a couple
of people over in Fairfax while they were asleep in bed. Said they found
the guy on his shredded mattress, still alive about three hundred feet
from the house. His wife was dead on top of him. The housekeeper was
killed, too. Said, there were arms in the trees and body parts strung
everywhere. They got him to the hospital in Fairfax, but he was dead,
too, by then." She stopped to take a much needed breath.

"Oh! My God! Who was it?" Father asked. "Did I know them?"

Lydia nodded. "Yeah, you know her. It was Rita and Henry Smith."

Father Jack gasped and nearly lost his balance on the ladder. The ladder was weaving, and so was he.

"My gosh! Father Jack, be careful. Come down off of there. You're
absolutely white."

Somehow, the trembling priest got down safely off the ladder and sat
down on the stone wall, mopping his brow. "Yeah, I know her, alright.

That's Bessie WhiteOaks' daughter." He wondered if she could have been the sister of the woman in the confessional." Father Jack wiped his brow again. "Lydia, have you seen her sister, Mollie, around lately?"

Lydia shook her head. "I went to school with her. I liked her. We kinda ran together. She's my age, but no, I haven't seen her in years. Who knows? She'll probably turn up for the funeral."

Father nodded. "I wonder what this investigator Bill Vaughn's waitin' on. You know he used to be a Tulsa judge? You'd think he could put two and two together faster than this. Should be a pretty smart ol' boy."

She shrugged her shoulders. "I don't know. He came in and got some bullets for his thirty-eight the other day. Says he knows who the master-mind behind the killing' is, but he can't prove it, yet. I asked him who, but he said, he'd rather not say, yet."

Father Jack put his head in his hands, deep in thought. "Now, we're killin' Indians and whites. The FBI may decide to move faster now that the whites are involved. You know there's some folks speculatin' around town that it's ol' man Hale that's behind the plot."

Lydia stood up. "Oh really. Well, nothin' would surprise me. He's got his finger on a lot of people with bank notes and all. Well, I gotta go, Father Jack. Take care and stay down off that ladder. You're too old for that." She laughed as she started across the street.

Father waved her off. "Get outta here. Go on, now." He wasn't in the mood for jokes. He put his tools and the ladder in the shed. He decided to ride up on the hill to the jail and see what Sheriff Cook knew and was willing to tell.

When the priest arrived at the white aristocratic structure on the hill, he tied his horse and buggy to the rail. He huffed and puffed his way up the steps of the court house. *Too many damn cigars*, he thought. He walked down the musty muraled corridor of justice and tapped on the glass door marked "Osage County Sheriff".

"Come on in," yelled a familiar gruff voice.

Father Jack opened the heavy door. There, in the big room amidst all the judicial debris of the county, sat Jake, Maggie, Sheriff Cook, and George Wright. He hesitated a second. "Oh, listen, I can come back later."

"Nonsense, Father. Set your not-so-holy butt down. It's about your flock anyways. Maybe you can shed some light on it for us. Maggie's up here to pick out the rapist in a line-up. They'll be ready in a minute."

Father closed the door and sat down. "How's Quinn, Jake?"

Jake looked at him. "Fine, Father. He's young. Doc don't even think he'll limp."

Father grinned. "Good. That's great." His mood sobered. "Say, Sheriff what's this I hear bout a house being dynamited over by Fairfax?"

Sheriff Cook was shuffling through some papers. "Yeah, it's true. Wasn't dynamite though, it was nitro."

Father looked stunned. "Nitro? Where'd they get that?"

"I don't know," The sheriff grimaced. "God, it was awful! There was body parts everywhere—Oh, pardon me, Miss Maggie!" He looked at Maggie's pale face.

Jake looked up. "Hey, maybe you better check old Bill Grammer's bootleggin' building. He had some soup—a quart or two the other day—when I was lookin' for some to shoot my well."

The sheriff nodded. "Alright, but it ain't going' help Henry and Rita Smith much, or their housekeeper for that matter. Henry's the one who sold Maggie the ring. We know that now. I really thought we had Henry and Lefty, too—

Mollie's husband. But now Henry's dead. I'm wonderin' if maybe he was gettin' ready to talk and spill his guts to Vaughn and they decided to knock him off."

"But my God, why?" Father Jack asked as he put his head in his hands.

Sheriff Cook stood up and leaned on both arms on the desk. "Because of these damn headrights. I've told you all this time after time.

These white swindlers marry these Indians, then they kill them. Look! Now, Mollie's just inherited headrights from her mother, her sisters, her brother, Bill, her grandmother, and her dead sisters that died of supposedly natural causes.

Vaughn's checkin' reports of those other two sisters to see if there's anything fishy surroundin' their deaths. I'm bettin' there is."

George Wright, looked disturbed. "The FBI telephone wires are burnin', now. It's gone too far. At this rate, there aren't goin' be any Indians left. I got a call from the State Attorney General saying he was willing to spend several thousand dollars to solve the murders, and asked the Osage Tribal Council to help out, too. They've agreed to spend five thousand dollars. So, we wired FBI Director Hoover this morning, and he's asked his Oklahoma office to give these cases full priority."

Sheriff Cook nodded. "That's true and Vaughn's uncovered some pretty startling facts. In 1907, when the roll was finished, there were 2,229 Osages alive. Now, sixteen years later, there's only 1624 Osages left. 605 people have died. Isn't it odd Pat Woodward, the Osage Attorney who handles all the probates, never brought that to anyone's attention?"

"Are you trying to say that this whole scheme could be masterminded out of our agency? Oh, my God." George Wright voice was slow and deliberate as the shock set in. He paced back and forth before the window muttering to himself. "Wood—ward—a crook."

"Well, we don't know yet, but the evidence is leaning in that direction. But even so, Woodward would have had to have a partner to pull the murders off. They probably split the money, somehow." Sheriff Cook said with a sigh.

As the group sat in a stupor, the door opened. It was Bill Vaughn. He looked wild. What was left of his hair was standing straight up and his clothes were rumpled to say the least.

"Guess what?" He stammered. "I just uncovered something big. You know who Lefty Kirk's uncle is?" Vaughn was almost out-of-breath. "A rancher by the name of Billy Hale." It came out in Kirk's interrogation downstairs. That's why he's here in Pawhuska. He said his Uncle had invited him to come to the oil patch. I said, 'and who is your Uncle,' and then he told me." The small group of people stared at him in disbelief. Jake stopped in the middle of lighting his cigar as the match burned his finger.

"Then, I discovered something else about Bessie WhiteOaks' two other daughters." Vaughn said in his high pitched voice. "Bonnie, her oldest daughter, died in childbirth. But Minnie, her second daughter, was married first to Henry Smith. She died in 1918 of an infirmity from something she ate. Hell, I'm sure it was poison. Then, her third daughter, Rita, married Henry, and they moved out of town for five years. Just recently moved back."

Everyone leaned forward in their chairs listening intently as he was forced to clear his throat. "Also, Bessie WhiteOaks' mother, Anna Brown died over in Grey horse last year after eating a huge dinner of steak and corn. The report said she was poisoned, but no autopsy was even demanded.

Bessie, it turned out, was married first to a guy named Tall Chief. They had two kids. The daughter died in childbirth, and the other one, a son, was the guy you found shot dead, Jake, in that Buick in the field that night at Elgin. His name was Charlie Tall Chief."

Vaughn paused for a second and hurriedly gulped down a nearby glass of liquid that obviously did not belong to him. He frowned and wiped his mouth with his sleeve as he launched back into his story. "Bessie's first husband died of alcohol poisoning. She then married Sam WhiteOaks. Then, lo and behold, he was found dead by a bunch of hunters in the woods over by Hominy. He was leaning up against a tree with a bottle. The report said, 'alcohol poisoning', but on closer examination, the mortician found he'd been shot in the arm pit with an overdose of morphine."

Father Jack stood up and began to pace, shaking his head in disbelief. Sheriff Cook was taking notes as fast as he could write.

Vaughn took a drag off his cigar. "My God! Now that her sister's been blown sky high that must make nine headrights now that Mollie, the fourth and last daughter, has inherited. She's worth a fortune—and she's married to Lefty Kirk, a rapist and attempted killer, who's sitting in this very jail. And he's none other than the nephew of Mr. Big Osage County rancher and banker himself, William Hale. Listen, folks. I know all of this is true, but I can't prove it all yet."

There was surprise written on all their faces as the truth slowly soaked in. Vaughn leaned back in the chair and kicked his feet up on the sheriff's desk and puffed on his cigar. He waited for his words to take effect. In the silence a clock ticked importantly from across the room. Father Jack was in shock, but the sheriff was having a hard time trying to keep from showing his elation at the prospect of someone nailing Hale—especially Agent Vaughn.

"I had about come to this same conclusion about Hale, but what's the deal with Pat Woodward?" Jake asked. "He had to have known all this. He's covering up something. He has to be furnishing names and important inheritance information to the killers."

"Yeah, and what about that Indian I found buried in the rocks up to his neck on Fred's road?" Father Jack asked. "Ed something or other."

"Oh, yeah." Sheriff Cook said. "That was Ed Tall Corn!"

From the corner of the room, Maggie made a gasping noise. "Oh, my God! Ed Tall Corn's dead? Then the only one left of that family is Katherine Little Bear. She was the only cousin of Tall Corn."

Jake thought a minute as he but the pieces together. "She's right!"

Vaughn got his second wind. "Yeah, now listen, George. You need to keep your mouth shut and your eyes open. Woodward should've reported all this stuff. He was in the perfect position to capitalize on all these deaths. Now, I need to know if Woodward's a guardian, too."

Agent Wright put his head down in dismay. "I already know the answer to that one. I'm afraid he is. I don't know to how many, but there's several."

The web of Osage murder stories was unraveling. That was just one inheritance line of Osage families about to be uncovered. They still didn't know about the other six hundred Indians who had died.

A deputy opened the door. "Ready for the line up, Sheriff!"

"Alright, Deputy. We'll be right down!"

They all stood up as Jake took Maggie's cold clammy hand. She walked as close to him as she could get. They filed to the room where, behind a crude window glass, they could see five men. Jake didn't even have time to look at them all before Maggie held up her finger. "That's him. Number four. Get me out of here, Jake." She started sobbing hysterically.

Jake scooped her up as she fainted in his arms, but before he left the room, Jake looked at the line-up. Number four was indeed, Lefty Kirk. George, Sheriff Cook, and Vaughn stayed behind in his office going over more details, but Father Jack, Maggie, and Jake had had enough.

They stepped outside as Maggie came to, and they all sat on the pedestals of the courthouse steps. It was a chilly day. From their high perch, they could see the whole agency town down below them. The leaves were mostly gone from the oaks, and they could see the Indian ghosts dancing behind each of the barren trees, inquisitive as to whether anyone would dare discover how they, too, had been murdered. The trees knew. Grandfather Sun knew. The killers knew. And it was Jake's suspicion that the Osage agency and the Osage's richest rancher had to know, too.

Chapter Twenty-nine

Spring was newborn. Just a hint of wild crocus and yellow daffodils around old farm houses was visible. The red bud trees were almost in bloom, a hint of pink on their branches. The oaks were still bare. It was still too soon to risk their fresh, new leaves. It was February 1924.

Jake had drilled three more wells, and he had gotten a piece of the action on each of them with the money he'd made from his eighth of the "Maggie T" well, as he called it. Red and Jake had two new rigs and brand new strings of tools. Quinn was about to turn six, and was back to full throttle. Maggie was happy, too, even though, she never missed an opportunity to reassure him that Quinn was not spending any more time at the oil well sites.

The tribe had appointed another Osage—Paul Red Eagle—as temporary chief to fill out Chief Ne-Kah-Wah-She-Tun-Kah's term. Fred would have to run again in that year's upcoming election. Fred was even glad for the reprieve.

The murders were still being committed and investigated. The latest one to shock the little agency town was Bill Grammer, kingpin of the Osage bootleggers. A month after the Smith explosion, Grammer's Cadillac was found crashed and burned on a lonely road. The brakes had been tampered with, but he'd been shot under the armpit, or so the coroner had reported. It appeared that his nine lives were finally used up. His illustrious cowboy neck had been broken, and in his pockets they had found cash totaling nearly ten thousand dollars.

The newspaper account had said that he was a famous forty-two year old world champion roper. He had performed from Pendleton, Oregon to Madison Square Garden in New York City. He had traveled with the 101 Ranch Wild West Show as a gun marksman and steer roper, as well. But what the paper had failed to add was that he was a real suspect in a day-light robbery at a Coffeyville bank.

He really hadn't needed the twenty-five thousand dollars. He had sufficient money since he was an Osage squaw man with a big lucrative ranch. Besides, he had admitted to killing several men, including Bill Berry of Pawhuska. In fact, there was no-telling how many men he had killed with his quick-draw expertise.

Jake's own thought on Grammer's murder was that he must have been right about the bootlegger's involvement with the Smith explosion and his nitro. The kingpin must have been through with him. No need asking him to testify.

Vaughn's investigation was going well. Jake and most everybody else in town really liked and trusted him. Lefty Kirk's trial was scheduled for that year. Vaughn was close to an arrest on Billy Hale and maybe even Pat Woodward. He was planning to go to Oklahoma City to report his findings before he made the arrest.

That night, Tom Fisher, Katherine, Maggie and Jake were having dinner to celebrate their up-coming wedding. The wedding was planned for early March, just before the big lease sell. The two couples sat enjoying their dessert and after-dinner coffee.

"Are you going to have the Osage Me Shin wedding ceremony, Katherine?" Maggie asked as she carefully replaced the china coffee cup in its saucer.

Katherine smiled mischievously. "Oh yes. It will be good for Tom to get acquainted with our Osage customs right away."

Tom winked at Jake. "And what's this ceremony?"

Katherine looked at Maggie and blushed. "Well, you have to bring food for two days to impress my family. The greater the food, the greater our impression will be. But since I don't have any family, I guess you'll just have to impress me." Katherine giggled.

"And the horse deal, don't forget," Jake reminded her.

"Oh yes! On the morning of the wedding I ride to your place on horseback, leading an extra pony. My Indian lady attendants race along side of me on foot to your place. The winner gets the pony. The second place winner gets all my clothes. Then a couple of the men carry me into your place and set me on a blanket. Okay, now, here's the good part. You present me with lovely new clothes symbolizing that you will always take good care of me."

Tom and looked at Jake and raised his eyebrows as his bride-to-be went on. "Maggie, explain to him about the Osage traditional wedding clothes."

Maggie eagerly took up the conversation. "Oh yes, Tom. The wedding robe is a military wool coat like the ones army generals wear, complete with gold-fringed epaulettes on the shoulders and brass buttons."

"Get to the hat, Maggie." Jake laughed out loud.

Maggie shot him a dirty look. "Well, it's a beautiful top hat. It has a black narrow brim with rows of colored ostrich feathers and silver bands that rise to a crown about two and a half feet high."

The look on Tom's face made them all laugh. "Oh golly. How did that practice ever start?" Tom asked cautiously.

Katherine thought a moment. "Well, let's see. It goes back to Thomas Jefferson's time. A delegation of Osage chiefs had gone to Washington. After their meetings, they were given military uniforms and top hats as presents. They, in turn, brought them home, and gave them as gifts to their wives and daughters. They were their prized possessions. For some reason, it became the ritual for the bride's attire." Katherine continued on, despite Tom's perplexed look. "It'll be fine sweetheart." She patted him fondly on the arm. "Later that afternoon, we'll go to the church and have Father Jack marry us.

"Jake and I will host the marriage feast at the Lookout ranch in your honor following the ceremony." Maggie's voice was filled with happiness.

Katherine beamed, "Oh that would be wonderful, Maggie."

Jake was happy for them both. She and Tom were all smiles and obviously in love. "Where are you going for your honeymoon?"

Tom blushed. "Frank Phillips and Aunt Jane are sending us to New York City. They have given us a suite at the Waldorf Astoria." Jake raised his eyebrows. "Gosh, Tom, I'm impressed. The oil boom sure has been good to us all."

Tom laughed. "Yeah, we should get back just in time for the lease sale, March 18th, I believe. I can't miss the sale. Boy, that one quarter up by Lyman is the one they all want. I shudder to think how high the price'll go."

"I wonder, too." Jake said. "You know I won the lease rights on a piece of ground up there near the Noble-Osage county line in a poker game about a year and half ago. So I'm anxious to see just how good everyone thinks it looks."

Tom rolled his eyes. "My gosh, Jake. That's worth a fortune. It's in the red-bed. Marland's geologist says that the pool on 14-27-4 is going bring the highest price ever recorded. You may be a rich man, Jake. Of all the luck. You gonna drill on it?"

"Yeah, I reckon."

Maggie nudged Jake on the arm with her elbow. "Jake, you didn't tell me, you'd won that lease."

Jake tweaked her nose. "Now, Maggie, I don't tell you everything." They all laughed.

"Boy, it's really wild up there around Whizbang," Tom said. "Cot houses, whorehouses, killins, shootins, and brawls, I hear."

Jake nodded his head and winked at Maggie. "Yeah, I'd rather just drive through the wild place, but I guess I'll just have to force myself to go up there and do a little wildcattin.'" They all laughed heartily, except Maggie, who pretended to pout.

"Say, Katherine, not to change the subject, but are your folks both dead now?" Jake asked intently studying her face.

"Yes. Mother died ten years ago and Daddy died in a car wreck over by Shidler six years ago."

"So you and Tom are going to live at your ranch?"

Katherine looked at Tom. "I guess so. They left me several headrights, his Pierce Arrow, and the ranch. It's just me left, now. I only had one cousin, and, he's gone now."

"What was his name?" Jake asked. He seemed to be concentrating on her every word.

"Ed Tall Corn. He was murdered. Father Jack found him along side that country road on the way to the Lookout place, remember?"

Jake nodded. "But Katherine, who was your guardian?"

"Mr. Woodward, the attorney for the Indians up at the agency, and he still is. He's been real nice to me over the years. After my folks died, he told me he had adopted some of the other orphaned Indian girls only on paper. There was some legal advantage or formality, but I can't remember now what he said it was. So he said he would do the same thing for me. I turned twenty-one a couple of months ago, and I needed to get my competency papers, but I just haven't done it. Mr. Woodward told me there was no hurry, since he was handling it all. Maggie do you know him? He's got the most beautiful white hair and dresses like a man of world-class."

The conversation concerning Pat Woodward continued but Jake had ceased to listen. He suddenly felt sick. *My God! She is the only one left of this line of Osages. I'd better warn Tom. Katherine could be in real danger.*

The two happy couples left the hotel arm in arm. The eight o'clock performance at the luxurious Constantine Theatre was nearly ready to begin. They were to see Isadora Duncan perform in person. The girls had been anxiously awaiting her performance. She was a great showgirl dancer. Even Jake couldn't wait to see her do "Second Hand Rose". She reminded him of Ruby Darby's slightly shady extravaganza that Red and he had attended in Burbank at the invitation of Al Evans. They found their seats in the theatre and Tom and Jake went back out to smoke. The girls were still lost in wedding plans.

As the two friends stood outside the theatre on West Main Street looking up Kihekah Street past the Triangle building, they watched ladies and gentlemen parking their big cars and strolling toward the theatre. The ladies were wrapped in their mink and ermine coats and hats, graciously trailing on the arms of the well-tailored men. They looked like they just stepped out of a band box—a whole town dressed in the best oil money could buy. Tom and Jake both lit up a cigar. "Tom, your life's really turned around in this town in the last year."

He smiled. "Jake, I'm so happy. I've loved Katherine from the first time I ever saw her. She was standing by Julia Lookout at the peyote church. I owe you one for taking me with you that day."

"I know," Jake said, puffing hard on his cigar, trying to figure out how he was going to broach this subject. "Tom, I don't know how to tell you this, but I'm more than a little alarmed about Katherine."

Tom nearly choked on the smoke. "Why, Jake?"

"Well, I personally hold Pat Woodward, the Osage Indian attorney, in real suspect as an accomplice for some, if not all of these murders. She says he's her guardian and now handles and manages her money. He even encouraged her not to be in a hurry about filing her competency papers. Now she tells me he adopted her on paper. Then I discovered she's the only one left of her family, and that Ed Tall Corn was her cousin. Tom, we know he was murdered. I'm afraid, they'll make an attempt on Katherine's life before the wedding."

"Oh my God, Jake! No. This can't be happening. What'll I do?" Tom asked. "I can't keep her in my sight every minute. Lord, Jake!" The absolute panic was written all over his face. "What do I do? I can't tell her. It'll scare her to death."

Jake nodded with a somber look on his face and stubbed out his cigar. "I know. We'll just have to be real careful and watch after her. You need to make sure you alert Sheriff Cook, and then keep your eyes open for anything suspicious. Come on. Stub out your cigar. They're blinking the lights. The performance is ready to begin."

They rejoined the girls along with the late-comers scurrying to their red velvet seats. The dark red velvet curtain opened and they became engrossed in the cast of characters. Jake knew the joy of the evening had been dimmed for Tom, but he had to know the truth.

The early spring days brought March in like a lamb. The wedding plans were progressing well. It was the talk of the little agency town. The nice young oil man and the beautiful Indian lady was a story book romance.

Father Jack was elated at the thought of a happy event in the parish instead of another miserable funeral, and spring was definitely in the air.

Five more days, Tom thought at breakfast that Tuesday morning in the Duncan hotel dining room. The Me Shin was to take place Saturday morning, and then the church wedding that afternoon at four o'clock. He took a deep breath. After Jake's warning he'd been a nervous wreck, but they had nearly made it safely to the wedding. He was a little concerned, though. Katherine and Maggie were taking the Midland train to Tulsa to pick up the wedding dress at one of the fancy Tulsa stores. They were so excited about the trip. How could he have put a damper on it? They were to return later that evening. Jake and he would have dinner together, and then meet the eight o'clock train to pick them up. Tom had to go over to Burbank and meet with Frank and the geologist most of the day in preparation for the lease sale. Marland already had his refinery in Ponca City, so it was going to be a fight to see who got what lease. Frank wanted him to go with him to look it over.

Deep in pre-wedding frenzy, Katherine and Maggie had excitedly boarded the six o'clock train in Tulsa to return home. They were wrapped head to toe in furs. The excitement of their full day of shopping was apparent in their pink and happy faces. They settled themselves in the dining car and ordered a light supper. The porter had boarded the train with box after box of wedding finery. As they ate, they discussed their wonderful finds. "Katherine, your dress is the loveliest I've ever seen. I can't believe you had it made in Paris."

Katherine giggled. "I know, it was terribly extravagant, wasn't it? But with Aunt Jane and her guest list, it had to be special. After all, I have to keep up my Vanderbilt reputation, don't I? Then I had to buy some nice things for afterwards when we go to Philadelphia to meet Tom's parents. Especially since they can't come for the wedding." She sampled the pork tenderloin and Maggie was enjoying her baked flounder. They toasted each other with a glass of dry white wine. "This is so great! Here's to our last girl fling before I become Mrs. Tom Fisher."

It was only after the meal was winding down that Katherine looked at Maggie, strangely. Maggie noticed she hadn't eaten much. "You know, my stomach is kinda upset, Maggie. Is yours?"

Maggie shook her head. "No. It's probably all the excitement of today, plus the rickety ride on this train, weaving us back and forth."

Katherine looked even more peculiar. "I don't know. I felt fine all day, but oh golly, I feel really bad now. I think I'm going to throw up, or faint, or both. I think I need to find the ladies' room."

Maggie looked at her face. She was white as snow and her eyes were glassy and feverish. Her face suddenly began to twitch. "I'm really getting concerned, Katherine. Do you suppose your food was spoiled?"

Katherine rolled her eyes. "Oh, I don't know. I feel so bad. I really am going to faint! I need some air!"

Maggie started to her feet. "Let me help you to the rest room!"

Katherine waved her off. "No! No! I can make it! You finish your dinner. It's right through that door." She stood up and steadied herself for a moment. Then she walked, weaving from side to side with the motion of the train toward the ladies' room.

The train car was about half-full. Maggie looked at the rest of the passengers, one by one. No one else seemed to be sick. It had come on Katherine so fast. Maybe she'd feel better when she got back. Five minutes, then ten minutes passed. Maggie was beginning to get really concerned. She got up to go see if she was still the wash room. She knocked on the door. "Katherine, it's Maggie. Are you alright in there?" There was no answer. She knocked again, then the door opened so abruptly that it scared her, and she jumped backwards.

A huge middle age woman stepped out of the rest room. "Are you in such a big hurry, you can't wait?" She asked her in a haughty voice.

"Oh, I'm so sorry! I was looking for my friend. She was ill, and I was checking to see if she was alright.

The heavyset lady pressed by her. "Haven't seen her."

Maggie searched the car and then asked the porter, but no one had seen her. She'd disappeared into thin air. Maggie was hysterical by now, and she pulled at the porter's sleeve. "Where are we? Are we close to Pawhuska?" She yelled over the loud clickety-clack of the train.

"We're 'bout a half-hour away, ma'am. Your friend will turn up. Just calm down."

The next half hour, Maggie paced up and down the aisle of the train asking everyone if they'd seen her tall beautiful, Indian friend. She couldn't keep from crying as he train was slowing down. *Thank God!* she thought. *We must be back in Pawhuska. Jake and Tom will be at the station.* The porter sympathetically told the distraught woman to go find her husband. He would bring her many boxes along. She gratefully thanked him as she leaped, crying from the train. The train was still moving as she screamed. "Jake! Jake!"

Jake heard her piercing scream from the depot. Tom and he started running, as Maggie fell into his arms. "What is it Maggie?"

"It's Katherine! I can't find her! She's missing!"

"Oh my God." Tom whispered. He started running on toward the train while Jake managed to get the story out of his terrified wife.

"Sit here a minute on this bench, Maggie. I'll be right back."

"Hurry, Jake!" she sobbed into her linen handkerchief. Next to her, the porter piled high, the boxes of their long forgotten buying spree.

Jake ran to the train, too. He found Tom, and together they searched everywhere. Jake told him the story as Maggie had related it to him. "She's not on here, Jake. They've poisoned her food or the wine, and as she went to the ladies' room, they've pushed her off the train to her death. Oh God! Why did we let them go alone?" Tom was absolutely beside himself.

"Come on, Tom," Jake yelled over the train's wheezing noise. "Let's go find the sheriff. We'll find her."

They ran back to Maggie and gathered her and all the boxes, and quickly dropped her by the Duncan Hotel. "Get a room, sweetheart, and wait for me." Jake hastily told Maggie. He and Tom were already out the door in search of the sheriff.

They called the sheriff from the lobby. He was at his house, by some stroke of luck, on Purdum Street. He answered on the first ring. "Sheriff, this is Jake Knupp. Can you meet me and Tom at the train station?" Jake asked with a tense edge to his voice. "Katherine Little Bear is missing off the train."

"On my way, Jake. Be there in ten minutes." Sheriff Cook never even bothered to hang up the phone as he grabbed his hat and gun and ran out the door.

Jake knew they had to hurry. They wouldn't have long. The poison would work fast. Jake's next call was to Doc Lewis. He related the story to him. "Can you meet us at the depot, Doc?"

"Oh my God! Yes! Yes, just give me a few minutes." Since he suspected poison, Doc had gathered up his stomach pump, some charcoal, and barbiturates in his black bag. True to his word, he showed up in his buggy on the allotted time.

In the meantime, Tom and Jake had grabbed a couple of horses at the livery stable, and rode to the depot. Sheriff arrived shortly with a couple of lanterns. They were grateful that the moon was nearly full. Searching would be more than difficult, especially for Doc, who was forced to straddle the rails with his buggy. They rode as fast as they dared, scanning on either side of the tracks for what seemed to be miles with no luck.

They had to be nearly to Nelagoney, a small town where the Midland Valley and Katy Railroads met. The little town sat about seven miles southwest of Pawhuska. There was a saloon, a post office, and a few shacks, but that was about it. They continued to search on through the town about a mile and a half. "This has got to be the area, according to the time the porter give me," Jake yelled to the others.

"Spread out! Look over there!" Sheriff Cook motioned. There was nothing but leaves and buck brush for miles.

Tom was beyond frantic. They had to find her soon. The railroad bed followed a wide curve in the road as they rounded the bend. Everyone was waving their lights. "There—there she is!" Tom yelled as he jumped from his horse.

When he reached her she was lying face down in the weeds. He knelt beside her, not even daring to breathe. "Katherine! Katherine!" He gently rolled her over. He felt of her neck and then put his ear to her chest. She was still alive. In the light of the lantern her beautiful Indian face was white and her black long hair was snarled with twigs and burrs like she had rolled quite a distance. Her dress was torn at the sleeve and her shoes were gone. "She's alive!" Tom shouted. "Hurry, Doc! Hurry!"

Doc jumped out of the buggy, grabbed his black bag, and ran to her side. Sheriff Cook and Jake were right behind him. He knelt down beside her and lifted her eye lids. He'd seen vomit in a couple of spots on the ground and on her dress. "She's been poisoned, alright." Doc looked up at the three men.

"We'll have to run this tube down to her stomach and dump her full of charcoal. Then we just have to hope for the best. These crazy bastards usually use a low dose of strychnine as poison, so I brought a shot of barbiturates to use as an sedative. I just hope that's what it is. We've got to keep her knocked out till the poison runs its course. If she wakes up, she'll go into terrible convulsions. That's what'll kill her. I just hope we found her in time." He got the stomach tube and hurriedly inserted it into her mouth down her throat to her stomach. It took only a few minutes until it was finished.

Sheriff Cook and Jake left them to look for clues where she might have been thrown from the train. Doc gave her a shot of the barbiturate. "Now, just hold your breath and pray, Tom. Cover her up with that blanket. Let's let the medicine take effect for a few moments before we try to move her to town."

Tom sat there along the railroad track, holding his bride-to-be and his broken heart. *How could this be happening to their beautiful perfect lives, five lousy days before the wedding?* As he held her in his arms, he smoothed the black tangled hair from her face. "Katherine, please live. Please fight, darling. Don't leave me. Oh God, help her. Don't let her die because of these evil, greedy men. Fight, Katherine. Please, for me." He could no longer keep the tears away. Suddenly, this country wasn't exciting anymore.

It was desolate, dangerous, and god-forsaken. There would be no more oil excitement in the Osage if he lost his beautiful bride to murder.

About twenty minutes went by. Then, her body started wrenching back and forth, and she opened her eyes. The pain was still there, but as her eyes focused on Tom's face, she smiled a gentle, slight smile. No sound came from her lips as she mouthed the words, "Tom, I love you!"

Tom bent his head to touch her lips as the tears rolled from his eyes. "Oh my God! Katherine! I—I—love you, too, my beautiful Katherine. Doc! Doc! Hurry! She's awake. Thank God!"

Doc came running up. "Well, hallelujah. Okay, Tom! Let's get her back to town." The men carefully lifted her in Doc's buggy and rode back the long way to Pawhuska. The murderers had lost this round. Their Indian victim was still alive.

The search party arrived at the hotel and took her up to a room next to Tom's. Jake found Maggie, and she was so thankful and elated, she was hugging everyone. She helped put Katherine to bed as Doc checked her over again. When she was settled, and still heavily sedated, Tom, Sheriff Cook, and Jake came in and sat by her bed as the girls pieced together the story.

When Katherine had been on her way to the ladies' room, she had felt so ill that she knew she wasn't going to make it. She could remember two men standing in the aisle before she blacked out. Evidently, they had known that she'd be coming shortly to the toilet within half an hour of eating. They had been waiting for her. When she had blacked out, they had simply dragged her to the coach door and thrown her off the train to die. She couldn't remember anything except that there had been two men.

Doc stood up. "Well, that's enough for now. Everybody out, but Tom. Let her get some rest. Probably the only thing that saved her life was when she was thrown off the train, she hit her head on a rock and it knocked her out. So the convulsions never took hold of her. We were real lucky on this one, Sheriff. Tom, I'll think she'll sleep for a while. The medicine will keep her real sedated. I'll be by tomorrow to see how's she doing."

Sheriff Cook and Jake left together to talk in the hall. "Looks like you might be right about Pat Woodward. He's still her guardian. Looks like Woodward adopted her and some other girls unbeknownst to anyone. That's castin' some real guilt on him. George Wright's havin' a hard time buyin' it, but Vaughn is convinced of it, I think. By the way, Vaughn's going to Oklahoma City on Monday to report his suspicions to the State Attorney General and the FBI. He's got a lot of documented evidence to present."

"That's good." Jake smiled. "We need to get this killin' stopped once and for all."

After everyone left, Tom sat down in the dim light next to her bed. "Katherine." He took her hand. "What if I'd lost you? I couldn't have lived without you. Darling, we'd better put off the wedding, don't you think, till you get your strength back?"

The beautiful Indian girl laid there and formed the word, "No!" as she put her fingers to his lips to hush him. "I'll marry you, Tom Fisher, this Saturday, rain or shine." She smiled and closed her eyes as he bent to kiss her again.

Tom sat down on the sofa and leaned back his weary head. *Thanks God. I'll take good care of her, I promise.* And in the long run the young man's word seemed to be good enough for Grandfather Sun and Wah'-Kon-Tah, too.

CHAPTER THIRTY

Saturday, Grandfather Sun was up early, ready for the wedding celebration. Dawn seemed to burst forth and spring was on its heels. Due to events of the past few days, the Osage wedding Me shin was to be cut short. The couple had dispensed with the two day ritual of food. Tom was to be at Fred and Julia's when Katherine arrived by buggy from her ranch with the extra pony. She was to be clad in her Osage wedding regalia.

Katherine's friends and Maggie rode in the buggy with her, all dressed with their tall Osage feather wedding top hats and military coats. Katherine was almost her old self again as she and the girls could be heard singing and laughing, while Tom, Fred, and Jake waited for them to approach the Lookout house. Fred and Jake met them at the buggy and unloaded the girls. Then they carried Katherine in their arms to officially give her to Tom as a sign of her absentee parental approval. Tom looked astounded and amused as the Osage Me Shin wedding custom unfolded before his eyes. The big military coats and the feathered top hats created a picturesque memory to be stored forever in his mind. *No one in Philadelphia, Pennsylvania would ever believe this*, he thought.

Everyone joined in and had a light lunch of soups and Indian meat pies as they relaxed and visited before the four o'clock church wedding. The Lookouts were in charge of the wedding feast after the ceremony at the ranch. Women from other clans had started gathering about noon to start the racks of meat cooking. It would be a huge gathering. All the Osage full-bloods had been invited and many of the mixed blood families, as well. The oil patch was represented by Marland, Skelly, and Frank Phillip, and many of the Phillips senior executives. All of the agency officials and prominent professional people in town had RSVP. Everyone wanted to come to see the beautiful couple united in marriage.

It was three-thirty. Father Jack had donned his white marriage vestments, and the four altar boys were robed to match. The organ was playing something romantically spiritual, and the church sanctuary was banked with the most exquisite European urns, filled with the largest mass of pink gladiolus and white roses that oil money could buy. The long, tapered brass candlesticks on the altar were all lighted and other brass candelabras framed the kneeler where the two would speak their vows. The long white aisle cloth was stretched clear to the back with pink floral pieces and ribbon dramatically marking each pew.

The church's double front doors were open, and the fanciest cars in the state lined the curbs for blocks. Pierce Arrows, Cadillacs, Buicks, Stutz Bearcats—each bearing Indians and other dignitaries all in their royal trappings. Royal trappings were indeed straight from the European market, or, at the very least, New York's Fifth Avenue. Fabulous silks and furs, along with custom hand-made purses and shoes was the dress of the day. They streamed into the Osage Cathedral. Each couple seemed to be more beautiful than the last. The saintly stained glass images in the dome above the altar had to have been duly impressed with the prestigiousness of the wedding guests.

It was four o'clock, the appointed hour. The guests were all seated. Pat Woodward was seated in the front row on the left. Julia Lookout was escorted down to the front pew on the right. Her great stature and floor length lime green lace gown with her ermine stole thrilled the onlookers.

Father Jack came out on the altar flanked on both sides by the acolytes. They were followed by the resplendent bridegroom, Tom

Fisher. He glanced at the crowd In awe. His eyes seemed to water as the memory of the past week flooded his mind. Jake was the last to enter as his best man. They were dressed in their formal black tuxes with gray ascots and white rose boutonnieres.

Suddenly the music became more aggressive, and every pipe resounded with grandiose tones to Lohengrin's "Wedding March". The guests rose to their feet and turned to watch Maggie Lookout Knupp in her crimson silk and satin gown, created in one of Paris's most chic design houses. *She is so beautiful.* Jake thought. *There is only one other, more beautiful today.* Maggie smiled at Jake and he winked back at her as she came through the altar gate.

As the organ thundered mightily, every eye was upon her. There she was—the most beautiful Osage Indian girl in the world. The breathtaking moment was captured in the musical magic of the old ornate Catholic Church.

Walking on the arm of the majestic Indian Chief, Fred Lookout, was Tom Fisher's bride—Katherine Little Bear.

Her dress was not bobbed short, as was the style of the twenties. Created in Europe with layer after layer of silk, the skirt fell to the floor, long and full, taking up the entire width of the aisle. The train followed ten feet behind her and the bodice was captivating with pearls and beads. The neckline and puffed sleeves were breathtakingly reminiscent of a Queen Ann design. Katherine's face was pink and radiant, and her hair was coiffured into cascading curls, while other unruly ringlets managed to escape down her back with interwoven ribbon and flowers.

There was an audible gasp from the guests, even over the sweet music, meant for only the ears of the angels. She was carrying a delicately fragrant bouquet of three dozen white roses and ribbons. In the candle light, she and Fred slowly walked toward the altar. It was portrait of royalty, indeed. The seven foot tall Indian was regal beside her. As she arrived at the center aisle, she flashed Tom a beautiful smile. It was a marriage made in heaven. Wah'-Kon-Tah and even Grandfather Sun were happily present.

This Osage Indian affair was happy and blessed as Father Jack invited the guests to share the time with them. "Do you, Tom Fisher, take this woman, Katherine Little Bear, to be your lawfully wedded wife, to have and to hold, from this day forward, in sickness and health, till death do you part?"

Tom smiled down at Katherine. "I do."

Father Jack turned his gaze to the bride. "Katherine Little Bear, do you take Tom Fisher as your lawfully wedded husband, to have and to hold, from this day forward, in sickness and in health, till death do you part?"

Katherine raised her eyes to Tom. "I do."

After the rings were blessed, Father Jack pronounced them man and wife. "Tom, you may kiss the bride."

Tom, still deeply emotional from the ordeal of her attempted murder, tenderly put his arms around Katherine, bent his head to hers, and kissed her long and passionately to the pleasure of the entire congregation of oil men and Osage Indians.

Father turned them around with a flourish. "Ladies and Gentlemen, may I present to you, Mr. and Mrs. Tom Fisher."

As the recessional soared, the church was filled with music and applause. The Indians congratulated the oilmen and oilmen congratulated the Indians. It was finally a happy day in the Osage.

Grandfather Sun even stayed around long enough to bless them before he faded off to another part of the world as the wedding feast and their honeymoon unfolded.

Dawn came slowly Sunday morning. It was six o'clock and Father Jack was hung over from toasting the wedding couple a few too many times. In fact he hadn't been to bed at all. He looked and felt like hell. He was planning to catch a few winks in the confessional before Mass. Business in there had been slow lately. He had given up trying to get his hair to lay down. He threw down his comb in disgust and wandered out of the rectory to the church.

He unlocked the doors and turned on a couple of lights, threw his stole haphazardly around his neck and made his way to the back of the church. He entered the confessional and sat down with a thud that made even his hair hurt. He grimaced as he put his head in his hands. In a few short moments he had dozed off when a slight movement opened the screen on the penitent's side.

"Bless me Father, for I have sinned," said a small feminine voice close to tears. "I need help, Father. My husband and his uncle killed my mother and my sister—and—and—they're going to kill me next—" The sobbing was enveloping her now. "For—for the Indian money—"

Father Jack sat bolt up straight, upsetting his breviary on his lap and it fell to the floor upside down. "Mollie, Mollie is that you?" No answer. Again. "Mollie—speak to me."

Finally one tiny almost inaudible word. "Yes."

"Oh Mollie. I've been so worried about you. Let me help you. Tell me who is the mastermind behind the murders. Is it Billy Hale? Please don't be afraid. Try to stop crying, my child."

The sobbing voice tried to continue. "Yes, he is—my—husband's—uncle."

"But why, Mollie?" Father whispered.

"He wants all my family's headrights. I'm the only one left. If I die my husband inherits all nine of my family's headrights. But what my husband doesn't realize is that ultimately Hale will have to kill him too, in order for Hale to inherit them all. That's the plan—"

Father had pressed his head so hard against the window, his circulation was cut off from his ear. "How do you know it's Hale, Mollie?"

"I heard them talking about two weeks after my mother died. Hale came over to the house about midnight. They thought I was asleep and they talked about getting the nitro from Grammer to blow up my sister, Rita and her husband, Henry's house in Fairfax. Lefty said they were going to have to waste Henry cause he was getting close to rattin' on them to the sheriff. Hale said Henry had threatened him. He said he was going to blow the whistle on them to the sheriff that they had killed my moth—er—" The sobbing was vibrating her whole body. Father Jack could feel it through the thin partition.

"There, there Mollie. Don't cry please. Is there anyone else involved in the plot, that you know if?"

Mollie blew her nose softly in her handkerchief. "Yes, I think so. Hale talked about raising some payment money for some big shot up at the agency."

Father Jack caught himself just in the nick of time to keep from screaming. "Who?"

Mollie hesitated. "I'm not sure—I think he's some big lawyer up there. Wood-something. I think Hale said."

"Father jumped up to his feet in his small compartment, "Woodward, Pat Woodward, is that it?"

"I—I believe so, Father Jack." The tiny woman forced the words out.

"Okay, Mollie. You have to come with me after Mass and give me permission to help you. We'll go see the sheriff together."

There was absolute silence. "I can't—I just can't. Lefty's out on bond—he'll kill me—I'm so afraid—"

Father Jack's whole body was sweating and trembling. Everything was riding on his words to persuade her to come forward with the story.

"Mollie, please, I'll hide you at my friend's for protection. No one will know where you are. Trust me, Mollie. You have to trust somebody."

After what seemed forever, a small feeble "Okay" came from the other side followed by hysterical crying.

Father raced out of his door, glanced quickly around the empty church, and threw her door open. He covered her with his arms as he consoled her sobbing body. "Come with me." With Mass totally forgotten, they raced out the side door toward the rectory. Safely in the kitchen be grabbed the phone. "Come on Lydia—pick up the damn phone."

The groggy voice at the other end said. "Hello."

"Lydia." Father screamed. "It's Father Jack. Come to the back door at the rectory quick. No questions please. Hurry." And he slammed down the phone.

Five minutes later, Lydia came through Father Jack's back door. A coat thrown over her nightgown and she had worn-out cowboy boots on her feet.

Her blond hair was standing straight up. "What the hell's going on Father Jack—I was sound asleep—"

"Lydia, do you remember Mollie WhiteOaks? Didn't you go to school with her?"

She whipped around and looked at the Indian woman huddled in the corner by the kitchen table softly crying. "Mollie. Mollie. It's me Lydia. Are you all right?" The tear stained face raised to meet her eyes and she stood up in the middle of Lydia's outstretched arms.

"Now listen, Lydia. Mollie has given me permission to tell this." Father Jack ran his fingers through his disheveled hair and took a deep breath. "Her husband, Lefty Kirk is the man who raped Maggie. That part we knew. But she says Lefty is going to kill her next. He's out on bond right now. He is Billy Hale's nephew and they stand to inherit Mollie's whole family of headrights. She over-heard Lefty and Hale discuss the killing of Bessie, Mollie's mother as well as the plan to buy the nitro to blow her sister, Rita and her husband's house up over in Fairfax." Father stopped pacing while he watched Lydia's reaction,

"My God, what next. Mollie, this is horrible." Lydia managed to find her voice.

"Mollie." Father Jack coached. "Tell her that they are in cahoots with Woodward up at the agency and together they're responsible for most of the Indian murders. Isn't that right?"

The Indian woman murmured "yes" and nodded her head. She collapsed in the chair in tears.

Lydia had heard enough. "Okay Father Jack. I'm going to take her with me to my place. I've got my double-barrel shotgun. You go find the sheriff and meet us at my place."

Father Jack nodded. Lydia grabbed Mollie's hand and they raced out the rectory door. The adrenaline was flowing as Lydia climbed up on the horse. She reached down for Mollie's hand and swung her up behind her as Lydia slapped the horse with the reins and they flew north down the alley behind the Catholic Church.

Praise God! Thank you, Jesus. Father Jack sat down for a minute while he caught his breath. Finally it was going to be over. The murders would end.

CHAPTER THIRTY-ONE

Tuesday, March eighteenth, 1924, was a red letter day. The birds were singing, the red buds were in full bloom, and the oaks had voted to show their tiny green leaves for the first time that year. It was definitely show time.

That day marked the Osage's twenty-second oil and gas sale, and everybody knew it was going to be the biggest ever. The Osage was on the map. Oilmen—big shots and new faces—had been in town for two days, wining and dining all over town.

Colonel Walters, the colorful auctioneer, was coming from his home in Skeedee, Oklahoma. Indians were everywhere, afraid they'd miss something if they didn't show. The weather man had promised a real spring day. Earlier that week, Mother Nature had scared everyone to death by predicting the possibility of a late winter blizzard. But fortunately, it had been averted.

The sale was scheduled to start at ten a.m. Six hundred thirty-three leases were slated to go under the hammer. The Duncan Hotel's lobby had resembled a political convention the previous night. Tom, Frank Phillips, and Jake had milled around talking to the other cigar-smoking, bullshitting storytellers till the wee hours of the morning. At any given time, there were probably two hundred oil men gathered around the giant up-to-date map of the Osage tacked to the wall in the lobby. It showed the leases already developed and the ones offered for sale.

The Midland Valley Railroad announced to the "Pawhuska Daily Journal News" that record crowds had come in Monday to infiltrate the retail businesses with some real oil money. The "Muskogee Special" was set to arrive at nine o'clock that morning. The banner across West Main Street read in big bold print "Welcome to Pawhuska, our wealthy city." Word on the packed downtown streets was that this sale could top the one-hundred million dollar mark for an all time total lease sale held in Pawhuska. The lease sale on June 28, 1922 had reached $10,889,700. Colonel Walters told all interested parties up at the hotel that 300 of the 633 leases comprised an area of 47,507 acres beginning east of range seven. There were 298 tracts with 47,198 acres lying to the east of range seven with nineteen tracts of 3000 acres lying to the west of range eight. These would be the last offered, but they were figured to be the choice pieces of oil land in the United States. It was suspected that tract 625, the SW 160 of 11-27-5, would bring a record price.

The agency had been crowded with men at each other's elbows gathering useful oil field data. Scouts were everywhere trying to appraise and value the land. Neat little folders had been provided by the U.S. Secretary of the Interior and the Commissioner of Indian Affairs, C. H. Burke. Each folder issued by the government included the rules and regulations for the sale. The sale usually took place up at the million dollar elm tree on the agency hill, but today, because of the chilly weather, it would be held on West Main at the Constantine Theatre.

And the old Constantine lady was certainly packed to capacity. Marland's men from Ponca City filled one whole area to the right of the stage, while Phillip's staff had the left side of the theatre. The excitement centered around the newcomers—Stewart and Baggley from New York. They had the front rows filled. It seemed to be a mystery how anyone from New York had ever found that wide spot in the road. Skelly's and Sinclair's outfit, Prairie Oil and Gas, Beacon Oil, Kewannee people,

Twin States Oil Company, Carter Company, Cosden Company, and Midland Oil filled the other seats.

From Jake's vantage point, he could see representatives from all the big metropolitan papers. The Kansas City Star, The Daily Oklahoman, The Tulsa World, and The Wichita Eagle all had reporters, and several additional members of The Associated Press were also in attendance. Looking around, Jake could even pick out several well-dressed representatives of oil magazines from across the country. The telephone and telegraph wires were humming already.

Tom Fisher was on tap, looking fresh as a daisy from his honeymoon, in a brand new navy striped suit. He had a sheaf of papers ready to research at any moment, if the need arose. It was a little past time to begin and the crowd was getting unruly.

Colonel Walters stepped up on the stage to a thunderous round of applause. He was a striking man, tall and lean, with small spectacles, and as always, clad in his long sleeve blue and white stripe shirt. On his left hand was a big diamond ring. It had been a gift to him from the Osage tribe for his great auctioneering expertise.

The crowd quieted. "Welcome: Ladies and Gentlemen," came the clear concise authoritative voice of the colonel. "It is time to begin the twenty-second Osage Oil and Gas Lease Sale. May I have your attention, please. Now, you all have your folder provided by the Bureau of Indian Affairs. So I trust you are familiar with the rules and regulations. I intend to adhere to them closely."

Again the crowd applauded and whistled loudly with enthusiasm. "Simmer down, now, gentlemen. Let's get down to business. We are going to auction off schedule A first. Let's start with tract 107, the southeast quarter of 27-29-11. Do I hear an opening bid of five hundred dollars, gentlemen?"

And there it was. The great oil gentlemen's high-stakes poker game was off and running. The price quickly rose to two thousand in fast and furious auctioneer rattling. Jake watched all of the powerful oilmen make some small insignificant signal, that could have been attributed to fly swatting, as they bid higher and higher. "Do I hear $8,000? How about $10,000?" Scanning the crowd, the Colonel pointed to the middle of the theatre. "$15,000. Yes, by Beacon Oil."

Colonel Walters waved his long arm and pointed with his sharp pencil to lure another bidder. Colonel Walters knew Cosdon wanted it bad. He had done his homework with the bidders. He paused a moment, looking straight at the Cosden camp, "Gentlemen, do I hear twenty? Yes. Back to you, sir." He looked straight at the Beacon oil vice president. "Do I hear twenty thousand, five hundred dollars? Yes, I do. Come on, now. Do I hear twenty-one thousand? Yes, the Cosden Company has bid twenty-one. Do I hear twenty-one five? Thank you, Beacon Oil. Do I hear twenty-two? No, do I hear twenty-two?" Cosden never moved a muscle. After what seemed an eternity, Cosden shook his head.

"Alright, gentlemen, $21,500 dollars, going once, going twice, going three times. Sold to Beacon Oil company for the low, low price of twenty-one thousand, five hundred dollars."

The crowd's enthusiasm was high. Everyone was having a great time. The back slapping could be heard all over the building. By noon, the bidding had netted $81,600. Colonel Walters closed the session for lunch and the oilmen scattered to enjoy the chicken dinners provided by the churches.

At promptly one-thirty p.m., everyone had returned to their theatre seats. Excitement was riding high and their full stomachs had prepared them for the high-stakes afternoon game. Colonel Walters walked on stage and a hush fell over the crowd. "Gentlemen, did you hear the story about the rich guy, driving a new Cadillac along one of these old Osage County roads?"

The whole crowd was instantly with him and even the big shots relaxed a little. "Well, there was a guy with a old Model T Ford broke down along side the road, over there bouts by Whizbang. So, the Cadillac driver, being a nice Osage County resident, stopped and asked him if he needed some help? The farmer gratefully, thanked him and said that he had a rope if he could just give him a pull. 'Fine', the Cadillac driver said. So, they hooked 'er up and took off with the Cadillac pullin' the Ford. Now gentlemen, there was only one problem. As the Cadillac driver was headin' down the road, he happened to notice he'd just passed the one thousand mile mark, you had to have before the car was broken in. '*Hot dog*'! he said to himself, and without another thought to the Ford, he opened her up. He was travelin' along at sixty miles a hour, then, seventy miles a hour, then, seventy-five. The poor Ford man was going crazy. Still, the guy in the Cadillac hadn't remembered he was back there. Well, they sped by this house and the sheriff was sitting there watching for speeders. He could tell he was going too fast for him, so he raced in the farm house and called to the next town—Lymon, I believe, it was. 'Hey, I've got a live one, headed your way. It's a guy in a Caddy, runnin' full bore. Hell! He must be goin' seventy-eighty miles a hour. But I'm not too worried about him. It's the guy in that model T Ford behind him. He's right on that Caddy's tail, standing up, screaming at the guy, to let him pass'."

Everyone laughed uproariously, probably from sheer nervousness, Jake thought, as the colonel went on. "Well, that 's enough joking around. Let's begin the afternoon's session with tract 307."

Beyond the crowd's wildest expectations, and before their very eyes, they watched the bidding skyrocket to an $605,000. The winner was the president of Twin States Oil, who was now mopping the sweat with his fine linen handkerchief like he might die at any moment from the stress. *Boy,* Jake said to himself. *My lease is real close to Lymon, too. My deal may be sweeter than I thought.*

Next, Colonel Walters introduced tract 309, the S.W. quarter of 13-27-5. That was one of the top leases. Jake knew Frank wanted it, and he aggressively opened his bid at $50,000.00. The tension was heavy. Half of the men were holding their breath, and the other half was laboriously breathing. Carter Oil's man jumped in at $100,000. It bantered back and forth between Carter, Phillips, and Prairie Oil Gas Company at breakneck speed—"$150 thousand, $250 thousand, $500 thousand, one million, one million-two." Every man was sitting on the edge of his seat. Even the unshakeable voice of Colonel Walters was filled with excitement as he tried to keep them focused on the next higher number. He was really pushing them. Finally, in a last ditch effort, Prairie Oil and Gas was proclaimed the winner with the uncontested bid of $1,825,000 for a one hundred and sixty acre lease.

Colonel Walters, master that he was, realized that he had them all on an expensive roll, as he immediately launched on tract 310, SE quarter of 14-27-4.

"Here we go again, gentlemen, a chance to bid on the hottest piece of land in the United States. Let's see what we got here."

Even the Indians sat up, no longer resting with half-closed eyes. Earlier most of the oilmen had shed their coats, but now their sleeves were rolled up, their ties were long gone, and their hair was wild. Perspiration beads had reached epidemic proportions on each 'high-roller's upper lip. Phillips, Marland, and Prairie Oil were at each other's throats. Back and forth, and with each giant leap in bids, the crowd would audibly gasp. Colonel Walters was working in a dead heat, and pressing them hard.

Finally, when it seemed these wheeler-dealers had bid more money than anyone had in the world, Cosden Oil and Gas Company, who had had their heads together and their pencils flying, jumped up and fairly screamed to the absolute delight of the audience, "We bid, $1,955,000."

There was silence, then the crowd started cheering. Phillips looked at his men. Then he wadded up all of his scrap paper and threw it on the floor, shaking his head. Marland sneered in disgust as he, too, waved off the colonel. Colonel Walters took a deep breath, knowing he'd just put the bidding over the top. He was in the record book. "And the winner, ladies and gentlemen, of the SE quarter of 14-27-4, near the town of

Lymon, Oklahoma, the most lucrative piece of ground in the United States, has just been awarded to the Cosden Oil and Gas Company."

The day was over, and the final results brought down the house of the Constantine Theatre. The grand total was $8,342,600. Everyone was standing up, shaking hands and slapping each other, winners and losers, on the back. They were declaring to one another that they needed a drink of whiskey and a good cigar.

The media ran over everyone, racing to the telephone and the telegraph office to get a head start on the world's top oil story. Jake wandered to the back of the theatre deep in thought. He had come out the real winner. He was sitting on a Lymon lease worth about two million dollars on the auction block, and he'd won it all on a full house hand of poker. Things were definitely lookin' up. With a definite spring in his step, he walked up to Fred Lookout and Bacon Rind standing in the back.

"Well, Jake, at least money stays good for our people for awhile longer. I guess that means the murders will continue," Fred declared.

Bacon Rind looked at him through his tiny spectacles. "Yeah, murders are liable to pick up. Wait till the headlines in newspapers carry bigger and better money tales—Osage famous, now! Gotta go, Fred. " Bacon Rind sauntered out the door. History had unfolded.

Jake slapped Fred on the back. "Come on, Fred. Let's go get a cup of coffee and a piece of chocolate cake up at the cafe. There's five hundred people milling around here. They'll be talking in the streets and at the Duncan Hotel all night long."

They walked up the street dodging the excited oilmen. They all seemed to be reliving the historic moments of the afternoon, over and over. Tom Fisher waved as he and Frank headed toward the Duncan hotel. He dashed over to Jake for a moment, "Wasn't that history in the making? Frank's not too happy. Course, he's got more than his share of good leases—he and Marland, both. I think it's just the idea he wasn't in the winner's circle today."

Jake laughed. "Pretty good poker game, eh, Tom?"

"You bet." Tom ran to catch up with Frank. "Gotta dash! See you guys later. I wouldn't have missed this for all the tea in China. No siree."

It was after eight o'clock as two men entered the café. "Lordy, old Colonel Walters really did it today didn't he?" Jake asked, as Fred nodded in agreement. Jake laughed. "Good thing Bacon Rind gave him that diamond ring from the tribe awhile back wasn't it?" They sat down at a booth near the window. "Bring us two coffees and a couple of slices of chocolate cake, please," Jake yelled to Ginger. "Well, I wonder what kind of luck Vaughn had in Oklahoma City on Monday? I haven't seen him, have you?"

"No, I haven't even seen Sheriff Cook," Fred replied. "Don't know what he's up to."

"Well, I haven't seen him since the night we found Katherine Little Bear."

Fred took a drink of his coffee. "Jake, do you think Woodward's the kingpin over Hale and Kirk?"

Jake finished pouring the cream into his cup. "Yeah, Fred, I do, but sooner or later, there's got to be a showdown between Hale and Woodward, cause Hale's getting too bold. And that's not Woodward's style. He won't put up with that. I figure Hale will rat on him before long. Course, they're working on two different Indian families, so maybe they'll stay clear of each other's territory. Sides, Hale's about got it all now with Mollie being the only heir left, unless he decides to get rid of Lefty, too, which would be alright with me."

Jake and his father-in-law finished their dessert and left the restaurant. They walked back down Kihekah Street to West Main. It was impossible to move through the crowd in front of the Duncan Hotel. Yet somehow, Tom spied them a block away. "Come on in! I've got a bottle of Frank's best in here. He's over talkin' to Sinclair. They're commiseratin', I guess. They both just wanted to be top dogs today so bad.

He told me awhile ago to just carry on. He's going to New York to see Fern!"

"Who's Fern?" Jake asked. "His mistress, Fern Butler! You know, I've told you about her. I guess he needs a little consolation." That remark brought on belly laughs from them all.

"Hey, Fisher!" Bill Skelly yelled. "Will you give me a ride back to the train depot? I need to take the midnighter back to Tulsa."

"Sure, Mr. Skelly! Come with me, Fred, Jake, both of you. Mr. Skelly, I'd like you to meet my friend, Jake Knupp, an independent driller, and his father-in-law, former Chief of the Osages, Fred Lookout."

"Howdy, Jake." Skelly smiled, "Sure, I know Mr. Lookout! How you doin', Fred?" Fred greeted him and shook his hand. Skelly looked at Jake. "So, you're an independent driller round here."

"Yes, sir. I've drilled some for Frank, but I don't think I've had the pleasure of drilling for you, yet."

He looked straight at Jake sizing him up. "Well, I may be needin' another driller before long. I'll give you a call."

Jake thanked him as they grabbed his suitcases and walked briskly to the back entrance of the hotel to the car.

Jake had parked his yellow Packard in the rear, so he tossed Skelly's grip in the trunk and Tom and Fred crawled into the back as they took off to the station. "Well, how to you think it went today?" Jake said to Skelly as the car pulled out into the street.

"Oh, 'bout what I expected. Cosden's got more money than brains. I doubt if he'll realize that kinda money out of the deal. But hell. It's just a damn big poker game with outrageous stakes. A guy just gets caught up in the game."

Tom leaned over the seat, "Marland's bet everything on that crack geologist of his, but I still think it's going to fall off sooner than they think. But I guess we'll see."

They drove the few blocks to the depot and the train was just pulling in. Jake saw Sheriff Cook over by the porter. He had a wagon pulled up close to the train. He was leaning on it rather nonchalantly. Jake casually wondered what was going on. The men talked a few more minutes with Bill Skelly. They said their good-byes, gathered his suitcases up, and shook his hands as he boarded the train. One car ahead of him, Jake could see some commotion out of the corner of his eye.

"Come over here, Tom." Jake motioned him. As they got closer, Jake could see Sheriff Cook and the porter carrying something off the train.

"What's he doing, Jake?"

Jake shook his head. "I don't know. Looks like a body wrapped up in a blanket. Hey Sheriff!" Jake called.

"Yeah, who's there?" Sheriff Cook yelled.

"It's me, Jake! Tom Fisher and Fred, too." The men reached the wagon tucked away in the shadows.

"Good! Come over here and help me. Give the porter a hand. Grab hold." Tom and Jake each grabbed a part of the bundle.

"Is this a body by any chance?" Jake asked.

Sheriff Cook looked up at him with a real sober face. "Yeah, you guessed it. A white guy this time. Someone killed him in his upper berth—shot him under the arm." They loaded the heavy bundle into the wagon. "I'm taking him up to the corner's office."

Jake's curiosity had finally gotten the better of him. "Okay, I can't stand it, Sheriff. Who is it?"

He looked at Jake from under the brim of his big hat. "Sure you want to know?"

Jake looked at Tom and Fred, as he nodded.

Slowly, Sheriff Cook unwrapped the blanket from the man's face. Tom and Jake both gasped. There, staring blankly ahead, was the empty face of Investigator Bill Vaughn.

"Guess he never made it to Oklahoma City," Fred said in a low dark voice.

"Nope," Sheriff Cook said. "Someone must a thought he was on the right trail. Guess what they didn't know was that Vaughn had mailed a full report into Oklahoma City earlier in the week just in case there was trouble. I had already gotten notification that the FBI would be here tomorrow to pick up Hale and Woodward. Ol' Vaughn did a good job. He had em' cold especially since he and I got Mollie's full report incriminating them all including her husband."

Jake and Tom's mouth hung open in absolute shock. "How? When?—Mollie's report?"

The sheriff had to laugh. "You boys fell down on the job of investigatin' while the big sale was going on. I've had her in protective custody with a wild woman guarding her with a gun for a week, now."

Fred and Jake stared at him incredulously. "Oh, God. Not Miss Lydia—"

As Sheriff Cook boarded the buggy, "Yep. You got it. Sure too bad for ol' Vaughn here. Hale could have saved a little money on a hit. He's goin' need it for a few good lawyers."

Tom put his hand on his arm. "I'll ride with you, Sheriff, if you'll drop me off at the hotel. Maybe you can explain this better to me on the way."

"Sure, Tom." The sheriff slapped the horses' rump, and they disappeared down the street.

Jake and Fred just looked at each other in disbelief as they stood alone outside the train station. "Now, what?" Jake asked. "Vaughn's dead. Is it over? Now that the price of oil is sky high, the worth of a dead Indian's headright'll continue to go sky-high with it."

The old Indian looked tired. He walked slowly to the Packard with Jake. His face was strained and wrinkled. Jake started the car, and they drove to the corner. Jake looked down the street. He could still see the oilmen standing out front of the hotel. He could still hear the sounds of the giant expectations of their soon-to-be-made fortunes. As he looked beyond the little agency town, he could still see the dancing spirits of the Indians as they watched from behind the trees. Jake took one final look as he turned the car the opposite way toward the Lookout ranch.

Fred looked at his son-in-law. "My people unhappy, Jake. First, we have no buffalo, no game, and no land. Now the pendulum swing other direction. We have too much land, too much oil, too much money. Yet, evil still plague Osages. Each day we try hard to follow Grandfather Sun, but we lose. Osages go to same fate as buffalo. White man kill buffalo, they kill game, and now, they kill us. My people are proud people, but whether we rich or poor, no matter, Osage lose."

Suddenly, Jake could feel the sadness that plagued Fred's heart. It plagued his, too, but today was over. Grandfather Sun had even agreed to put it to bed. "Guess now there'll be a big trial to look forward to. You have to admit Fred, if nothing else, there's always excitement in the Osage."

The old Indian nodded. "Never same two days in row, history say it."

Jake looked at Fred. "But oh God! Not Miss Lydia with a gun guarding our prize witness." And together they burst into laughter until the tears ran down the wise old Indian's face. Then, without a second's hesitation, Jake stomped his foot hard on the accelerator, blew out the cobs on his twin-six motor, and listened to her roar. The two of them raced history full-bore along the lonely dirt road, each claiming to be the winner. The shadow of the tall oil derricks were blurred by their huge dust clouds. Engulfed by it all, the oilman and the Indian laughed again as Jake raced the big yellow Packard for all she was worth toward home, back to the northwest quarter of 29-25-11 deep in the Osage.

Chapter Thirty-two

It was three a.m. on no one's clock. The untried path was brush-covered with tangled thorn covered vines that created a one way in and a one way out maize. There were great gnarled grapevines draped dramatically over the trees. The smell of dankness was hanging in the air. The crickets were held captive in their own territory by fear and made not a sound. Yet there were footsteps felt but not heard upon the land.

Hidden on a half-gnawed log that had been washed up from the creek sat a figure. The outline of a dark wide-brimmed hat in the shadows could have been traced if there had been any living thing in motion in the deep Osage woods. By the size of the crouched form, nature would have surmised it to be a man. The sound of a popping sound broke the night's stillness. *Damn, these bugs never sleep.* The big man slapped the back of his neck and grumbled. He'd waited an hour and he was sick of it. *Damn swamp down here anyways*, he thought. He knew that his cohort was no doubt waiting and watching him right now to see if he'd been followed.

A twig broke behind him. He whipped around as the sweat beads leaked out onto his forehead. "Oh, there you are. Damn it's about time. You kept me waitin' forever."

"Well, I'm here now. Settle down. Can't be too careful." The voice said from the shadows.

"Did you bring the evidence? You said you had proof? I want to see it for myself." He uttered.

Dressed in a black slicker and hat, the person emerged still hidden from the shadows and threw down a package on the closest stump. The man with the hat broke open the string and unfolded the brown paper. There in the box was a fine powder. "All right. So you've got ashes. How do I know whose they are?" he asked.

"I figured you wouldn't believe me, so I brought a little insurance policy for myself." The voice answered.

"Let's see it," he was beginning to get excited. The sweat was beginning to bead up faster.

From behind the tree, the person in the shadows held out a huge sealed jar. "Here it is. Hope you're happy."

The man struck a match and in the glow he looked at the contents of the jar. "So it's a pickled arm. How do I know it's hers?"

"Look again, it's the arm with the spider tattoo. It's matches the spider her mother, Bessie had on her arm. Each family has a particular kind of spider. You know that."

Taking a closer look, the man examined the pickled arm and its grotesque design floating in its sea of formaldehyde. "Alright. You did real good. You drive a pretty hard bargain. He took a deep sigh and relaxed. "So right under the sheriff's nose, we nailed Molly Kirk dead. Vaughn may have turned me in, but at least we have the headright. I'll get me a good lawyer and I'll beat the rap."

"Yeah, but you promised me my share of her headright, up front, remember? So where is it, Billy—fifty-fifty for ten years."

"Okay. Okay it's right here." He threw a bundle down on the log.

"Light another match, Billy. Let's see." The glow from the match provided the figure in black a quick view of the bills. "Five hundred thousand. Seem like it's all here. Better be."

"Now, is your business all finished?" Billy Hale asked not waiting for an answer. "Well, then come on over here, darlin'. Let me feel that gorgeous body." The man reached for the shadow and the two people became one in a torrid embrace. The money and the jar with the mangled arm were forgotten as he tore open the long black rain slicker. Even in the darkness he could see the soft curves of her unclothed body. He kissed her passionately and laid her on the ground. The softened mud was perfect for their getaway bed deep under the covers of the Osage. After a few moments of heated passion, Billy Hale gasped for breath and collapsed on the woman. "My God. Lydia, you are the best damn lover in the Osage."

ABOUT THE AUTHOR

 Jamie S. Eccleston was born and raised on the Osage Indian reservation in Osage County Oklahoma and was adopted into the Osage Tribe. She grew up in an oil field camp with her oil producing father and grandfather. In addition to her writing, she has enjoyed a wide spread variety of career interests. While raising her four children, she became a gun dealer in rural Osage County. Later, she became a co-owner of the Sunnyside Bed & Breakfast in Eureka Springs, Arkansas. Currently she is a co-founder of Mary Martha Outreach in Bartlesville, Oklahoma that provides free food, clothing, and furniture for the poor.

Printed in the United States
77747LV00003B/88-126